Coming of Age

Also by Jonathan Havard

Blood and Judgment
The Stockholm Syndrome

Coming of Age

JONATHAN HAVARD

Heinemann : London

William Heinemann Ltd
Michelin House, 81 Fulham Road, London SW3 6RB

LONDON   MELBOURNE   AUCKLAND

First published in 1988
Copyright © C. Havard 1988

British Library Cataloguing in Publication Data

Havard, Jonathan, *1924–*
Coming of age.
I. Title
823'.914 [F]

ISBN 0 434 31392 0

Printed and bound in Great Britain by
Richard Clay Ltd, Bungay, Suffolk

To my Mother and my Father who never heard me say how much I loved them

Acknowledgments

Having had the privilege of being born into a mining family who brought me up to respect the law, it has been my desire not to write anything that could be construed as being unjustly biased by either the miners or the police. For their guidance in my efforts to achieve this end, I would like to acknowledge with gratitude the help I received from Dr Kim Howells and Inspector Stan Sulman.

1

'To be a good surgeon, you've got to be a bit of a bastard.'

Jonathan Brookes smiled to himself. They had all been in the bar at the Royal Westmere, comfortable in quiet companionship after a round of golf and a few beers. He could still see Dai Jack Williams, the anaesthetist, his father's closest friend, sitting there. There had been nothing flippant about his remark. He was notorious for making outrageous statements that had no basis in personal beliefs when he felt the conversation flagging, but this had not been one of those occasions. One could always tell when Dai Jack was joking by the tiny crinkles at the corners of his eyes. Neither had there been any malice in his face, simply the look of someone who had just come to a conclusion after years of experience. Jonathan had looked across at his father, expecting resentment at most, at least some quick riposte in keeping with more than twenty years of friendship. He had been surprised to find neither, only a quiet smile, almost as if his father had taken the remark as a compliment.

His father a bit of a bastard? Jonathan would have been as ready as any son in showing filial loyalty in a father's defence, but there had been no need – there had been no doubting Michael Brookes's ability as a surgeon, everyone locally would have accepted that. But, his father some sort of a bastard? Jonathan simply couldn't believe it. And yet, his father had raised no argument; he had actually nodded his assent. So, this man to whom Jonathan had always looked up as the epitome of all that was straight and honest, what possible reason could he have had for agreeing? His father had winked at him and grinned, as if Jonathan should not take old Dai Jack too seriously, that he was always pulling someone's leg. But it was too late; the seed had been sown; Dai Jack had meant it and his father had agreed.

Jonathan laughed out loud. A strange time to be thinking of that. Odd how the mind wandered while waiting for a kettle to boil. He clambered out of the companionway, a steaming mug of coffee in each hand, handed one to Susannah and sat on the cockpit coaming, wedging his back against the guardrail.

'What were you laughing about?'

'Nothing much. I was just thinking of something one of your lot said a few months ago. It's not often an anaesthetist says anything very profound; I think that's why it's stuck in my memory.'

Susannah Ridgeway, one of the Royal Liverpool's anaesthetic registrars, stuck out her tongue. 'What did he say?'

'He said, "You've got to be a bit of a bastard to be a good surgeon."'

Susannah thought for a moment. 'Yes. I think I'd go along with that.'

Grinning, Jonathan was about to say something facetious when he changed his mind, holding his inspired breath in surprise. She wasn't joking either.

'Who said it?' Susannah asked.

'Dai Jack, Dr David John Williams, consultant anaesthetist, Dunbridge General Hospital, to give him his full title. You must come up and meet him one day. He's good value.'

The conversation lapsed, giving way to the steady thump of the diesel. Jonathan put his head back and closed his eyes for a moment, feeling the sun on his eyelids.

'Bloody gorgeous, isn't it?'

They had crossed the bar at Barmouth together many times over the previous few years. It wasn't always like this, gliding in on a flood tide on a blazing August day, the estuary a placid lake of glinting ripples. They had hurtled in on seething rollercoasters, fighting to keep their craft straight ahead of hissing surf that raced to engulf them, hanging on, grinning their apprehension. But today, Susannah drank her coffee as she steered, the tiller between her knees, swivelling her hips from side to side as she weaved her way down the busy fairway. The world and his wife were out on anything that would float and Susannah smiled quietly back at the friendly greetings attracted by the handsome pair in the spanking new racing cruiser.

Jonathan had read somewhere that the only journey more beautiful than that up the Mawddach estuary from Barmouth to Dolgellau was that back down from Dolgellau to Barmouth. He looked to starboard, up towards Cader Idris, benign in a late summer sun, and shivered. The world, his world, was at peace. He was back in a job he loved. He was afloat in a beautiful, fast, responsive boat. He was with a woman who made him ache just to look at her. He had recognised a couple of boats up from New Quay, so there would be beer and good company that night. Who could ask for more?

'Did you see those New Quay boats?' he asked.

'Yes, I did.'

'Looks like a good night,' he grinned.

She said nothing. Tall and strong, Susannah Ridgeway looked relaxed, as much in control of herself as the boat she steered. Her jeans were expensive looking, close fitting without being tight, her figure good enough to look slim inside the red and black striped jumper, buttoned high on one shoulder. Dark brown eyes, strangely restless in someone so calm, blended with skin that still tanned like a child's. The texture and colour of her long black hair made up for the total lack of wave or curl. She had never been seen to wear a hat, even in the coldest of weathers. If it rained, she might put the hood of her jacket up but – Jonathan had noticed it many times – where others ducked the flying spray, she seemed to welcome it as it whipped across the deck, closing her eyes as if uplifted by its stinging scourge. It was at such times, with eyes closed and skin glistening wet, that the scar, puckered and jagged across one eyelid, stood out, marring her otherwise flawless features.

They had met when 'on the house' together at the Royal Liverpool, Jonathan in one of the prestige posts, Susannah, a year older, lucky to get one of the unpopular jobs. For Susannah there had been a gap of a year since qualifying in Cambridge and she would not have got her professional toe in the Liverpool door except for such a brilliant student career. It had proved no hindrance also that her father was rich, influential and Chairman of one of the neighbouring Area Health Authorities. She had introduced Jonathan to sailing, taught him all he knew, watched it grow into a passion. There had been weekends in the Ridgeways' holiday home at Abersoch, looking across the wide sweep of sea to Tremadoc Bay and Harlech, its castle backed by the grandeur of Snowdonia, blue on blue in the hazy distance. There had been the trips *en famille* to France in the company's forty-five-footer kept at Lymington for the purpose of entertaining rich clients, but Susannah and Jonathan had preferred the relative quiet of Cardigan Bay. There had been visits to the London Boat Show, staying at the company's pad in Belgravia, with nods of recognition from Mayfair head waiters and bills settled, without looking, at the flourish of a signature. To Jonathan, considered rich by his peers, it had been another world. There had also been the quieter times, the murmuring hours in the corners of friendly pubs, the gentle rocking at anchor on a warm night.

But they had never shared a bed. In the idiom of the Royal Yacht Club, they had never made it; in the patois of coarse sailing, he had never got his leg over.

No one would have believed them. In this permissive age? Who would accept that there had never been a party where both had had too much to drink? Except that Susannah never drank, always drove home, had no trouble fending off beer-driven passions from someone basically too gentle to be troublesome. And, in the cold light of day, they were kept apart by Jonathan's hereditary inability to express his emotions and Susannah's manifest distaste for all things superficial, interpreted by many as downright frigidity. Her eyes rarely held another's for long but, when they did, they flashed a warning, not a welcome.

It couldn't last. They were not brother and sister. There was nothing incestuous about the way he felt. He wanted her, straight, no frills, with a gut ache that at times crippled him. And he was scared, scared that soon, if nothing happened, she'd get bored and tell him to get lost, something he did not know how he would handle. He would miss the lifestyle – he would be the first to admit that – but that would be nothing compared with losing her. Please God . . .

He jerked up and threw the dregs of his coffee over the side. 'I'd better call the Harbourmaster, ask if we can go alongside.' He smiled. 'If I remember, there's no nipping in and out without paying with this one.'

'It's worth it – it's a comfort to know someone has seen us come and go. We'd better try to be outside boat if there are any others alongside. I've had enough of your friends from New Quay climbing all over us in the early hours. In fact, I think we'll anchor out tonight to make sure of a bit of peace. Ask the Harbourmaster what time he expects it to dry out alongside tonight.'

There is never a shortage of hands to take ropes from a boat coming alongside with a beautiful young woman at the helm. Within minutes, they were tied up. A few minutes more and Jonathan was renewing acquaintances over cans of beer while Susannah busied herself at the galley. She swore quietly to herself at the rocking caused by Jonathan showing his friends over the new boat. They all warmed themselves in the envy of those who teetered to the quay's edge to peer down at them. The chilli con carne was hot and needed another can to wash it down. They cleared away, climbed the vertical steel ladder and walked along the beach, sitting to watch the tropical brilliance of a west coast sunset. Jonathan became restless, throwing stones fitfully and aimlessly. Good drinking time was passing – if they were going to anchor out, time was a precious commodity – but he hesitated to complain. They rarely argued, Susannah seeming only too glad to steer away from emotional intensity of any kind, bringing a tranquillity to their relationship that Jonathan cherished. But there was more than the usual reserve in her mood and she flickered her irritation as Jonathan finally stood up.

'Come on, let's go and find where they are.'

Susannah had no need to ask who 'they' were and had little trouble finding where 'they' were, simply entering the first pub they came to that vibrated in rough unison. A place was found for her in a corner and she managed a smile at the jokes about the orange juice Jonathan handed across to her. She watched Jonathan dispatching beer even faster than his friends and there seemed a desperation in his drinking not altogether explained by the falling tide. She endured the inevitable bawdiness as they left early and took the brunt of Jonathan's unsteadiness as his shoulder jostled hers on their way back to the harbour. He cast off with the assurance of the inebriated and Susannah sighed her thanks for the lifting keel as the boat slid away in not much more than two feet of water. She watched anxiously as Jonathan staggered on the foredeck as he lifted the anchor over the side.

Susannah always slept in the privacy of the bows, the double berth closed off from the cabin by a mahogany door, and Jonathan hauled the sail bags out through the forehatch to empty it for her. They had sailed together often enough for her to become accustomed to the sound of Jonathan passing urine over the stern but, this time, it seemed longer, louder and cruder than usual. By the time he put his head into the cabin, Susannah was closing the door behind her. She reopened it a fraction to say 'Good night, Jonathan,' and then shut it, firmly.

Jonathan searched in the locker for another can, opening it with a sulky tug. He imagined the warmth and the companionship back in the pub. He tried to compensate by enjoying the sensation of being afloat under a clear starry sky in one of the most beautiful parts of Britain and all it did was to make him randy. He squirmed and ached and threw the empty can over the side, envying its serenity as he watched it glide away into the darkness on the ebbing tide. His mind made up, he climbed through the companionway, forgetting in his sudden resolution to turn as he did so and pitching forwards down the vertical steps. As he picked himself up from the cabin floor, he had lost some of the impetus of alcoholic bravado and there was nothing macho about the strength of his knock on the door before he opened it.

He was drunk, but not so drunk as not to curse the wimpish tone of his whispered 'Can I come in?' There was no reply from the darkness, only the rustle of a sleeping bag. He put out a hand, searching, and found a knee that was quickly withdrawn. Knowing now at least where her head should be, he leaned forwards, both hands outstretched. 'Where are . . .?'

Slow-witted with booze, confused by the explosive suddenness in the darkness, he reeled back against the hull as a blur of spitting, scratching fury came at him. He felt the pain of a finger nail close to his eye, dragging its searing course down his cheek. The other hand found his hair, tearing at his scalp and forcing his head down and back towards the door. He put up his own hand to fend off the blows that now thudded into his face and chest as he tried to wriggle his way back into the cabin. Her 'Get out' was vented over and over again, not in any angry cry or shout but in a terror-filled shriek that rose higher and higher as Jonathan's bulk became jammed in the narrow doorway. Finally free, the door was slammed behind him. He heard the thud of her body collapsing against the other side, the brushing sound as she slid against it, sobbing, to the floor.

Jonathan sat in the cockpit, elbows on knees, head in hands. Voices carried across the still water of early morning and he raised his head. On one of the New Quay boats, someone was being cheered on as he climbed the mast to retrieve a pair of trousers tied to one of the spreaders. Jonathan dropped his head again without a smile. He looked up only when he heard Susannah lift herself out into the misty sunshine. She sat directly opposite him, leaning forwards, their heads no more than inches apart. They exchanged wan, silent smiles. Susannah stretched the few inches to kiss gently the livid weal down Jonathan's left cheek.

'I'm sorry, Jonathan.'

He shook his head. 'No, I'm sorry. I had it coming to me. Put it down to the beer. I'm so sorry.' His head dropped once more.

'D'you want some breakfast?' she murmured.

'Not really.' He raised his head as if it would be impolite to speak to the floor and found her looking at him with eyes that had lost their restlessness. Now steady with affection, not the anger or disgust he might have expected after her reaction to his pathetic attempts at seduction, he saw for the first time the tiny black speckles in the brown. 'I don't think I could swallow anything at the moment.'

'I owe you an explanation, don't I?'

'Of course not. There's nothing to explain.'

'Oh yes there is. Not everyone who has a bit of a grope in the dark is treated like that.' She smiled and got the glimmer of a response.

'It was meant to be rather more than a grope but I don't seem to be much good at that sort of thing. I wanted you and I was getting desperate. I can't look at you without aching. No one else does it to me. Only you. And I've sensed you getting edgy too and I felt that if I didn't do something about it soon, you'd be giving me the old heave-ho.' Jonathan stared at eyes that were now so close as to be difficult to focus on. 'And I honestly don't know how I would cope with that.'

Susannah didn't answer immediately, looking at him with a quiet, affectionate smile. 'I'm just trying to imagine how anyone so stupid got a Ph.D.' She studied the worried, earnest face so close to hers. 'D'you know what you are, Jonathan Brookes? You're a passionate puritan, that's what you are. You're the sort of man early morning cold showers and hair shirts were invented for. You should have been a monk, except that would have been a sad waste of a man. But it's really not your fault, it's mine. It's me. It goes back to when I was up at Cambridge.'

Jonathan put out his arms to take her hands in his. 'There's no need to explain anything. You don't have to. As I said, I had it coming.'

'I want to. I should have told you long ago. You probably don't realise just how lucky you've been. You can have no idea what it is like to be both rich and intelligent in an intellectual hothouse like Cambridge. Brains and no money and you're probably safe. Money and no brains, and, believe me, there are still quite a few of those up there even now, and you've still got a chance. But money and a hyperactive intellect you cannot switch off, night or day . . . Fall in then with the wrong lot and you're in trouble, big trouble. If you're fortunate, you're a theatre type, or you go in for sport or politics. But fall in with some of the Hooray Henrys of the social set and God help you. Swirling minds longing for rest, feeding off each other, sucking each other dry, striving for the super witty saying, eternally trying to impress. You get so burnt up you need a boost. One moment your mind's a roaring blowlamp, burning its way through some highborn party, the next you're searching for peace through meaningful conversations in kaftans and squats. And, when you're on a high, you crave sex for kicks; when you're not, you still want love, anyone's love.'

She laughed bitterly, banging their entwined hands against Jonathan's knees. 'Do you know how much I spent on cocaine alone in my last year at Cambridge?'

'Susannah, don't . . .'

'Over fifteen thousand pounds. Fifteen thousand pounds. The richer you are, the higher the price. And that was without all the trimmings. God knows how much I spent on pot and vodka. And, of course, the odd amphetamine. How I qualified so well I'll never know; the same way a lot of the high flyers in the City still manage to cope, I suppose, probably the only way some of them cope. And advertising; and TV. You wouldn't believe the sort of people I met at group therapy sessions; industrialists, stockbrokers. But it was after qualifying and before starting my first house job that it happened. You know the sort of parties that go on then.'

'I seem to remember marking the occasion with a few beers, yes,' Jonathan smiled wanly.

'A few beers,' Susannah laughed bitterly. 'I woke up in a clinic one morning to learn I had survived a cardiac arrest, courtesy of the dear old NHS. And the very last thing I could remember before that was a man, some faceless man, in the dark, climbing into bed with me. That's why,' she detached a hand to touch his cheek, 'Jonathan, poor gentle Jonathan, has that mark across his handsome face this morning. Please forgive me.'

'I'm sorry, I had no idea.'

'I should have told you before.' She touched her scarred eyelid. 'That's how I got this. If I hadn't had a rich and loving father, I would now be dead. It's not everyone who can afford to keep his daughter in the Charter Clinic for three months at over £6000 a month, is it? That's why I was a year late starting work, not taking a year to travel as I've told everyone. I had to say that if I wanted to do Medicine.'

Jonathan nodded.

'I don't think they'd have been very keen on me handling drugs if they'd known I'd been a junkie. And, of course, now I've gone and chosen anaesthetics, it makes it even more of a secret; so easy to become a sniffer, isn't it?'

'But you're cured now?'

'There's no cause and there's no cure; that was the first thing I had to learn. It's a complete waste of time looking for either. I'm an addict, full stop. That's why I have had nothing done about this.' She drew her finger over her scar once more. 'Daddy wants me to see a plastic surgeon about it but I won't. I still need this scar to remind me. Every time I get to feel a bit down, get a bit shaky, I look in the mirror and think back, just in case I need reminding I'm an addict who just happens not to be taking drugs at the moment. I'm still not sure enough of myself to work for Narcotics Anonymous – they have asked me – but I am afraid to go back and mix with those people again. That's why I reached out and grabbed at the first Jonathan Brookes that came my way.'

Jonathan's mouth thinned out as if ready for the worst. 'But what happens now? Where do we go from here?'

'Nothing. Nowhere.'

'But things can't go on the same.'

'Why not?'

'I can't go on taking from you. It's your boat, your house, you let me pay for very little. I give nothing in return.'

'You great big bloody fool.' She shook her head slowly. 'How can someone so intelligent be so stupid? I take from you far more than you ever realise. How many men d'you think would have been so goddam gentlemanly as you have? So I agree I've been uptight recently; but for the very opposite reason you imagined. I just couldn't believe you, even you, could stand this brother and sister business much longer, that you'd tire of my coldness and push off. I wouldn't have blamed you for a moment. And who would take your place then? Some man who almost certainly would not turn back after just a scratch, might even enjoy the sensation, look for more to add to his pleasure?'

Susannah sat back and stretched, running her fingers through the back of her hair, lifting it before letting it fall back in place.

'You and I, Jonathan dear, are emotional cripples – well perhaps cripples is a bit strong but we're certainly a bit lame, both of us. Why you should be, I don't know; but then I don't think you are quite as bad as I am. Perhaps it's because we're both poor motherless children. What is to become of us, I don't know, but, in the meanwhile, we'll sail and sail and sail and get our kicks from the sea while all our friends will have us in and out of bed together like yo-yos.'

'And what happens if we come to Barmouth again and I have too much beer again and come through that door again?'

'I can't promise you any different reception, except,' she smiled, 'I'll make sure I've cut my finger nails a bit shorter.'

'I'm no monk, Susannah.'

'I know. And I'm no nun – not that they'd have me now, I suppose,' she murmured sadly. She paused as if summing up her feelings. 'I too want to make love with you. You are certainly the only man I can imagine myself making love to at the moment. But not with someone who feels basically he's doing something that's wrong, someone who needs a skinful of beer to overcome his puritanical streak. Neither, for that matter, do I want to be raped by some unfeeling brute. I want to be . . .' She struggled. 'Dear, dear Jonathan, the trouble is you're too perfect. You're every man's idea of a son. That's why I feel so safe with you, why I owe you so much.'

'My pleasure,' Jonathan growled, hurt not so much by what Susannah was saying as his recognition of the truth of it.

'Don't look so sad. There's nothing I would love more than to take up this conversation with you some time again when . . . when you're a bit more of a bastard.' She smiled. 'Not a complete one – I would hate to lose the old Jonathan altogether – just a bit of a bastard. When you've found out what Dai Jack meant, come and see me – soberly – gently.'

2

Police Constable Taff Evans belched. He had intended to enjoy the experience and had given it all the impetus he could muster from a strong contraction of his belly muscles. The distension of his gullet produced by his self-indulgence seared his chest and made him wince.

'That hurt,' he complained, sitting more upright so that he could rub his breastbone ruefully.

'Serves you right, you disgusting little Welshman,' was all the sympathy he got from his colleague in the seat alongside him. Badger Kincaid's bulk, accentuated by the thick, unyielding police raincoat he wore, took his shoulders across the midline of the tiny Panda car. 'You shouldn't have had that second lot of chips.' He glanced quickly across and down before continuing his level stare through the windscreen. 'Though where all that food goes to beats me.'

'Did you ever see a fat thoroughbred?' Evans grinned before sliding back to rest, tilting the peak of his hat over his eyes to keep out the coldness of neon street lights. His slim-wristed hands with fingers of almost feminine length and slenderness came to rest on the steering wheel in front of him. At 5 foot 9 inches, he had only just reached the minimum physical requirements for entry into the police force, his reputation as an amateur boxer probably tipping the scales in his favour. His lack of academic distinction had gone hand in hand with his stature, the two O levels, of which he was inordinately proud, being insufficient to spare him from the Police Entrance Examination. The fact that he had scrambled through had left him with no illusions as to his prospects. He knew that to make Sergeant would be, for him, the pinnacle of success.

They accepted silence with the ease of two people happy in each other's company. Evans, dark and quick, was Kincaid's senior by two years, but he had taken to the rookie copper the first time he had seen him, standing, slowly blinking those fair eyelashes like an old, abandoned Labrador. He reckoned he could pick out the graduate entrants now. Line them up in a row and they stood out, older than the rest, older and more innocent looking, their faces fresh from open playing fields, in contrast with the more watchful, mistrusting faces of those straight in from factory floor, street corner or dole queue. The two young men got on well, drawn together by the mutual attraction of diametric opposites. They even pushed side by side in the local police rugby team, Evans, the Captain, a sniping flanker who made up for his lack of momentum with an obliqueness of attack that also served him well when meting out undetected retribution for any fouls perpetrated against his more ponderous, straight-running friend. Even so, it was still difficult at times to suppress a pang of jealousy to know that Badger had convinced the selection panel over the course of three days that, beneath that unflappable, almost stolid exterior, there was a mind sufficiently quick and intuitive to benefit from the twelve-month course at Bramshill Staff College. Evans, who had already failed his Sergeant's exam once, would have to put up with the sight of the coveted stripes on Badger's arm when he returned. Another three years would bring promotion to Inspector and there were already graduate entrants who had made Chief Inspector in their early thirties – out of reach of a simple, hard-working woodentop.

There were flurries of snow in amongst the drizzle of the February night and Kincaid had to lean across his dozing companion from time to time to switch on the windscreen wipers as he maintained his solitary vigil. The Ford was parked, blatantly white, in one of the three narrow streets that led to Scarsby's central bus station and the spray from the buses, sweeping irregularly into the sheltered bays, only distorted further the image of the group of youngsters they had been sent to watch.

'I'm bloody freezing,' complained a voice from deep in the raincoat beside Kincaid.

'Count your blessings, Taff. Just think, you could be on picket duty. Cortonwood can't be looking its best on a night like this.'

'At least they're doing something useful, not freezing their arses off watching a bunch of kids. Somehow I feel that February 1st 1985 is going to be a night not to be remembered.'

'Haven't seen you doing much watching.' Kincaid's remark was good natured. 'Just lying back there with your mouth open. I often wonder what's going through that tiny little Celtic mind of yours.'

A deceptively frail-looking hand was detached from the steering wheel and laid gently to rest on Kincaid's knee. Beneath the lowered cap, a grin spread as Evans's voice became husky. 'Can't you guess? I thought it was obvious. Surely the boys must have told you by now? And I thought, with both of us bachelors and that lovely blond hair of yours, that you . . .'

He got no further as the small car rocked with the force of the laughing, gasping maul that followed. As they both sat square again, breathlessly tidying up the disarray, Kincaid had to wipe the steamed-up windscreen to peer through once more.

'Blast you, Taff. He's there now.'

'Who?'

'That greasy looking devil, Morelli. Can't miss him with that leather jacket – you know – with sort of studs or rivets all over it and strips of leather on the shoulders. He's turned up while you were fooling about.'

11

Evans cleared his half of the windscreen to take his first interested look. 'That one? The one they call Chico? He's no different from the rest of the great idle gits. I've collared him more than once myself. Right little tearaway he was. I don't know why you go on about him.'

'He's different, I tell you. He's older than the rest; he comes and goes. We've watched that bunch of tearaways long enough now to know who belongs and who doesn't.' Badger shook his head. 'Don't these kids feel the cold? Look at that Morelli. What's he got on? A pair of jeans, a T-shirt and that leather jacket, that's all. On a night like this. And they say that rain is the best form of crime prevention.'

'Probably finds his Crombie overcoat a bit bulky climbing through some pensioner's kitchen window to nick her telly, I expect.' Evans snapped a chocolate bar with care, handing the smaller fragment to Kincaid. 'In bed all day, steal all night. I hate those little bastards' guts. You'd think they'd at least go and steal from the bloody rich, not from their own kind. Anyway, if he bothers you that much, why don't you pull him in? He's on a suspended sentence at the moment. Why don't you get him out of your hair?'

'I would, given half a chance.'

'Could be arranged,' Evans said quietly.

'Bollocks. I know you Welshmen are meant to be a devious lot but you've never fitted anybody up in your life and you know it. You couldn't do it if you tried, so don't be so stupid, talking like that.'

'Miserable gits,' Evans growled. 'Worst thing that ever happened when they played around with the sus law. Those kids know damn well we can't just go up to them any more and dust them down like we used to. Reasonable suspicion, my arse. Look at that bastard – how are you supposed to reasonably suspect he's got a Stanley knife under that jacket? He could have a bayonet up his belt for all we can tell.' He summed up his feelings once more. 'Miserable bastards.'

As if hearing the remark, the group of youths turned towards the car, agitated into a burst of excited bravado, to mill around, their obscenities muffled in the freezing air, their gestures crystal clear. Only the leather-jacketed figure remained still, centrally aloof.

'Fat lot of good we're doing here.' Evans yawned as he slid down once more. 'A lot of bloody nonsense, if you ask me. Just showing the flag, that's all. And all the result of those useless college friends of yours nosing around up at Northend.'

Scarsby Council's Northend housing estate, a sprawling maze of blotchy grey roughcast semis that had devoured acres of grassland on the northern fringe of the town, had been built in the 1930s with the intention of replacing the planner's anathema, the rows of terraced stone-built homes, so cosily protective to their occupants. Here and there, scattered haphazardly, painted walls proclaimed proud ownership. Occasional resplendent gardens were tended by pipe-smoking, slow-moving men, while, within some sombre walls, extremes of parental sacrifice guided cherished children through to success and escape from the graceless surroundings. Scarsby was a town built on coal, with entry to the pit a family tradition guarded as discriminatingly as acceptance into any Royal golf club – no black skin sweated beneath the coal dust as the miners spewed out of the cage and into the sunlight. As a result, it had been spared the racial problems of black enclaves – there was no need for police surveillance posts on the roofs of high-rise buildings – but the Northend estate had more than made up for this by attracting the low paid and the unemployed, the threadbare houses and neglected gardens infiltrated widely with the hardened villains of Scarsby and their young apprentices. It had been just the sort of corralled community that Badger's old university had been looking for when carrying out a survey into drug abuse and their findings that well over 10 per cent of the 16- to 24-year-olds on the estate were habitual users had surprised and shocked many, but not the local police. Northend was, under normal circumstances, the two young coppers' home beat and Taff Evans was of the opinion that he could have saved the long-haired college gits a lot of time and money if they had simply come to see him first.

'"Definite correlation between drug use and break-ins."' Evans pursed his lips as he imitated what he considered to be an educated accent. 'Gormless beggars. How else did they think they get the money? Can't see the wood for the trees half the time, these fellas. There's no doubt about it' – he settled further into the seat – 'there's nothing like a couple of years in college to cloud your mind. And what's happened as a result of squandering all that taxpayers' money? Just two of us taken off picket duty to sit here watching a bunch of kids who know they only have to wait until our shift is over. It's daft, I tell you. Give me a spell of picket-bashing any day and let those young buggers over there go to hell if they want to; that's what I say.'

Badger Kincaid smiled to himself. He had witnessed his friend's 'picket-bashing', a good-natured, red-faced pushing and shoving that had had nothing to do with baton charges. He had also seen the change in Evans's face as he had heard for the first time Welsh voices raised in anger against him. They were both too young to play hard-nosed, seen-it-all coppers and each had recognised compassion mixed with the disgust in the other's features a few nights before when they had dragged the emaciated, inert teenager from the Catholic Church Hall loo and helped lift her into the ambulance. There had been no doubting the violence in Evans's face then as the syringe had resisted the fury of his efforts to grind it into the concrete floor.

A sound emerged from beneath the lapel of Kincaid's coat, a flat metallic transmission of a flat monotonous chant from the girl in the Control Room. He thrust his gloved hand into the folds to acknowledge the call. Evans sat up, pushing his cap to the back of his head before stretching his hand to hover over the ignition key as they both listened. Report of a disturbance at the Butcher's Arms. Request for assistance made by landlord. Message timed at 23.14. Given with all the emotion of a machine reciting one's weight.

'Thank God for that.' Taff Evans made the wheels spin as he accelerated away but could not resist the temptation of a tyre-squealing arc into the bus station. The group of youths spread as the car approached, some sliding away into the shadows, others advancing within feet of the flashing blue light, fists and fingers extended in defiance. As Kincaid was pressed against the door, he turned his head to stare for a timeless moment into a face set in fearless mockery. As it was whisked away from his sight, he caught a glimpse of an ear lobe studded to match the jacket.

The Butcher's faced Theobald Way, the four-lane trunk road that rose gently northwards through Northend. There was little or no parking space; none was needed. The Butcher's was the locals' pub well within staggering distance of all its clientele. Visitors were not welcome and those who entered by chance soon got the message, drank up and got out. Jack Stringer ran a tough pub. He knew it. The police knew it and respected him for it. He sold the cheapest beer in Scarsby outside the clubs and provided the barest and most durable of amenities. An ex-professional wrestler, he looked after most of his own troubles and the police responded by turning a blind eye to some late drinking. They knew that to close his pub would only be to disperse Northend's problem drinkers from where they could keep an eye on them. And it was rare for Jack Stringer to ask for help.

He was standing at the door as Evans jerked the car to a halt. The grubby forecourt was empty of the usual knots of incoherent philosophers, too absorbed in fatuous argument to go home. Evans and Kincaid walked towards him, side by side.

'Evening, Jack. Trouble?'

A mixture of apprehension and excitement made the Welsh accent more noticeable.

'Out the back. Two of them.'

'Who are they, Jack?'

Stringer instinctively ignored the question. 'I've locked them in. No way they can get out. They're all yours.'

'Kind of you, Jack. Lead on.' Evans wiped his palms on his coat as they followed Stringer across creaking, beer-stained bare boards and waited for him to turn the key in the heavy back door. 'What made you call us for this one, Jack? It's not like you.'

'Because, the way they were going at each other, I reckoned one of the silly sods was going to get killed, that's why.'

'Sounds quiet enough at the moment,' Evans muttered as the door creaked open.

It took a few moments for them to adapt to the dim light shed by the one bare bulb high above the open door to a crumbling, brick-built shed. The stench and the sound of dripping water that came from within identified it as the Butcher's toilet facilities. Enclosed on three sides by high walls topped by a cruel tiara of broken glass sunk in concrete, the yard was littered with metal barrels and cases of empty bottles. Half crouched, Evans edged sideways while Kincaid stood erect in the doorway, slowly opening and closing his fists. They both heard the slobbering, snoring sound from the direction Evans was going.

'There's one of them over here. Out cold by the look of it. You stay there, Badger, in case the other makes a break for it. Shit!'

'You all right, Taff?'

'Ugh. He's covered in blood and vomit and God knows what else. As far as I can make out he's been glassed and then hit over the head. Watch out for the other one, Badger. We've got a right one here. Can you . . .?'

'Over here, I think.' Kincaid said quietly, sounding calm enough. 'Stay where you are.'

Out of the deep shadow there emerged a small thin man, the front of his tight-fitting two-piece suit and open-necked shirt, obvious even in the poor light, drenched dark red. A great deal of the blood must have been his own, judging from the jagged laceration that split his cheek from ear to mouth, gaping and closing unheeded as a vicious smirk contorted his face. Slowly, he advanced on Kincaid.

'Watch it, Badger, he's got a bottle,' Evans hissed from the gloom away to Kincaid's right.

'Put that down. Now don't be stupid.' Kincaid took a step forwards. 'Give it to me.'

Without a sound, his eyes never wavering from Kincaid's face, the man swung the bottle in an arc to shatter it against the corner of the shed. Before anyone could move, the jagged fragment remaining in his hand was raised at arm's length to point at Kincaid's throat.

The only change in Kincaid's expression as he continued to walk forwards was a clenching of his jaw that tightened a thick-lipped, generous mouth. Within reach, he suddenly stretched out his hand to grasp the man's wrist, the jagged glass slicing through the back of his glove as he did so. He had no difficulty in forcing the boncy wrist upwards at the very moment Evans flung himself at the little man from the side with all the force of a flanker finally catching an outside half who has been making a fool of him all afternoon. The moment the three hit the ground, the man lay submissively, not making a sound other than the grunt he gave as a knee drove into his lower ribs. The blow brought a frown to Kincaid's face as a look of deep satisfaction spread over his colleague's.

'Did you have to do that?' Kincaid asked as he hauled the man to his feet.

'Badger.' Evans paused to brush himself, only to smear the filth over his coat. 'For your own good, the sooner you're safely behind a desk, the better. You great stupid idiot, walking straight up to a guy with a broken bottle like that. Don't ever do that again. Call an ambulance. Let's get these two beauties over to the General. You'd better go with them in case they start their nonsense again. Give a call when you want to be picked up.'

Twenty minutes later, Kincaid followed as two trolleys were pushed into Scarsby General's Casualty Department by ambulance men as cheerfully detached as country postmen making a delivery. In the corridor, they were met by a Casualty Officer, a big man, almost as tall as Kincaid, though not quite so burly. His coat was virgin white, his face showing a degree of enthusiasm that, at that time of night, spelt novelty. He was a little older than Badger Kincaid would have expected for someone who, as the General's first line of defence at midnight, must be a junior doctor. They nodded to each other from opposite ends of the trolleys.

'Found them in a pub, doctor. That one hasn't moved since we found him. This one's quiet enough now but needs watching. Seems to be all right except for that gash on his cheek.'

The unconscious man had been turned on his side on the trolley and the Casualty Officer's hands came away sticky with blood as he cursorily examined pupils and reflexes. He looked up at the ambulance men and jerked his head.

'He's for admission. We'll sort him out later.'

The ambulance men gave an almost imperceptible nod of appreciation of a firm, quick decision. This young man was new to them and it was a comfort to them to know they were not stuck with a ditherer for the next six months. As the men bent their backs to the trolley, a head and shoulders reared on the other, suddenly demanding to know where they were taking his friend and what they were going to do to him. Wild-eyed, arms flailing, the wiry little man swung his legs down before being restrained. The doctor looked appealingly at Kincaid.

'D'you think you could stay and keep an eye on this one for a while? It's my first night here but the only sort of security we seem to have is a five foot nothing night porter who has gone to get some blood.' They smiled at each other with the generous condescension of big men. 'I've got a couple of other things to do before I can get to this one but I shouldn't be too long.'

'Of course, doctor. No problem.'

'Good. Let's push him in here then.' Between them, they trundled along the line of cubicles, past the pallid young student, silently longing for the mother she could never tell about the miscarriage, past the bus driver with the sore throat who had called in on his lonely walk home, and into the next vacant space. 'Might as well leave him on the trolley for now as we will have to take him to theatre later. I'll get a nurse to come and tidy him up a bit.'

Badger Kincaid stood, large and awkward amongst the quiet bustle but smiling with the instinctive camaraderie that exists in that exclusive trinity of police, ambulance men and Casualty staff. Only when the porter returned, a plastic bag of blood in each hand, did he detect the slight wariness of approach that he had now come to expect whenever he was in uniform. A good bit younger than Kincaid, his coat whiter than white against his black skin, he wore a pale blue, open-necked shirt. Short and slight, his jet black hair tight curled without a parting, he moved quickly, his feet making no sound as he did so.

Badger's smile intensified at the sight of the nurse who entered the cubicle, a tray in her hand. The one narrow stripe on her cap identified her as a first-year student and there was a tender diffidence in her touch as she set about clearing the grime from the unwashed, unshaven skin around the laceration. She smiled caringly at her patient who looked over her shoulder to give Kincaid a monstrous wink. The young girl leaned closer as she struggled to swab away some dried blood only to step back suddenly with a half-scream, half-sob of disgust. As she pulled herself away, her eyes closed, her face aflame, Kincaid saw the grimy hand withdrawn with alcoholic sluggishness from under the skirt.

For a moment Kincaid stood nonplussed, torn between a desire to comfort the now sobbing girl and to break the arm that still hung over the side of the couch. He began to move forward only to be pushed aside by an arm thrust out from a small, red-haired figure that strode into the cubicle.

'Stay where you are. Leave him to me.' Badger looked down to see a diminutive Staff Nurse, businesslike in transparent plastic apron and surgical gloves, take the tray from a nurse whose smile to a patient would never be quite the same again. 'Here, give me that. Stop that nonsense and go and help put the transfusion up on that girl next door. So you've just learned something you won't find in any of those textbooks you have to read these days. Never mind, it's not going to kill you.' Her voice softened though her face did not. 'And when you've finished next door, go and have your break.'

She turned to face the patient who, ever since her appearance, had indicated to Kincaid with grins, winks and nods that they had both better watch their step now. 'And now, my fine fella. You just try anything like that on me and see what it gets you. Come on, Romeo, let me try and get some of this mess off you, you great worthless lump.'

In spite of her none-too-gentle attention, as if soothed by the sort of talk he understood, the patient fell asleep and, as the Staff Nurse turned to leave, he began to snore. Before she left the cubicle, she turned to Kincaid. 'If you're going to stand there helpless, give me a shout if you get any more trouble with him.' Badger was still grinning sheepishly long after she had gone.

He watched the young girl wheeled away, a blood drip stand clamped to her trolley. He listened to the bus driver complaining how long it was taking to be seen. He was looking at his watch when the Casualty night porter came silently in. With a practised movement of his foot, he unlocked the trolley wheel but, before beginning to push, leaned over to whisper in the patient's ear. Badger imagined the few routine words of comfort to an anxious patient and was surprised at the hissing intensity of the last few syllables but there was no emotion in the face that was finally turned towards him. 'They're ready for him in theatre now,' the porter explained. 'Coming?'

Badger Kincaid swallowed as television screens of operating theatre dramas sped before his eyes. 'Yes, I suppose I'd better.'

'Please yourself.' The porter didn't seem too concerned about a policeman's finer feelings.

Kincaid had removed his soiled raincoat but he still looked down, pointing vaguely at his uniform.

'What about . . .?'

'Don't worry; nothing very grand. Just stand at the back. Keep out of the way.'

It was obvious from both the porter's and the Casualty Officer's attitudes to the patient in the theatre that they knew all about the young nurse's goosing. Their handling of the increasingly wary patient bore scant similarity to some baron of industry being helped on the operating table of some Wimpole Street clinic. But no one was totally prepared for the reaction that the sight of the syringe full of local anaesthetic produced. As the Casualty Officer advanced, syringe in hand, the patient retreated up the table, curling into a writhing, screaming mass and a flailing arm sent the Staff Nurse's instrument tray crashing. In silent fury, she glared at the three men standing around the table. In response, as if each taking a part of the body as his responsibility, the surgeon lay over the man's chest, Kincaid across the thrashing legs while the porter grasped a handful of lank, greasy hair. Still leaning on the chest, the surgeon brought the syringe to bear on one end of the torn cheek and, by delaying the needle's final insertion, could not resist enjoying a split second of malicious retribution, a split second during which three young men looked at each other and grinned.

3

On two days of the year, February 1st and August 1st, the Health Service undergoes a brief period of upheaval when almost all the most junior ranks take part in a process of vocational musical chairs which is anything but a game. A few, a favoured few – the gifted students, the fast talkers, the outstanding rugby players, the ones with contacts – do no more than change bosses within the safe bastions of the Teaching Hospital. Others, the majority, decamp ten, twenty, one hundred miles to settle gratefully for at least another six months' security. A small band of intelligent dissidents, student oddballs, overseas graduates and plain lazy bastards finally grab those unpopular, unfilled jobs that hold no future for anyone, leaving a tiny final residue in embittered limbo.

Friday, February 1st, 1985 was no exception.

Jonathan Brookes drove his dark blue Golf GTI into Scarsby General's Casualty yard, weaving between the parked ambulances with the assurance of someone who had quietly, anonymously, reccied the place on foot the day before. He knew exactly where to park. He had seen the space reserved for the Casualty Officers marked out on the oil-slicked tarmac, the words, chipped and dirty, painted roughly on the old stone wall above. The walls of the yard were festooned with the external plumbing of the wards above, the constant drip from pipes leaving long-tailed stains on the stones, steam hissing from leaky joints adding to the sound of tyres on wet tarmac. The incontinent death throes of a well loved old centenarian that had served Scarsby well.

Isolated in a no-man's-land between the spheres of influence of the

Liverpool and Manchester Teaching Groups, considered too tactically unrewarding to be fought over, Scarsby General contained no specialised units staffed by ambitious young extroverts, no research projects to bring financial spin-offs for the hospital as a whole. Neither did it possess the lucrative private practice to attract the profession's thrusters to its consultant ranks. Scarsby, root, line and branch, was embedded in coal, with none of the private industry that begets executives with BUPA membership amongst their perks. Absent were the powerful industrial lobbyists with political clout and rich bored wives given to good work with the Friends of the Hospital. The male wards, where miners were cared for by the wives and the daughters of miners, throbbed with the ribald comradeship of the coal face, and anyone taking up a permanent appointment, young and naive enough to strive for change, was doomed to certain disillusionment. But, at last, the bulldozers were out on the outskirts of town, clearing the site for the new hospital that would be the excuse for no further money to be spent on the General in its declining years.

To the disinterested onlooker a dismal sight; to Jonathan Brookes, strangely exciting. It might as well have been Guy's or Bart's. He pulled into the space next to that reserved for the Casualty Consultant. The car that occupied the space was parked at an angle, its front wheels transgressing the white line, making it difficult for Jonathan, a fastidious driver, to open his door. His face twitched in a half-frown, half-grin as he looked at the vehicle, a rusting MOT-doubtful, sporting a hugely dented front wing; it had little in common with the consultants' cars he had been accustomed to seeing at the Royal Liverpool. Looking inside, he saw the driver's window half open, the seat wet. He glanced upwards. The rain had stopped but the sky looked heavy with snow. He walked round, found the driver's door open and ran the window up. He almost expected to see the keys in the ignition. He returned to his own car to take out a white coat – he wasn't too sure whether Scarsby General would provide one – and with this in one hand, a stethoscope in the other, Jonathan Brookes, one of Scarsby General's Casualty Officers for the next six months, presented himself at the Casualty Porter's desk.

'Yes, sir. Can I help you?'

The welcome was immediate and polite if unsmiling. Jonathan's excitement heightened a fraction. To attract that degree of respect at the Royal, one had to be well up the promotion ladder.

'Mr Bannerman. Where can I find him?'

'Straight down the corridor on the right, sir. Between Casualty and Casualty theatre.'

'Thank you.'

Jonathan felt the porter's eyes on his back, drawing in a first impression.

The long Casualty corridor was already heaving with early morning activity; the night shift worker with the split finger, the bawling child who knew the pain of having a burns dressing changed, the local Eleanor Rigby, patiently waiting for someone to find time to dress her varicose ulcer, a small service for which she was always so grateful. One or two nurses were not too busy to turn their heads as the tall, well-built young man with the white coat over his arm went by. Was he one of the new Cas Officers? Today was the day they all changed over. Jonathan found the door and read the plaque – Mr Robert Bannerman. He knocked.

'Come.'

The summons was instantaneous, loud and brisk, as if given with the intention of impressing. Jonathan Brookes opened the door and found he had to close it again behind him before he could reach the front of the desk. He put out his hand across space fogged blue with stale tobacco smoke.

'Good morning, Mr Bannerman. My name's Brookes. I've been appointed one of your SHOs for six months.'

If the room had appeared small as Jonathan had walked in, it seemed to shrink even further as the man behind the desk stood, leaned forward and shook his hand. He was no taller than Jonathan, who stood well over six feet, but his vast bulk made the younger man suddenly feel puny.

'Welcome to Scarsby General, hub of the universe.' Jonathan laughed politely at the remark, feeling, for some reason, more sadness than amusement. 'Sit yer down.'

Jonathan had to remove several files from the chair before he could comply. He had difficulty in finding somewhere to put them, such was the clutter. Bannerman made no move to help him and Jonathan finally solved the problem by piling them on the floor. As he bent, he came close to knocking over a squash racket propped in the corner. Sitting to face his new boss, he saw the plaster cast surrounding Bannerman's left wrist and thumb, the rugby team photograph on the wall above his head.

'So what possessed you to come to this God-forsaken part of the world?'

Jonathan felt his jaw sag, almost allowed his mouth to gape in surprise and disappointment.

'Well, sir ... I ...' he stammered. 'Basically, I suppose I've come to do the six months Casualty I need to comply with the College's requirements for the final Fellowship, but I am also keen to do it for its own sake. I'm really looking forward to it.'

'Hm.' Bannerman did not sound convinced. He stretched for the smouldering butt of the cigar on his desk. Heavy jowled with thick, deeply wrinkled skin, his high colour intensified with the congestion of a deep

21

rattling cough as he inhaled appreciatively. Jonathan waited in polite silence until the spasm passed. 'Yes, but why here, for pity's sake?' Bannerman wheezed on. 'I mean, with your background, your contacts, I would have thought you could have picked somewhere with a bit more class.'

'Well, sir, it's not quite . . .'

'And for God's sake, stop calling me "sir",' Bannerman broke in. He scowled, smiled and scowled again in a matter of seconds. 'The name's Bob, all right? We don't go in for that sort of thing around here anyway, but when it comes to people as senior as yourself it becomes downright bloody embarrassing. Right?'

'Yes, of course, si. . . Yes, of course.' Jonathan shifted in his seat. He would have preferred someone like the others he had worked for so far, those that had put a distance between themselves and him so that he had known exactly where he stood. He had a sudden, instinctive mistrust of so much fraternity so soon. 'Fact is, it's not so easy to get enough experience in trauma to satisfy the College without joining a rotation scheme that includes more orthopaedics than I want to do. Added to that, so many of the pure Casualty posts are filled by the GP vocational schemes now that jobs such as this are not that easy to find. But this has worked out very well; I am starting a General Surgical Registrar Rotation back in Liverpool in August and this couldn't have fitted in better,' he added hurriedly. 'But that doesn't mean I'm not looking forward to doing this job. I really am. I have just finished a General Surgery SHO post in Liverpool but you know what it's like in the teaching hospitals, hardly get to assist at an appendix. I'm looking forward to getting close to patients for once.'

'As long as you can stand the smell, now and again,' Bannerman growled and Brookes's young face frowned. 'You did Anatomy for a while; got a Ph.D., I believe?'

'That's right,' Jonathan agreed modestly.

'What on earth for?'

'I fancied myself as an anatomist at one time.'

'What made you change your mind?'

'I enjoyed the teaching, the students, but I got to miss the action. I found the department very quiet during the long vacs. Corpses don't talk much. They tend to lose their charm after a while.'

'It means you were a bit late starting to do surgery, weren't you? How old are you now?'

'Twenty-seven. I'll be twenty-eight in July.'

'And you got your Primary Fellowship while you were there?'

Jonathan nodded.

'First time?'

'Not difficult under those circumstances.'

Bannerman recalled the number of visits he had made to Queen Square and grunted. 'And how's your father?'

'He's very well, thank you, Mr Bannerman.' Jonathan wondered how this man whom he judged to be no more than in his early forties, could be so familiar with his father and the wary, protective note in his reply got through to Bannerman.

'Got over that spot of bother he had a few years back, has he?'

There was a kindliness in Bannerman's voice but Jonathan heard only morbid curiosity, felt threatened invasion of a privacy.

'He's fine, thank you.'

'The bastards,' Bannerman muttered. 'You watch it this next six months, d'you hear? You watch your tail. The swine will be after you too, given the slightest chance. Don't imagine it couldn't happen to you. D'you play squash?'

The sudden change of tack confused Jonathan.

'Yes,' he smiled. 'Not very well, but I do play.'

'Good. Perhaps we could have a game sometime; I should be having this off next week.' He waved his plaster cast. 'In the meantime, I suppose we had better get you organised, show you around, introduce you to your partner. We work in pairs here. You'll be working with the fair Janet. She's been here for six months and is staying on for another six so she knows all the ropes, will soon fill you in. And,' he grinned as he ground out his cigar, 'I'm afraid you're on night duty tonight. Just worked out that way, I'm afraid. Sorry. Comes of being the new boy.'

Jonathan smiled and shrugged his shoulders. 'It happens,' he said, good naturedly.

'Is there any Mrs Brookes to complain?'

'No.'

'That makes it easier then, doesn't it?' Bannerman heaved his bulk out of the chair and Jonathan glimpsed the belly, the belt and the sagging trousers. No pinstriped doyen. Bannerman looked out of the corner of his eye at Jonathan as he came round the desk. 'How come you've had such a good run then, big good-looking fella like you, twenty-seven and not married. Not one of these bloody poofters are you? Don't look like one.'

'No,' Jonathan laughed, adding, with a shudder, 'Thank God.'

'Right, then, come on.' And Bannerman led the way, his crumpled white coat fluttering loosely behind him, dispelling, like some invisible vapour trail, the cigar aroma that clung to it. His voice resounded down the corridor, turning heads, as he called wheezily for his departmental Sister.

Sister Gaunt was well named. Almost as tall as Jonathan, she was a poker-faced beanpole of a woman with rounded shoulders, a small lace cap pinned to the most obvious wig Jonathan had ever seen. Her large flat-heeled shoes had been split at the sides to accommodate her large flat feet, old companions that together had trudged many a corridor mile.

'Morning, Maisie. This is Dr Brookes, a born again surgeon who has wasted a few precious years contemplating his navel in academic retreat. We'll have to wait and see what he's like at trauma but if there's anything you would like to know about any part of your anatomy...' Bannerman gave a bubbling chuckle as he walked on but there was no amusement reflected in Sister Gaunt's face. In fact there was no emotion of any kind in her features as she nodded to Jonathan, just the flat, fatalistic stare of the afflicted.

Bannerman stopped in the centre of the long corridor, well within earshot of groups of patients who sat on long hard benches bolted to its walls, the degree of patience on their faces ranging from abject acceptance to smouldering anger.

'This is what passes for our waiting room.' He waved his arm expansively. 'It's not long since we had one of those know-it-all TV programmes here. D'you know what they told us? That we should install TV and those penny-in the-slot machines to amuse the patients who have to wait so long to be seen. Stupid bastards. I tried to tell them they haven't made bolts strong enough to fix the things to the wall. They didn't believe me when I told them they wouldn't last a week. Anything that isn't too hot or too heavy just goes. Isn't that so, Maisie?'

Bannerman did not wait for an answer as he slid back a door that rattled on its rollers. He stretched out his arm. 'Have a look at Sister's pride and joy.'

Jonathan saw a small windowless room, the central stainless steel couch surrounded by emergency equipment, all gleaming with the redolence of efficiency, the ambience that spells out, to the cognoscenti, frequent, skilled usage. No expensive high-tech showpiece, rarely used except to impress. And Jonathan, accustomed to a Teaching Hospital's banks of switches, cables and dials, saw the minimum of monitoring equipment that could not be denied, even in Scarsby.

'What Maisie calls her Intensive Care Unit; what I call her Expensive Scare Unit,' and Bannerman roared his way down another corridor. After a tour of the Casualty theatre, a Victorian, marble-floored, high-windowed old veteran, followed by the plaster room and various small clinics, they came to the department's core, the row of cubicles between whose curtains stood the hard-worn couches, body warmed throughout the day, sometimes the night. They crowded between curtains filled with the heart-rending howls of a small boy, struggling manfully against his mother's cooing restraint. They watched over a doctor's bent back, saw her remove a dressing stuck to the scald on the boy's chest, the red raw surface gleaming accusingly at a mother for her one moment's lapse in watchfulness at the end of a long and tiring day. As the doctor unwound, she turned towards them and Jonathan had the first impression of bright blue eyes beneath fair, almost ginger eyebrows. The upper tapes of the mask that covered half her face disappeared into auburn hair whose tight curls looked as natural as the fresh complexion over her cheekbones. As she cleaned the wound she kept up a chirpy conversation with Bannerman, seemingly oblivious to the strong young lungs bawling in her left ear. Satisfied, she nodded to a nurse to replace the dressing and walked away without a glance at child or mother. Outside the cubicle she stripped off her mask to reveal a small but humorous mouth in a pert, almost cherubic face devoid of makeup.

'Janet, this is Jonathan, Jonathan Brookes, your new sidekick. Jonathan, this is Dr James, a physician given to caring for moral wounds as well as physical, given half a chance. So watch your step; you have been warned.' Bannerman watched as they shook hands, relieved at an obvious immediate rapport. They looked as if they'd get on together without much trouble. 'Show him the ropes, would you, Janet, there's a good girl? Only watch out; he's twenty-seven, single and, by the look of him, probably drives a fast car. That's why I've put him with you; keep him on the straight and narrow while he's with us. Who knows; perhaps by the time you've finished with him, you'll have him banging a drum with you. What d'you say, Maisie?' There was affection in the nudge from Bannerman that made the tall, austere figure totter but, though she said nothing, Jonathan sensed the first flicker of resignation in Sister Gaunt's eyes. 'He's volunteered to do tonight, Janet. Nothing I could say would talk him out of it.' He turned. 'Come on then, Maisie; let's get stuck into those follow ups. How many wingeing woebegones have you got there for me this morning?'

Janet James saw the bemused look on Jonathan's face as he watched Bannerman disappear through the door. 'He's all right really,' she winked reassuringly. 'Heart of gold under that stupid front. Welcome to Scarsby.' She put out her hand and Jonathan felt a forthright grip. 'Are you really happy to do tonight? I'll do it if you want time to settle in.'

'Not at all.' Jonathan stood beside her as she washed her hands. 'I'm anxious to get stuck in.'

'Where are you staying?'

'Actually, there's no problem; I haven't had to move. I have a small house in Lymm. Means I can travel every day.'

'I'm impressed,' Janet said, and looked it. 'It's not often we have a career surgeon working here, let alone someone from the stockbroker belt. Everyone else has come to us from the GP vocational training scheme, each with a mortgage and about seventeen kids. We'll all have to watch our steps with you looking over our shoulders.'

'Rubbish. I'm the one who'll be glad of the advice.'

'I'm afraid your reputation has already gone before you. You already have something to live up to – Ph.D. in Anatomy and the Primary first time. One SHO scheme in a teaching hospital under your belt and accepted back there as a registrar six months in advance. Doesn't happen to everyone now does it? You're obviously going places.'

'What about you?' Jonathan asked. 'What d'you plan to do?'

'Whatever the Good Lord has in mind for me.'

Jonathan found nothing to say that would match the quiet sincerity of her reply.

'Perhaps you could give me a hand until lunchtime; it gets pretty hectic at times in the mornings. Then I suggest you go home and get your head down for a few hours. You might not get much tonight.'

The next four hours were a jumble of faces, arms and legs, twisted joints and X-rays, putting sutures in blood-sticky scalps, probing in jerking ears, noses and throats, trying to be civil to a stroppy, fat-gutted drinker with a headache he could have cured himself in any chemist, pulling him aside as a trolley sped on juddering wheels to the intensive care unit. Only once, and then only on a local procedural problem, did Jonathan seek advice from Janet James, finding her serenely helpful amidst all the purposeful bedlam that surrounds a miner who has had his chest stove in under a roof fall.

He stayed close to Janet as they ate a stereotyped hospital lunch in a stereotyped hospital canteen, surrounded by stereotyped hospital staff. He could pick out the other newcomers, carefully reading a menu they would know by heart in a week. Back in Lymm he tried to catnap and failed. He was an hour early for duty when he drove back, sleet flurries slanting across his headlights.

He did not see Janet again. There was no handing over of responsibility – no log to sign, no ceremony of the keys so honoured by the nurses – neither was there any formal introduction to the night staff. The Staff Nurse whom Jonathan had seen taking the report from Sister Gaunt passed him without a glance, a diminutive figure, rolling up her sleeves as she disappeared into the theatre. It would matter little to Peggy Wells to find that Jonathan Brookes's middle names were Adonis Croesus if he was no good at his job. She would reserve judgment until she had seen him under pressure, tired and stressed at 4 in the morning. He looked big enough, something in his favour; it had always been a comfort to have someone his size around with the drunks, but now – with some punk high on glue . . .

The night porter was more friendly, a black, slim young man who walked on the toes of his soft shoes with the gliding stealth of a gymnast, all his energy seeming to be spent economically in propelling him forwards in the horizontal plane with no detectable waste of effort in the vertical. Jonathan grinned to himself. Only bend his knees, he thought, and he would look like an athletic Groucho Marx. They had exchanged nods and smiles during the late evening rush, the tired hours of the day at the blurred interface of work and rest when human errors are rife. They came together in a lull when the corridors were silent, the cubicles empty.

'Welcome to the madhouse, Dr Brookes. Settling in? Anything you want to know, give me a shout.'

'Thank you.' The porter's accent was local but Jonathan wondered from what sun-scorched latitudes those genes had started their long journey to give such skin, eyes and hair. 'Are you on your own here at night?'

'You see before you, Dr Brookes, the night Casualty Porter, in other words, doorkeeper and bouncer, stretcher bearer and body humper, theatre orderly and lavatory attendant, messenger boy and telephonist.' He grinned engagingly as Jonathan took a second look at such an articulate porter. 'Oh, and I forgot; I'm an expert on cardiac arrest too, can get a tube down while a new Houseman is still scratching his arse, wondering what to do. No offence, Dr Brookes – you don't look that sort of chap – it just rankles a bit when you see the pay slip at the end of the week.'

Jonathan nodded sympathetically. 'Are you permanently on nights? Or are you on a rota?'

The porter shook his head. 'Up until now it has suited me. Perhaps shortly . . .' He stopped abruptly as they both heard the short, urgent ring from an ambulance. 'No peace for the wicked. Here we go again.'

The young woman's face was ashen with the stillness of shock and fear as she was wheeled into a cubicle. Jonathan took one end of the canvas as they transferred her on to the couch, smiling in surprise at the ease with which the porter lifted the other end. He looked at the doctor's letter, three words scribbled on the back of a prescription form by a weary general practitioner.

Studying Medicine had been no great hardship for Jonathan Brookes. He had had little difficulty in mastering all the various subjects, finding some deeply fascinating, others less absorbing, some downright boring. The study of Obstetrics and Gynaecology had been the sole exception and he had finally closed those textbooks with a sigh of relief that no more would he have to deal with something he had found distasteful, as if he had been a reluctant voyeur of something so privately feminine as to demand attention solely by other women. As he put his questions to the young woman, there was a tender diffidence in his voice that was not lost on the Staff Nurse standing opposite him.

'What's your name?'
'Annette.'
'How old are you, Annette?'
'Nineteen.'
'And what's your job?'
'I'm a student.'
Jonathan had to bend to hear the whisper.
'Where?'
'Manchester.'
'And where's your home?'
'Bristol.'
'Do your parents . . .? Would you like us to . . .?'

Tears welled up in eyes opened wide in alarm. She shook her head violently as Staff Nurse Wells screwed hers up, looking closely at the doctor opposite her, wondering whether they were dealing with another of those cocky bastards of doctors who always knows what's best.

'All right, all right,' Jonathan Brookes smiled. 'Don't worry; we'll look after you. We're not going to do anything you don't want us to do.' His tone became slightly more hesitant, as if apologising for the intrusion of her private life. 'Have you taken anything? You haven't done anything, been anywhere . . .? Did you want the baby?'

'Did?' There were the signs of agitation again. 'Does that mean I've lost it?'

It was impossible to say whether the agitation was due to relief or despair, and Jonathan cursed himself for his tactlessness.

'Honestly, I just wouldn't know. I'm not an expert but I would have thought you should accept the possibility with that amount of bleeding. But you can never tell. We'll get one of the obstetricians down to see you as soon as we can and he'll be able to tell you more accurately. But don't worry, you're going to be all right.' He tousled the fair hair above the pallid forehead, the maximum permitted caress between young doctor and attractive patient, a gesture that put him in credit with the Staff Nurse.

No mention of the embryo's other progenitor. It was as if Jonathan was reluctant to dispel the possibility of a virgin birth in someone so young and so alone.

Outside the cubicle, nurse turned to doctor.

'You won't get the gynae registrar for a while; they've only just gone into theatre with an ectopic. What do you want to do with her?'

'She obviously needs admission but I thought it might save a bit of time to send her straight to theatre from here, if that's what they decide is the right thing to do.' Jonathan resisted the temptation to ask the Staff Nurse what she thought. 'We'll let them know she's here but we'll get some blood up on her while she's waiting. Can you fix that, Staff?'

Peggy Wells's only answer was to reach for the blood forms for Jonathan to sign. 'Cut hand in theatre, Dr Brookes; they took him straight in,' she said over her shoulder as she bustled back into the cubicle, syringe and bottles in hand.

Between cases, waiting for theatre to be made ready, Jonathan paced the corridor, stretching cramped legs, when, for the second time, an ambulance's warning ring sent a surge of adrenalin to wash away fatigue. Minutes later, still in the corridor, he was examining two drunks brought in by the police after a bottle fight. One, deeply unconscious and bleeding from head wounds, he admitted direct to the ward – no point in getting the intaking firm down to see him first. The other one looked as if he might be trouble and Jonathan asked a hefty young copper if he would stay and keep an eye on the patient while Jonathan saw to another couple of cases first.

Jonathan had just found the broken-off needle in a diabetic's thigh when Staff Wells stormed in to give him her unsolicited opinion of men in general and one drunken groper in particular. Jonathan knew exactly which nurse had been involved, he had already quickened to her innocent, friendly smiles, and his mental picture of a grimy, bloodstained hand against a cool-skinned thigh drained his face of any compassion as the porter wheeled the trolley into theatre. The young copper, large, bulky and incongruous, was pushed to one side by the Staff Nurse as she closed the door. Transferred from trolley to table, the patient became more and more watchful, wary eyes moving slyly from side to side. At the sight of the syringe of local anaesthetic in Jonathan's hand, he began a moaning sound that rapidly became a scream as he writhed and flailed his way towards the top of the table. Jonathan found himself taking a certain delight in doing nothing more than holding the needle aloft until driven to take action by the fury of Peggy Wells's look as her instrument tray went crashing.

As if more fearful of the Staff Nurse's wrath than any thought of physical injury from the patient's wildly swinging fists and feet, the porter gleefully grabbed some hair while the policeman threw his considered weight across the legs. Jonathan leaned over the heaving chest and, in one exquisitely lingering moment of retribution, held the needle in full view. Suddenly alarmed at the possible reaction of his assistants to such uncharacteristic callousness, he looked around only to see two broad young grins of approval.

4

Gavin Prescott was a real bastard, not by nature but by birth. It was an estate of which he was not particularly proud but he had grown up in a sufficiently realistic world to appreciate that there were worse things to be. He accepted that it would probably tell against his chances of getting into the Royal Enclosure at Ascot but then there were other adverse factors at play there – like being black and having no money. A young man who thrived on adversity, he frequently counted his blessings. He could have been born deaf or blind or mentally deficient. As it was, the only hereditary trait left him by his fleet-footed father, apart from the colour of his skin, was a nimble brain that had been denied the education it had deserved by the grinding burden of a stupid mother and her dependent family.

'Ma, are you getting up?' he shouted up the stairs.

Eva Morelli stuck a podgy hand out of the grey sheets, pulled the emaciated eiderdown up over her shoulder and rolled on her side, trying to get away from the bitter cold of a February morning.

Gavin tried again. 'Ma, are you getting up this morning? Do you want a cup of coffee?' He waited, heard nothing, shrugged his shoulders and went back into the kitchen to sit at the table where supper and breakfast were being eaten simultaneously.

'I'm not surprised, the time she came in last night.' The teenage schoolgirl, spotless in grey skirt and V-necked jumper, her long fair hair hanging over the collar of a freshly ironed blue shirt, sank her teeth into her toast with more than relish. 'Had me out of bed at two o'clock 'cos she didn't have no key.'

'Linda, I'll thump you if you don't learn to speak properly. It's "didn't have a key" or "had no key", not "didn't have no key". The fact that you are going to be a doctor doesn't mean you don't have to speak properly. You'll be starting to have your interviews soon; what chance have you got of getting into medical school if you talk like that?'

His half-sister, the first child Eva had conceived in wedlock, didn't look unduly chastened. 'Whichever way you say it, I still had to get up and it was bloody cold, I tell you.'

'You also swear too much.' He looked affectionately at his sister with all the pride and joy of someone regarding his one prized possession. It was well after nine o'clock but there was no call to be worried. She was never late for school; she must have a free period to start the day. 'What about Wayne? What time did he come in?'

'God knows. I never hear him.'

'Does he have a key?'

The chewing stopped only long enough for Linda to pull the corners of her mouth down. 'Shouldn't imagine that bothers him too much. Doesn't seem to have much trouble getting in anywhere, does he?'

Their eyes met in an atmosphere of 'us' and 'them', two of this world's survivors sharing unspoken fears of being dragged down by two of its losers. Gavin wagged his finger across the table. 'Don't ever leave the doors unlocked for anyone when you're here on your own, d'you hear? Don't open the door until you are absolutely sure who's outside.'

'Can't open the front door anyway; it's stuck.' Linda gulped her mug of tea, glancing at the raucous alarm clock that stood slowly rusting away in the greasy dampness above the stove. Perhaps she was late after all.

'And those things in his ears,' Gavin grumbled.

'What things? Who?'

'Your brother. Those brass stud things. What on earth does he want those things for?'

Linda gave him one of her rare smiles, slowly. 'You're getting old, Gav. You'll be voting for Maggie Thatcher next. Anyway, they're not brass, they're gold.'

'Gold, did you say. Gold? Where did he get that sort of money from, then?' Gavin asked and his question went unanswered except in doubt and fear. He watched the smile fade from her face as slowly as it had come. He saw with sadness the worldly, womanly look on the face of someone who should still be a laughing innocent. There had been the early years when she had been just that, a grubby-faced tomboy, oblivious of a drab, threadbare existence in her unquestioning enjoyment of being alive. But there had come the time when open-faced trust had suddenly been replaced by questioning doubt, itself slowly moulded into watchful, determined prematurity. Now, she never laughed.

Gavin watched her stand up and pull on her duffel coat, slinging a bulging school bag over one shoulder. At least he could give thanks for one thing. She was no tight-skirted, gum-chewing, flint-faced punk as so many of her erstwhile class mates had become. He said nothing as he saw her leave her dishes for him to clear away and add to the pile left from the previous night. He was content in the knowledge that in that school bag lay his sister's passport out of Northend, work completed without bidding late into the night in the head aching fumes of the old paraffin stove in her bedroom. It was a stove he would lovingly refill before he himself went to bed, knowing that in its warmth germinated the hope of escape not only for Linda but for himself. He would have turned his back on Northend long since had it not been for his determination never to leave her defenceless in Northend again.

31

'I'll have your tea ready about six.'

'You working again tonight, Gav?'

'Yes.'

'Right. See you then, Gav.'

'Take care, love.'

The slam of the side door left Gavin Prescott with no human contact apart from the creak of a bed upstairs. Where others might have sighed he clenched his jaw a little harder and cleared away. He washed and dried the dishes, ran lightly up the stairs to his bedroom, returning with books, pad and pencil case. These he spread on the kitchen table and began writing in the dwindling vestige of warmth remaining from their meal. It was not long before the same books were slammed shut with angry frustration as tiredness and cold overcame determination. He climbed the stairs once more to pause at the door to his half-brother's bedroom. He thought about going in, decided there was nothing to be gained by doing so, and passed on. Stripped to T-shirt and pants he climbed into bed, having closed worn unlined curtains that were about as effective at keeping out the daylight as a pane of frosted glass. He picked up a book once more and fell asleep without turning a page. When he woke, the light was failing. He drew the curtains to see the rain giving way to snow flurries.

Downstairs, walking into the kitchen, he was enveloped in a soft billowing blanket of inertia. Gazing down reluctantly at an ironing board, carefully placing her cigarette in an old chipped scallop shell at just that angle that would send a thin acrid column of grey smoke up into the cold, still air, stood his mother. Eva Morelli's head, her uniformly blonde hair corkscrewed into curlers, was covered in a pale blue muslin scarf tied at her forehead. Flaccid, atrophied breasts hung braless beneath a threadbare petticoat, hirsute nipples clearly visible as she bent forwards in a fit of coughing. She wore an arcuate bruise above a prominent collar bone like a badge of honour. Sitting on the table, his feet on a chair, Wayne Morelli rocked gently to a rhythm being pounded into his skull by a Walkman, slapping his thighs in time to the music, making the frills along the seams of his black leather jacket dance. Neither registered Gavin's entry by word or glance.

'Ma, you'll catch your death like that. Why don't you put some clothes on?'

'Hullo, love.' His mother smiled as she looked up. 'Sleep well, did you?'

'Why haven't you lit the fire? It's like an icebox in here.'

'Didn't see the point, Gav, seeing we're all going out later. Anyway, it wasn't laid, was it?'

'And I don't suppose it occurred to you to lay it yourself for once, Ma? Or get Wayne to do it?'

'What, Wayne?' She looked placidly at both her sons with equal affection. 'Don't you remember the right bloody mess he left last time he done it? Any road, I'm not sure there's enough coal left.' She didn't seem too concerned by the possibility. 'You'd think they'd put in central heating these days, wouldn't you? All them houses up Tennyson and Milton Roads have got it now. Talk about a Labour bloody Council. Are you going to make our Linda's tea?' She didn't wait for an answer as she inhaled deeply, smiling her thanks through the reluctantly exhaled smoke. 'That's right kind of you, Gav, is that. Don't know what I'd do without you, straight I don't.'

Gavin winced at the thought of his mother and instant warmth at the flick of a switch. 'Are you out again tonight, Ma? I don't like the thought of Linda alone in the house so much.'

'Linda? She's all right; nice and snug she is, up in that bedroom of hers. Got plenty of common sense as well as brains has our Linda. She can look after herself. I won't be late. If she's worried she can always knock the wall for old Foggie. Very fond of our Linda, them two in their way, you know. Stuffy pair of old buggers at times but not bad hearted really.'

Fred Boardman and his wife, retired after thirty years foot slogging the streets of Northend, militarily erect, to read the electricity meters, now enduring patiently the bitter months until he would be able once more to plant the rank and file of his beloved garden. A respectable couple, bound to honest routine, that had found themselves living cheek by jowl with the Morellis in the housing lottery of a working-class council estate. Wall-to-wall loving comfort and cold, feckless existence, one brick apart.

'I've got to make the most of it while I can.' Eva winked at her son, moving the ironing board a few inches to allow him to get to the cooker, a packet of mince in his hand. 'Not long now and your father will be home and then, by heck, it'll be look out; have to behave myself then. Have to do what I'm told then like, won't I?'

'Why do you keep calling him my father, Ma? You know I don't like it. He's not my father.'

'He'd like you to think of him as your father, you know, Gav. Always been very generous, Gav. Got to be fair, like. Not many men would have taken a woman in with a kid like he . . .'

'With a black bastard in tow, you mean?'

'No, I never meant that, Gav. You shouldn't be so hard on yourself. What I mean is . . .'

As Gavin began to peel potatoes, quietly cursing the fact he had been too tired to do it earlier, he let his mother drivel on while he recalled bitterly his step-father's generosity, just how liberal he had been with his hidings, his curses and, perhaps most wounding of all, his indifference.

33

His very first memory of his step-father was one of pain and hatred, all arising from the matter of Gavin's dove, his tiny china dove. He could still feel its hard, smooth wings set in rigid flight. The planners had made generous allowance for Northend's mortality rate and the earliest tenants of the vast graveyard, their tombstones askew in grassy neglect at the far periphery, their peace now shattered by the vibrating roar of a motorway, had provided ideal cover for a child, be he cop or robber, cowboy or injun. It was at a time when he was still young enough for his street gang to think nothing of the colour of his skin as they had raced and hidden and banged and shot and killed and died and resurrected in seconds amongst the weedy hillocks and pitted marble. But the dove had been his own secret, lying in the long grass, tethered with rusting, fragmenting wire to the white china flowers beneath their glass dome. He had longed to set it free, to give it warmth, and he had braved the spooky darkness of a December night, stone in hand, to shatter the glass dome amongst the frost-hardened tussocks.

It had been Christmas Eve when he had found his secret hiding place bare. It had been a grinning Wayne who had stood behind his father as he had demanded to know where the little bastard had stolen it from, had watched with delight his father's futile attempts to beat the information out of a mute defiance. Gavin Prescott could still hear the sound of the dove being ground to powder on the bare boards, still hear the sound of the key being turned in the bedroom door, the prelude to a lonely, hungry Christmas.

There was a pause in his mother's monologue and he turned to see her lighting another cigarette.

'Do you have to smoke in here, Ma, especially at meal times?' She might as well have been stone deaf. 'When exactly does he get out?'

'Two weeks yesterday, love. I think I'll go down and meet him off the ferry this time if I've got the money. It's been a long stretch for him this time, him not getting no parole an' all. I think he'd like that.'

'He's a violent man, Ma. He could easily have killed that warder. He was lucky not to get another stretch. Do we have to have him here?'

'It's his home, i'n't it, Gav? Where else could he go? And that screw had it coming. They're all the same, them bastards.'

'We didn't see much of him last time, only when he wanted money.'

'But he had to give a proper address, like, Gav. They'd want to know where he was going, wouldn't they?'

'So they can keep an eye on him you mean. Means we'll have half the Northend nick crawling over this place again.'

Gavin lit the gas under the two saucepans. He turned to slide two plates and tarnished cutlery across the formica table. He put his hand in the small of his brother's back, pushing him off the table, feeling the bar-tight muscles through the thick jacket.

'I don't like him in the house here with Linda. You make sure he's never left alone with her, d'you hear, Ma? If he so much as puts a finger on her, I'll shop him, I give you my word, and then, with his record, they'll throw away the key. But I can't be here all the time.'

'You do go on about that, love. I'm sure he didn't mean no harm. He was very fond of our Linda; he just used to like a bit of a cuddle now and again. You kids never show no affection, ever. Don't even send a Christmas card, you don't. Wayne there, well you can't expect much can you, on the dole like that. But you and Linda; you never show no affection.'

'I'm just giving you fair warning, Ma; one word from Linda that he has so much as looked at her and he'll be back inside before he knows what's hit him.'

Gavin had been barely 17 when he had heard the sobbing, had gone into his step-sister's bedroom, had seen the man in her bed, had finally recognised a drunken step-father. In spitting fury he had hurled himself on the bed in a flurry of arms and legs only to be thrown off and hurled back into his own bedroom to nurse a split lip and loose tooth, burying his head in his pillow to shut out all sound. He had taken to sleeping with his sister, feeling nothing other than protective to the soft pubescent girl alongside him, sharing her degradation as he had been turned out in the early hours, enduring her shame as he had listened to his father's drunken groaning and to her silence.

Respite had come, suddenly and savagely. The sledge hammer through the front door and the policeman's shoulder bursting through the kitchen door had been simultaneous. There had been the legalised ransacking of the pitifully fragile furniture as they had searched and gleefully uncovered the stolen goods that had cost a night watchman the sight of one eye. And then the long, silent, poker-faced wait. It had been early in the morning before they had heard the steps outside, the drunken farewells. The scuffle had been vicious but brief. To Wayne Morelli, watching his idol being dragged away, it had been bitter proof that the police persecuted the poor in their task of protecting the wealthy and the powerful. To Gavin Prescott it had all the sweetness of revenge. When it came to informing, he had been taught by the best.

For six years, a degree of peace had settled over a divided house. And now Patrick Morelli was coming back. But six years had passed, time that had not been wasted. Another year; just one more. That's all they needed. Time to get Linda into a medical school as far from Scarsby as possible, where Gavin could find a job too. Neither would have the slightest trouble in walking out on their mother without a backward glance. Years of

35

neglect had slowly eroded all respect. There would be nothing to hold them back. He gave a little shiver at the thought of slamming that kitchen door for the last time. Then he could work days, would not need the extra money the night shift brought in, would be able to sign on for night classes, maybe even the Open University, would be able to train most nights, not just two in seven.

He called up the stairs to Linda and returned to the kitchen. He attracted his brother's attention by facing him squarely, mouthing words as if speaking to the deaf.

'What about your tea? And your Ma's?'

Wayne Morelli lifted one earphone and one eyebrow without missing a beat of his head.

'What about your tea and your mother's?' Gavin repeated.

'Go up the Chinkie.' The earphone was replaced.

'Have you got money?'

Gavin was ignored, his brother's eyes focused somewhere above his mother's head.

'These take-aways are expensive,' Gavin shouted and there was overt irritation in Wayne's face as he took the earphone away for a second time.

'Eh?'

'Where are you getting all this money?'

'Had a few jobs on the side, haven't I?' Wayne grinned.

'Work, my arse. You're in bed most of the day. Where did you get the money for that Walkman? And those things in your ears, are they gold? How did you pay for those?'

The thick leather jacket creaked as Wayne leaned forwards. He spoke slowly and deliberately, equally deliberately letting the earphones spring back into place.

'Why don't you sod off?'

Gavin Prescott's night shift was from 10 p.m. to 7 a.m. The cold night air cut through the worn tracksuit as he closed the door behind him. He shivered in the darkness as he walked along the side of the house and across their tiny front garden, his feet instinctively finding mud patches trodden into uncut grass. He stepped over the sagging wire fence between the only two privet bushes that had survived the attentions of Northend's stray dogs. There was an unaccustomed tension in his stride as he set out on the four-mile run to Scarsby General; there were icy patches on the uneven paving stones and a broken ankle would have catastrophic results on his razor edge economy.

He changed into the clothes Sister Maisie let him keep in a locker in the unit store room. There was no question of a shower however; the sweat, now cold, would have to dry on him. There would be no question of hot water for a bath at home either. There were times when he went as long as a week between those exquisitely prolonged soakings at the sports centre and he often worried how he must smell during humid summer nights. He pulled on a clean white coat, taking care as he pinned his identification and NUPE badges to its lapel. He exchanged respectful nods with Staff Nurse Wells and went in search of his first sight of the new Casualty Officer and was relieved to find a big man with the look of someone anxious to make friends. He was always happier working with big men, those with nothing to prove. This one looked at him as if he'd seen him, not his skin, as if he would not be above talking to a porter, even a black one. His first impression was confirmed as they chattered during a lull between cases.

'Seems a nice chap, Staff,' Gavin observed later as he watched Peggy Wells take blood with deceptive ease from the collapsed veins of a shocked young girl not much older than Linda.

'Who?'

'Dr Brookes.'

'So far, so good.'

'You're a hard woman, Peggy Wells,' he smiled. 'What does someone have to do to impress you?'

'Early days yet, Gavin. They're all anxious to please at first in case they need some help. Don't take long to start their tantrums as soon as they find their feet. Here, take these up to the lab.' She handed him the forms and bottles. 'Quick as you can. Bring the blood back with you; we can manage down here for a while.'

When he got back, a unit of blood in each hand, he found a vast policeman standing amongst the cubicles. Though the copper looked prepared to be friendly, Gavin felt the inevitable turning inwards of his mind that he found impossible to prevent whenever he got too close to blue uniforms and silver buttons. To him they represented something to be shunned, innocent or guilty. He delivered the blood on his way to theatre. He returned later to find a tear-stained student nurse and a furious Staff Nurse, one dumbly distressed, the other only too ready to give her views on the matter. He had helped hand over the shocked patient to the gynaecologists and had pacified a whingeing bastard of a bus driver with a sore throat before he walked into the cubicle that reeked of booze, blood and body stench. Pointedly ignoring the policeman standing just inside the curtains, he leaned to whisper in the patient's ear.

'I think it would be better if you and I were to understand each other from the start, matey. You are now dealing with someone fortunate enough not to be bound by the ethics of a great profession. And don't be fooled by the way I talk. I come from your world; I know your type well.

37

So let's get one thing quite clear from the start, shall we? One more word out of line from you and I'll screw your balls off.' He wiped the cold hatred from his face as he turned to the young copper. 'They're ready for him in theatre now. Coming?'

Gavin Prescott helped transfer the patient from trolley to operating table. Normally he would have left but he stood to watch the new Casualty Officer at work. This one had the air of someone already quite experienced, but you never could tell. The first few sutures and you could be pretty sure what you had got for the next six months, even the way he put the local anaesthetic in. Gavin had another reason for not leaving; he was enjoying the patient's obvious terror, taking delight in the slightest pain given to someone resembling in so many ways an animal he so detested. He was relishing the scene when an instrument tray went crashing and a few well chosen words from Peggy Wells sent him scurrying willingly to the man's head. It was not solely the greasiness of the man's hair that made him take such a vicious grip to turn the head sideways. It made the man yelp, drunk as he was, and Gavin Prescott made no attempt to hide the smile of satisfaction on his face as he looked up, only to find it mirrored by the two hefty young men lower down the table.

5

Only drunks shout after dark. In any hospital ward, day or night, it is unforgivable to raise one's voice, but Casualty Departments such as Scarsby General's were always built some distance from the nearest wards. During the day, with working clothes, howling children and dripping umbrellas, they are only one degree removed from the street outside and it is not unknown to have to shout the length of a corridor to make oneself heard. But, even in Casualty, night duty is always endured in a hushed, almost whispering fatalism by those who feel they are simply holding together strands of existence between episodes of the real daylight world. Permanent night staff in a general hospital are a breed apart, a quiet, unobtrusive, self-possessed coterie often preferred by the patients as bringing peace from the exhausting hurly burly of a hospital day. Private people, they come and go, facelessly, taken for granted. They suffer the same torpidity as anyone who cannot sleep at 4 in the morning, the only difference being that they do it for a living.

The door of the white police Transit van was slammed shut, there were a few subdued grinning profanities between the driver and Badger Kincaid before the van drove off to leave Kincaid and Brookes in the doorway.

'How will you get back?' Jonathan asked.

'I ring Northend nick and my oppo will come and fetch me.'

'D'you feel like a coffee?'

'Wouldn't say no, doctor. I'm due for a break about now.' He suddenly thrust out his hand. 'Name's Kincaid, doctor; Badger Kincaid.'

Brookes took the hand and shook it. Of similar height, they faced each other squarely. 'Brookes; Jonathan Brookes. Let's go and see what we can find.'

Staff Nurse Peggy Wells saw them descending on her down the now deserted corridor. She saw all the signs. Stern and unsmiling, she jerked her head.

'All right. Go in Sister's room. What d'you want, tea or coffee?'

Sister Gaunt's room still had a fireplace. Though cold for more than thirty years, it had survived when the old coal-fired donkins with their highly polished tiled surfaces had been removed from the middle of the Nightingale style wards. Its rusting bars still held their strange attraction however and Peggy Wells found the two men sitting facing the fireplace when she came in, carrying, with difficulty, three hot mugs. Kincaid jumped to his feet to take one from her, standing as if offering his seat as she gave another of the drinks to Brookes. Slowly he sat once more as she ignored his good manners. She put her mug on the old cast iron mantlepiece to rummage in a large shoulder bag.

'It's tea, all right? Some thieving beggar on days has nicked our coffee. Where the hell are my matches?' She lit her cigarette without offering one to the men. She inhaled deeply. 'That's better; I've been dying for a fag.' Mug in one hand, cigarette in the other, she lowered herself on to a small stool where she sat, knees agape. Kincaid, sitting facing her, shifted his chair to one side, honest embarrassment flushing his face. Together they surveyed the empty fireplace until Jonathan Brookes broke the silence.

'That sort of case frightens the life out of me,' he admitted. 'It's the classical set up, isn't it? Man brought in drunk with a head injury; can't be certain if there has been a period of unconsciousness; is it just head injury or something more? Poor devil of a casualty officer decides he's just drunk and the patient is found dead in the cells the next morning from an extradural haemorrhage. Many's the promising career's been blighted like that. The way to avoid it is, of course, to admit every drunk overnight and you can imagine the fuss that would cause.' He turned to Kincaid. 'Assuming I've been lucky tonight, what will happen to that bright little beauty in the morning?'

'Night in the cells, charged tomorrow morning, probably out on bail to appear before the Magistrates. It'll depend a bit on whether he's got any form or not. By the look of him, I wouldn't be surprised if he's had free board and lodging from Her Majesty at some time or another.'

'What will you charge him with?'

'I don't really know but I'm sure the Inspector will think of something. He doesn't take too kindly to people coming at us with broken bottles. Intent to inflict grevious bodily harm, causing an affray, obstructing a police officer in the course of his duty, disturbing the peace, drunk and disorderly – take your pick. If the Inspector's got a hangover or quarrelled with the missus,' Kincaid grinned, 'he'll probably throw the lot at him. And, of course, there's the other guy. He might want to bring charges when he regains consciousness though he probably won't remember a thing about it. Not that they take action against each other very often, these people. They tend to stick together, don't shop each other very often.'

'Like the police, you mean?' Peggy Wells did not flinch from looking directly at Kincaid whose forehead furrowed in honest concern. 'Perhaps we should have counted all his cuts and bruises before he left, compare them with the ones he's got tomorrow morning.'

'That doesn't go on very often,' Kincaid said, his frown now so deep that blonde, bushy eyebrows almost met. 'I'm not going to say it has never happened but it's not as common as people make out. I've never seen it.'

'Don't get me wrong.' The Staff Nurse took some of her tea in forthright, noisy swallows. 'In here, I treat everyone the same. They're patients – full stop. If Prince Charles walked in here with a cut head, as far as I was concerned, he would have to wait his turn.'

'I can believe that.' The frown dissolved into a broad grin.

'But, outside, I wouldn't be above taking an animal like that round the corner and teaching him a lesson. It's the only language they understand. But it's different if you take it out on someone just because you have a grudge against him. That, I think, is vile.'

Jonathan Brookes decided it was time to change the subject.

'Forgive me for saying so but that's an unusual name you have.' He looked at Kincaid as if he hoped he was not offending him. 'Badge, was it? Badger?'

'Badger.'

'Never heard that name before,' Peggy said. 'Is that your Christian name?'

'Yes and no. Please don't laugh but my real name is Cecil, Cecil Kincaid. Now who ever heard of someone called Cecil Kincaid?' He waited patiently for the inevitable good-natured sniggers to subside. 'Sir Cecil Kincaid, now that's got a ring to it – I'll be all right when they make me Chief Constable – but when you're in school with a name like that, and no alternative, you've got to be big and in the school fifteen, you've got to be one of the sixth form louts, otherwise you get hell. The only possible reason I have for liking it is that I'm named after my grandfather who was killed underground when I was 2. But it seems that 'badger' was the nearest I could come to saying "grandpa" when he was alive and the name stuck. Now you can't blame me for encouraging that, can you? Anything is better than Cecil.'

Jonathan nodded. 'I think I can understand that. How long have you been in the police?'

'Not long. Still a bit of a rookie, I suppose.' Both doctor and nurse looked at him enquiringly and he went on, hesitantly, as if he doubted their interest. 'I got fed up with teaching.' They still said nothing. 'I got brassed off, living in digs and taking stick from a bunch of louts in a London East End Comp.'

When, once again, they said nothing, looking genuinely interested, he relaxed, smiling. 'I'm not saying there weren't a lot of good kids there, I'm sure there were. But these days you don't find yourself teaching the really talented youngsters when you are just out of university with only a red-brick two two in geography to offer. I tried,' he laughed. 'My God, how I tried. I stuck it for about two years. But the kids I ended up teaching were more into drugs and foreplay than the finer points of second phase possession on the rugby field. In the classroom I tried being friendly, being the father figure. When that failed I tried brute bloody force but, when one of the boys finally drew a knife on me, I cracked. I reckoned they didn't pay or protect me enough for that. So I joined the force as a graduate entrant and I haven't regretted it for a moment; I'm enjoying every minute of it. I'm just coming to the end of my two years on the beat and then it's Staff College, I can't wait.'

'So, how old does that make you?'

'Twenty-six, nearly twenty-seven.'

'Interesting,' Jonathan said while Peggy Wells looked again at the copper with the fair, almost albino eyelashes lowered in genuine modesty. She tried not to see him with truncheon and shield and failed. She sniffed; they were all the same, drilled stupid in what they called discipline. It didn't matter much what he was like before he joined, by the time they'd finished with him, he'd split a miner's scalp and laugh at it, like the rest of them.

'I suppose,' Jonathan mused, sliding down the chair, his chin on his chest, 'I've done much the same sort of thing. I tried teaching too, had a taste of the academic way of life, though I must admit,' he looked up with a smile, 'I never had anyone come at me with a scalpel.'

He, in turn, became the centre of interest in the silence of the high-ceilinged, dusty old room.

'I'm not given much to hero worship, something I've rather picked up from my Dad. But there is one exception, my old Professor of Anatomy; I must admit I've come near to idolising him at times. He offered me a research post just as I was finishing my house jobs and I jumped at it. And I loved it, working for a man who had my total respect, doing something I found fascinating, teaching young, lively medical students. Then I got my Ph.D. and I lost some of my drive; then I began the same teaching course all over again for the fourth time to a lot of students who were identical to the previous lot except for their faces. I could see that stretching ahead of me for the next thirty years. So I got out too but for the very opposite reason to yours; it was the peace and tranquillity that drove me out.' He grinned. 'Perhaps I could say the deathly silence got to me.'

He finished off the dregs from his mug, throwing his head back to do so.

'I must say the Prof took it well, helped me get a good job back in the medical school. But then, he's that sort of a guy. I tried to explain. Told him I wanted something more, more . . .' Jonathan struggled for the word, 'active, more physical.'

'Macho. That's what you mean.' Peggy Wells stubbed out her cigarette against the fireplace. 'All the bloody surgeons are the same, they all like to think of themselves as the macho branch of the profession.' She saw Badger Kincaid snigger. 'Just like the police. You're just the same. You two should get on well together.'

'And the miners?' Badger asked gently but, getting no more than a pout in reply, he turned to Jonathan. 'Do you come from this part of the world, doctor?'

Jonathan found himself saying something Bannerman had said earlier that day, something that had made Jonathan uneasy. Perhaps it was different between two young men of similar age. 'For God's sake stop calling me "doctor". The name's Jonathan. No, my home is up in Dunbridge. My father is a general surgeon up there.'

'Runs in the family, then,' Badger said, kindly.

'I suppose so. My mother was a doctor too although she never practised. She died when I was quite young.'

Silent, gentle sympathy stopped the conversation for a moment.

'Something we differ in then, d ...' Badger managed not to say the word but could not yet use the Christian name. 'I'm afraid I broke the mould when I joined the Police.'

'Oh?'

'Yes; I come from a mining family. My grandfather was killed underground, all his brothers and all my uncles were miners and I have a brother a miner. My father didn't actually work underground but he was a mining engineer.'

'Did you say you have a brother a miner?' Peggy's sharp question cut into the dialogue between the two men.

'Yes.'

'And is he out?'

'Of course.'

Peggy Wells noted the pride in the curtness of the reply and her eyes narrowed as, for the first time, her voice softened. 'Then that must be very difficult for you, both of you.'

'It's had its moments, I must admit.'

Jonathan suddenly felt that he was standing aside, irrelevant, as two minds met, albeit for a moment.

'And you? Any miners in your family?'

'Two brothers.' She looked at Kincaid as if daring him to ask if they were out.

'No doubt where your sympathies lie then at the moment,' Brookes smiled at Peggy Wells and was made to realise what a stupid remark that had been by the look she shot his way. 'I mean, I expect you have had quite a few injured picketing miners in here recently?'

'You might say that.'

Jonathan glanced towards Kincaid, trying to be the honest broker. 'And, no doubt, one or two police as well.'

'I haven't seen any yet,' Peggy was too quick for Kincaid.

'As you can see, Jonathan,' clear blue eyes looked at Brookes from under the fair lashes, 'you won't find much sympathy to spare for the poor bloody coppers at the moment. Is there any mining up in Dunbridge?'

'No.'

'So you won't understand,' Peggy said.

'That's not fair, Staff.' Jonathan might be the new boy but he was not prepared to take everything lying down. 'Dunbridge is not exactly Cheltenham or Bath. It's got quite a bit of heavy industry around.'

'But no mining?' Peggy persisted.

'No.'

'Then you won't understand.'

Peggy's attitude was dismissive, almost damning, brooking no argument.

'What Staff Nurse means,' Badger began – he hesitated, seeing her anger that he should presume to know her that well – and ploughed on doggedly. 'What she means is that, now you are working here, you are going to have to decide; are you with them or against them? The miners I mean, obviously; no one around here is for the police. And, if you want to get on with the staff here, the sooner you learn to understand the miners, the better.'

Jonathan said nothing, tacitly inviting Badger to go on.

'The first thing you must realise, Jonathan, is that the miner is unique and proud of it. He is ... He is, within the working class, perhaps a bit like the surgeons in medicine, if what Staff Nurse said just now is true. He is the macho worker, proud and fearless, very jealous of his image, very protective of his own. That's why to be a scab is to be an outcast. He cannot accept that anyone who calls himself a miner could possibly break ranks. He is so used to physical danger that, man to man, he'll die before he gives an inch. That's what's so pitiful now, he's so bloody obstinate he can't see that, this time, he's bitten off more than he can chew.'

'Rubbish.' Peggy Wells tried to make the word incisive but there was sufficient doubt in her own mind to dull its edge.

'It's all very sad,' Badger said, quietly, and, this time, Peggy Wells did not disagree with him. They both fell silent and Jonathan Brookes searched for something else to talk about.

'That young nurse earlier tonight, Staff; that was unfortunate, wasn't it? Is she still very upset?'

'She'll survive.' Peggy Wells saw his look of disapproval. 'Look, after you have been down here for a while, you'll learn to take things as they come. If you are going to get concerned about a thing like that, how are you going to feel about the 4-year-old girl we had in last week, violently raped by her uncle?'

She waited for an answer and got none.

'As I say, she'll survive. Save your emotions for the ones that matter.'

'But don't you have any sort of security down here at night? As far as I can see, all you've got to protect you is that sawn off little coloured porter chap.'

Peggy laughed. 'Black,' she said. 'For God's sake don't call him coloured. He's black and proud of it. And believe me, you'll soon find that that sawn off little coloured porter chap, as you so patronisingly describe him, is no ordinary porter. For one thing, he's very bright and very knowledgeable; all self-educated. He's certainly the best NUPE branch secretary we've had in this hospital in years.'

'We?' Jonathan asked. 'You're a member of NUPE?'

'I am.' There was enough defiance in the voice to silence a young doctor still not used to the idea of any nurse not belonging to the Royal College of Nursing. 'And, for another thing, be warned; he's a black belt at karate. He's a second or third Dan or something like that – he tried to explain to me once. What I do remember him saying is that he won't be happy until he's got his fourth Dan and, as there are apparently only about six of those in the whole of the UK, he must be pretty good. They say he's far and away the best instructor in the county but it seems he'll only train children. Young boys or girls, he doesn't mind which, but he can't be bothered with adults.'

'I beg his pardon,' Jonathan smiled. 'Thanks for the warning; I'll watch my step. Perhaps you had better fill me in about some of the others, Staff; Mr Bannerman, Sister Gaunt. For God's sake don't tell me Sister Gaunt is a black belt as well.'

'Now I don't want any jokes about poor old Sister Gaunt.' The tone was as severe as ever but there was a smile twitching at eyes and mouth. Jonathan glanced sideways at Badger to find him staring at the diminutive figure, entranced. 'She's pure gold.'

'Under that wig, d'you mean?'

'Stop it now. Don't let appearances fool you. You might not believe it but our Maisie is an opera buff. All right, so you probably won't see her in evening dress at Covent Garden too often but you should see her collection of records; absolutely fantastic. And d'you know how she spends all her time off and her holidays?' She waited as if inviting them to guess. 'Does voluntary work in a local home for autistic children. I won't have a word said against Maisie, right?' Again she paused, as if giving fair warning of the consequences. 'As for Bob, well . . .'

Jonathan leaned forwards, listening more intently as her voice trailed away, trying to assess the significance of her sudden silence. He wondered whether any Staff Nurse in Dunbridge would be so familiar with his father's name. In his mind's ear, he tried to hear the words and couldn't. There would be too much respect.

'He's a good surgeon, an able chap in many ways, I'm sure. I used to think he was a bit wasted down here. Perhaps he feels the same; perhaps it has got to him, rather given up.'

Jonathan got the impression of a generous person struggling to find good things to say about someone.

'But he doesn't do much of the acute stuff now – perhaps that's because he has so many good juniors these days – does the odd fracture and follow-up clinic, the occasional minor op on one of his golfing cronies – but he's still good value if he's around when something big comes in. Seems to know all the corners he can cut, has a feel for a case, picks out the essentials just like that.' Peggy Wells snapped her fingers. 'But, like all men, he rather hankers after his lost youth, I think.'

'Oh?' Jonathan's single syllable was heavy with suggestion but he was to be disappointed.

'No, none of that nonsense. Quite safe to be alone in a room with him. Not one of these pinch-your-bum, order-you-around-the-next-moment, sort of bosses. I've met a few of those in my day. Even so, I believe it's true that he was the guilty party in his divorce.'

'He's divorced?'

'And remarried. Married a much younger girl – could almost be his daughter. Pretty girl she was. A secretary from the Path. department. I rather think he must have been quite a good athlete at one time. Still fancies himself, I believe.'

'I've already been challenged to a game of squash,' Jonathan laughed. 'Is that how he got his fractured scaphoid? I take it that is a scaphoid plaster he's got on?'

'Yes, it is a scaphoid; no, he did not get it playing squash,' Peggy answered slowly, suggesting that there was more to tell but that she was not to be asked. It was obvious to doctor and policeman that nurses too could close ranks and they pressed her no further.

'He may be a good surgeon but he's obviously a lousy driver,' Jonathan remarked. 'Judging by the state of his car, that is. I must admit I was a bit nervous of parking alongside him. He doesn't look too careful.'

'Was that your car I saw in the yard when I came on duty?' Peggy asked. 'Not the usual Casualty Officer's car, I must say. Thought we must have some visiting consultant. You'd better watch it. Hospital car parks are notorious for having cars stolen, isn't that true?' She turned to Kincaid who nodded, laughing.

'True enough and here am I, desperate for someone to steal mine so that I can claim the insurance and nobody looks at it. For God's sake don't tell my Inspector but I don't even bother to lock it. One good bang on the roof and all the four doors and the boot fly open.'

He sat back and enjoyed their laughter.

'Do you play any sport, Jonathan?' he asked. 'How do you keep fit?'

'The answer is I don't,' Jonathan laughed. 'Bit of a lazy bastard, I'm afraid. Occasional game of squash in the winter. But I have to admit to having one passion outside surgery and that's sailing. I help sail a friend's 27-foot racing cruiser out of Abersoch in the summer. Any exercise I do is simply aimed at keeping fit enough to do that, I'm afraid.'

It was as if a veil had been thrown over their faces, solidifying their expressions, dulling their interest. He had wandered into a world where their experience, even their vocabulary, could not take them. He suddenly felt isolated from two people to whom small boats meant nothing more than trips around the bay. He sensed that to persist in the subject would only widen the gulf, to become a sailing bore would positively alienate them.

'That must be great fun, I should think,' Badger said, generously, and Peggy sniffed. 'I went on a school trip to Pwllheli once; beautiful country, North Wales, isn't it? Do you play rugby by any chance?'

'I used to.' Anxious to be one of them again, Jonathan's answer was immediate but guarded, anxious not to commit himself, looking at Kincaid from the corners of his eyes.

'Who for?'

'I haven't played for some years now, not since I qualified, but I used to play for my medical school, mostly in the seconds. I could never be bothered to train.'

'What position?'

'Number eight.'

'Fancy the odd game while you're here?'

'I'm not so sure. Getting a bit old.'

'How old are you?'

Peggy Wells took an interest in the answer to that.

'Twenty-seven.'

'That's not old, not for a number eight. Just about at your peak. Why don't you come and have a game with us? We've got a good bunch of lads.'

'Who would I be playing for?'

'The local coppers.'

'But I couldn't do that.'

'Nobody would know. We've had all sorts of people turning out for us. There are so many on picket duty at the moment that we have great difficulty fielding fifteen cripples. Nothing serious, I promise you, Jonathan.'

'I'll see.'

'Good.' Badger made it sound as if Jonathan had made him a promise. 'And now I'd better ring and get someone to come and fetch me. Now comes the bit I hate, all the paper work. May I use your phone?'

Later, as they walked together towards the entrance, Badger called towards the policeman approaching them.

'Hey, Taff. We've just found a new number eight. This is Dr Brookes.'

Taff Evans stopped blowing through his hands, began to rub them together and nodded to Jonathan as he looked him up and down, measuring him along his Mervyn Davies scale. 'Poor bastard, pushing against his

47

backside.' He jerked his head in Badger's direction. 'Wouldn't wish that on my worst enemy.'

Jonathan watched them walk away from him, pushing and shoving an erratic course to the exit and out.

Gavin Prescott heard the crash as Badger's push sent Taff Evans thudding into the half-open door as they went out. The sound, reverberating up the corridor, reminded him of other doors, other coppers. There had been no joking then. Not that he held any grudge; they had only done to his stepfather what he would have dearly liked to have done himself many times. He was not a man to bear grudges. Incidents that produced envy and malice in others, particularly if they had the same colour skin, only fuelled a quiet determination. It had been quite acceptable to be there, holding the patient down, feeling and sharing the comradeship of the other two young men. But when it had come to intimacy, the sharing of youthful thoughts and dreams, there had been no doubt, as he had seen Staff Wells go off with the steaming mugs, that his place had been with the junior nurse, clearing up the empty cubicles. It would have been the same if his skin had been white, he accepted that. But, one day, he would be able to walk into such company without an eyebrow being raised, that he swore.

He laughed to himself. As if that could be the apogee of anyone's ambitions. The Dr Jonathan Brookes of this world were going to be stepping stones, no more.

6

Micky Dunn didn't look like a saint. But he was, or as near to one as an ordinary citizen of Scarsby could aspire. Bald, stocky, powerful and hyperactive, with a rolling gait and deep, commanding voice, he might have been a man of the sea, which he was not. Micky was Northend's Youth Organiser, a true profession for which he had trained during his time as the most popular scrum-half Swinton had had in decades. One of the many characteristics for which the Swinton supporters had taken him to their hearts was his ability to absorb endless punishment and still come up smiling, mandatory qualities for any successful Youth Organiser. Five years of the thankless task of trying to imbue the rougher element of Northend's youth with some sort of social responsibility had done nothing to dull his enthusiasm and he put the key in the lock of the Community Centre with the pride of someone opening his first Rolls Royce.

He opened the door by pulling on the key as it was turned in the lock; none of the Centre's doors had external knobs or handles of any kind. Without a key, the only way to get in was with a crowbar and Micky grinned affectionately at the gouged doorpost. The windows, set in the streaked, mustard-coloured roughcast walls, were partly bricked up, the remaining glass covered over with heavy gauge metal grilles. The red burglar alarm above the door and a high, spiked, vicious-looking metal fence enclosing the unkempt grass and mud surround, gave the impression of a determination to keep people out which could not have been further from Micky's intent. Micky had but one fear, that, one evening, he would open the Centre and no one would come in.

Inside, there was a struggling cleanliness about the place, like a down-at-heel old pensioner who worries that her underwear is clean in case she is knocked down by a car, the paint on the walls amateur and garish, like cheap makeup on a face desperate to maintain proud dignity alongside more prosperous neighbours.

He unlocked his office and went in. Micky liked people, not material objects, and his heart sank as he looked at the untidy heaps of paperwork that spread from his desk to the rough shelves on the wall behind. Peeping from beneath the paper he saw the box file, seemingly all important to the Education Department in their research into the social behaviour of habitual truants. His heart lifted once more as he looked at the notice board, plastered with out-of-focus photographs of himself, surrounded by irregular groupings of rebellious youngsters he had taken on trips abroad. Pride of place went to the group with the golden domes of St Basil's Cathedral towering above their shoulders.

He sat to fidget with some of the papers for a few minutes, turning the box file to hide the label on its side, as if, by doing so, the problem would go away. He stood, sighing gratefully at the sound of footsteps in the hall outside, picked up a bunch of keys and went out.

'Evening, Angela. Cold night.'

'It is that, Micky. Feels nice and warm in here though.'

'At least I was able to convince them up at County Hall about that. I told them we didn't have a hope in the evenings if we didn't keep the place warmer than the local pub. How's it going?'

'It' was the twice weekly drama session run by social worker, Angela Muldoon, a rowdy, tempestuous struggle to fire the imagination of young people who saw a future in nothing.

In her battered old briefcase lay photocopied scripts, pruned to the bone for youngsters who never laid a hand on book or newspaper. In the last week she had lost her leading lady who had found herself 'in the club' and she fought a constant running battle with the louts of the weight-lifting class in the next room. Only one thing, or rather one person, kept her going – Danny – a small, black-haired, dusky faced extrovert with quick, darting eyes who would have made a sensually attractive girl had his genes not cast him into the body of a boy.

'Danny here yet?' she asked, almost fearfully.

'Haven't seen him yet.'

'Not in trouble again, is he?'

'Is he that good, Angela?'

'Fantastic, Micky. You must come and hear him. Fifty words from him at times and he has even a hardened old bag like me swallowing hard.'

Micky Dunn laughed but was diverted as a gum-chewing youngster thrust himself between them, a fatalistic challenge in every word and stride.

'What you got for us tonight then, Micky?'

'Are you in the drama group?'

'Me? In with that poncey lot? You've got to be joking.'

'What about some weights, big strong lad like you?'

'Got this back, like, haven't I? What about a video then?'

Micky sighed. 'I'm just going to fetch it.'

'What you got tonight then?'

'*Star Wars.*'

'Bloody hell, not again, Micky. Dead boring that is. Can't you get us something a bit more saucier. Me Dad brought a cracker home for his mates last Sunday. By heck, you should . . .'

'Spare me the details,' Micky laughed, 'and come and carry the screen for me. That's if that back of yours will stand up to it.'

'What's the matter with you then, Micky? Why don't you carry it? You got sudden paralysis or something?'

Dunn, tuning himself to the young man's level of banter, not expecting vintage Oscar Wilde, was still laughing as they crossed the hall. He turned his head as the front doors creaked open and an upright figure in corduroy slacks, check shirt and high necked jumper pushed his way in. The lad with the allegedly bad back saw him also and melted away into the pool room.

'Evening, Badger.' Micky Dunn put out his hand. 'Nice to see you again. Thank you for coming. Go and sit in the office. I've just got to put the video out and I'll be with you.'

After setting up the video and making sure someone was prepared to take the few pence at the tiny coffee bar in the corner, Micky made his way back to his office. He saw in Badger Kincaid the epitome of everything he was trying to achieve in the youngsters he dealt with, a straight-backed, honest young man, healthy in mind and body. Micky thought of Badger, with his over-full lips and almost white eyelashes, as handsome rather than good looking but then Micky didn't altogether trust men who were too good looking, he had known too many dashing young villains. But there had been immediate rapport between the two strong men when the young copper, looking even brawnier in his uniform, had come, knocking diffidently on his office door some months before.

Badger had come to help, not to snoop. Not all the Centre's habitués believed that but Micky did. Finding that his uniform tended to empty the place, Badger had taken to looking in at irregular intervals when off duty. In time he had gained enough of their confidence to hold what he called 'question time', when he would sit and take the flack from members of a subculture to the majority of whom all police were pigs. What did he think of the filth who had beaten 'me Dad' up in the cells just because he was drunk? Didn't the police ever get drunk? What was wrong then with being drunk? And their brother, just because he was walking down the street, carrying a car radio . . .

He watched Micky Dunn sit behind his desk, the only place in the Centre, Badger thought, where he looked out of place. 'Sounds like a pretty full house tonight, Micky.'

'Not too bad,' Dunn smiled. 'I like to hear the noise. Problem is, on drama night, keeping the lads who fancy themselves with the weights away from the rehearsal. As you can imagine, they don't exactly gel. But I much prefer the noisy ones; I can always tell where they are, what they're up to. It's the quiet ones I don't like. Much more difficult to handle.'

Leaning forwards, elbows on knees, Badger lifted his head. 'I reckon you're doing a great job here, Micky, I really do. How you stick it, I can't imagine.'

'Comes of getting kicked on the head so often in my playing days.' Micky grinned. 'But I'm glad you've come tonight; there are a couple of things I'd appreciate your help with.'

'Sure, Micky, if I can.'

'One's pretty straightforward, the other not so easy.'

'Let's have the easy one first.'

'We've been given two old scramble bikes by the local garage owner – we did a bit for his son some years back – and the son has agreed to come about once a fortnight to teach the lads a bit of simple maintenance. Would you come and give them a few lessons on road safety, give them a few tips how to pass their tests; that sort of thing?'

'No problem. What's the other?'

'Not so easy, Badger. I don't quite know how to put it. The last thing I would want to do is get you into trouble. You have no idea how much I appreciate what you are doing here but that doesn't mean I should take advantage of you. So, if ever you think I'm pushing you too far, you back off, d'you hear?'

'Fair enough. I promise. How can I help?'

'You know, don't you, Badger, that I've always made it quite plain to the lads – I don't know why I keep talking just about the lads – and the girls too, that, if they break the law in this place, then I report them to the police – no messing?'

'Yes, I know that. I remember that time when one of your staff had her handbag stolen.'

'That's right. Violence, well, I can usually sense it building up and I can then head it off. If I can't prevent it, I can usually handle it on my own. But theft, vandalism, things like that, then I'm on to your Inspector straight away. However.' Micky hesitated and pulled a face.

'Look, Micky. I promise you that anything you tell me in this office will be off the record. If I think at any time that you are going too far, then I'll stop you and forget anything you have just told me beforehand. Fair enough?'

'Fair enough.' Happy to know where he stood, Micky Dunn relaxed. 'As you can imagine, I get to hear all sorts of things in this job. In many ways I like to think that it's a sign of success when they take me into their confidence. Now, if I were to go to the police about the umpteen minor offences I get to hear about outside these premises, then I'd lose their confidence and I might as well shut this place up.'

Badger nodded.

'That doesn't mean I'm turning this place into a thieves' kitchen, because I'm not.' Micky looked aggressively at Badger. 'But these kids have got no one to talk to, I'm *in loco parentis* to a lot of them.' He saw Badger grin and grinned back. 'What's the matter? Didn't expect that sort of language from an old Swinton scrum-half, did you?'

'Come on, Micky; get to the point.'

'It's this boy, Danny.'

'Danny who?'

'Never mind that for the moment. Let's just call him Danny. He's 15, a bright kid who's got into trouble now and then but nothing serious. He has spent the odd night in the cells but that was only because the police

52

had no one to hand him over to. They've kept him there for his own protection really. His parents refused to collect him, said a night in the nick might do him a bit of good. They're that sort of people – father's got form, mostly GBH, mother's no good. But the main problem is that Danny plays truant and each time the school reports him, he gets a leathering from his Dad. So they've stopped telling anybody. Now he wanders the streets all day and spends his evenings in here. Then he found that he was getting a hiding if his father was drunk anyway, whether he went to school or not – fifty-fifty chance who got it, his mother or himself. So he's walked out. He's living rough.'

'So, tell me something new,' Badger said. 'Plenty of those around. He should be rounded up and put in care. No problem really. Does he go home at all, when the father is out, I mean?'

'No.'

'So how does he eat? Where's he getting the money? He's got to eat.'

'Theft.'

Poker-faced, Badger Kincaid absorbed the word. 'All right,' he said, slowly. 'Hardly a minor offence, Micky, but go on; where do I come in?'

Encouraged, Micky sat forwards. 'It seems he's a brilliant little actor.'

'Aren't they all?'

'Yeah, I know what you mean, but this is for real. Angela, the girl who runs our drama for us, she's convinced he's in a class of his own. And she's got him there.' Dunn clasped his hand, palm up, in front of him. 'She thinks he might be dyslexic, that's why he's doing badly in school. He's intelligent enough to know he could do better but doesn't know how. So he runs away from school as much out of frustration as anything else.'

'You still haven't told me how I can help.'

'Danny won't go into care, I know that; he'd rather live rough. But sooner or later, they're going to catch up with him and then he'll be gone. I reckon he'll hitch his way to London and that'll be the last we see of him. And I'm sure I don't need to tell you what might happen to a young boy down in the smoke.'

He paused to look at Badger, his eyes searching for signs of understanding.

'The kid's on a knife edge, Badger. He's no saint; he's got some form, mostly trivial stuff; nothing vicious. I wouldn't want to con you over that but then I imagine you'd check on him as soon as you got back anyway. But he's also talented and, so far, he hasn't got into any deep trouble but, as things are, it's only a question of time. If we don't help him now, it will be too late. The first thing we have got to do is get him home and that's where I think you could help.'

'How?' Badger asked.

'Have a word with the lad first, get his confidence. Then a word perhaps with his father? Breathe on him a bit? Say you'll be calling to see Danny now and then? If you really got to Danny, you might be able to find out from him a few things about his father that's not already on his form sheet, enough to have a hold over him; there's no love lost between the two. And then, if we can get Danny home, we can get him seen by some expert, see if he is dyslexic. I don't know who would look after that but I expect his GP would help there. What d'you say?'

'Do you know where to find him?'

'Yes.' There was still caution in Dunn's voice, not prepared to give anything away until he was certain of Badger's help.

Badger stood up. 'Let's go and have a word with him then, shall we? Where do we find him?'

His face radiating his delight, Micky Dunn stood to face him. 'You know that old quarry behind here, the one they've begun to fill in?'

Badger nodded. 'Aren't there plans to grass it over, make a football field for you?'

'That's right. They reckon it will take about two years altogether. Perhaps you've noticed the old derelict sheds left over from the quarry days?'

'Don't tell me he's in there.' Badger looked horrified. 'There's usually one or two alkies dossed down in there. It's one of Maggie May's favourite haunts.'

Micky reached for a hand torch. 'Come and see. He gets in and out through the gap in the quarry fence. All the poor bastards sleeping rough know about the huts. So do the Council who probably don't do anything about them as they at least give the poor devils a roof over their heads.'

Badger had difficulty keeping up with Micky as they stumbled towards a small distant light across a rough path worn in the foul smelling refuse by the scramble bikes. If the young riders fell off, they were at least assured of a soft landing in that part of the circuit. Micky tried to light Badger's way and the sweeping beam sent a rat scurrying away into the darkness. 'Never short of company out here,' he whispered. Nearer the hut, he shouted, 'Danny, it's Micky. Can I have a word with you?'

The light was doused and there was no reply. They crept within feet of the rotting walls.

'Danny, d'you hear me? I'd like a word with you.'

'What d'you want?' The young voice was wary but defiant.

'Are you coming to drama? You're late and Angela wants to get started. I said I'd come and see you.'

They saw the first trace of success as the light flared and they were close enough to hear the hiss of a gas jet.

'Are you coming?' Micky tried again.

'Dunno.'

'Can I come in, Danny? It's bloody cold out here.'

There was the grind of a sheet of corrugated iron being shifted and the chink of light became a widening shaft, shuttered abruptly once more as Dunn added, 'I've brought a friend of mine to see you as well, Danny.'

It took another five minutes of wheedling before both men coaxed their bulks through the gap Danny made for them.

'What happened to the door, Danny?' Dunn asked.

'Couple of winos broke it down the other night.'

'They didn't hurt you?'

'Nah. They were all right. Just stank of shit. I think one of them had crapped himself. They left again in the morning. What you want then, Micky?'

Badger had been looking round, his heart aching at the child's attempt at self-sufficiency. He had cleared one corner where a stained mattress, chewed at one corner, lay on boards that somehow he appeared to have brushed. In the noisy light of a camping gas light, he saw a tattered khaki blanket, a golden satin cushion, incongruously clean, acting as a pillow. Danny saw him stare.

'Me Mum's, i'n't it? I took it when she wasn't looking. Who are you anyway? You really a friend of Micky's?' He took a long, searching look in the dim, yellow light. 'You're a bloody copper, in't you?'

Badger's silence only confirmed a child's clear perception. 'You're a bloody copper.' Danny repeated, backing into a corner. 'What's all this then, Micky? You in with this lot now? I thought you said we could trust you? You two-faced bastard, bringing . . .'

The two men, blocking all hope of escape, let Danny's anger spend itself. 'This, Danny,' Micky said, 'is PC Kincaid. And you're quite right, he is a friend of mine. But, I promise you, Danny, Badger here is not your usual kind of copper.'

'Badger? What sort of a stupid name is that then?'

'We can't all be given a name like Danny.' Badger sat on the floor, his back to the wall, his arms around his knees, settling himself as if he had no intention of leaving without having his say. 'Which would you prefer, a nickname like Badger or go around being called by my real name, Cecil?'

The young boy almost smiled but managed to suppress it in time.

'What's your surname?' asked Badger and knew immediately, from the twitch of young lips, that, inadvertently, he had scored a bullseye. 'Danny what do you call yourself?'

A flushed, shame-faced grin spread below downcast eyes.

'Well?' Badger persisted.

'Shufflebottom.'

Danny raised his eyes slowly, there was a pause, and all three laughed. 'It's all right for you, i'n't it?' Danny looked at Badger. 'You're a big bugger. Imagine what it's like for me in school with a name like that. It's hell, is that.'

'We'll have to find another name for you, Danny,' Micky broke in. 'You're never going to break into the Royal Shakespeare Company with a name like Danny Shufflebottom, now are you? They'd never find a theatre big enough to put that name up in lights.'

The young lad, a brittle outer protective shell already cracked, had no real chance against the experience of two dedicated adults. Badger watched, fascinated, as Micky, slowly and skilfully, transformed a trapped, wild animal into a quick-witted, articulate youngster. Danny's thoughts might be transmitted in the obscenity-spattered patois of Northend's no-hopers but there was no denying the frustration that drove him. It came home to Badger, watching the black, close-curled head bobbing as he spoke, what a sense of liberation the youngster must feel when set free amongst the language Angela so painstakingly laid in front of him. To a deprived, highly intelligent boy like Danny, he thought, a rat-infested shed must be a palace compared with the bonds of ignorance.

'But I'm not going into care, Micky. I just bloody well won't go. I'd rather top myself first.'

'Now don't talk like that, Danny. That's just stupid and you know it. You've got to go home. You're bright enough to know, Danny, you can't live like this for ever. But there's another reason for you to go home. Angela reckons she knows what your problem is.'

'Glad somebody does then.'

'She reckons you're probably dyslexic.'

'Dys what?'

'A problem with reading and writing.'

'Well we all know that, don't we?'

'But it doesn't mean you're stupid, Danny. Lots of clever people have suffered from it. Have you ever heard of a man called Albert Einstein?'

'Course I have,' Danny retorted, though he wasn't too sure he had.

'Well he was dyslexic and you don't come much cleverer than him. It's something you're born with and it's something that can be put right. We can get you seen by an expert, get you expert help. But you would have to go home first.'

'What exactly is the problem at home, Danny?' Badger asked.

'Come on; do me a favour.' Danny was scathing. 'Me Dad's half pissed most of the time and he belts the shit out of me. There's no great mystery.'

'Would you go back home if I promised to do something about that for you?'

'What could you do?'

'For one thing, I could call and have a chat with this Dad of yours.'

'What good would that do?'

'You'd be surprised. Could make it a regular occasion, different times of day, amazing how often we get reports of a disturbance round your way. Has you Dad got a car?'

'Might call it that.'

'MOT up to date is it? Tyres OK? Paid his TV licence has he? Got a dog? Neighbours ever complain? Ask him if he's heard of knock-on offences; obstructing a police officer in the course of his duties, that sort of thing? I thought everyone had heard of police harassment by now. Won't take long to get through to him. If it does, then I'll have to spell it out to him; one finger on you means a couple of hours down the nick with me.'

'That's all very fine, but what about when he comes home on a Saturday night with a gutful. Not going to be around then, are you?'

'No, but I think I can do something about that for you too. How big is your Dad?'

'Big enough.'

'I know, but how big, really?'

'Well, not all that big but you don't need to be, do you, not with someone my size?'

'Size needn't be all that important, might even be an advantage not to be too big. I think I know someone who might help you.'

'Who's that then?'

'Black belt at Karate. Fancy learning Karate?'

Micky Dunn didn't give Danny a chance to answer. 'D'you mean Gavin Prescott?'

'Yes. D'you know him?'

'How many black belts d'you think there are in Scarsby? Of course I know him. Been trying to get him to come and give a few lessons at the Centre for the last couple of years but, for some reason, he won't. You could get him to give Danny some coaching?'

The incredulity in Micky's voice made Danny look at Badger with a new respect.

'I can but try. If what I'm told is true, Danny is just the sort he likes to take on.' Badger turned to Danny. 'And he's not much bigger than you are; I've seen him. What d'you say, Danny? How would you like to give your father a surprise one Saturday night and kick him in the balls?'

It was not entirely reflected light that shone now from Danny's eyes. He nodded.

'But you must go home first.'

He nodded again.

'Right then.' Badger struggled to his feet. 'No promises but I'll do my best. One more bargain, Danny.'

'What's that?'

'I'm famished. If you let me sit through your rehearsal, I'll drive you down to the chippie afterwards. Don't fancy going in there on my own this late.'

'OK Badger; as long as you park round the corner. Wouldn't do around here to be seen eating with the filth.'

As they watched Danny's back disappear into the welcoming bedlam of the rehearsal, Dunn put his hand on Badger's shoulder. 'I'm grateful to you, Badger.'

'No need, Micky. Makes me feel good. Makes a change from hounding the poor little devils all the time. One thing surprised me though when I saw him in here, under a decent light.'

'What was that?'

'His clothes. Not at all what I expected for someone sleeping rough like that. He looked quite smart.'

Mickey Dunn smiled. 'Angela Muldoon has a boy about the same age.'

The house looked like any other Northend house. Badger pressed the bell but heard no ring and saw no movement through the small glass pane as a result. The door knocker had been wrenched off, the wood around it split and dented, looking as if someone had taken a sledge hammer to it in the past. He thumped a panel with his fist. Moments later, he heard someone curse as the door was not so much opened as disimpacted; it was strange how many of Northend's inhabitants used the side or back door rather than the front. It crossed Badger's mind whether this might be related to criminal tendency. He grinned; an interesting basis for a personal survey perhaps. The door gave way suddenly and two men faced each other.

'What the hell do you want?'

Badger had had worse receptions in Northend.

'Good evening, sir. I wonder if I could have a word with you?'

'Dear God, can't you think of anything more original to say? As soon as you people put on that uniform, you become just a bunch of bloody robots. Haven't you got minds of your own?'

Badger laughed. 'Sorry about the uniform, Mr Prescott. This is not anything official but I was passing on my way off duty. I wonder if I might come in for a moment?'

'I suppose you'd better. And you can cut out the Mr Prescott rubbish. You know the name's Gavin. Should do by now, the time you spend in Cas. Everyone's half expecting you to move your bed in.' Gavin stopped his chatter for a moment to grunt as he put his shoulder to the door. He looked accusingly at Badger. 'Never been the same since a bunch of your flat-footed colleagues forgot to knock some years ago. As I was saying, why an intelligent girl like Peggy should take up with a copper like you beats me; I've told her, silly cow. Still, there's no accounting for tastes, I suppose. Now then, what can I do for you?'

There seemed little hope of being invited beyond the tiny hallway and Badger, partly out of good manners, partly to make the visit seem less official, took off his cap. He smiled at Gavin, pointing to his tracksuit. 'Still running to work, I see.'

'I'm sure I look divine but somehow I don't think you've called to get the name of my tailor. What d'you want?'

'I've called to ask for your help.'

'Makes a change, I must say.'

'Lad of fifteen, basically a good lad, very talented, having all hell beaten out of him at home, runs away and is living rough.'

Gavin looked long and hard into Badger's face, matching up Badger's words with data so readily accessible in his own memory banks. 'Come in the kitchen,' he said, softly, the brashness gone for the moment. 'I have to go in a few minutes so there's no time for coffee. What can I do?'

They stood in the kitchen, just as they had in the hall, but Badger appreciated the modest gesture of welcome. 'We've managed to get him back home and to go to school at the moment . . .'

'We?' Gavin interrupted.

'Micky Dunn from the Community Centre and me.'

'Oh, him. He's a pain; always after me to teach those thugs of his to be even more violent.'

'That's a bit hard, Gavin. They're not all thugs by any means. There are a lot of good youngsters going there.'

'Please yourself.' Gavin gave a dismissive toss of his head. 'What's this kid's name?'

'Danny Shufflebottom.'

'Poor little sod. He'll need all the help he can get with a name like that. You'd better tell him to come and see me.'

'Thanks, Gavin.' Badger turned to leave. 'When?'

'Tomorrow, about the same time, perhaps a bit earlier? How big is he?'

'Not very big.'

'Thank God for that. Not one of your macho boys?'

'No. In fact he's a bit the other way, how can I put it . . .?'

'How would you put it?'

'Well, you know, sort of . . .'

'What's the matter, scared of him?'

'Certainly not.' Badger didn't know whether to look amused or angry. 'Why on earth should I be scared of him?'

'Not afraid he might seduce you, are you?' Gavin gave a little cluck of irritation. 'Oh, skip it,' he snapped as he saw Badger's jaw clench. He led the way out into the hallway again as a clatter of feet on threadbare stairs echoed hollowly in a house devoid of softness. A young man passed between them on his way to the sitting room and the TV set visible through the open door. Gavin stepped back to allow him through though his eyes did not flicker in acknowledgment of the man's existence as he did so. The young man ignored Gavin equally, his grin concentrated on Badger as he delighted in the naked surprise caused by the sight of his grease slicked hair, golden ear rings and leather jacket.

'Good evening, officer.' Though the young man smiled arrogantly, his lips down turned, it was with the lower half of his face only, his eyes remaining cold and motionless, a combination of disdain and hatred Badger had witnessed less than a week before in the frosty murk of Scarsby's bus centre.

Gavin took a perfunctory tug at the front door and Badger, his attention still attracted to the broad, leather-clad back bent over the TV, heard him say something about using the side door like everyone else. Having passed back through the kitchen, Badger found himself once more out in night air that felt no colder for being appreciably fresher than that inside. He turned and thanked Gavin but did not walk away. Slowly wedging his cap over the thick, blonde hair, a born copper once more, he peered closely at Gavin, silhouetted now in the doorway. 'Wasn't that Wayne Morelli?'

'As ever was.'

'Chico Morelli. Does he live with you?'

'We share the same house.'

'But you're not related?'

'I didn't say that. He's my brother.'

'Brother? But your name is Prescott.'

'We do not only share the same house but have the doubtful honour of sharing the same mother. We're half-brothers. Send this Danny of yours to me. I'll look after him.'

The door shut in Badger's face.

7

That subtle combination of hush and clamour had stopped Jonathan's chatter about Manchester United, aimed at allaying a 10-year-old's fear of a loaded syringe. Alone with the lad, he had delayed for a moment the insertion of the dreaded needle into the grit-filled wound over a bony knee, had raised his head as he had absorbed and analysed what he had heard. Although the casualty theatre was a little distance from the main corridor, there had been no mistaking the clamour; the rattling rhythm of trolley wheels oscillating violently from side to side at speeds for which they were not designed; running feet, sliding at the corners; the crash of trolley against door post; breathless voices raised without shouting. The hush had come from those patients who had stood back, holding their breath as, for a moment, they had thought of someone's troubles other than their own, silently wishing the inert shape on the trolley God's speed.

Jonathan had resumed his argument over the relative prowess of Liverpool and Manchester United but he had worked with a thoughtless professional efficiency, his mind occupied with what might be going on in the Intensive Care Unit nearby. He had almost completed his suturing when Sister Gaunt's head had appeared around the door.

'You all right, Dr Brookes?'

'Yes, thank you, Sister. Bobby Charlton here is as good as new, aren't you?' He turned to put a gloved fist close to a snub nose. He turned again to the door. 'What was all that about just now?'

He had already come to accept that he would never see anything but sadness on Sister Gaunt's face and he wondered how she would ever cope with good news. As it was, her doleful expression was apt to her words. She shook her head.

'B.I.D.' Sister Gaunt observed the ritual of not informing a live patient that another had been brought in dead. 'Young woman. Probably cervical spine, they think. When you're finished there, there's a nasty scald in three; needs to go to the burns unit, I think.'

Coming from someone else, spoken in different tones, and Jonathan would have bridled at someone telling him his job. But it was Maisie and her hangdog voice and Jonathan smiled.

'Be there in a moment, Sister.'

At the theatre door, Jonathan restored a limping child to a grateful mother. Grinning his farewell, he stuck out his tongue at the boy, enjoying the moment as the lad returned the compliment in an act of forgiveness.

He turned towards the corridor en route to the cubicles, hesitated and turned again. He slid the door of the Intensive Care Unit aside just enough to sidle through into the stillness. He closed it behind him.

He walked across the terrazzo floor, stepping carefully as if anxious not to wake someone. There was no sheet over the body; there had been no ritual covering of the face to signify defeat. All around were the signs of final, reluctant submission to the inevitable; the discarded drip set, hanging limp and impotent; the endotracheal tube, still attached to its tubing, trailing on the floor; the resuscitation tray abandoned in total disarray. Doctors and nurses, dumb with failure, had walked away. Now, it had become no more than a leisurely administrative problem of a body subject to due process of law. It had been brought over the hospital's threshold and so had to be admitted to the hospital's records to await the Coroner's pleasure. Jonathan walked to her side to stand, his hands thrust deep into coat pockets, and look down on her.

She still had the warm body aura of life, not yet the chill indifference of a corpse. Her eyes were still open, clear and unglazed, looking up at the ceiling, a slightly puzzled look on her face like someone unable to get to sleep. She wore jodhpurs, well cut and expensive looking. A heavy gold chain and locket hung around the neck of her cashmere polo-neck jumper and Jonathan imagined the pictures of the children within the locket and wondered who would meet them from school that day, take them home in the Range Rover and break the news. He saw the expensive material slit from wrist to shoulder as someone had searched desperately for a vein with no time to admire the large diamond solitaire. Her hair, thick and golden with the sheen of robust health, had been carefully brushed and Jonathan wondered at her thoughts as she had made up her face that morning; had she been worrying about school examinations, the dinner party she was due to give? She looked elegant, unmarked. Just dead.

He wondered where she had come from; she was not the usual sort of Scarsby General patient. Without doubt she would be a member of BUPA. He imagined her, gin and tonic in hand. 'My dear, I wouldn't be seen dead in the General.'

Jonathan gave a sad little sound, heard movement and turned to find Sister Gaunt standing beside him.

'Dr Brookes, are you . . .?' She saw his face and stopped in mid-sentence, staying to gaze with him for a moment. She had already been impressed by the young man's ability. Now, as they walked away slowly, she knew he also cared.

'Stupid bloody waste, don't you think so, Sister?'
'I couldn't agree more, Dr Brookes.'
'Who's got the job of breaking the news to the family?'

'No one. According to a friend who came in with her, she's separated from her husband – they haven't been able to trace him yet – and her only son is a no good junkie, bumming round London somewhere.'

A tall young man, broad of shoulder, narrow of hip, a good-looking bachelor with money, intelligent with an obvious future stretching before him, Jonathan Brookes was going to have no trouble finding nurses to share his leisure hours. To bring into the equation a gleaming new Golf GTI was like taking a sledge hammer to crack a nut. He brought the car to a halt outside the Nurses' Home. He stretched to turn off the ignition but a tiny figure was already standing under the light at the door, holding her anorak tightly around her neck to keep out the cold.

Jonathan had made the trip back into the General late one evening, haunting the department until he had had a chance to talk to the girl alone. The secret had been 'leaked' throughout Casualty within minutes of Jonathan making his move and 'Didn't know you went in for cradle snatching, Dr Brookes,' had been Peggy Wells's terse comment as she had passed him in the corridor.

Perhaps Peggy had been right, but the young nurse had looked so much more mature in uniform, so in need of protection that first night. Jonathan looked at the flouncing fair hair as the girl opened the car door and jumped in. Smiling outwardly, he winced as, in her excitement, she slammed the door, making his beloved new car shake. The outward journey was punctuated by fitful banalities, though three vodka and lemonades loosened her tongue and brought an entrancing glow to her face as Jonathan nursed his beer.

On the drive back, she talked incessantly, her speech slurring temptingly. Half turning to him, she crossed one thigh over the other, her skirt high above a rounded knee. The miles ticked away and the exit sign to Lymm reared in the headlights. Jonathan sighed his relief as he maintained his speed, watching from the corner of his eye the slope of the exit road that would surely have led to something he would have regretted.

Outside the Nurses' Home, he switched off ignition and lights. He turned and, in the darkness, stretched a hand which found a shoulder. Jonathan encountered neither compliance nor resistance as his hand slid under the anorak, searching out the gap between jumper and skirt. Encouraged, he turned his attention to her hip, her thigh, feeling for the rounded knee. This time he felt her move, the upper thigh slide back, his fingers falling against the inner silky smoothness. And he saw another hand, filthy and bloodstained, lecherously groping, but without all the trappings of position, money, expensive cars, food and wine. He wondered suddenly where was the difference between himself and the drunken animal he had despised. Gently, he withdrew his arm.

'It's late. I think you had better get back. I don't want to get you into trouble.'

'I don't mind.' It was obvious from her tone that it was not the thought of getting into trouble that she did not mind.

Jonathan reached across her to let her out, saying nothing as he did so. He watched until she appeared under the light over the door but heard distinctively the snigger that had come, like some derisory epitaph, from the darkness between. He drove home slowly and let himself in to the silent house. He undressed, walked into the bathroom and, with no one in the house, closed the door behind him.

On rare occasions Casualty Officers can be found standing with nothing to do in the centre of a department that is seething with activity. At times, competent, experienced young doctors can work their way through a backlog of patients to leave a trail of people waiting for their tetanus injections or to have their dressings renewed or their sutures removed. For a while they can stand and watch others working hard. Janet James and Jonathan Brookes were doing just that, leaning to face each other across a high, lectern-like desk, when they heard the sound of running feet. Janet was easy to talk to, the sort of woman destined to be the favourite maiden aunt who would understand all the problems of children she herself had never borne. She was also the one person in the hospital who had never been known to refuse to take on for an hour the duties of the house surgeon desperate for a game of squash or the house physician who simply must have her hair done. Hence the cardiac arrest pager clipped to her coat, its weight dragging at the top pocket. The footsteps got nearer until a plump, bespectacled, curly headed man burst through the door, saw them and hurled himself towards them.

'My wife,' he spluttered and got no further.

Jonathan raised his eyebrows in amusement while Janet James simply transferred her smile from Jonathan to the man. They waited for the man to go on but he simply turned towards the door, making furious signs that they should follow him. When they did not move, he came back to stammer his alarm once more.

'What's the matter with your wife?' Jonathan asked.

'She's having a baby,' came tumbling out.

Suppressing the facetious remark that flashed through his mind, Jonathan asked, 'So what's the problem?'

'I'm telling you, she's having a baby.'

'When?'

'Now. Don't you understand, she's having a baby now, outside.'

'Outside?' Both suddenly stood upright. 'Where?'

'In the car.'

For a split second Jonathan and Janet looked at each other, taking in a sharp breath of surprise and delight before leaping for the door to the corridor outside. Both here and at the door to the casualty yard, Jonathan gave way to Janet, partly from ingrained good manners and, as he laughingly admitted afterwards, partly from the fear that he might otherwise arrive on the scene first. They saw the car, a small family saloon abandoned haphazardly in the corner of the yard, a woman's back disappearing into the open rear door. Janet took the place of the bypasser who had heard the cries and was doing her best to help while Jonathan opened the opposite rear door and put his head in. He felt the breath on his face as the woman panted and grunted her apologies.

'Oh, I'm so sorry, doctor.'

'Don't be silly,' Jonathan heard Janet say. 'How many is this?'

'Sixth, doctor. I was very quick with the last two but I . . .' Her voice faded into renewed gasps.

'Now don't push for a moment. Let me have a . . .'

The nasal tones of a cardiac arrest pager are urgent enough without amplification inside the confines of a small car. 'Arrest, Attlee Ward, arrest Attlee Ward, arrest Attlee Ward.' Even the sounds of childbirth seemed to stop for a moment.

'All yours, I'm afraid, Jonathan.' And he heard the sound of Janet's running feet.

Hurrying around to the other side of the car, Jonathan saw a huge woman bent double in the cramped space, her knees jammed against the backs of the seats in front. Presented towards him was an ellipse of scalp, wet, crinkled and swollen, downy black hairs slicked and parted. The ellipse widened for a moment until the gasping subsided once more. Breathlessly, the woman gave a little laugh. 'My husband will kill me, making a mess over his precious car.'

'Don't be ridiculous. Now don't . . .'

Precipitate labour takes no account of time, place or person. Jonathan knew that matters were beyond his control as the next period of gasping and pushing began. He simply put out his hands to support a tiny head as it made its entry into the world with a spluttering rush.

'Don't worry, Mrs ... Everything is fine.' That was all he managed before the head was followed by a fine pair of shoulders. Jonathan had his own knees now firmly fixed on the lower door frame and tiny legs were already kicking vigorously when the infant confirmed his arrival with a lusty bellow. Instant recall of training in a subject he had hated made Jonathan look to the baby's airway, clearing out the tiny mouth with the tip of his little finger. With the slippery bundle precariously crooked in his arm, he was glad to hear the voice of an ambulance driver behind him.

'You all right, doctor? Anything I can do to help?'

'Yes, please. Two large artery forceps, Kochers if they've got them. Quick as you can. And scissors.'

'What kind did you say, doctor?'

'Any big artery forceps; don't be too long.'

They waited, silent except for a bawling baby that Jonathan was trying to keep warm in the thin nylon of his coat.

'What is it, doctor?' she asked.

'What's what?' Jonathan replied before realising his stupidity. 'Oh, it's a boy.'

'Red alert, Dr Brookes. Motorway pile up,' Maisie intoned solemnly. 'And they've asked for a medical officer out on site. Looks like you're elected.'

'Oh, hell, no. Really?'

As if Maisie would joke about a thing like that. As if Maisie would joke about anything.

'Janet's in theatre. I'll go and get the crash box for you.'

'What about Mr Bannerman?' Jonathan was having trouble keeping a slight tremor out of his voice.

'Not in yet.'

'But . . .' Jonathan looked at his watch, '. . . it's gone half past ten.'

His only answer was a momentary lifting of Sister Gaunt's downcast eyes as she intensified for a second their weary message.

The fog had been dense when Jonathan had driven to work, more like a November morning than the middle of February. He had edged his way on to the motorway, happy to stay in the slow lane for the short time it took him to reach the exit to Scarsby. 'Bloody fools,' he had muttered to himself as cars had zipped by, nose to tail, in the fast lane but he had had the honesty to wonder what he would have done had he been a rep with a monthly quota to reach and already late for an appointment fifty miles away.

'Police car's waiting outside, Dr Brookes.' Jonathan had heard the familiar slapping, unhurried steps in the corridor as Maisie had returned with the box. 'Good luck.'

The first of the ambulances from the pile up was heralding its approach as Jonathan walked across to the waiting police car. 'Nasty morning, doctor,' was the emotionless greeting from the stocky traffic cop who slammed the door of the white Rover behind Jonathan. It was also the sum total of the conversation apart from growling gossip between the driver and his navigator over which crackled the intermittent descant of the radio controller. Jonathan tried to sit back and look at ease but tense muscles arched his back. His father had done this once, years before, back when Teflo had blown sky high. He must ring him, tell him all about it, tell him that only now did he appreciate just how dry a mouth can suddenly become. But his father had been forced to take an arm off to get a man out. For God's sake, he couldn't do that. He wondered what they kept in the box he had across his knees; he should have asked to see when he was shown round that first day; Bannerman should have shown him; it was too late now. Once more he made a conscious effort to relax, look like the men in front, but it takes more than one motorway crash to produce faces like that.

They had left the gloom of Scarsby's streets for the thick fog outside. Even allowing for the circumstances, something seemed odd and, within such limited horizons, it took time for Jonathan to sort out what was so strange. Slowly it dawned on him that the double crash barrier of the central reservation was on the wrong side, with the cars and lorries beyond it travelling in the same direction as they were going. They were driving the wrong way up a deserted motorway. Blue flashes reflected off the fog and an ambulance glided by in the opposite direction. He thought of Janet back at the General; had they called the other Casualty Officers back to help her; had Bob Bannerman turned up yet? He leaned between the seats in front.

'Have you any idea what the problem is? What do they want me for, d'you know?'

'Bus full of flying pickets gone over an embankment trying to avoid the pile up, doctor. Scargill's Air Force crash landed, you might say. They've got most of them out but there are one or two still stuck, likely to be grounded for a while, by the sound of it.'

'Two of Arthur's bombers failed to return,' his colleague added, chuckling. They both laughed.

A mass of twisted, blackened metal loomed out of the fog as if a barricade had been thrown across the road.

'That's as far as we can take you, I'm afraid. And the best of British luck to you, doctor.'

Jonathan stretched for the latch to find the door opened for him from the outside. The man looked huge from slapping thigh boots to glinting helmet.

'Thank you for coming, doctor. This way, please.'

The fire officer did not even glance at the human form beneath the blanket at the road side but, just behind the leading edge of the pile up, there was no denying the two blackened shapes, bolt upright like charred dummies, in the front seats of what had been a family saloon. Accustomed as he had now become to the smell of burnt human flesh, the sight still

67

sickened Jonathan; they looked as if, should someone give the wreck a good shake, their heads would fall off like coconuts at a fair. The fireman nodded at them.

'Still too hot to get them out. Not one of the pictures they'll see on the six o'clock news, doctor. Sometimes I think they ought to show them; make them realise it's some poor sod's job to get them out; might slow some of the maniacs down a bit. Though I doubt it,' he added, mournfully.

They walked silently, side by side, weaving between the jumbled heaps of twisted metal, picking their way over spilled oil and petrol, sand, fruit and toilet rolls from overturned lorries. One lorry driver, calm and grey faced, stared balefully down at them as firemen struggled all around to free him. They crossed a bridge below which Jonathan, through the fog, could just see either a small river or a canal.

'It went down here, doctor; didn't actually hit any other vehicle but must have spun and gone down backwards, mowing down a couple of pretty substantial trees as it did so; hence its stove-in back. They all ended up in a heap and most of them got out unhurt but there are two down there, I imagine in the back seat, trapped by their legs.' He pointed to a massive recovery lorry backed up to the crash barrier, heavy chain disappearing over the grass verge. 'The bus is hanging over the edge of the canal a bit but, with that chain on it, I don't really think there's much chance of it sliding into the water. But, each time we try to pull it out, they start screaming and, the way it's lying at the moment, our lads can't get at the back with jacks and cutting equipment.'

'What about from inside?' Jonathan asked, surprising himself with the calmness and authority in his voice.

The fire officer shook his head. 'We can get down to them but there's no way we can free them from inside.' He swung his legs over the crash barrier. 'Careful on the way down, doctor, the grass is very slippery.'

The bus had been no luxury coach to start with, more accustomed to struggling as far as Blackpool on the miners' outing than long distance motorway travel. But now it was a sorry sight with scraped sides, broken windows and crushed roof. With its front wheels reared off the ground, it was held in graceless equilibrium by the chain that disappeared back up the way they had come. To Jonathan the fire officer's 'hanging over the edge a bit' seemed the understatement of the year but he was given no time to argue the fact as he became the centre of a group of men with grimy, unsmiling faces beneath their helmets. 'What we'd like you to do, doctor, is to keep them quiet somehow for a few minutes while we pull the bus up far enough to get at the back. Do you think you could manage that? There's only room for one in there so there will be no one to help you. We've managed to get two Entonox cylinders in there for you. We've used them from time to time but we can't seem to keep them asleep long or deep enough. Is there anything else you want?'

'I don't think so, thank you.' Jonathan's eyes focused on a silver button as he asked as nonchalantly as he could. 'No doubt about being able to get them out, is there; once you've pulled the bus up, I mean? You're not going to ask me to do any guillotine amputation or anything dramatic like that, I hope?'

'No problem, doctor. You look after them as we pull and we'll do the rest.'

'Thank God for that.' Jonathan felt he was allowed that much overt emotion as he placed the crash box on the grass and tried to look as if he did that sort of thing every day. He struggled not to show the tremor that he felt in his hands as he fumbled with the catches, watched critically by a group of hardened professionals. He didn't know exactly what he was looking for; all he could think of was morphia. He hid his relief as he found the drug compartment, saw the phials and the syringes in their sealed plastic bags. He closed the box once more. 'Right,' he said, 'How do I get in?'

Instead of answering, the fire officer went to the bus door, high above his head, and shouted, 'All right, Sandy, you can come out now. The doctor's coming in.'

Minutes later Jonathan was taking advice from a stocky young fireman who looked him up and down. 'Bit big for this sort of caper, aren't you? What we need is some sort of medical ferret. Go down feet first, doctor. Once you are down there, you've got no hope of turning round and you won't manage standing on your head.'

Jonathan found himself being lifted bodily and pushed in through the door. The crash box was handled with far greater care as it was handed up to him. He swung his legs in line with the aisle between the seats and felt as if he were hovering at the top of a children's slide. He prevented himself from falling by wedging his feet against the seats on each side as his white coat, already filthy, telescoped in folds around his chest. He thought of taking it off and decided it was too late for that. Half way down, the roof had caved in and Jonathan had great difficulty forcing himself through the gap but beyond, the box still sliding and bumping against his head and shoulders, the space opened a little and he found the two miners.

His mental picture had been of two men, sitting neatly side by side, their feet equally neatly disappearing at their ankles beneath some metal bar. In reality, the two men had been pitched forwards, their legs doubled up behind them and invisible from somewhere above their knees under the seats they had been occupying. Lying in a tangle against the twisted seats in front, they were face down except for the amount they had been able to twist their trunks. One had an arm across the other's back and both leaned pallid cheeks against the rough comfort of the uncut moquette of the seat in front. The man nearer to Jonathan opened his eyes.

'Thank God you've come, doctor. I'm that pleased to see you. I don't think I could stand this bugger's halitosis much longer, straight I don't.'

Jonathan had heard of a miner's gritty sense of humour but his first real experience of it left him dumbfounded. The other man, equally grey and sweaty, his eyes closed against the pain, was not to be outdone.

'While you've got him tied down, doc, d'you think you could go through his pockets, like; find the five pounds he owes me. The only way I'm likely to get it off the mean sod, is that.'

Finding it strangely difficult to speak, Jonathan told them not to talk, hating his voice of pampering bedside etiquette, cursing himself for not being able to speak their language.

'That'll be the . . .'

The voice trailed away into a gasp of pain as the bus eased a few grinding inches on the end of the chain.

'I'm going to give you both an injection. I don't know whether I shall be able to but I'm going to try first to put it into a vein. In any case, we will need to wait ten minutes for the drug to work and then they'll pull the bus up and get you out through the back. As they're moving the bus, I'll give you some anaesthetic from these cylinders to help the pain. They've got some laughing gas in them, help you see the funny side of things.'

He felt his attempt at humour had been inept, a pale reflection of their own, but it brought its response.

'Give him a double dose then, doc, miserable bastard. And get his arm off my back, would you? I think he's getting ideas.'

Opening the crash box, Jonathan took out the carton of morphia. He checked the name on the label, Cyclimorph 15. It was a preparation of morphia that contained an anti-emetic. His patients didn't look the types to vomit but it would do them no harm. He clucked his tongue. A pity. He knew the adult dose was 10 to 20 milligrammes but they were very big men and would undergo considerable pain; he would have liked to give them more than the usual dose. But 30 milligrammes, he hesitated to give them that much. He looked in the box again and found another carton of Cyclimorph 10. Problem solved. One ampule of each and he could give them 25. Leaning awkwardly on his elbows, he filled two syringes and laid them down in readiness. 'Now then, who's first?'

A conversation he had had with his father raced through his mind. 'If you can, always do the difficult part of an operation first; leave the easy bit for when you're tired.' It hardly applied here but Jonathan saw the hand stretching towards him across the other man's back, asking to be injected first, and decided instead to tackle the arm belonging to the man nearer to him but doubled up beneath him to help support the weight of a vast paunch. He took from his pocket a length of old rubber tubing, an old friend he had carried in his white coat pocket since his house surgeon days. He hauled the arm out, slit the clothing with scissors and applied the rubber tourniquet. The veins, warmed and congested beneath the man's bulk, stood out, and, minutes later, he was withdrawing the needle to the accompaniment of a whispered 'Thanks, doc.'

The easy hand defeated him. Uncovered in the cold and with the vasoconstriction of shock, no rubbing or smacking would produce a vein capable of being injected and Jonathan had to admit his failure. 'I'm sorry,' he said as he plunged the needle deep into powerful muscles. 'Just means we will have to wait a bit longer for it to work, that's all.'

'That's all right, doc. Always was bit of an occud sod.'

The two minutes it took to pull the bus clear of the water seemed to Jonathan endless. Stretched across both men, a mask in each hand, he struggled to keep them breathing as much of the gas as he could. With only equal parts of nitrous oxide and oxygen, he knew there was no chance of such big men being put to sleep, the gas would have an analgesic action only, and their shouts and curses, only partly muffled by the masks, mingled with the shouts and curses of those outside, all deadened by the din of buckled metal grinding and grating. There followed a half hour of gentleness and brute force as the two men were freed and Jonathan followed them out through the hole cut in the rear panel. He was brushing himself down as he saw the second stretcher start its climb up the embankment. It stopped and an arm was raised towards him. He went over, took the hand that was offered and accepted in its leathery grip a reward far greater than any fat fee.

Entering any hospital department, be it ward, theatre, clinic or laboratory, Jonathan strode head up, shoulders back, walking heel and toe with total confidence, happy in his chosen métier. As he crept down the maternity department corridor, slightly hunched and on his toes, he was ready to whisper his apologies to anyone who might bar his way. The place had an aura, a smell, all its own that made Jonathan strangely ill at ease. It was not a department he would go to without good reason but he had an overwhelming desire to see once more what had become known as the back seat baby. Jonathan found him cradled in an adoring mother's arms.

'Isn't he beautiful, doctor? He's our first boy, did you know that? He's a bit premature and a bit jaundiced – that's why they've kept us in for a few days – but they say he's perfect. Aren't you my lovely?'

The beloved bundle was held up for Jonathan's inspection and approbation and he made the appropriate noises even though his first impression of the tiny face was that of a yellow prune.

'I'm ever so grateful to you for being there to deliver him, doctor. I don't know what would have happened without you.'

'I didn't do anything, really,' Jonathan said, modestly enough. 'It wasn't so much delivering him as catching him in the slips.'

He hadn't expected his flippancy to provoke peals of laughter but he looked for a smile and found none. It then occurred to him that her whole conversation had been strangely low key, lacking the usual joyous overtones of a new baby. Perhaps this was the way you welcomed the arrival of your sixth child but it was their first boy and there had been nothing sham about the mother's loving adoration. The dialogue became stilted, began to peter out, and Jonathan made slowly for the door. He was about to go through it when a quiet voice called him back.

'Doctor, would you do me one more favour?' Her eyes were fixed on the end of the bed as she spoke.

'Of course. If I can.'

'That call the lady doctor went on, when that buzzer went off, just as my baby was born, that was for what you call a cardiac arrest, wasn't it?'

'Yes.'

'And the patient died, didn't he, doctor?'

'Yes, that's true. But he was a very sick man, had been for a long time. It wasn't altogether unexpected.'

'How old was he, doctor?'

'Nineteen.'

'Nineteen.' She hung her head in sadness. 'So young. Do you think they'd mind . . .' She hesitated. 'Do you think you could find out his name for me? I would like to call this little one after him. D'you think they'd mind? D'you think she'd mind, his mother, I mean? Could you ask her?' She became agitated. 'I wouldn't want to see her. But could you ask her for me? Perhaps she would feel as if a part of her son was living on. Bit like a transplant,' she added as if just thinking of it.

'I'm sure she wouldn't object,' Jonathan smiled. 'I'll see what I can do.'

8

'Right then, young Jonathan, are you ready?'

Bob Bannerman stood, battered old sports bag in one hand, squash racket in the other, in the midst of the surge of patients that always seem to appear just before lunch when tempers shorten on empty stomachs. Jonathan, clutching a clip board burdened with notes, looked despairingly at him.

'Come on.' Bannerman seemed totally insensitive to the glances from patients who, until then, had endured a long wait with no thought of complaint in the face of so much honest endeavour all around. 'Where's your kit?'

'In my car but . . .' Jonathan held up his clip board as if no explanation was necessary.

'Nae bother. Janet will sort those out for you. Let's go.'

Scarsby's squash club had, in its heyday, been famous for its squash and notorious for its drinking. A small nucleus of dedicated athletes had been good enough, in the most unlikely of surroundings, to have members competing at national level while the small galleries above the twin courts had known the packed excitement of demonstration games with some of the Khans. But, with the opening of the new sports and leisure centre, they had moved out, leaving the drinkers to play just sufficient squash to justify the periodic renewal of their liquor licence. What had not changed was the smell, the miasma of beer and sweat unique to any small squash club. It enveloped Bannerman and Jonathan as they pushed open the rotting front door, seeming to breathe new life into Bannerman while bringing a wrinkle to Jonathan's nose.

Jonathan was changed and ready by the time Bannerman had stripped down to baggy underpants, the perished waist band disappearing into a deep fold below a sagging paunch. The skin over his chest was lax, with two pads of fat that drooped like an old woman's breasts, but there were signs too that, in younger days, Bannerman had been a powerful man; the girth of his thorax, the wiry hair over shoulder and back. Jonathan watched him pull on an old rugby shirt with broad black stripes, wondered whether one complained to one's boss about wearing a shirt the same colour as the ball and decided it wasn't worth the bother.

Jonathan had been truthful when he had told Bannerman he was no expert, though he was still of an age when he stayed reasonably fit without any great deal of training. He was co-ordinated and had a good eye but never seemed to have mastered the angles and change of pace the game demanded. Any attempt at a drop shot was usually a point lost. But he had a competitive spirit, belied by an easy-going manner, that drove him to chase shots through the last stages of exhaustion, searching out the ball amongst the black spots that spattered his visual fields. Not that he imagined he would need to drive himself that far against a man with a belly the size of Bannerman's. He wasn't quite sure how to play it. Do you always let your boss win, however bad he might be? It was not in Jonathan's nature to give a game away but, under the circumstances, might it not be wiser? Let him have the first few points perhaps; that wouldn't be too difficult.

Jonathan was six points down before it came home to him that he was playing against someone who, in his day, had been a far better player than he could ever hope to be. By the time he had tightened his grip, he found he had lost the first game nine – six having been twice knocked flat by a barging Bannerman who had promptly demanded the let. As Bannerman leaned against the wall, head down so that sweat from nose and forehead dripped rhythmically on to the boards, Jonathan decided he was a man that he would have to beat to keep his self-respect. The next few points were evenly fought but, as the second game wore on, the pace slackened as Bannerman tired. Jonathan only had to relax to run out a comfortable winner.

'The decider?' Two words at a time was about all Bannerman could now manage. Jonathan looked at him, bent, hands on thighs, his eyes sunken and his jowls sagging to keep a dry crusted mouth permanently open. He had fully expected to see Bannerman vomit. Now he was more concerned he might have a cardiac arrest on his hands if Bannerman went on playing.

'Do you really feel like it? I'm quite happy.'

By way of an answer, Bannerman walked to the corner and served. Jonathan took the first seven points despite Bannerman skinning his knee in a desperate gasping dive into the corner and Jonathan was faced with the likelihood of whitewashing his boss. He lobbed the ball to bounce back gently centre court. His opponent hurled himself at it to strike it with all the strength he could muster into a corner where Jonathan found no difficulty in missing it. He looked up to see a face, grey with dehydration but snarling in naked hatred.

'Don't patronise me, fuck you.'

The match won and lost, they made their wordless way back to the changing room where Bannerman slumped exhausted on a bench. He leaned his head back and closed his eyes. He was still there when Jonathan had showered and changed and Jonathan, wondering how Janet was coping, had to spend another twenty minutes, sitting, fully dressed, in steamy discomfort as Bannerman went through a similar process.

'What are you going to have?'

Jonathan had realised how slim was the chance of passing the bar on the way out but he felt he must at least try.

'I really feel I should be getting back.'

'What are you going to have?' The words were repeated, staccato, the tone ascending to ring around the nicotine-stained ceiling of the otherwise deserted lounge. The steward rose slowly from where he had been sitting reading the racing page to stare at Jonathan.

Jonathan dropped his bag on the floor as if in capitulation. 'Pint of orange juice and lemonade, please.'

'Do you know how to make one of those, Alf?' Bannerman laughed as he took his glass from the steward. 'Cheers. Thank you for the game.'

As Jonathan watched, Bannerman emptied his glass without taking breath, pushing it back over the bar. 'Proper one this time, Alf, please. That one was just therapeutic, now I can start enjoying them.' He settled on to the bar stool as he lit his cigar. A voice came from the other side of the cloud of smoke that covered his face. 'I hear you're taking Gorgeous Gussie out tonight.'

'Good God,' Jonathan's jaw dropped. 'How d'you know that?'

Bannerman's chest heaved up and down in half-laugh, half-cough. 'Everybody's been wondering how long it would take you to get round to her.'

'You do mean Staff Wilks?'

'That's right. Known as Gorgeous Gussie for her frilly knickers – but then you're probably too young to understand the connection.'

'Well, I'm damned.'

'Lucky beggar. I only wish I was twenty years younger. And then again, perhaps I don't. A much over-rated pastime. I think nowadays I would prefer a good pint.' He waved his almost empty pint glass and Jonathan took the hint.

'Please, let me.'

'Only if you join me.'

Jonathan looked at the curling corners of the sandwiches under their finger printed plastic cover, the long forsaken pork pies in their crumpled packets, and decided he was hungry but not that hungry. 'I'll have a half.'

A wink from Bob to Alf and the half ordered became a full pint delivered. The drinks paid for, Jonathan sat on the stool to face Bannerman as the steward picked up his paper again.

'Well, and how are you enjoying medicine out in the bush?' Bannerman asked.

'I'm enjoying it very much.'

'Lying beggar.'

'It's the truth.'

'You don't think we're leading you into bad habits then? Surgical, I mean, not sexual.'

'Not a bit. I'm learning a lot.'

'Hm. No criticisms of any kind?'

'Not really.'

'You're lying again. I can tell by your voice.'

Jonathan's concern at the lack of day-to-day anaesthetic cover in the department surged to the surface but he suppressed it. A squash club bar seemed hardly the place to express it. Anyway, a few months and he would be out of the place. He was startled by Bannerman's next words.

'But why should you worry? Another couple of months and you'll never see the inside of a Casualty department again. No one puts a foot in the place unless they have to. You won't either, once you're a famous general surgeon; no time for pathetic rejects like me then.'

'That's a bit hard, isn't it?'

'Is it? Take a damn good look at me.'

Jonathan did just that, wondering what was coming next, watching Bannerman rattle his glass on the bar.

'Can't take any more of that, Alf. Give me a gin, there's a good fella – the usual. And put it on the slate, would you?' He turned back to Jonathan. 'Different, isn't it, if you want to be a Casualty Consultant right from the start like most of them. They're happy enough. But it wasn't what I wanted. Difficult to believe, isn't it, that I looked just like you years ago. Can't imagine it, can you?'

Jonathan didn't answer.

'Well I was. Greatest orthopaedic surgeon Manchester had ever seen, Harry Platt and all, that's what I was going to be.' His eyes narrowed. 'The bastards. So perhaps there is at least one thing I can teach you before you leave.'

'And what's that?'

'Keep your nose clean.' He turned his head, his voice now curt, less friendly towards bar stewards. 'I'll have another panatella.'

Jonathan raised one eyebrow.

'There's no need to look so bloody innocent. You know exactly what I mean. It's not all to do with ability, you know. Your face has got to fit, that's the most important thing.'

His circulation still speeding as a result of the exercise, the alcohol absorbing directly through the walls of an empty stomach, Jonathan's face flushed. 'Oh, come on, there's got to be more to it than that. I'm sure the really able ones make it in the end.'

'All right; but don't say I didn't warn you. I'm not saying the ones who make it aren't able; I'm sure they are. All I'm saying is, you watch out. All those mates of yours, you know, all those who seem so friendly even though you're all competing for the same jobs. You watch 'em.'

Jonathan listened, fascinated, making no attempt to prevent the barman from refilling his glass.

'Let your hair down in hospital a couple of times and a word from one of them to your Prof and you'll begin to wonder why you're not getting the jobs you're after. Take my advice, don't crap on your own doorstep. And, of course, if you've got one of these holier-than-thou Profs, then . . .' He waved his hand vaguely, inviting Jonathan to use his imagination on that one, then adding, in case Jonathan had missed the point, 'You end up practising your medicine somewhere beyond the Styx like Scarsby.'

'That can't be all bad.'

'End up at 35 to 40, with perhaps thirty years to go, doing a job you can do with one hand tied behind your back, while the guys you used to meet, waiting for the interviews, pull in their merit awards on top of their private practice.'

'There have got to be compensations.'

'Tell me one.'

Jonathan leaned forwards, his face earnest. 'You get so much closer to the local community out here. You never really feel you belong in the big hospitals – they're so impersonal.'

'You'd soon get tired of that, start longing for anonymity. I worked for a chief once, there were times he didn't know the sex of the patients he was operating on, let alone their names; hadn't seen his ward for years. That's the way to work, chum.'

'I hope and pray I will never agree with that.'

'I don't really mean that either.' Bannerman's voice became softer. He slumped a little further to lean towards the younger man. 'You're a good lad, Jonathan, so take a bit of advice from someone who has seen it all. Don't trust any of your colleagues and don't get too close to your patients. Keep the swine at arm's length.'

It was past three o'clock when Bannerman announced his return to the department at large, his voice echoing as he called for a coffee. Jonathan followed in his train, still conscious of the impression they were having on both patients and staff but less anxious about it than when walking out earlier. A few strides behind Bannerman, like an heir apparent, Jonathan suddenly found the door to Bannerman's office closed in his face, leaving him to bear the full brunt of Sister Gaunt's silent disapproval. He looked for Janet James but could not find her. He began to deal with the few casualties waiting, for the first time in his life turning his head away from a patient, aware of the smell of beer on his breath. In a wave of remorse, feeling degraded by the thought of something of Bannerman rubbing off on him, he swore to himself that, consultant and his boss though Bannerman might be, he would never play with him at lunchtime again. He looked sheepishly at Sister Gaunt.

'Do me a favour, Sister. Find Janet and tell her not to worry. Tell her I can manage the rest of the session.'

'And I should think so too, Dr Brookes.'

Jonathan did not find Staff Nurse Ellen Wilks any easier to talk to than the first-year nurse. Not that it mattered, as there was no question of putting someone at her ease. Neither was there any problem of attuning himself to an atmosphere of innocent expectancy. Staff Nurse Ellen Wilks sat in the passenger seat as if she had done it many times before. She was soon adding to the ash left by Bannerman.

Jonathan had eaten virtually nothing all day and the effect of the beer had worn off to leave him furry tongued and with a slight headache. He drank nothing but orange juice but this had little inhibitory effect on his partner who drank anything he suggested, adding a few ideas of her own. The effects of the drink were minimal, doing nothing to stimulate the conversation and producing no sign of drunkenness apart from slight sluggishness of eye movements. As the evening wore on, however, her smoking accelerated to the point of a chain reaction throughout the sweet and coffee stages. Dead sober, Jonathan wondered how her breath would smell.

Halfway back to Lymm, Jonathan changed direction back towards Scarsby, a decision made. He was too sober. Perhaps, another time, he would confirm whether or not Bannerman had been correct about her knickers. Frilled or plain, for some reason they had suddenly lost their appeal. As if reading his mind and understanding, the girl alongside him, without a word, put out a hand which came to rest high on his thigh. The stroking and scratching had its inevitable effects and she turned to bring both hands to bear. As Jonathan slowed, steering with white-knuckled care, she brought him to a gasping climax with practised artistry. Neat and dexterous to the end, she closed the zip for him, the gentle, concluding pat that of a contract sealed, an account settled.

Staff Nurse Wilks lit a cigarette and inhaled deeply, settling back in her seat with the contented air of someone with all debts paid. To Jonathan it seemed a silent age until he dropped her outside her door. Her 'Thank you, Dr Brookes,' as she got out, was all encompassing.

He watched the door close behind her before driving away slowly. There was a hard frost and the tiny gardens of the houses that bore in on him from both sides were already beginning to sparkle in the street lights. He opened his window and welcomed the cold that bit into his flushed cheeks. He felt sticky and uncomfortable – that he knew was readily put right – but what no sluicing shower or soaking bath could hope to reach was the grubby, brutalised opinion of himself that produced in him a loneliness that had nothing to do with being alone.

9

The Butcher's Arms was, in its way, a club as exclusive as any in Pall Mall, with the added attraction of having no entrance fee or annual subscription. Any hard drinker with a grudge against society was eligible to join. Non-smokers were frowned upon. There were no temporary members and no resignations; the only way to break away from the membership's influence was by death, usually from alcohol-related diseases, or violence in some form or other, or by penal servitude. Any observed voluntary association with the forces of law and order meant being immediately blackballed with almost certain penalties to be paid in full. A few members kept themselves in humble obscurity never having graduated any higher than the local Magistrate's Courts after being heaved out of some gutter by the police for their own protection. Many of these had been born to better things, dragging their anchors from family and peers on their Odyssey into oblivion and were only tolerated on the outer fringes of the society out of grudging admiration for their drinking and, even there, an inborn snobbish pride in the pseudo-intellectual arguments they sometimes provoked.

The usual Saturday night crowd was almost complete; Jack Stringer could have checked his watch against their entry. Outwardly, this was just another Saturday night, the beginning, middle and end as predictable as a bad thriller. But Jack was uneasy. His regulars were all creatures of habit; anything unusual made them confused, suspicious, quite often spelt trouble. Above all, they liked to sit in the same place, week in, week out. No crusty old salt of an admiral in his favourite old leather back was more possessive. Even the dogs knew their place. The spheres of influence were the large log fire and the bar, the local Woolsack being the stool at the end of the bar nearest the fireplace. The qualifications that decided just how near one came to occupying that high office was the length of time one could boast behind bars and the ability to settle any differences of opinion with one's fists or a broken glass. Hence Jack Stringer's unease.

Jack had heard that Patrick Morelli was out, had got out a day or so before. And that stool was Pat's. It was only a question of time before Pat came back to claim his own and it would not be Pat Morelli's style to creep in early. He would want to savour the acclamation that a Saturday night crowd would give to the return of one of its folk heroes. And Snudge had got used to that stool, really fancied himself.

Jack's regulars shared his expectancy and the conversation was subdued, dropping to a hush as heads came up each time the doors on to the road outside swung open and crashed shut. It was after half past nine when their vigil was rewarded and Patrick Morelli, a poor man's Godfather, rejoined his people. He stood for a moment just inside the door, bathing in the flood of acclaim due to anyone who had survived years of incarceration unchanged. And who knows? Perhaps he had graduated an even better villain. Behind him and to one side, stood his proud consort, tottering on stiletto heels with thin, plastic straps around her sturdy ankles. Behind him and to the other side, equally proud, stood his son. Snudge joined in the welcome from the corner of the bar.

Within minutes, Pat Morelli was the centre of a back-slapping, drink-buying ring of toadies, anxious to allay any misconceptions he might have been mulling over in Parkhurst. Some of those around Snudge looked anxious, wondering whether to hedge their bets. A couple of pints later and the two groups merged and spread, opening up an area to allow Pat and Snudge to confront each other.

'Pat.'

'Snudgie.'

From his vantage point Snudge surveyed his rival. Pat Morelli was not all that big – what he lacked in size, he made up for in viciousness – but that son of his had grown to be a big sod. He was such a big lad that Snudge would have doubted his parentage if he hadn't seen his eyes. Like his father's they showed the compassion of a hungry stoat. Snudge had seen him in the Butcher's, taking his beer like a man, not saying much. But he had not been around so much recently. The talk was he was into other things, but that was no business of Snudge's.

'Looking a bit pale, Pat. Not much sun down the Isle of Wight this time of the year, I imagine.'

'Not much, Snudge; no.'

'Look after you well, did they, old, respected customer an' all?'

'Service in't what it used to be, Snudge. You been keeping well?'

'Can't complain. Managing to keep out of trouble.'

'How's that then, Snudge; found yourself a bent copper or something?'

There was precious little mirth in Snudge's laugh. 'How come you took so long to come and see us, Pat? Story is you got out a few days ago. Naughty of you, is that. But then,' he leered at Eva Morelli, 'no doubt you've been busy like, haven't you. First things first, after all.'

Eva simpered at the compliment until she saw her husband's face. She wondered why he didn't do something about that bastard Snudge sitting in his place. But he'd been funny all evening, he had. She'd been all ready to go by seven o'clock and there he was, stuck in front of the telly and nothing she could do to shift him, sitting there, nothing to drink, sober as a bloody judge, he'd been.

Snudge, on the other hand, had been there early to stake his claim and Pat watched as he began to squirm. Another half pint and he slid from the stool. 'Must have a piss,' he grinned. 'Must be getting old. Now don't go away, Pat. You and me got a lot of talking to do.'

When Snudge got back, he found Pat Morelli had conformed with his wish and not gone away. In fact, as if to make plain just how long he intended staying, he had perched on the stool so recently vacated by Snudge. Jack Stringer watched anxiously from behind a bar that had suddenly become a lonely place to be.

'Feeling better?' asked Morelli, kindly.

Unsmiling, Snudge stared. In a straight punch up, he had always been more than a match for Morelli, even more so now with Morelli so thin beneath his Parkhurst pallor. Where he had lost out to the smaller man was in his last split second hesitation at driving his boot into an undefended kidney or face, a petty consideration that had never cramped Morelli's style. But there was his boy, Chico, silent and patently unafraid, now standing in front of his father, his drink resting on the bar, one hand hidden menacingly in the pocket of his leather jacket. Snudge looked quickly over both shoulders for similar support and found none. He forced his lips to smile.

'Nice to see you back in your old place, Pat. Just like old times.'

'It's nice to be back.' Morelli slid his hand under his buttock. 'Thanks for keeping it warm for me.'

Jack Stringer, sighing in relief, slid a drink towards Morelli. 'On the house, Pat. Welcome home.'

Without taking his eyes from Snudge's face, Wayne stretched for his drink, still keeping one hand concealed. Feeling the young man's idolising protection, Morelli relaxed.

'Met a couple of old mates of yours, Snudgie; send their regards. Made a few contacts of my own this time; thought you might be interested. They're getting out in a couple of months. From over in Liverpool...'

Gavin Prescott turned the handle and pushed, but the kitchen door stayed shut. With wide, draughty gaps around it, this one, unlike the front door, was usually easy to open and he tried again. There was light in the kitchen window and he banged with his fist. 'Linda, are you there?'

Fear was transmitted through the door. 'That you, Gav?'

'Open the door. It's me.'

Linda had trouble turning the rusting lock. Gavin couldn't remember the last time the door had been locked. There were two good reasons why no one in Northend would have been stupid enough to break in to the Morelli house, one was the fear of retribution, the other the common knowledge that they were unlikely to find anything worth stealing.

'You all right, love?' Gavin asked as he closed the door again behind him.

'I'm frightened, Gav.'

'Where are they?'

'Where d'you think? You're not working tonight, are you, Gav?'

'No. What time did they go out?'

'Not till quite late. It was funny. Mam was all tarted up for hours but couldn't get Dad to move. He just sat there staring at the telly, not saying a word. He's horrible, Gav. I think he's worse than before. He's hardly said a word to me.' Linda was close to tears. 'Gav,' she said. 'Is it wicked to hate your father the way I do?'

'Don't worry, Linda love. Join the club.' He threw his sports bag on the floor. 'I've had something to eat. What about you? Did you eat with them?'

Linda gave Gavin one of her 'do me a favour' looks. 'I found some sausages; I fried those and had them with some bread and butter.'

'Cup of tea then?'

She shook her head. 'Think I'll go to bed, Gav. You're not going out again, are you?'

'No. You're quite safe, Linda. Just bolt your door from now on. I'll be here. You just keep your head down, get those A levels then we'll both get out of here. It won't be long, now.'

'It's difficult to concentrate, Gav, with him in the house. Couldn't we move out somewhere?'

'Difficult, Linda. I have thought about it, I promise you, but it would be very difficult the way things are. Just a few more months.' He smiled at her. 'I'm depending on you, you realise that, don't you? Just think, medical school somewhere hundreds of miles away from here, never see Northend again. I'll get a job in the same hospital, on days, to look after you. After that, who knows?'

'Would be nice, Gav.'

'If you want something badly enough, it will come. Now, you go and do an hour's work before they come back.'

At the door to the hallway, Linda turned. 'What about other nights though, Gav? What about the nights you're on duty?'

'You're a big girl now. He wouldn't dare.' It was obvious to Gavin that Linda was not convinced. 'You've got those bolts I put on the door; you'll be quite safe.' Linda still said nothing, making no move to leave. 'If he ever touches you again, Linda, I promise you, I'll put the police on to him.'

'That wouldn't be much good to me, now would it, Gav? It would be all over by then, wouldn't it? And,' her voice began to tremble, 'I don't think I could tell the coppers about all those things he used to do to me. I think I'd almost rather things went on like before than do that. Can you imagine them all, sitting round laughing in the canteen afterwards, making jokes about it? Why are men to disgusting?'

'They're not all like that, Linda.'

'What?'

'No, they're not. And I think I know one copper now who would understand and look after you, make sure they treated you right.'

'Can't be a real one then. And the women coppers are no better. I've seen them on the telly, interviewing these rape victims and that; all as hard as hell really, just trained to look sympathetic.'

'They get to see some pretty horrible things in that job, Linda; bit like us in Cas. They've got to be a bit hard.'

'And in court. I couldn't stand up there in court and tell everybody what happened. I'd rather die.'

Six years before, Linda had been too young to ask for help, even from Gavin, against something she had had no means of understanding. Now silence settled between them for a moment as minds sifted data provided by the first open admission between them that anything beyond the normal had ever occurred. Up until then, there had always been a dumb, agonising acceptance of reality without either being able to spell out his or her feelings.

'Fair enough, Linda, love,' Gavin said, quietly. 'In that case, we would have to make some other kind of arrangement, wouldn't we? Now then;

off with you. An hour's work, d'you hear, and then bed. Sure you don't want that cup of tea?'

'Yes, thanks, Gav. See you in the morning.'

In the living room, the stale smell of the unwashed made Gavin wrinkle his nose in distaste. It was a room in which he spent very little of his time. He was obliged to make contact with his mother and Wayne in the kitchen – he had to eat. But for the rest of his time in the house, he lived like a lodger, disappearing into his bed-sit, his only loving contact Linda, almost as isolated in her room across the tiny landing. He tried to revive the dying embers of a miserable fire and turned on the TV. He stared unreceptively at the screen, fixing his gaze so that he did not see the beer stained mat beneath his feet, the peeling wallpaper beside the fireplace. He tried to take an interest in the late night film, anything to blot out self questioning as to why he should bother to wait up for people he loathed.

He stood up and turned off the TV as, from the street outside, came sounds he had not heard for six years, the shouting, the irregular, stumbling footsteps. The kitchen resounded to one of his mother's skittish yelps and beer cans rattled as they dropped on hard Formica. His mother was first into the room.

'Hullo, Gav, love. You missed a night tonight, you did,'

'Not over yet, neither.' Pat Morelli brought a delighted shriek from Eva as he came in behind her, one shoulder colliding with the doorpost as he bent to run a hand up her skirt. He had not totally regained his balance as he fell into the chair beside the fire. He looked up at Gavin, now standing above him. 'Fetch me another beer, Eva. Gavin here's the only bastard who hasn't drunk with me yet.'

'How many bastards have you met tonight then? Real ones like me, I mean.'

'Sorry, Gav; no offence. Drink with my eldest son then.'

'I'm no son of yours, Pat. I'd rather be a bastard. And I don't drink,' he added.

Pat Morelli was drunk, his reactions unpredictable. He stared, his eyes uncoordinated, at this young man he had last seen as a stubborn, rebellious kid. Six years ago, a remark like that and he would have fetched the little bastard one that would have rattled every tooth in his head. Not that he was much bigger now, he hadn't grown much, not like Wayne. Now there was someone who had filled out, the young sod. Really grown into a man. Real chip off the old block.

'You shouldn't talk to your father like that, Gav, you shouldn't. It's not nice, is that. And him just out an' all. Where's your consideration?'

'Shut your face, Eva. I'm sure I can get him to change his mind.' Pat still faced Gavin as he spoke to his wife. 'Get me that beer.'

'No need, Dad.' Wayne walked in to drop four cans, still tethered in their plastic rings, into his lap. He pulled one from another group of four and thrust it towards Gavin.

Gavin shook his head.

'What, not going to celebrate your father's homecoming then?' Two beer cans spluttered open almost simultaneously as Wayne sank into the chair opposite his father.

'I see no cause for celebration in that.'

Pat Morelli's trunk jerked forwards but his legs were slow to follow. Half way out of his chair, it got through to him that Gavin no longer shrank back, his shoulders hunched, his eyes half closed in expectation of the blow that was to follow. He saw a man, alert and relaxed, as if begging him to try. He sat back, slowly, as Wayne watched, looking for a lead from his father.

'I'm going to bed.' Eva, almost forgotten, sounded miffed.

'Best place for you, an' all.'

'Is our Linda in, Gav?' Eva asked.

'She's in bed.'

'All right, I'll go up then. Good night all.'

Completely ignored, Eva left the three men, one clear-eyed and watchful, standing between the other two who sat, red and truculent with drink. Without quite knowing why, Gavin sat between them on the settee, his fingers unconsciously searching out the cigarette burns in its hard plastic covering.

'Yes,' Pat said. 'Our Linda. There's somebody else who's grown up while I've been away, by heck she has; really filled out. Not really had a chance to see her yet.' And Gavin suddenly knew exactly why he had sat down with two men he loathed. 'What's she been up to while I've been away?'

As Gavin sat and watched can after can opened, drunk, crushed and discarded beneath their chairs, he knew he must stay until they were both in bed, however long the period of mind-numbing banality he had to endure in the process. He felt that that first night would set a pattern, lay down new ground rules for the weeks and months to come and that the slightest sign of weakness would bring its own harvest in due course. He knew that, in the steel blinkered minds he was dealing with, even a quiet, sober retirement to bed would be interpreted as evidence of submission. He must stay and see it out, start again at least on level terms the next morning.

'What are you going to do with yourself, now you're out?' Pat Morelli looked like going to sleep in the chair and Gavin spoke sharply, trying to prevent him doing so.

Morelli snorted awake to stare balefully at Gavin. He was having difficulty coming to terms with this scrawny little bastard talking to him with a new confidence. He should be up in his bedroom by now, fearfully hoping to avoid a thrashing, not sitting there as if he owned the place.

'What d'you mean, do with myself?' The few moments' sleep had been sufficient to dull the euphoria of drink and replace it with a head-aching, foul temper. It had been a long day for Morelli, full of excitement, and he resented Gavin's interference in what he wanted to do, which was simply to fall asleep where he was. 'What d'you mean, do with myself? I'll show you what I'll do with myself. I'll bloody well . . .' He bent forwards suddenly in the act of getting out of his chair, one fist clenched, his face suffused with anger. He stopped, halfway out of the chair, surprise and irritation replacing the anger on his face as he was doubly incontinent. 'Oh, shit.'

It was only as Morelli staggered and shuffled his way to the loo that Gavin realised just how drunk he was. Through the open door, they heard him curse as he tried to clean himself up.

'Bit out of training, i'n't he?' Wayne sniggered.

Hoping to divert Morelli upstairs as he came from the loo, Gavin stood and went into the hall but Morelli pushed him aside as he returned to his chair. Gavin followed to stand over him, recoiling from the waft of foul air that surrounded Morelli.

'You're drunk. You ought to go to bed.'

'Piss off.' Morelli looked up at Gavin as Wayne sat, laughing, enjoying the fun. Morelli pursed his lips, rocking his head from side to side. ' "What are you going to do with yourself?" ' he imitated. 'As I said, what the hell has that got to do with you?'

'Because I am the only one bringing any money into this house, that's what it has got to do with me. I have a right to know.'

'Right to know, my arse. But, if you must know,' pride spread sluggishly over Morelli's face, 'I've got a couple of business deals coming up, over in Liverpool. Won't be for a couple of months, but then . . .' With a laborious wink, Morelli left the rest to Gavin's imagination.

'And then you'll be back inside.'

There was a silence as Morelli took a long hard look at Gavin. Slowly, he spelt out a considered opinion. 'You hate me, don't you?'

For a second, Gavin stared at his step-father incredulously before bursting into a short, cynical laugh. 'Whatever gave you that idea?'

'Yes, you do.' The whining tone of the maudling drunk rose as Morelli went on. 'You've always hated me; me, who's always looked after you, kept you straight like as if I was your real father. You and Linda. She's always hated me too. And that was because of you. You turned her against me, my own daughter. Too stuck up by far, our Linda, with all these ideas you've been giving her. Your mother's been telling me about you and her, spending all that time together in that room of hers. Ain't natural, is that.'

Gavin's eyes had narrowed with every word. 'That, coming from you ...' he hissed, but Morelli seemed not to notice in his self-pitying mutterings.

'Wouldn't even come and have a drink with her father. Never came to visit me. Her own father.' With explosively sudden violence, he lifted himself out of his chair and brushed Gavin aside. 'Haven't even seen her. Going to see her.'

He rushed out of the room and was halfway up the stairs before Gavin caught up with him, shouting at him to go to bed. At the top of the stairs Morelli turned and kicked viciously at Gavin's face but the movement was slow and Gavin swayed away out of harm. He watched Morelli grasp the handle to Linda's door and saw the blind fury as Morelli found it locked. He shook it furiously. 'Linda, open this flamin' door.'

'Go to bed.' The softly spoken words, coming from Gavin, standing close behind Morelli on the tiny landing, sounded like a last warning but Morelli's only response was to take one step back before charging the door with his shoulder. The bolts held and Morelli stood back, the fury on his face replaced with thin lipped evil.

'I said, go to bed.'

Frustrated by the door, Morelli turned his fury on his step-son. A strangled grunt of hate in his throat, he raised his fist high above Gavin's head in a movement that brought back all the pain and unhappiness of a young man's childhood.

Morelli never saw Gavin move. Arm still raised, fist still clenched, he found himself falling, just glimpsing Gavin's snarl before hurtling backwards down the stairs. His descent was halted momentarily halfway down as one ankle caught in the banisters. There was a loud snap and he slid the lower half, head first, to buckle against the wall where the lower two steps turned at right angles.

The silence that fell momentarily on the whole house was shattered by a scream and Gavin turned to see his mother standing in her bedroom door, muscular thighs and calves tense below the hem of a pink, see through nightie. She joined him at the top of the stairs. Her voice rose hysterically. 'Gav, you've killed him. You have. You've killed him. He's dead, I tell you. He's dead.'

Gavin heard the bolts being drawn on Linda's door. He shouted above his mother's screams. 'Stay there, Linda. Keep out of this.'

Devoid of all feelings of guilt or anxiety, Gavin descended the stairs, stepping with difficulty over the inert figure crumpled in the corner of two walls. He saw movement in Morelli's chest and was feeling for his carotids when Linda's voice, curt and urgent, came from above him.

'Gav.'

He saw her gaze, fixed as if hypnotised, and followed it back over his shoulder. Wayne stood in the hall, a knife in his hand, his arm fully extended in the direction of Gavin's throat, his tongue slowly circling his lips. He held the knife, not out of the back of his hand, but along his palm and fingers as if holding a torch. He said nothing, his eyes glazed.

'Watch him, Gav. He had a couple of lines early on, I saw him, just before he went out.'

Gavin had time to feel surprised. He had often wondered how he would react to the real thing; would he just fold up? The art of arresting a lethal karate blow, centimetres from its target, was one thing when practised in the courteous ritual of the gymnasium, to have someone come at you with a knife for real was another. He was gratified to find he felt no fear as he descended the last two steps into the hall, moving away from the stairs a little to give himself room. Totally relaxed with no tenseness in his shoulders or knees, his breathing was gentle and shallow, ready to inhale with the block, exhale again with the finishing manoeuvre. He watched his half-brother back off a few feet as if to give Gavin a sporting chance.

When Wayne's lunge came, it was as sudden as it was silent, aimed unwaveringly at Gavin's jugular with no split-second deviation simply to frighten or to wound. It was a movement violent enough for being driven by years of pent-up hatred without being boosted by the twisted excitement of cocaine. Equally, Gavin's reactions were no longer those of the skilled instructor, revelling in his physical fitness, taking pride in his ability to harness lethal power. He knew that, so long as he kept cool, he had nothing to fear from his attacker; he could take the knife from Wayne like a bum taking a handout. But there was a score to settle, years of petty meanness that went as far back as the serious matter of a small boy's china dove. Gavin was in no doubt that he was going to maim his half-brother and enjoy it. What he had to be careful about was that he did not kill him.

He swayed to his left, blocking Wayne's arm as it passed over his right shoulder. Grabbing his jacket, he used Wayne's momentum to pull him onwards, hurling him into the living room doorpost, rolling over as he did so. Before Wayne could recover, Gavin had regained his feet, bent over him and brought his arm down in a scything arc. Gavin's Kiai, the sharp exhalation that tensed his belly muscles to give his hand its added power, preceded by milliseconds Wayne's scream of agony as his arm fractured. Gavin derived a deep gut satisfaction from both. The knife fell free from the right hand and Gavin, with all the time in the world, picked it up. With one cheek pressed to the floor by the pressure of Gavin's knee between his shoulder blades, Wayne watched in terror as Gavin raised the broad blade, held it aloft for a second before driving it downwards, to leave it quivering in the floorboards, inches in front of Wayne's eyes.

He leaned down so that his lips were close to Wayne's ear. 'The Japanese are a courteous race,' he whispered, 'given to such stupid concepts as dignity between enemies and honour towards a foe who has fought well.'

Wayne's eyes closed as he began to moan in pain but he opened them sharply, giving a squeal of agony as Gavin shook him.

'Pay attention, dear brother, to what I'm saying to you. The great masters have always taught that karate is a discipline of the spirit and the mind as much as of the body. The power to inflict terrible injuries is of secondary importance to them. They are reluctant to talk now of Ikken Hissatsu or killing with one blow. But we're not Japanese, are we, dear brother? You're a fine upstanding Englishman and I'm a black God-knows-what. So we don't have to conform, do we? We can make the rules up as we go along, can't we? So just remember, should you ever be so stupid as to try a thing like that again, that could have been your neck I broke, not just your arm. Be grateful for the pain, dear brother. If that had been your neck, you would now be beyond all pain.'

For a Saturday night, it had been surprisingly quiet – the usual pulped face or two from some bar fights, an overdose, a fractured neck of femur – run-of-the-mill cases only to be expected, with nothing to make the adrenalin flow. Jonathan Brookes was putting some catgut sutures on the inside of a through-and-through mouth laceration, his sense of smell never fully adapting to the mixture of vomit, blood, beer and saliva that stuck to his fingers. Peace reigned. It had been so quiet that Staff Nurse Peggy Wells, looking slightly sheepish, had told him she was going to put her feet up for half an hour. Jonathan had seen Police Constable Badger Kincaid, looking equally sheepish, slink down the corridor towards the sister's office, as far, that is, as any fourteen-stone man can slink down anywhere. It had to be too quiet to be true. It couldn't last and Jonathan looked up from washing his hands and sighed as he heard the tell-tale short ring of the ambulance siren. Making his way back to the cubicles, he saw Gavin walking towards him.

'What on earth are you doing here? I thought it was your night . . .' He didn't finish as he saw Gavin's face. 'What's the matter? Trouble?'

Without answering, Gavin took him into a side room. 'Who's on with you tonight?'

'Staff Wells. Why?'

'Thank God for that. I've just brought my step-father and brother in.

My brother has a broken arm but I think my father may have broken his neck.'

'Right.' Jonathan started for the door. 'How did it happen?'

'Let's just say for now that there was a fight and my father fell downstairs. He's broken his leg as well, by the look of it. They're both drunk. I must go and have a word with Peggy, ask her to be careful what she says or writes. Where is she?'

'She's in Sister's office. With . . .'

'Oh, God, no. That copper?'

'Yes. What about the police?' Jonathan asked. 'Was there anyone else involved? Any chance your father or brother will want to bring charges?'

'That's the last thing they'd want, Dr Brookes. Difficult to explain quickly but do you think you could get rid of him?'

Jonathan looked long and hard at a night porter he had known for such a short length of time. Why should be stick his neck out for him? Would Gavin do the same for him? 'Leave it to me,' he said, slowly, leaving no doubt about his reluctance. 'You go and help get your father in – make sure they don't move his neck more than they have to – and I'll find Staff Nurse.'

As Jonathan knocked on the door, he wondered that Staff Nurse Wells had not reacted to the ambulance ring – was love deaf as well as blind? – but she was already halfway to the door by the time he opened it. Jonathan smiled over her shoulder at Badger as he rose politely from his chair.

'Hullo, Badger, how are you? I'm afraid we need the boss for a while. I'm sorry.'

The door closed behind them and, a few steps down the corridor, Jonathan stopped. He jerked his head back over his shoulder. 'Get rid of him. Get him out of here.'

'He's not doing any harm, Dr Brookes. He's . . .'

'Out, Staff, now.' Peggy Wells was taken aback by an authority in Jonathan's voice she had not heard before, a curtness immediately replaced by his easygoing tone. 'Please, Peggy. I'll explain later. Just get him out of here, there's a good girl.'

Out of sight, they had already transferred Patrick Morelli very gingerly from trolley to couch when Badger approached the Casualty exit. He stood back as an ambulance driver came through the door, leading a grey-faced young man whose right hand supported his left arm as it hung in a sling. Grey or not, there was no mistaking the face if only for the cold hatred in the eyes and Badger's bushy eyebrows rose in surprise. Wayne reacted also. Drunk, drugged or shocked, or all three, Chico Morelli could always summon up a sneer at the sight of a policeman.

Badger turned and followed them, a few steps behind, to be confronted by Jonathan Brookes. They faced each other. No smiles.

'What's happened to him?' Badger asked.

'Just a broken arm, I believe.'

'How did he get that?'

'I really don't know yet.'

Badger moved to step around Jonathan and Jonathan moved to stand in his way.

'There's nothing here for you, Badger. Just another broken arm. Leave it. Go home.'

'He's a bad lot, that one, doctor.' Doubt was written all over an honest face. 'Perhaps I should . . .'

There was obviously no way he was going to get around Jonathan without physically pushing him aside and respect for Jonathan increased Badger's hesitation.

'Please, Badger.' Jonathan timed his plea skilfully and sighed his relief as he saw Badger, slowly and reluctantly, turn away and walk towards the exit once more.

Inside the cubicle, Jonathan pointed directly at Gavin. 'You too – out. I'll come and have a word with you when we've sorted them out. Until then – out.'

'He had a head injury as well as the rest, Dr Brookes.' Jonathan was struck by the clinical calmness of someone giving details of injuries to members of his own family. 'He was unconscious for a short while.'

'All right – but out you go. I don't want a member of the family breathing down my neck. Now hop it. I'll talk to you when we've finished.'

Later, in the dry-mouthed timelessness of the early hours, Jonathan found Gavin abstractedly cleaning an anaesthetic machine.

'Right,' Jonathan said. 'Let's do the easier one first. Your brother . . .'

'Half-brother,' Gavin corrected him.

'All right, half-brother. I noticed the difference in the surnames. Your half-brother – he's got a transverse fracture shaft of humerus; looks as if it snapped like a carrot. We've fixed that up and he does not seem to have any other injury. He's a big strong chap and you can take him home with you but I think he needs help, Gavin. He's hooked on something. That's not just beer he's had. You must know that as well as I do; we've both seen enough of them. There are what look like old needle marks on his arms, nothing fresh, but he's on something, no doubt about it. We've taken bloods.'

'Cocaine.'

'I beg your pardon?'

'Cocaine, doctor.'

'You know about it?'

'I live with him. I sleep in the next bedroom.'

'And you've not done anything about it?'

'What about the other one?'

Mentally, Jonathan was left floundering. Brought to manhood on a solid rock of parental loving care, his mind lacked the basic format to interpret what he was hearing.

'You mean your step-father?'

Gavin nodded, looking irritated; as if he could have meant anyone else.

'Not so easy, Gavin. We will need to keep him under observation for his head injury, of course, but there is no immediate worry from that. He has a fracture left tib and fib, junction of middle and lower thirds. That's going to need reduction, possibly open fixation – we'll ask the orthopods to see to that. But it's his neck that's the worry. He's pretty restless and the x-rays are not too good but there's little doubt he's fractured a couple of cervical transverse processes. What I'm concerned about most is that he looks as if he may have a hairline fracture of the body of C3 as well. He has some weakness of his left arm and it's impossible to tell if he has weakness in his left leg because of the fracture but he could well have significant permanent paralysis – you must be prepared for that. One thing's certain, he must be treated as if he has a broken neck until proved otherwise. And, of course, if he has, that means some considerable time in hospital, perhaps even a bone graft.'

'Good.'

Jonathan's disbelief must have been obvious as Gavin smiled sadly. 'I'm sorry to shock you, Dr Brookes. But you can have no idea of what it's like living in a family like mine. He only got out of jail a few days ago. That's why he was celebrating, that's why he was so drunk. How can you, with your background, possibly imagine what it's like to have a father who has spent half his life in jail?'

'But how did it happen exactly? Frankly, it's difficult to fit both men's injuries together. I can't see any sort of pattern to them.'

'I did it.'

'You what?'

'I did it. It's true, the bit about him falling downstairs but I threw him. And I broke my brother's arm. And enjoyed it. He was coming at me with a knife at the time.'

'Good God.' Jonathan shook his head as understanding slowly dawned. 'Of course. Staff Wells told us. A black belt, or brown or something.'

'That's right. I have certain skills which come in very useful at times like that. Now perhaps you can see why I wasn't too keen on having Peggy's boyfriend around. Not that I imagine they'd be too concerned about a little dust up like this, just so long as we keep it in the family.

Somehow I don't think they'd mind a couple of Morellis less about the place; probably their only regret would be that I hadn't broken both their necks while I was at it.'

Jonathan looked at a man who could stand so relaxed and composed after he had just broken one man's neck and another man's arm. He remembered Peggy Wells saying he was no ordinary hospital porter and he laughed softly.

'What's so funny, doctor?'

'Nothing. I was just a little anxious whether this makes me an accessory after the fact or whatever they call it.'

'I wouldn't worry too much about it, Dr Brookes. I wouldn't let you get into trouble like that, not for those two bastards. But there is a strange code of ethics between these villains, you know. If my step-father were to go to the police with a complaint like that, he'd immediately lose all credibility in the incredible world he lives in. He will be quite happy to go along with the story that they were fighting at the top of the stairs and both fell down together; and Wayne will do anything his father tells him. Anyway, if he looks like being at all troublesome, I have something on him that would put him away for a long, long time. Don't worry, doctor. I'm grateful to you and I'll make sure you come to no harm as a result of what you have done tonight. As it is, it couldn't have worked out better. It's all we need, just a few more months.'

'What d'you mean?'

'It's a long story, doctor. Perhaps, one day . . .'

10

'Out of sight, out of mind' applies to aspiring young surgeons as much as to anyone. Although Jonathan Brookes had the comfort of knowing that his next job was already assured, he was not so foolish as to think that he could bury himself in Scarsby for six months without thought of keeping his face well and truly in full professorial view. A low profile and surgical ambition are contradictions in terms. If one's presence could be audible as well as visual at any surgical meeting, so much the better, but, if one can't be heard, one must at least be seen.

In fairness to Jonathan, neither this nor the free drinks and buffet provided by the drug company was the sole reason for his attendance at Liverpool's Clivedon Hotel to watch the film on microsurgery and listen to the discussion afterwards. He had now seen enough trauma to take an intelligent interest in the subject. It was also an opportunity to meet his peers who, at least on the surface, remained remarkably friendly in spite of the cut-throat competition.

He ran up the steps and into the still warmth that fell on him like a blanket. The sound of his feet disappeared into the carpet to be replaced from above by Mantovani's tranquillising tones. He began to follow the signs towards the meeting only to be diverted into the bar by two young men who had preferred to buy themselves draught beer than avail themselves of the drug firm's sweet sherry or white wine. Within minutes, he was standing alongside them, a pint glass in his hand. The bar was full, mostly with guests waiting to go through to the restaurant beyond, and Jonathan had, from time to time, to stand aside to let them pass.

The sudden, hurried movement in the midst of so much muffled torpidity caught Jonathan's eye. All three looked towards the door, their conversation suspended in mid sentence. Though Susannah Ridgeway had stopped so abruptly that the man behind her had walked into her, pushing her forwards a step, her gaze never wavered from Jonathan's face, her eyes at first startled, then defiant. A whispered word over her shoulder and they turned and left with all the laboured theatricals of a couple who have suddenly changed their minds.

The previous topic of conversation was dropped. Jonathan's two friends agreed that that had been downright bad luck, picking on a hotel the night of a drug do like that. But hadn't they seen the signs on the way in? But then love was blind, they sniggeringly agreed. There was a hell of a lot of it about amongst the senior staff, it seemed. Quite an epidemic. And not just surgeons. But who ever thought a dermatologist would have it in him?

Jonathan tried to quell the pain in his chest enough to fake a laugh.

How many children did he have, three? Wasn't one only a few months old? The old ram. They went on relentlessly, agreeing it was getting pretty blatant. How did he manage it? After all, there weren't that many night calls in dermatology. Still, they supposed dermatologists were only human. What they couldn't understand was how these fellas managed to keep it secret from their wives for so long. Always seemed to be the last to know. Fat lot of chance they'd have with ... They were still discussing it as they carried their beers into the meeting.

The video droned on in a blur as Jonathan sat, crushed by sadness. The film he watched but did not see was a good one, the discussion it stimulated spirited and lengthy. It was after ten when they were let loose on the food, after eleven by the time Jonathan had shaken off the attention of an intense senior lecturer who seemed to be taking a genuine interest in Jonathan's future. His mind spinning from the effort of talking surgery when all he could see was Susannah's face, he finally sucked in the winter night's air as he walked to his car.

He drove the streets, turning right or left at random, as if Liverpool was a maze from which he could find no exit. With no precise idea as to his own intentions, he parked the car in front of the block of flats, counted down the row of buttons in the dim light alongside the door and pressed. He had to wait a long time and had turned to walk away when he heard the hiss as the microphone came alive.

'Yes?'

The voice had a sharp, metallic tone over and above that given it by the instrument.

'It's me, Jonathan.'

There was no sound except the hollow, hissing echo from the wall and Jonathan was about to speak again when it stopped and he heard the lock turn in the door. He took the lift from the marble-lined hall to the third floor. The door to Susannah's flat was open.

He had been there many times before. The furniture, the pictures, the decor were unchanged but the atmosphere was. Susannah sat in her usual chair but he had never seen her sit quite like that before. She still had on the dress she had so elegantly worn as she had walked into the hotel but it looked crumpled. There was a faint smell in the air and Susannah had a tumbler in the hand that hung over the arm of her chair.

'I've been half expecting you.' Susannah jerked her drink aloft, spilling clear fluid on to the arm of the chair which she began to rub laboriously with her free hand. 'Drink? Only got vodka I'm afraid and you're not much of a vodka man are you? Good old macho pint of beer is more your tipple, isn't it? There's some lemonade there,' she giggled. 'I won't tell anyone I saw you drinking it. While you're at it, you can pour me another one of these.'

As Jonathan watched, Susannah emptied her glass, sitting forward so that she could put her head back to do so. She held her glass at arm's length towards Jonathan but he shook his head.

'Miserable beggar. Get my own then.' The way she struggled out of her chair and the time it took her to steady herself explained the delay in answering the door bell. 'You haven't come to preach to me, have you?'

'I don't quite know why I've come. I just wanted to make sure you were all right.'

'Kind of you but look – ' she spread her arms wide ' – you need not have worried; no evidence of rape. Satisfied?' Susannah returned to her seat with the bottles, placing them on the table beside her so that she would not have to get up next time. The vodka bottle, half empty, and the lemonade bottle, almost full, stood stark and crude against the polished mahogany and the velvet. Susannah's dress slid above her knees, the bow at her neck was lopsided.

'Who was that guy?'

The question caught Susannah in mid-swallow and her short, bitter laugh made her choke. She placed the glass on the table with exaggerated care.

'That's my Jonathan; straight to the point. What the hell is it to you who he is – or was?'

'I just don't like seeing you making a fool of yourself. And I don't like seeing you drinking like this.'

Susannah looked sideways, smiling at the bottles as if suddenly recognising old friends. 'One thing at least I'm good at.'

'Is it true he's got a wife and three kids?'

'Had a good old natter about us, did you? Yes, quite true. And you needn't worry; he'll be safely tucked up with the brave little woman by now. Running into you lot in that bar was the final straw.' She reached for her drink at the thought of it. 'Hilarious really, when he finally decided to cut and run. I didn't even get a farewell dinner out of it. Poor John.'

She put her head back and closed her eyes. For a while there was silence and Jonathan thought she had fallen asleep. When her head came up again, her eyes were sluggish and her speech lazy and slurred.

'He was nice. Wanted so much to be the gentleman and be sexy at the same time. Older version of you, I suppose. I won't be the last, that's for sure. He'd better have a very understanding wife or they're in for big trouble.' As of old, the alcohol had slowed her movements but had done nothing to dull her perception and she saw the pain she was causing. 'But you needn't worry, Sir Galahad. My honour was preserved. I saw to that however hard I tried not to. Must have been very frustrating for him. Though I suppose, in some ways,' she added, bitterly, 'he was lucky – at least I didn't scratch his eyes out. That treatment I reserve for my friends.'

'Susannah.'

The half-plea, half-reprimand was rung from Jonathan as he saw her pour neat vodka. Before he had time to cross and take the bottle from her, she had thrown the raw spirits into the back of her throat. She watched sullenly as Jonathan took the bottle into the bathroom, pouting as she listened to the contents gurgle away into the washbasin.

'What if he hadn't been a married man?' she asked him as he returned to his chair. 'Would you still have called?'

'No.'

'Perhaps I felt safer with a married man.' A whirling mind that was looking for oblivion at the same time fought off the overwhelming desire to sleep. 'Perhaps I thought a mature man might help me over the hurdle. He was so gentle.'

'And what if he hadn't been so gentle?'

'I'd have been in trouble then, wouldn't I? I'll just have to be extra careful in my choice. Problem is, you can't always be sure, can you?'

'What d'you mean, choice?' Jonathan stood up, his face tight with distaste and disapproval. He fidgeted as if looking for a fireplace to which he could turn his back and ended up looking down at her awkwardly.

'Aren't you careful who you choose?' she asked.

'Don't be ridiculous. That's different.'

'Is it? How?'

'Because . . .'

'Because you're a man and, as everyone knows, all red blooded men need sex of some kind or another pretty regularly, while I'm a woman who must keep herself pure for the likes of you when you decide to settle down. Poor Jonathan; you were born about a hundred years too late. Women have orgasms now, haven't you heard?' She spelt out the forbidden word, watching him wince, letter by letter. 'They're allowed to enjoy it. Or so they tell me.' She sat up abruptly, wobbling now in her chair. 'I rather think I'm going to be sick. Can't drink like I used to.'

When Jonathan offered his hand, she leaned back and closed her eyes. 'Like to tell me about all those doting nurses in Scarsby who have come your way? Few more notches on your stethoscope are there? And that's not fair either, my passionate puritan. You're as bad as I am really. What you need, perhaps what we both need . . .'

Susannah's eyes opened wide, staring ahead unfocused. She struggled to sit upright, then stood only to sink on one knee. Jonathan caught her, preventing her from falling further, heaving her to her feet and propping her tottering steps to the bathroom. With one arm around her shoulders, he knelt besides her as painfully she retched and heaved. 'Come on. Let's get you to bed,' he murmured as the last racking spasm passed.

On rubber legs, Susannah let herself be manoeuvred out of the bathroom and into her bedroom to sit slumped on the edge of her bed. She fumbled impotently with tiny buttons until Jonathan took over the task, heaving her to her feet once more for the stained and crumpled dress to slither into a heap at her feet. He managed to keep her upright just long enough to turn back the bedclothes, slipping off her shoes as he lifted her legs onto the bed. He heaved at her shoulders, turning her well on her side before tucking the clothes around her. Picking up the dress, he carried it to the bathroom and dropped it in the bath.

He stood and looked around him, reluctant to begin what he felt he must do. Susannah had drunk enough, fast enough, for someone who had not had a drink for a couple of years to pass out so quickly – there was no need for there to be anything else involved. There had been that slight smell, long since lost in his sensory adaptation, when he had walked into the flat – but that could have been anything. Could he really bring himself to look through her things with her lying there unaware? And what would he be looking for? Mental pictures of syringes, glass phials, tablets, cigarette papers, small heaps of white powder, raced through his mind. And if he was to be sure, where must he look, behind lavatory cisterns, behind books, in her underwear drawer? Didn't they tend to hide these things away, even in their own home?

Loathing himself as he did so, he worked back systematically from the most distant point of the bathroom, feeling grubby as he went through her clothes, trying to leave no trace of his search. By the time he finished with the drawer beneath her bedside table, he felt not so much relief as guilty self-reproach. Pulling the stool from in front of her dressing table, he sat at her bedside to gaze at her face sunk into her pillow, too tired to analyse his feelings. All he knew was that he must stay and watch, not leave until he knew she was safe. The only risk she now ran, that of inhaling vomit, was a remote one – he realised that as he laid his chin in his cupped hands, his elbows on his knees – but he must not leave her until he . . .

'Go home.'

He had no idea just how long he had dozed off when the whispered words woke him. There was a trace of a smile on the half of Susannah's face that Jonathan could see. An eye flickered open momentarily.

'Go home. Go to bed. I'm all right.'

The card in its envelope had obviously been delivered by hand. It lay just inside the door as Jonathan arrived home after night duty.

'Scarlet woman, seeking redemption, wishes to contact kind, understanding male, over six feet, late twenties, good looking, to hear her confessions over dinner this Saturday evening. Successful outcome essential to prevent early return to Russian waters. Ring 051-7072231.'

11

The man was in his mid forties, tall, lean and blue chinned, with a shiny grey suit and black heavy shoes. He had a prominent Adam's apple which accounted for the deep voice.

'Dr Brookes?'

Jonathan Brookes looked up, too busy to hide his irritation at someone trying to jump the queue. It was amazing how many people thought themselves too important to join those sitting in what passed for a waiting room in Scarsby's Casualty Department, the benches bolted to the corridor walls. Jonathan saw the pens clipped to the man's breast pocket, the neatly trimmed moustache that went with some desk job, the confident, head-up stance of some jumped-up pen pusher.

'I'm sorry. There's a long queue out there, I'm afraid.'

The friendly and understanding smile he got in response, self-assured without being offensively cocky, made him doubt his first impression.

'I'm not a patient, Dr Brookes. Thank God,' he added hastily, as if anxious not to tempt providence. 'My name's Dangerfield. I'm from the local NUM. Could I see you for a moment?'

'The NUM? To see me?' Jonathan held his pen in his teeth as he shook hands. 'What on earth for?'

'It'll only take a moment, doctor.'

'Hang on then; let me fix this up first.'

As Jonathan sorted out the problems of the patient he had just seen, Dangerfield stood, perfectly at ease, watching with interest the bustle going on around him. 'Exciting place you work in, doctor,' he remarked as they walked out together.

'Could do without the excitement now and again,' Jonathan smiled. 'Now, how can I help you?' They had turned into a length of disused corridor, closed off at one end and used to store spare trolleys. They wedged themselves into the only privacy they could find and Jonathan apologised. 'Sorry about this. I'm afraid Scarsby General doesn't run to consulting rooms for the likes of us.'

'That's all right, Dr Brookes.' Dangerfield looked round affectionately. 'Still plenty of good music to come out of this old fiddle yet. Now then; I've come with an invitation.'

'Really? To what?'

'The lads from Broadoak colliery would like to show their appreciation for what you did out on the motorway the other day.'

99

'That's very kind of them but there's really no need. I expect you know one of them lost his foot?'

'Yes. I've just been up to see him. But the other one is going home today and the lads at the club, as I say, they'd like to say "thank you".'

There was a swell of pride and pleasure within Jonathan that overcame the thought that he would be alone, the centre of attention amongst total strangers and he had said 'Yes, thank you, I'd love to come,' before he had given himself time to think.

'Fine. It will be at the Working Man's Club in Firth Street. Eight o'clock? I'll pick you up? You'd better not drive,' he added, ominously.

'Yes, that'll be great. But what night?'

'Sorry, doctor. Stupid of me. Saturday night. That all right for you?'

Jonathan had now had time for second thoughts and wondered whether he should say he was on duty. Spending his Saturday night in a working man's club, even The Working Man's Club, suddenly didn't seem such a good idea, but his voice still emerged keen and grateful.

'Yes, that will be fine.'

Dangerfield turned to edge his way out between the trolleys when suddenly he turned. 'Don't expect too much, will you, doctor. They'd like to have bought you something but money's a bit short at the moment, as you can imagine. A few drinks, like.'

'Of course. I really would have been most embarrassed if they had gone to the extent of buying anything for me. I appreciate the gesture. There was no need for them to do anything. I did so little.'

'One other thing, Dr Brookes. They're pretty down at the moment. Things are not going well for them. I hope you'll understand.'

Dangerfield opened wide the driver's door of the battered and rusting Cavalier. 'Afraid you'll have to get in from this side; the lock is broken on the passenger door. Can you manage?'

With a quick look of longing at his own car, parked at the far end of the yard, Jonathan struggled to lift his legs over the gear lever.

'Sorry about this,' Dangerfield grinned, 'but Arthur's borrowed the Jag and its my chauffeur's night off.'

Jonathan laughed. 'Don't tell me Scargill's going to be there tonight, is he?'

'Not much chance of that. Wouldn't be too sure of his reception at the moment.'

'Is that so?'

The car ground its way out of the hospital while Jonathan waited expectantly, hoping perhaps for a rare personal insight from the driver into a conflict that had battered a nation's emotions and reason for nearly a year. But he was to be disappointed and had to listen instead to a blow-by-blow description of how Dangerfield's long back had given way under the strain of mining. The union man was still describing how difficult it had been to screw his compensation out of the mean bastards when they drove into the club's cramped car park. Jonathan decided he was glad, after all, that he had not brought his own car as the rust-crazed Cavalier squeezed between others of similar vintage.

The Working Man's Club had been one of Scarsby's smaller cinemas. As Jonathan climbed worn steps between crumbling concrete pillars, he could imagine the wartime queues trailing away around the corner of the dirty grey building into the drizzly blacked-out darkness. The only splash of colour came from a pithy exhortation to Sir Ian MacGregor, the work of a local graffiti artist on the front door and the foyer walls were bare except for dry, warped panels that carried the tarnished names of past officials. Through what had once been the ticket window Jonathan saw the tight, whiter than white curls of the elderly lady taking coats. Footsteps resounded, particularly the ones that approached Jonathan. Only the fact that he had taken a firm grip of the hand that shook his prevented his own from being crushed. A powerful man, beginning to run to fat, was introduced by Dangerfield as Jack Formby, the club secretary.

'Thank you for coming, doctor.'

'Not at all.' Jonathan had been impressed by the dignity of so many of the older miners' speech. So many he had met had paid him the courtesy of a full title, not the 'doc' so beloved by the snobs of all classes. 'It's very kind of you to ask me like this.'

'The least we could do, doctor. Come and meet the Chairman.'

Jonathan followed Jack Formby but Dangerfield did not. 'I'll leave you in Jack's capable hands then, Dr Brookes. I'm afraid I have a meeting I must go to but I'll be back later to take you home. I won't forget you.' And he was gone, leaving Jonathan with the daunting thought of an open-ended evening ahead in the company of total strangers amidst a culture as foreign to him as a meeting of nuclear physicists.

Formby led him into the hall and along a false corridor between rooms without ceilings, constructed out of wooden frames and chipboard panels. Through one door Jonathan saw what he took to be a committee room, from another section came the unmistakeable click of snooker balls. Tables of varying sizes and shapes were spread out haphazardly over the remainder of the hall and Jonathan, as they emerged from the corridor, saw a rough stage, its thick faded curtains closed, at the far end where he imagined the screen had been. Along one side wall stretched a vast bar. The hall was half empty and there hung overall an oppressive atmosphere, the low background muttered conversation falling away almost to nothing as

Formby and the stranger were seen to weave their way towards a table, longer than the rest and parallel with the wall opposite the bar.

An untidy man, his back to the wall in the centre of the table, stood up as Formby introduced Jonathan. His coarse grey hair, bushy eyebrows and moustache, his crumpled collar and tie, the saliva that leaked from the corner of his mouth around the stem of a blackened old briar, all gave him the appearance of someone totally unselfconscious. Even the tattooed coal scar across one cheek, worn with the pride of a Prussian sabre cut, was jagged and untidy. George Butterworth was also a man of few words.

'Come and sit down, doctor. Move over, Maggie luv, and let the doctor sit between us. Doctor, this is Maggie, my missus.'

Squeezing between knees and table, Jonathan finally settled with his back to the wall.

'What can I get you, doctor?' Jack Formby asked.

'A beer would do fine, thank you.'

'Any particular kind?'

'Not fussy.'

It was as if his answer to the question had been vital, like some crucial point in a viva voce examination. He could almost sense the sigh of approval from those around him.

'What about you, George?'

'I think I could manage another one, yes, Jack.' Jonathan could hear the wheezy laugh but missed the wink. 'I think entertaining a local hero can justifiably come out of committee funds, don't you agree, Jack?'

As Jack Formby headed for the bar, Jonathan had his first full view of the faces turned his way. As they saw his embarrassment, one by one they looked away, picking up their conversations once more. But one face remained, eyes focussed brazenly on his. He would have noticed her anyway, if only for the mass of red hair, but there was an amused challenge in her stare that picked her out from her background like a bright flower on a dull day.

'Thank you for coming, Dr Brookes. The lads appreciated what you did for them, that they did.'

'My pleasure, Mr Butterworth. It's very kind of you to ask me.'

That brought the conversation to a halt and there was an uneasy silence until the beers arrived. There was no sign of it being picked up again after they had taken their first mouthfuls. Jonathan tried Maggie Butterworth, sitting demurely to his left.

'Do you come here most Saturdays, Mrs Butterworth?'

'Yes, mostly like.'

Silence fell again and Jonathan listened to the juicy bubbling as George sucked on his pipe. He felt ill at ease as nothing more was said until suddenly he realised he alone felt that way, George and his wife gazing quite contentedly around the room which was now filling up, the background buzz of conversation rising. It gave Jonathan time to look at the woman again. The cascade of red hair was immaculately groomed but with sufficient artifice for Jonathan to wonder what it would look like after being caught in a sudden squall in an open boat. She wore little makeup over a fine complexion with no sign of the blotchy skin that sometimes goes with such flaming hair. She wore a green, tight-fitting jumper and matching slacks and it was no coincidence that Jonathan was looking at her as she half stood to throw a paper ball at a nearby table, revealing a trim figure. Jonathan was close enough to see the wedding ring.

The man sitting alongside her looked like her brother. His uncombed hair was a duller reflection of hers, his beard, coarse and full, trimmed untidily to a point. But, where she radiated vitality and challenge, he sat, morose and still, gazing dejectedly at his beer, slopping the contents of his glass with nervous twitches of his fingers.

The woman was one of the first to rise and clap as a burst of applause came from the back of the hall. Jonathan, unsure of what was happening, stood in company with those around him. There were cheers, whistles and clapping as a man on crutches, laughing and ducking under a hail of backslaps, came into view, manoeuvring a path through the crowd to stand in front of Jonathan. Balancing on his good leg, both crutches grasped in one fist, the man thrust the other hand across the table and Jonathan shook it to another burst of applause.

Taking his pipe from his mouth and holding it aloft, George Butterworth called for silence and cleared his throat.

'I'm sure I speak for you all when I say how glad we are to see Tommy here back with us. By the look of that plaster on his leg, he won't be playing skittles for a while so perhaps we'll stand a chance of winning the odd game for once.' He waited for the cheers to stop before changing the tone of his voice and speaking through the murmurs around him. 'We're only sorry that Frank isn't with us as well tonight but I've been to see him today. He says they're looking after him right champion at the General and he hopes to bring what's left of him round to the club as soon as he gets out. Which brings me to a very pleasant task.' He turned half left to look at Jonathan. 'You will all have heard how Dr Brookes here helped get lads out and I'm sure you will all want to show him your appreciation in the usual way.'

Jonathan stood head down, a modest flush on his face but enjoying his moment of fame as hands were clapped and beer glasses rattled on table tops.

'We'd all like you to know Broadoak's right proud of you. You haven't

103

been with us long but I can tell you now, straight, you're our kind of doctor, Dr Brookes, and I hope your stay in Scarsby will be a long and a happy one.'

Butterworth sat down amidst murmurs of 'Here, here,' and a final spatter of applause, leaving Jonathan standing, suddenly terrified that he was being expected to reply. He was mouthing his gratitude when the injured miner came to his rescue. Sitting in a chair, he swung his injured leg high to crash the plaster down on the table, making the glasses shake and rattle.

'Sign please, Dr Brookes.'

Gratefully amongst the laughter, Jonathan reached for his pen and added his signature to those already scrawled over the uneven surface. By the time Tommy had bought Jonathan a beer and more signatures had been added, the room was full and noisy, the atmosphere warm and smokey. In the far corner there were sounds of a scuffle and the Chairman's peace-making ability was urgently demanded. As Jonathan sat back, he found that Maggie Butterworth had also made her escape, now sitting at a table surrounded by other quiet, watchful elderly women. At a loss, he took a drink and played with his glass, trying to look at home. He looked up to see the red-haired woman, without a word to the man beside her, stand, turn and walk unhurriedly towards him. She came round the table to take the seat vacated by the Chairman's wife. She turned towards him, leaning her left elbow on the table.

'And how does it feel to be a hero, Dr Brookes?'

'Embarrassing.'

'Rubbish; you're enjoying every minute of it.'

Jonathan admitted it with a smile.

'You know my brother-in-law.' The statement was made confidently by someone sure of her facts. 'Badger Kincaid.'

'Oh, yes. I met him my first night here. I've met him several times since then – he seems to be very fond of one of our Staff Nurses.'

''Bout time he had a woman' – not 'a wife' or 'a girl friend' but 'a woman'. 'Time he cut himself off from his Gran's apron strings. My name's Victoria Kincaid; they call me Vicki.'

No mention of a husband as they twisted awkwardly to shake hands.

'My name's Jonathan.'

'I know.'

'You haven't got a drink.' Jonathan struggled to stand up. 'Do you think I'd be allowed to buy you one if I went to the bar?'

'Where d'you think you are, the Athenaeum? Just make sure you don't find yourself buying the whole bloody club a drink. I'll have a gin and Martini, seeing you're a rich doctor an' all.'

'Sweet or dry?'

'Sweet.'

Vicki Kincaid had not been far from the mark about the drinks. He found himself surrounded by miners who broke off from eyeball-to-eyeball, chest thumping arguments to put comradely arms around his shoulders at his offer of a beer. He found he had drained another glass as he talked and had to buy another to return to his table. As he paid, he tried to conceal the size of his wallet, feeling guilt amongst that company at just how much money it contained. It was the best part of ten minutes before he could break away and return to the table where Vicki Kincaid sat, alone and totally composed. He sat by her side, uncomfortable in what now seemed like a no-go area around them and half wishing for the return of even the Butterworths' silent friendliness.

'I've been trying to keep out of your brother-in-law's way,' Jonathan laughed.

'Why's that?'

'He's after me to play for his rugby team and, up until now, I've always managed to be on duty but I rather think I've let myself in for it next Saturday. I've just run out of excuses.'

'What, you play for the coppers?'

'Yes. Why not?'

'God help you, that's all I say.' She looked round as if it was not a subject that interested her. 'Well, and what do you think of the miners, Jonathan?'

'Salt of the earth.'

She looked at him as if weighing his reply. Appearing satisfied, she agreed. 'They are that.' There was a long pause before she added, almost in a murmur, 'Poor bastards.'

'Why do you say that?'

'It's over. They won't admit it but it's over, they're going back in droves.'

'What, at Broadoak? Is that what that fight was about just now? Was that someone who's gone back to work?'

Pity and scorn spread over Vicki Kincaid's face. 'For someone so brainy, you don't learn very quickly, do you, Dr Brookes? They've had no more than a handful of scabs at Broadoak and, by heck, they'll live to regret it; they'll never, never put a foot through these doors again. No, that was probably an argument over whether they should go back or not, but of one thing you can be quite sure, when Broadoak decide to go back, they'll all go back together.'

With a grin at the flushed intensity on her face, Jonathan put out his hand. 'Let me get you another drink and then you can continue my education.'

'I won't say no.' She drained her glass. 'A good drink is that but, in case I make a right fool of myself, it had better be tonic instead of Martini this time.'

By the time Jonathan made his third trip to the bar, it was as if he had been a longstanding member, shouting snatches of conversation above the din as he elbowed his way back to Vicki. He sat face to face once more with a woman, extremely articulate within the bounds of a limited vocabulary. He hardly got a word in as she put him straight on what she called a real miner's philosophy. He was touched by her loyalty to the Union that survived intact in spite of all the criticisms she was only too ready to thump out against its leadership.

'Don't get me wrong,' Vicki said, both of them now having drunk enough to be shouting at each other though inches apart. 'The fact I sit here and criticise Scargill all night doesn't mean I'm not all for him, because I am. I think Arthur's God. The only problem is, Arthur agrees with me.'

'I take it your husband is a miner?'

Vicki Kincaid nodded.

'Is he here tonight?'

'No.' Her eyes never wavered but there was the first note of insincerity in her voice, obvious enough to convince Jonathan she was lying. He was pondering boozily why she should bother when her excitement returned.

'I'll tell you one thing this strike has done. It may turn out to be a disaster for the men but it could be salvation for us wives.'

'In what way?' Jonathan looked up to thank someone who slid another drink across the table to him, someone who took a second look at the animated pair and backed off.

Turning, Vicki jerked her thumb in the direction of Maggie Butterworth's table, the first lady of Broadoak sitting upright and still amongst the turmoil, her cronies around her as flushed and as mute as she. Vicki asked, 'Do you see me ending up like that?'

'Frankly, no,' Jonathan laughed.

She turned her full attention back to him. 'And yet, if I had asked you that question just a year ago, I suspect you might have been polite and given the same answer but I'm sure you would have thought differently.'

'Why?'

'Because . . . Here, give me some of your beer.' She reached and drank from Jonathan's glass, shaking her head at his offer to fight his way to the bar once more. 'I had a good job in a shoe shop when I met Reggie. I reckoned another year and I'd have been manageress. But, when we married, like all good miners' wives, I gave up my job so that, like all the rest, I could look after my husband, cook his food, wash his clothes, bring up his kids. Yes, and take the odd hiding from him too. Miners don't like their wives to work, you'll understand; not good for the macho image, is that. I was lucky; at least I didn't have to bath him. D'you know there were lots of old miners who resisted pithead baths because they said it would lessen the wife's traditional role in the home? I tell you, the miner is the biggest bloody conservative you've ever met.'

'Oh, my God.' Jonathan's reaction was not to what Vicki had said but to the sight of another beer coming his way, 'compliments of the Chairman'. He was already having trouble focussing on the face so close to his.

'Here, let me help you.' Vicki took his partly finished glass from him as he grasped the full one. 'Not that I had such a bad time of it compared with some. A well paid husband doesn't always mean a well paid wife, you know, by heck it doesn't. But I couldn't complain there. We had a nice car, nice house, foreign holiday every year; I don't remember me complaining much in those days,' she laughed, a bitter edge now to the passion.

'And then the strike started and I had Reggie around the house most of the time. Some of us women went on the picket line once or twice but we didn't feel we were accomplishing much, just being sworn at by foul-mouthed coppers. And then, this woman came to the door, talked to me and gave me this pamphlet about a meeting of what they were calling the local Support Group. And I went and I talked and I talked and I talked; and I haven't stopped talking since. Well, you've had a sample of it tonight, haven't you?'

Jonathan nodded, smiling, his nose in his glass.

'Before I realised what was happening, they'd made me what's known as Area Coordinator and, since then, I've been to meetings all over the North and down to London.' She put her head back and laughed. 'When I think of it now, how I used to bargain sex for my Reggie's permission to go to the meetings. And then it came home to me that there was bugger all he could do about it anyway. So Reggie had his oats and I went to London, no nonsense.' Her voice dropped in theatrical terror. 'By heck but I was scared going down to London. Them and their fancy accents; like those Suffragette women you see on the telly. But, d'you know, by the time I'd finished, they couldn't get a word in edgewise. They're always on about the South beating hell out of the North – and it's true – but, when it comes to arguing, and knowing what you're arguing about, the North beats hell out of the South. All we need up here is confidence in ourselves, we always sell ourselves so bloody short, always a bit ashamed of a Northern accent.'

'If you're so sure you can beat hell out of the South, why don't you both go down there where all the money is?' Jonathan asked.

'Why don't you? You could make more money down there in London, couldn't you?'

The sharpness of Vicki's counter took Jonathan out of his stride. 'Well, I . . . I . . .' he stumbled before Vicki answered for him.

'Because you're a Northerner. Why should we have to go down there just to make an honest living? We pay the same taxes as them buggers down South. Why shouldn't we have the same slice of the cake, I say? Well I'll tell you the reason. The South sees the North as a bunch of ignorant working men who only know how to drink away a week's wage packet. They don't think we deserve any better. And, to some extent, they're right. So we've got to change things.'

Her open-mouthed swallows as she drained the remainder of the beer looked natural in the surroundings, more honest than any thin-lipped sips from a champagne glass.

'It's never going to be the same, not if I have anything to do with it. We're not going back to the way we lived before the strike. I'm a thinking woman now and what's the use of thinking if you can't put your thoughts into practice? They all talk of the miners' wives being behind their men a hundred per cent. Well, we've always been that but that's not good enough for us any more. We want to be alongside them, not behind them. It's not going to be enough any more, just being dug out for the soup kitchens in a strike and then being put back again. Nobody asked us what we thought about coming out and we certainly won't be asked about going back. Women aren't even allowed near a Union meeting, let alone join it but, by heck, if we were, Arthur would have something to contend with, I tell you. It wouldn't be a question of telling a bunch of sheep what to do then. Men have always dominated the working class but I reckon it's the lasses who really have the brains. And they talk better. The only reason people think Arthur talks a lot is that he hasn't had a couple of women to compete with at the top. Poor bugger wouldn't get a word in edgewise if we were only given a chance.'

'For the first time, I feel sorry for Scargill.' The words slurred. 'Do you reckon they'll get rid of him after this strike?'

'No. I reckon he's got things wrong at times but he's honest, most of the miners think that. Make no mistake, when this strike is over, give it a year and, like he says, Broadoak will be closed. And that'll be the end of Scarsby. That'll be the end of all this.' She waved at the vibrant human contact all round. 'No, you've got to stick with the Union, right or wrong. The miner hasn't got a thing the Union hasn't won for him. The owners never give a damn thing they're not forced to.'

She became quieter. 'I am sorry, Dr Brookes, I am that. You didn't come here expecting a Union meeting. But I get so wound up these days.

To think, a year ago and I wouldn't have dared say boo to you. And I can't go on about it much at home at the moment, so you rather walked into it head on tonight.'

'Why can't you talk about it at home? Does your husband not approve?'

'Him? No, he's no problem now. It's Reggie's Gran; she's one of the old school, doesn't exactly approve of me gadding about, shouting the odds. If I said half the things to her I've said to you tonight, she'd throw me out of the house.'

'She lives with you, I take it?'

'No.' Vicki laughed as Jonathan, slow witted with beer, tried to work it out. 'We live with her, her and Badger, that is. As I said, we used to have foreign holidays, nice house, nice car; Reggie said he couldn't do the early shift without a car. We just lived over the top and I was more than happy to go along with it. Well now they're all gone, we're in debt up to our necks, and, when the house was repossessed, we had to move in with Badger and his Gran. But I was lucky. I managed to get a part-time job in a supermarket quite quickly – just on the check out, you know – and, for the last few months, they've taken me on full time. Makes it a bit hard going, like, what with the Support Group work an' all, but I manage. Means I haven't seen much of Reggie, down to London on my day off, that sort of thing. But it does mean we're paying a few bob off our debts and things are beginning to look up. And when we get out, I'm going to hold the purse strings, make no mistake about it. And I'm not giving up my job when this strike's over, neither. It's not just a question of money, you'll understand. It's having friends of my own. I'm not giving those up just to go back to be a kept woman.'

'What about your in-laws? Can't they help?'

'Killed in a motor cycle accident when the boys were quite small.' A quiet defiance subdued her voice as she added, 'Their Gran brought them up.' Her eyes screwed up as if she were assessing the wisdom of something she wanted to say. 'You ought to meet her.'

'Who?'

'Gran. Come and have Sunday dinner with us tomorrow. As far as I know, Badger will be there. Will you come?'

'Yes, I'd love to. What time?'

'Any time about one. There was a time when dinner started whenever our lords and masters came home half pissed from this place, depending on how much of a run for their money the stripper had given them up on the stage there. But that's over, is that. From now on, if Reggie's going to be here on a Sunday, then, by heck, so am I, not slaving in the kitchen, watching good food going to ruin and then listening to complaints that the joint's burnt. We'll expect you about one o'clock then; 48, Bradbury Street; I'll be interested to see what you think of our Gran.'

'What was the address again?'

'48, Bradbury Street.'

Dangerfield took it that all young bachelor doctors live in hospital. It had never occurred to him to ask where Jonathan was sleeping. He drew up in the casualty yard, pulled on a twanging brake lever but made no move to let Jonathan out through his door, leaving him with a feeling of being trapped.

'Enjoy yourself, doctor?'

'Very much.' Jonathan felt a cramp in his jaws as he began to salivate.

'Rough fare by your standards, I expect, but genuine for all that.'

'Not at all. Very gentlemanly compared with some rugby clubs I've known.'

Dangerfield laughed but still showed no sign of opening his door. His outsize larynx rose suddenly as he swallowed nervously. 'Don't take it amiss, Dr Brookes, but may I give you one word of advice?'

'Of course.'

'Take care with that woman. Don't get involved.' He raised his hands as if to ward off a hostile reaction. 'Please don't be offended – just a friendly warning. But she could be trouble.'

'I think I can keep my hands to myself but thanks for the warning.' Jonathan suddenly longed for a bed, any bed, anywhere horizontal.

'I don't mean that. There's nothing like that about her; I know; some of the lads have tried. But, take it from me, that's one hell of a high tension family – you'd best keep away, doctor – and she just loves to stoke it up. I'm sure Reggie doesn't recognise her as the girl he married, poor bastard. As if he hasn't got enough problems.'

'What's that?' A sudden realisation that the vomiting reflex had reached its irreversible stage made Jonathan totally disinterested in Reggie's troubles. He started to push at Dangerfield's shoulder. 'Excuse me, Mr Dangerfield, but I must go . . .'

Dangerfield took one look at Jonathan's face, saw the bulging cheeks, and got out hurriedly. He laughed to see Jonathan just make it in time to one of the drain gratings and drove away, the roar of his blown exhaust failing to drown completely the sound of painful retching.

12

Looking for any sign of an early spring in Bradbury Street would be a waste of time. As far as the eye could see along its gently sloping length, there was a total absence of vegetation, not so much as a molecule of chlorophyll to relieve the overwhelming grey of stone, slate and concrete. There was a small amount of red brick around the windows and doors of the old primary school that divided the houses on one side of the street. One or two of the houses had had their roofs renewed in red or green, their ugly modern tiles thick and gross, standing out from the Welsh slate like keloid scars. Here and there doors had been painted in garish, almost luminescent colours. But all these modest attempts at vivifying the outlook had succeeded only in highlighting the overall drabness. The front doors opened directly on to the street, the paving stones appropriate to each house having been in their time the object of as much pride and attention as any front garden in wealthier areas. Bradbury Street had seen the day when housewives, on hands and knees, had holystoned their own pavement, grown men being forced, by flint-eyed glares, to take to the road rather than walk across the freshly wet flagstones. Number 48 was still such a house and Jonathan sensed an aura of pride even before he knocked on the door. It was opened by Badger Kincaid.

'Hi! Come in.'

The narrow passageway that served as a hall was hardly big enough for someone of Badger's size to turn round in. Adding to the problem was a highly polished, sturdy old mahogany hall stand, laden with coats. Badger, too good mannered to turn his back on a visitor, had to step into the door to the front parlour to allow Jonathan to enter. Faced with the foot of steeply rising stairs, Jonathan turned half right into a room that gave an immediate impression of permanence. Cold, tidy and polished, it looked as if it had not been disturbed for years, memorabilia of two world wars giving it the atmosphere of a shrine. There were heavily framed, black and white portrait photographs on the wall, faded faces of men, looking down sadly on chairs they had only been allowed to sit in on Christmas Day. One wall was occupied by a heavy book case, its glass doors tightly shut and locked against anyone who might feel a sudden urge to read.

Badger joined him. 'How d'you feel?' he asked, almost in a whisper.

'Rough.'

'I heard you had quite a night,' Badger laughed. 'What time did you get home?'

'I didn't. I managed to find a bed in Residents'. There's always someone on holiday or away for the weekend. I even had to borrow a razor and I didn't have a clean shirt. Do I smell of vomit? I had a couple of quick sicks when I got back last night. Then I ran foul of your girlfriend as I was trying to creep in through Cas; gave me her opinion on my mental age in no uncertain terms.'

'I can imagine,' Badger grinned ruefully. 'I've come in for a bit of that myself. Have you had any breakfast?'

'I've only just got up. Strangely enough, I feel quite hungry.'

'Thank God for that. Gran's got one of her famous Sunday dinners. Come on, come and meet her.'

Warm air fanned Jonathan's face as Badger opened the frosted glass panelled door that led to a stone-floored kitchen, small enough to appear already crowded by the three people in it. There seemed little space for two more large men. A poor light filtered through the window, looking out, as it did, on the whitewashed stone wall of the neighbouring house that denied all direct sunlight. Sitting with her back to it, wedged between it and the table, was Vicki Kincaid. She looked up from cleaning carrots into a tureen.

'Morning, Jonathan. And how d'you feel this morning?' she asked brightly.

Jonathan had no time to answer, would probably not have answered had he been given time, as he was suddenly confronted by the compelling presence of a diminutive old lady. Standing proud and erect, she hardly reached Jonathan's shoulder.

'Gran, this is Dr Jonathan Brookes I told you about.'

'I'm pleased to meet you, Dr Brookes. It's not often I get the chance to meet Badger's friends.'

She stood for a moment, unashamedly sizing Jonathan up. Smiling, sensing she would respect rather than resent a similar response, he looked her up and down too. Steel grey hair, centrally parted and taut, was drawn back from a small, sharp face and held in a tight bun by a tortoiseshell comb. The skin over her cheekbones was remarkably smooth, giving her the appearance of someone much younger than Jonathan reckoned she must be. She wore a large cameo brooch at the neck of a simple white cotton blouse, a wash-worn apron, dusted with the flour that covered her hands, partly hiding a thick, black, ankle length skirt, its waist band high above a small but rotund belly that Jonathan could imagine her holding when she laughed. There appeared to be mutual approval.

'Sit down, my boy. Badger, I'm sure Dr Brookes would like a beer.'

'I'm not too sure about that this morning, Gran,' Badger grinned and was about to obey when, almost as an afterthought, he said, 'And this is my brother, Reggie. Reggie, this is Jonathan Brookes.'

Beyond the table, in the cramped space between it and the heavy, iron fireplace with its old fashioned oven and water heater, their brass taps and handles in bright contrast to the polished blacking of the metal, Jonathan had seen the one armchair in the room. Over the back of it, he had noticed the top of a man's head. Slowly, the man rose half out of the seat, half turned towards him. Without a smile, he murmured 'How do,' before silently slumping back out of sight. Jonathan had seen only part of his face for no more than a few seconds but there had been no mistaking the red hair and heavy beard of the man sitting with Vicki in the club the night before. He looked across at Vicki to see her face crinkled in amusement.

'Sit there.' Jonathan did as he was told, sitting where the old lady pointed, finding he was on a very hard sofa, so low that even Gran Kincaid could look down on him. She paused in her mixing of the Yorkshire pudding as if the provision of beer for the men was of more importance. 'I like to see a man with a beer in his hand. Never met a real man yet who didn't drink a drop too much now and again. Badger's grandfather there,' she indicated Badger with her mixing spoon as if there might be some confusion, 'he always used to have a barrel in the house Christmas time, even if we had to go into hock to get it. I remember the Christmas they knocked the wrong bung in first and we had beer everywhere,' her hand swept the room, 'wasted half of it. They were trying to lick it off the ceiling, just about.' And she did just what Jonathan had imagined she might, held her round belly in two hands as it bounced in time with her laughter.

Vicki did not join in and Jonathan saw her raise her eyes to the heavens as if she had heard that story once or twice before. She extricated herself awkwardly from the table, carrying the carrots in one hand, the parings in the other. She stepped over Jonathan's feet to get to the door alongside the fireplace and out to where Jonathan could hear the sounds of a meal cooking. She returned to help herself, unasked, to a beer. Not for one moment had she attracted so much as a flicker of attention from Gran Kincaid. 'Any moment now, Jonathan, and you are going to hear all about the old days. Coming into this house is like stepping back into the twenties. Just about every other house in the street has had some renovation of some kind or another done. But not this one.'

'At least I've got my own roof over my head, my girl, which is more than you can say for yourself.' Gran waited proudly for Vicki to come back at her but there was no reply, just a bitten lower lip and a glare at the back of an armchair that called unavailingly for a husband's support. 'And it's not true either.' Gran Kincaid used the spoon as a pointer once more, prodding it backwards over one shoulder. 'Badger's built a beautiful kitchen and bathroom on for me, out there at the back.' She turned to Jonathan. 'You must come and have a look at them afterwards. But, in here, no. Changing all this would take all my memories away, and why would I want to do that? Giving me all new furniture would be like asking me to dress like that.' She pointed to the same bright colours Vicki had worn the night before.

'At least you could have put in central heating as Badger wanted you to.' Vicki had returned to sit at the table. 'My feet are that cold, they're like blocks of ice.'

'There's nothing to beat a good coal fire.' Gran gave Jonathan a mammoth wink. 'You can always spit into a fire. There's many a poor collier who has coughed his lungs up into his own fireplace.'

'Charming,' Vicki grimaced. 'Just the thing to give us an appetite for dinner, is that.'

Jonathan began to forget his hangover as he took on the role of fascinated voyeur. He was intrigued by the old lady's accent, unmistakeably North Country but with a subtle difference he had noticed amongst several of his aged patients. It was not Scouse, nor Mancunian nor solid, honest Lancastrian. He found eyes twinkling at him as if trying to read his thoughts.

'What's the matter, Dr Brookes; you look puzzled.'

'Forgive me.' Jonathan had a feeling he was in a house where secrets were short lived. 'It has become a bit of a hobby of mine. We have patients from all over the country come in to Casualty, not just from around here, and I often amuse myself trying to guess where they come from, either from their surnames or from their accents. And there's something about your accent, I must admit, that's got me foxed.'

Gran laughed. She put one floury hand up close to her head, sweeping it backwards. 'You'll never believe it but my hair was the same colour as theirs when I was that age.' She pointed first at Reggie, her hand then lingering over Badger. 'Though where that one came from I don't know, must have been Sweden or Germany or somewhere. No, Dr Brookes, my family came from Ireland and there are a lot of the older members of the families around here who have never completely lost the old blarney. A lot of Irish came over during the famine and settled round here; they reckoned this was about as far as they could walk from Liverpool before dropping from hunger. You won't find any in Yorkshire because they were too weak to climb the Pennines. Did you know, Dr Brookes – I'm sure, you being a doctor, you'll be interested in this – that, what with the big families and the terrible death rate, the average age of the people around here at that time was 20? When I was a child, the average age at death was 17, 17, Dr Brookes. It's difficult to . . .'

The tiny figure dominated the conversation throughout the meal. As Reggie, the elder son, was brought to sit at the head of the table, his back to the heat of the fire, Gran stood, carved the joint and dispensed the vegetables, poured out the gravy and assessed the portions before sitting herself. Jonathan noted the major shares, particularly of the meat, had gone to the men, the piled plates possibly favouring Badger, while Vicki's slim figure was in no way endangered by the amount apportioned to her. Gran had given herself a minute amount which she patiently minced between long descriptions of times when she had been a child, recalling the hardships she had endured as one of the last of the pit brow lasses. Reggie ate almost equally from knife and fork, head down, sullen and mute. Badger snatched sideways glances at Jonathan, half-proud, half-embarrassed at his Gran's dominance, while Vicki appeared at times to be struggling to keep her mouth shut in the presence of a guest. Inevitably, the conversation turned to the miners' strike and, perhaps equally inevitably in that household, its comparison with the General Strike. As Gran vividly described watching her husband diving in the canal for coal that had fallen from the barges and the starvation of bare-footed, rickety children, Jonathan had the impression of an old First World War sweat boasting that the casualties at Arnhem had been nothing compared with the Somme.

'Not that I'm saying there have been no casualties this time.' Gran put her hand gently on Reggie's shoulder. 'Poor boy.'

Sensing a story behind the gesture, but too polite to pry, Jonathan tried to change monologue into discussion. He turned towards Vicki. 'How d'you think it's going to end, Vicki?'

She was given no time to answer, the old lady's scorn reducing her to pale-cheeked, fist-clenched fury. 'No good asking any of the wives today, Dr Brookes. Half of them are more concerned with their own position in society than their men, off at meetings all the time instead of being where they should be, looking after the lads. They're only making things worse for the boys.'

'That's a bit hard, isn't it, Mrs Kincaid?' Jonathan had become genuinely involved in what the old lady had been saying despite suffering under the combined effects of a late night's drinking and a huge plate of thick, creamy rice pudding. 'I don't see how they can possibly make things worse.'

'Don't you?' The words were spoken with a sharpness that amazed Jonathan, coming from someone who must be nearing 90. 'Let me explain something you won't hear mentioned by any one of those so called experts on the TV. The miners are not as afraid as all that of losing their jobs when they close the pits.'

'Come on, Gran; that's got to be crazy.' They were the first words Badger had uttered for half an hour.

'It's not. You don't seriously believe anyone enjoys digging coal out, do you? You don't think anyone looks forward to going underground, do you? It's a filthy, hard, dangerous job; always has been. People think they can imagine it but they can't. Would you like to work where you have to be careful where you sit to have your meal out of a tin because someone might have squatted there earlier to have his bowels open? The only reason sons followed fathers was that there was nothing else for them to do around here. Why has education always been so important to the miner if it wasn't to get his children out of the mines?'

She paused to take breath and to change the tone of her voice.

'But that doesn't mean they're not proud of their job, because they are, no one prouder. But their pride is in their strength; without his strength a collier is nothing. He has also got the pride of anyone who does a dangerous job but, above all, it's sheer physical strength he admires most. And that's why he's afraid, not just that he will be out of work but what type of work is he going to be offered in its place. A miner's power is in his back, his shoulders, his arms and his legs; he loves to haul, to heave and push. And what does he see in these Japanese firms that have taken over the old pit sites? He sees people sitting at a bench, their muscles wasting away; he sees them working with their fingers, not even with their hands, sticking tiny pieces of wire together. And who does he see doing it, nine times out of ten? Women. And where are those women's proud husbands? Pushing the Hoover. And that one over there,' she pointed accusingly across the table, 'is all for it.'

Vicki sat, tight-lipped and silent, with none of the bright-eyed enthusiasm of the previous night. In Jonathan's mind there could only be two reasons for her silence in the face of such provocation – either she was being polite, reluctant to argue in front of a guest, or she had been totally subdued by the old lady's personality. It did not take him long to make up his mind as he watched the two women, Gran poised like a cat over a dying mouse, ready to strike again at the slightest sign of movement. He tried to imagine the conflict that had preceded such total capitulation and found himself making excuses for Vicki. She was isolated with a nonentity for a husband and Badger, at best, neutral. She had no home of her own, was in debt and living on a shoestring. They had just eaten a large joint of beef, not the sort of food bought out of part-time wages from a supermarket or a Social Security pittance for a striking miner but more likely to have come out of a young policeman's wages, grown fat with overtime from picket duty. It was not so much an ill wind, Jonathan thought grimly, that blew through number 48, Bradbury Street, as the cold blast of charity.

The table cleared, Vicki left to wash the dishes. Gran looked disapprovingly at her elder grandson as he got out of his chair to help her. Still sitting at the table, Badger and Jonathan began to discuss the following Saturday's rugby match. Driven to the stage where all excuses were being brushed aside, Jonathan had finally promised to turn out when they were disturbed by the sound of loud snoring. Looking up, they found Gran Kincaid fast asleep, bolt upright in a hard, high-backed chair, her lower jaw sagging in uncompromising, forthright snores. Badger looked at her affectionately, then grinned at Jonathan.

'Stubborn old devil.'

With Reggie back in his chair and Gran immovable in the only other chair near the fire, Vicki took her place at the table once more. Their voices, subdued as they tried not to wake the old lady, added a welcome softness and intimacy as their heads came nearer.

'I'm sorry about all the argument, Jonathan,' Vicki said, 'but it's not easy, living under the same roof.'

'I can appreciate that.'

'It's not easy for these two either.' She nodded her head at the two brothers. 'Particularly since Reggie was arrested. It's a fortunate thing that Badger here is not your usual kind of copper.'

'What d'you mean, not your usual kind of copper?' Badger's back straightened, his blonde eyebrows bristling. 'What d'you think Reggie would say if you told him you didn't think he was your usual kind of miner?'

Jonathan came between them. 'Did you say Reggie was arrested? Is that what his grandmother meant when she talked of him being a casualty?'

'That's right. It's a long story, and I wouldn't want to bore you with it, but it was over at Orgreave, back last May. I suppose it was the ultimate confrontation between the miners and the police. They really drew up their battle lines and there's no doubt, they outmanoeuvred us from the start. Looking back in years to come, they'll probably look on it as Arthur Scargill's Waterloo. They reckoned there were some ten thousand miners there and who had to be one of those arrested but my Reggie? He says he was doing nothing and, by heck, I believe him, even though he had lorry drivers waving ten pound notes in his face.' The words were spoken with bitterness, not pride. 'He was always a hard-working man, I'll give him that, never missed a shift – started on the bank and worked his way up from datal lad like everyone else.'

'Started on the surface and then did odd jobs underground,' Badger translated with a smile.

'But he'd never been to a Union meeting in his life, said there was no point, that it was all cut and dried anyway. What he really meant was he didn't have it upstairs. Otherwise he might still have one of the jobs on the safety teams that are still working every day; because you can imagine who's had those, can't you. And, of course, he's got no other skill so he can't tell both Coal Board and Union to get stuffed and go off somewhere else. Wouldn't be right, would that, he says; mustn't leave the lads now.'

Jonathan looked at the back of Reggie's head and wondered just how much more a man could take from his wife without a whimper.

'Poor old devil,' Vicki went on. 'As far as I was concerned, he went off to Orgreave on the bus like a day trip to Blackpool, but he just didn't come back. We had no idea where he was. In fact, he'd been herded into a police cell somewhere near Rotherham and he reckoned there were miners in there with him whose arms had been broken after the police horses had rolled on them. After a few days, they were brought before a magistrate in batches and he finally turned up, on bail provided he didn't leave the house, and was charged with riotous assembly. It was only when I got a book out of the library and read about it that we found he had been charged with something that carried a possible life sentence. Life. Can you imagine it, my Reggie being defended on a charge carrying a life sentence by some toffee-nosed Tory barrister who wouldn't know a lump of coal if you hit him with it, when he's done bugger all wrong in the first place?'

As Vicki's voice rose in her indignation, Gran stirred, muttering angrily in her sleep. They held their breath until she settled again.

'That's why Reggie wasn't really there when you saw him down the club last night,' Vicki explained. 'If he had been there, then, technically speaking, he would have been breaking his parole. Can you imagine what it must be like for an innocent man to be confined by law to the house for months on end with no idea when his trial might be? He can't even go picking coal off the tips like the rest of them. Can you wonder the poor bastard is depressed? And it's not easy for Badger here either. He knows Reggie breaks his parole, going down the club, going to the Welfare canteen to help with the washing up. And can Reggie ever trust his brother again after hearing what barefaced bloody lies the police will swear to in a witness box? That was a revelation, I'll tell you.'

Her head drooped as if, for the moment, her passion had burned out. She smiled sadly across the table at Jonathan as he began to make the early sounds of leaving.

'What must you think of us? Don't judge us too harshly, Jonathan. It's a difficult time and we are not unique by any means. There must be lots more like us. Just try to imagine what it must be like to belong to a family where one son is out and the other has gone back, or an old-time father and a scabbing son.' She smilingly tendered the inevitable peace offering. 'Don't go just yet. Stay and have a cup of tea. Please.'

The gentle comfort of ritual tea drinking did a great deal to soothe the passion of beer and underdone beef. Gran was woken with soft proddings to sip drowsily and even Reggie was encouraged to give his opinion as to who would make it to the 85 final at Wembley. But, as Jonathan observed all the farewell niceties of the well mannered guest, he wondered just how long the fragile truce would last after he was gone.

13

Linda had shown the lump to Gavin with a simple trust that had touched him. He had looked on it solely as a reward for years of protection until he had had time to think about it. Linda was an attractive girl, a bit old for her age, her features a little too mature for a schoolgirl, her manner a little too wary and withdrawn. But an attractive girl for all that, one who should have been in and out of love many times by now, not standing back as if touching anyone male would make her throw up. Yet she had shown her breast to him as if they still at times shared a bed together. There had been many occasions on his nights off, long after Pat Morelli had been safely shut away, when Linda had crept into his room, silently sliding between his sheets, looking for the kind of warmth that had nothing to do with temperature. Linda, someone to whom the male body was a thing of abhorrence, had clung to him, sleeping the sleep of complete trust. And it had worried Gavin, when he had thought about it, his total absence of any reaction to her soft breast, her firm thigh. He had reassured himself with the thought that she was, after all, his sister. But only his half-sister. He had laughed to himself; at least half of him should have reacted, or the whole of him half-reacted.

His concern for Linda was genuine but was not the only aspect of the matter to occupy his mind. Up until now, his priority had been survival, both for himself and for Linda, in Northend's hostile environment. Hanging over them both had been Pat Morelli's return but things were changing; there was light at the end of the tunnel. Another few months and they would be free. It was time to think ahead; grasp any opportunity that came his way; see advantage in the most unlikely places. Like Linda's breast lump, for instance.

The time was coming when he must dedicate as much time and energy on his mind and his ambition as he had on his body. It would not be enough to be physically balanced, poised to strike at any weakness. He must train his mind along the same lines. He knew he was too late to become an educated man in the accustomed sense of the words but he must find the time to arm himself with the specialised knowledge for what he wanted to do. For that, he was going to need guidance. He must also learn the art of using people. He wasn't going to make it alone and Gavin had grown up in a sufficiently hard school to know that no one was going to volunteer to help. He saw nothing wrong in using people. To use someone was not necessarily to take advantage of that person, or so Gavin reasoned with himself. The other person need not necessarily end up any the poorer as a result. What did Linda call them, catalysts? It was not Gavin's intention to rob anyone. Didn't they do it all the time in big business, use people, the old school tie, buy some guy a drink in the golf club? Few men joined a Country Club out of love for the countryside. The invitation to the yacht in Monte Carlo for the Grand Prix – there was usually a price to be paid sooner or later. It was time Gavin began to learn how never to forget a face, instantly remember a name. But where was he to start?

'Dr Brookes, could I see you for a moment? I'd like to ask you a favour, if I may.'

Gavin Prescott's shift finished at seven, Jonathan's day shift began at eight, and so, unless Jonathan was doing his stint of night duty, their paths rarely crossed. Jonathan showed his surprise.

'What are you doing here? I thought you would have been at home and in bed by now.' He looked at Gavin's tracksuit. 'Don't tell me you run home as well after working all night?'

Though he smiled, Gavin gave the impression that it was too early or too late for pleasantries, depending on which way one looked at it. 'I'd appreciate your opinion, Dr Brookes.'

'Sure. Fire away.'

'Somewhere more private?'

Jonathan looked at the follow-up patients already dribbling through the door in the vain hope of first come, first served.

'Won't take a moment, Dr Brookes.'

Behind closed doors, Jonathan looked a little apprehensively at Gavin Prescott. Was this to be some dreaded aftermath of the affair in which he had become involved with the Morellis? Jonathan could already see himself in the dock, could already hear the cell doors clang shut behind him. Gavin read his mind.

'No. Don't worry; nothing to do with that. But you seem doomed to be involved with my family one way or another. It's my sister, Linda, this time. I wonder if you'd have a look at her for me?'

'Why, of course.' Jonathan stood up straight, looking alert, the picture of professional competence. He looked round though well aware the room was empty. 'Where is she? What has she done to herself?'

'She's not here.'

'Oh?'

'She's at home. I wondered whether you would be kind enough to see her at home for me?'

'Oh.' The tone was now that of doubt, not surprise. 'I don't quite understand.'

'I believe you were a breast specialist, when you worked in Liverpool, I mean.'

'Hardly that,' Jonathan laughed.

'But didn't you do some research on breasts? I'm sure Janet told me you did; she was going on one night about how clever you were.'

'I don't know that it was grand enough to be called research,' Jonathan said, modestly, 'but I was building up a series, comparing the findings on mammography with . . .'

'So you saw a lot of women with lumps,' Gavin cut in.

'Two clinics a week.'

'So, would you please see my Linda for me?'

Reluctance dragged at every word as Jonathan answered, looking down at dark brown eyes set in a satin smooth face. 'That's not really possible, Gavin. In here,' he waved his hands around him, 'no problem. You could always say she had fallen and knocked herself. But I can't see her at your home. Casualty Officers just don't do that sort of thing. I could get in awful trouble if I did. Why can't she come up to Outpatients like everyone else? She wouldn't have to wait long, not with anything like that.'

'Very difficult to explain, Dr Brookes, but she's got this thing about men. I can't even get her to go and see our GP about it.'

'I'm a man. What's so different about me?'

'I know, Dr Brookes, but I've explained about you, how understanding you were over that spot of bother with her father. I've told her how sympathetic you are to the patients.'

Struggling not to be affected by blatant flattery, Jonathan swore to change his ways.

'What about a domiciliary visit? I realise your sister is quite fit enough to come to hospital but, under the circumstances, I'm sure it wouldn't be too difficult for your GP to find some consultant who would agree to go and see her.'

'No chance. Linda would be more likely to agree to her GP seeing her.'

'Who is your GP?'

'Old Dr O'Connor.'

'Can't say I've heard of him,' Jonathan admitted.

'Doesn't know his arse from his elbow.'

The medical profession closed ranks. 'Come on, Gavin. I'm sure that's not true.'

'Don't get me wrong, Dr Brookes. O'Connor's great; never too busy to see you, never gives you the impression you're wasting his time; his older patients worship him, the Catholics especially. You know the type, just bangs a bell and shouts "next" and everyone in the waiting room immediately feels better. But he's knocking eighty and not much good on lumps in the breast, I shouldn't think.'

They faced each other in silence, Jonathan feeling boxed in.

'How old is she?'

'Seventeen.' Gavin smiled inwardly, knowing he had got his way. 'Doing her A levels this summer.'

'What is she hoping to do?'

'Medicine.'

'Medicine?' Jonathan looked surprised.

'Why not?'

'No reason at all, Gavin, none at all. All right then, I'll come. But', Jonathan added as he saw the smile break the surface, 'only if I can square it with this Dr O'Connor first. I'll ring him this morning.'

'And what time will you call?'

'About six? That do you?'

'That'll do fine. I don't really think it's anything to worry about but you know how worked up these kids can get. Felt all right to me.'

'You've felt it?'

'Yes, I have. Bit of a lump there but it doesn't feel too bad.'

Jonathan didn't know whether to look surprised or disapproving and ended up doing both. 'Are you sure you want me to look at it?'

'Thought I'd better have a second opinion,' Gavin grinned. 'Can't be too careful can you? See you about six?'

Dr O'Connor was delighted, wasn't he now. And wouldn't that be a great help, going to see the dear child in that way, save so much trouble with the hospital and it was so kind of Dr Brookes to take an interest. An unfortunate family in many ways. That Morelli woman had seen hard times, so she had. Delivered her, didn't Dr Brookes know; remembered it well, snowing hard, quite a difficult forceps. And was Dr Brookes any relative of Bill Brookes down in Chester? No, of course not; dead long since, was Bill.

Standing in the hallway as Gavin struggled to close the front door, Jonathan saw, through the living room door, the glistening DA haircut. He walked over to put his head into the fetid atmosphere. 'Hullo, Wayne. How's the arm?'

Though his shoulders remained firmly applied to the back of the chair, Wayne sluggishly afforded Jonathan the courtesy of turning his head away from the TV. 'All right.'

'Getting a bit of movement back?'

His answer was an arm that was moved in an arc that surprised Jonathan both in its range and apparent painlessness.

'That's very good, Wayne. That's doing better than . . .'

'Just proves the truth of the saying, "Where there's no sense, there's no feeling", doesn't it?' Gavin took Jonathan firmly by the elbow. 'Shall we go up and see Linda?'

Jonathan followed him up the echoing stairs, trying to re-enact in his mind the fight between two drunks and the slim figure that led the way. He saw the banisters where Morelli had broken his leg, almost heard the crack, and Jonathan wondered whether breaking one's neck made the same sort of noise. Gavin opened a bedroom door without knocking and Jonathan entered behind him, feeling paraffin-tainted warmth on his cheek.

The young girl lay on the bed on her side, propped up on one elbow, knees bent, her head down over a textbook laid flat on the blanket. Her eyes flickered to the door as it opened but returned immediately to the book.

'Here you are, Linda, love; I've brought Dr Brookes to see you.'

The eyes flickered once more but what she was reading seemed to be all absorbing. Gently, Gavin took the book away, leaving her defenceless. She curled a little more, looking warily at Jonathan who, in turn, took the book from Gavin. He glanced at it as he let the pages slowly cascade from his thumb.

'Oh, my God, calculus. Do they still expect you to do that?' He looked up but got no response. 'Can't say I ever really came to terms with it. How are you getting on with it?'

'All right.'

At least, that was a start. 'In my day, Physics was the compulsory subject. I reckoned that it was virtually the qualifying exam because, once you had got that brute, the rest was all downhill. Is it still the same?'

'No. It's Chemistry now.'

'What subjects are you taking altogether?'

'Maths, Chem and Biol.'

'Which one's your favourite?'

Gavin stood back, fascinated to watch his sister's defences being slowly prised open.

'Biol. It's fab.'

'You'll make a good doctor then,' Jonathan smiled.

'How d'you mean?' Linda swung her legs over the edge of the bed, beginning to take an interest.

'Because you're obviously more attracted to something alive than dead.' Jonathan threw the book back on the bed. 'Try and make a point of that when you go for your interviews; don't, for Pete's sake, tell them you want to do Medicine because you want to help people, they just won't believe you. As a matter of interest, why do you want to do Medicine?'

'Get out of this bloody place.'

'Linda,' Gavin snapped, but Jonathan only laughed.

'Where have you applied to? Who's your first choice?'

'I've got interviews at St Mary's and Edinburgh.' She looked across uncertainly at Gavin before adding, 'But Gavin's not so sure now. He's talking about Liverpool now. I don't quite know. Liverpool was my third choice.'

'Haven't quite made our minds up yet, have we, love?' There was a bland smile on his face as he spoke but he did not look at Jonathan as he did so. 'We'll have to wait and see what sort of grades you get first, won't we?'

'You couldn't do better than Mary's but Liverpool would be a bit nearer home.' Again he felt tension rise as if he had touched a raw nerve. 'It does mean you are making it a bit more difficult for yourself in the interviews if you are not completely clear in your mind where you want to go. How good are you at interviews? Have they taught you anything about the technique in school? Because there is a technique, you know. How would you like me to take you through a mock interview sometime? Would you like that?'

And the defences came tumbling down.

'Would you, Dr Brookes?' She glanced excitedly at Gavin and back to Jonathan. 'That would be brill.'

'We'd do it properly. You'd have to come to hospital to get the atmosphere and I'd sit there in my white coat and really put you through it, be a real swine, just like some of these people can be. We'll tape it and run it back, analyse your answers. You'll be amazed how daft some of them will sound.'

'Sounds smashing. When?'

'First things first,' Jonathan smiled. 'This lump of yours. Let's get that sorted out first. Gavin tells me it's on the right side?'

Linda nodded as she pouted. 'It's nothing really. He's just fussing.'

'I'm sure he is but how long have you had it?'

'Comes and goes, doesn't it? About a year.'

'No bleeding from the nipples?'

'Gawd, no.' Linda's face contorted with mock terror.

The answers to Jonathan's routine questions were given in terse, no-nonsense phrases, devoid of all trace of teenage innocence. There were no girlish giggles to impede a clipped, clinical account that would have shamed many a terrified 40-year-old.

'Right then, Linda; let's have a look, shall we?'

Gavin helped her take off the tight-fitting grey jumper. The blue shirt, buttoned to the neck, was pulled out of her waist band, a loose fitting bra slid upwards and a few square inches of bulging skin presented.

'One thing you will have to learn in your first few months in hospital, Linda,' Jonathan said, gently, 'is that, whenever a patient has got two of anything, you must always examine the normal one first. So, let's have the shirt and bra off altogether, shall we?'

Linda looked for reassurance from Gavin.

'Come on, Linda, love; I always said, if you didn't work hard and get into medical school, you'd have to get a job in a topless bar. Strip off, love. And don't worry about Dr Brookes; he's seen so many boobs in his time, he must be fed up with the sight of them.'

Not totally convinced, Linda's gaze did not waver from Jonathan's face as she let Gavin help her strip off, as if, at the slightest sign of human reaction from him, she would have instantly covered up once more. She lay back, still intently scanning his face, as he gently, methodically and silently examined her. He signalled he had finished by picking up her shirt and restoring her modesty himself. He sat on the edge of the bed and shook his head.

'Nothing.'

'What d'you mean?'

'I mean there's nothing there you need be worried about.'

'I have got something there but it's nothing to be worried about, that's what you really mean, isn't it?'

'You, Linda, are going to make a very good doctor,' Jonathan said, slowly, obviously impressed. 'It's not going to be easy to fool you is it? Yes, you're quite right, you have got a bit of mastitis but, I promise you, it's nothing to be worried about. Do you believe me?'

Tears welled into eyes that had not cried for years and Linda nodded.

Jonathan stood up, picked up the book and threw it into her lap. 'Good,' he grinned. 'In that case, I'll leave you to your calculus and I'll see you for that interview within the next couple of days, I promise.'

Out on the landing, he turned towards the stairs but was diverted firmly into one of the other bedrooms and the door closed behind them. Inside, he was diverted equally firmly into a rickety old easy chair at the foot of the bed. 'Which would you like, Dr Brookes, tea or coffee?' He was given little chance to refuse both.

'Tea, please.'

Gavin turned his back, busying himself with a battered electric kettle, while Jonathan, struggling to suppress a shiver, looked round the unheated room. Screwed to one wall were two rough shelves laden with dog-eared paperbacks. Jonathan was just too far away to read the titles on the spines but they didn't look like fiction. Stacked as bookends were a few textbooks of similar vintage, the gilt lettering long since rubbed away. Below the shelves and dated by the ink stains and cigarette burns in its wooden top, stood an old-fashioned desk, no status symbol of an academic snob, littered as it was with all the paraphernalia of serious study. Pinned to the wall between desk and shelves was a picture that closely resembled a famous Trade Union leader. The remaining walls were bare, and, apart from an upright chair beneath the desk, the only other furniture in the room was a small, portable, black and white TV propped on the table where Gavin had been pouring the tea.

Incongruously, the tea came in a delicate china cup and saucer, not the thick beaker Jonathan would have found more in keeping with what he had seen. He shook his head as Gavin offered him sugar in a matching bowl.

'I think you have just made my Linda your slave for life, Dr Brookes.' He nodded towards his sister's room. 'Thank you.'

'My pleasure. And do you think it could be Jonathan, at least out of hospital?'

'Thank you again.'

'I have to admit,' Jonathan sipped his tea, wishing it was beer, 'I don't go much for this Christian names habit when we're working. I still can't bring myself to call my consultant, "Bob". Bit old fashioned in that way, I'm afraid. But, out of hospital . . .'

'I couldn't agree more. I prefer it; at least you know where you stand. And what about Linda? What did you think? I imagine you were telling her the truth, weren't you?'

'Oh, sure. Just a bit of mastitis with small lumps everywhere, though,' he paused to shake his head, 'I don't think I can remember seeing changes like that in someone so young before. In the 30- and 40-year-olds, yes, but so young? Even so, I still don't think we should do anything about it.'

As they talked of A levels and interviews and a life far from Northend, Jonathan's mind split like a computer screen displaying two windows. While the upper half produced the words that kept the conversation alive, the lower half was occupied by the data fed in by the intriguing young girl he had just seen. Outside that school uniform there had been none of the frippery one would have expected in a teenage bedroom; no pop star poster, no lipstick, no battered cuddly bear. They were poor, yes; but that poor? And inside that uniform; much more confusing. The face, the worldly look on that face, those breasts. But, above all, her attitude of mind, her watchful seriousness, the grown-up way she had looked at him and read his thoughts. Suddenly, Jonathan had difficulty in preventing the two screens becoming one, his inner thoughts being put into words. That girl in the next room, take away her school uniform, was more adult than he was.

'It must be nice to have your future all mapped out for you.' Gavin's remark needed answering.

'Do you mean me?' Jonathan asked.

'Yes.'

'It's hardly that. The next two or three years, yes, but after that, who knows?'

'But you go back to Liverpool in August, don't you? You are only in the General so that you can take the Fellowship, aren't you?'

'Yes, that's true enough.'

'And your future has got to be in Liverpool, I imagine?' Gavin looked into the depths of his cup as he spoke.

'Hopefully, yes, but', Jonathan laughed, 'there are a few others around with the same idea, you know. Competition is horrendous for the plum jobs.'

'But you have got a good start,' Gavin insisted. 'This Ph.D.'

'Will be an asset, no doubt, but has held me up for a couple of years, let others get ahead of me, and it only needs for me to put up some small black to be thrown off the ladder. Like', he smiled, 'making a habit of seeing patients in their homes when you are a Casualty Officer.'

'But you must be hoping for one of the top surgical posts in Liverpool,' Gavin persisted. 'Is that not so?'

'Sure. That's what we all aim for but I'll probably have to settle for something slightly more modest, the sort of job my father has up in Dunbridge.'

'But somewhere in the north-west. You wouldn't think of going south?'

'No, certainly not. My roots are up here.' Jonathan decided to reverse the inquisition. 'I'm fascinated by your books, Gavin.' Gavin, sitting on the bed, turned his head proudly to look at his prized possessions. 'They say you can tell a lot about someone by his choice of books but I can't see the titles from here. Have you really read all those?'

'Not really. They look so dog-eared because they were all second hand.

But I have read most of them. That doesn't mean, unfortunately, that I have understood all I've read. I need desperately to get on a course of some kind, evening classes at a College of Higher Education, something like that.'

'I certainly don't see Gavin Prescott as a hospital porter all his life but I've never seen any nursing textbooks looking like that. So; what else might they be? Hospital administration? No, they don't look right for that either. I give up; what are they?'

Smiling, Gavin stretched and took a book seemingly at random and handed it to Jonathan who put his cup and saucer down to open it. He read out the title: *Industrial Town, Self Portrait of St Helens in the 1920s.* He flicked through the pages, stopping at the pictures. 'Pit brow lasses. That's a strange coincidence. I'd never heard of them before I came here and then I met one of the last of them only a short while ago. Badger Kincaid – you know, Peggy Wells's boy friend? – his grandmother; she was a pit brow lass.'

'That's another good one.' Gavin threw Jonathan another well-worn volume. '*Wigan Pier Revisited.* There's someone who can write, Beatrix Campbell.'

'I've heard of her.' Jonathan took up the second book with less enthusiasm than the first. 'Rabid women's libber, isn't she?'

'And what's wrong with that?'

The immediate censure in Gavin's voice startled Jonathan. 'Nothing. Nothing at all,' he said but now took less interest in the book than in its owner. He held it aloft. 'So, what does all this mean?'

'I want to do full-time Union work, become a full-time Union official. As I see it, that's the only way I'm going to make anything of my life. There's real power there, if you get to the top, that is. And I intend doing just that. I know there's good pickings in hospital administration – the money's good these days – but nothing like the power of the Labour movement. That's why I made Linda apply for London and Edinburgh, thought it would be best if I was in a capital city. But now I'm not so sure. Perhaps it might be better to go to Liverpool. I've got to get on some local Council, any local Council; get myself known in the local Labour party. That might be easier if I stayed in this part of the world. Then I want to specialise.'

Jonathan laughed, hearing the phrase with such an unusual connotation.

'Doesn't only apply to you doctors, you know. I intend to specialise in women – and no snide remarks, please. There are going to be more and more women in the work force from now on, if only part time, and you can imagine how they're going to be treated if you bloody capitalists get your way. Not that the Labour movement treats them much better either – the Labour movement has always been run by men for men. But I have a feeling that 1984 could have been a watershed in a working woman's life. It was the year the working man's wife took over from the articulate, toffee-nosed blue stockings down south and, if they let it all slip back to where it was before, then they deserve to be downtrodden all over again. All they need is a leader and that's what I intend to be. I'm going to be the part-time women workers' champion. No more pit brow lasses. Perhaps there's a place for a completely new union of part-time women workers. Just imagine being boss of a union of all the part-time workers in the country. The NUM would have nothing on us. We could bring the country to its knees in a week.' Although he made it sound an idea that merited serious consideration, he smiled. 'Perhaps that could be the ticket that's going to make me the first black Chairman of the TUC.'

'Why stop there? Why not the House of Lords?' A broad grin of understanding now on his face, Jonathan pointed below the bookshelves. 'So that is Clive Jenkins. I thought it was, though, for the life of me, I couldn't see why you should have his picture on your wall.'

'My hero,' Gavin grinned too. 'He also worked nights at one time, you know, as a shift supervisor. An amazing man; only one thing wrong with him, he's not black. I've put him there, with that cocky grin of his, so that, every time I look up from the desk, he's looking at me, laughing at me, telling me I haven't got a prayer, that I'll never do what he's done.'

'I think he's thoroughly objectionable.'

'Well, you would, wouldn't you, privileged to be born and bred into the establishment as you are? But have you any idea of what he's achieved for his members, the committees he's served on, the books and articles he's written?' Jonathan shook his head but Gavin had not been looking for an answer, smiling affectionately at the picture, speaking out loud words he had muttered over and over again in cold, determined solitude. 'All right, master, I'll have that bloody smile off your face one day.' He turned to Jonathan once more. 'Having to look after Linda the way I have, I reckon, like you, I'm a year or two behind schedule, but, even though "a small black" has a slightly different meaning for me than for you, I still think I can make it.'

'I'm damn sure you can,' Jonathan said, and meant it. 'It must be hard going, working nights as you do. What do you do for holidays?'

The thoughtless stupidity of the question was brought home to Jonathan by the slow, forgiving smile that spread across Gavin's face, reminding him just how far divorced from his world was Gavin's.

'Never really had one, Jonathan. I pay the rent, feed and clothe Linda and myself, not much left over then for the Riviera on a night porter's wages.'

'I'm sorry; that was rather stupid of me. In that case', Jonathan spoke slowly, measuring in his mind just how far he was committing himself, 'how would you feel about a couple of days sailing? I don't imagine you've done any before?' He was more careful now about his phrasing.

With eyes half-closed, Gavin shook his head.

'I'm not sure of the exact date yet but, sometime towards the end of May, we are taking part in a race down to New Quay in West Wales. Why don't you come with us? About four days at the most. You're obviously very fit; I think you'd love it.'

'Who's "we"?'

'A girl friend of mine – she's an anaesthetic registrar in Liverpool – and I'm going to ask Badger Kincaid as well. He's made me promise to play for his rugby team and I mean to get my own back on him. Will you come?'

A few days away from Scarsby and the chance to forge further links with the nearest to a high flyer that Gavin had met to date.

Jonathan misunderstood his hesitation. 'I'm sorry it's rather an establishment sport but, I promise you, it won't cost you a penny; couple of beers maybe. Food's provided. So is the clothing. Cheaper than living at home. And you needn't look on it as charity because I go on exactly the same terms. Doesn't cost me a penny either. Will you come?'

'Whose boat is it?'

'It's a boat called Gelert. It belongs to Sir Warwick Ridgeway.'

'Sir Warwick Ridgeway did you say? Do you mean the Chairman of our local Health Authority?'

'I would have thought it extremely unlikely there are two Sir Warwicks.'

'Good God.' Perhaps his luck was changing.

While enjoying the astonishment on Gavin's face, Jonathan had no way of appreciating the thought processes that produced it.

'What about Linda?' Gavin worried suddenly that he was straying too far from the role of downtrodden protector.

'She'll be all right for a couple of days.'

'Her father . . .'

'Might not be out of hospital by then, the way things look at the moment. Even if he is, we can ask Badger to get one of his mates to keep an eye on her for you. Will you come?'

'Yes, I'll come. Thank you.'

'Dr Brookes. Do you think you could stay on for a few minutes after we finish in the morning? I'd like you to see something.'

'Yes, of course.' Jonathan raised one eyebrow in curiosity. It wasn't often that Staff Nurse Wells was coy or mysterious. When she had anything to say, she usually spoke plain English. 'Sounds interesting.'

He didn't expect an answering smile and did not get one. 'I'll come and get you after I've given the report.'

Her face was equally expressionless when she found him standing at the desk, changed into his navy anorak, yawning, his car keys dangling from one hand. 'Come and look at this.' She turned on her heel and Jonathan followed, amused and intrigued. At the door to the Sister's office, she stopped, knocked and walked in. She stood aside as Jonathan entered, closed the door behind him and locked it. It took Jonathan a while to work out what was strange about the way Sister Maisie was sitting in her chair. It was her uniform. It was unbuttoned down to the waist.

Peggy Wells stood behind Maisie's chair, leaned over and began to slip her uniform over her shoulders while Maisie's hangdog eyes never wavered from Jonathan's face. 'Just look at this, Dr Brookes.'

Jonathan leaned forwards but had difficulty controlling his facial expression long before the Staff Nurse had touched the stained, adherent gauze and cotton wool pad. His instinctive reaction was to close his eyes in acceptance of defeat as she began to peel it gently back. His nose had already given him a diagnosis he did not want to confirm with his eyes. Pyocyaneus. Now and again, he had caught a whiff of something as Maisie had passed close by, smiling to himself that perhaps Maisie didn't bath quite as often as she might. But he should have known. He'd smelt pyocyaneus often enough, you couldn't miss it, it stuck in your sinuses for days. It was the smell that screwed faces up and brought out the air fresheners if the patient was under an anaesthetic. But Maisie was very much awake and looking straight at him.

'What have you got hidden under there, then, Sister?'

Behind Maisie's back, Peggy Wells was having equal trouble controlling her expression as she folded the foul pad with her finger tips, placing it in a disposal bag as if red hot. 'Now, don't be cross with her, Dr Brookes. I've already given her a good wigging, haven't I, Maisie? She only showed it to me last night.'

'I'm sure Sister knows me better than that by now. Let's have a closer look for a moment, see what the problem is exactly.'

Putting his face close to her chest wall as if it smelt of roses, Jonathan made a play of detailed examination though one glance would have been enough for a first-year clinical student. The right breast was gone, replaced by foul-smelling ulceration that had eaten its way through paltry muscle to her ribs. The cancer had spread to the other breast, pulling and puckering the skin towards it like the crab it was. There was no need for the ritual feel for glands in the armpit, they were there to be seen, pushing their way through the skin.

'Let's have a look at your back for a moment, Sister.'

He leaned over her shoulder, raising his eyes in a snatched look of despair at Peggy Wells. Stretching beyond Maisie's spine, the skin was indurated and fixed, skin secondaries fanning out towards her opposite shoulder. Her whole chest was held rigid in *cancer n cuirass*, her breathing almost entirely diaphragmatic.

Jonathan nodded to the Staff Nurse who gently applied a clean pad, getting Maisie to tuck it to her side until she could bandage it properly. She pulled Maisie's uniform back over her shoulders. Though he hadn't touched her, Jonathan felt the overwhelming desire to wash. 'Well now,' he said, smiling his compassion, 'What are we going to do about that for you?'

'You wouldn't want to operate on that, would you, Dr Brookes?' Maisie broke her silence without changing her expression.

'No, of course not. That's the sort of thing that needs treatment, not operation.'

It was an answer that had to be given with confidence without implying the truth of which Maisie was perfectly aware, that her disease was far beyond any question of cure. Even in his short career, Jonathan had seen this picture often enough to wonder at the attitude of mind that could shut out such stark reality in a lonely world of blind fear. The fact that the patient was a nurse obviously did not render her immune to self-deception. It was obviously an exception to the rule that knowledge conquers fear. If Maisie, after thirty years of nursing, didn't know a cancer of the breast when she saw one, who did? But, even if he could not understand such a head in the sand attitude, he was already determined to treat such a mentality with compassion, not anger. She must have known the score ever since that awful moment of feeling the first lump, one, two, three years before.

Her treatment, palliative at best, would be straightforward, the handling much more complex. There was one easy way out, easy for the clinician that is, the way demanded by modern thought. Tell her she had been a fool, tell her to face up to things, make her admit to herself she was going to die, tell her to do what any intelligent woman should do, go home and put her affairs in order, methods designed by high intellects for high intellects but not for the Maisies of this world. If she had wanted the explicit truth, she would have sought it soon after feeling the lump. It was obvious to a sensitive young man that Maisie wanted it played her way and, if that was the way Maisie wanted it, then that was the way Jonathan was going to play it too. It was just a question of praying for the right words.

'You've got to be sensible and have some treatment for that, now haven't you, Sister? Something to clear up that infection.'

'Nothing to worry about, is it, Dr Brookes? I won't need to stop work or anything like that, will I?'

'You'll have to go to Liverpool for the treatment and I think it would be better if you were to go there to be seen first as an outpatient. Difficult to get you seen here without everyone getting to know about it. If I were to fix that up, could you manage it?'

'She'll go. I'll see to that.' The words, quietly determined, came from behind the chair. 'Time someone looked after her for a change.'

'You'll certainly need some tablets for that and, if they can clean it up enough, perhaps some radiotherapy.'

'But no operation?'

'No, Maisie. No operation.'

The hated name, constantly in each mind, was never mentioned, the future unexplored, the past never criticised. Maisie dropped her head to stare into a cold, black fireplace.

Outside, Jonathan turned wearily to Peggy. 'All I need now is for you to tell me you've got a lump somewhere. Please tell me you haven't.'

'Not bloody likely. I'm not having you putting your boney great hands all over me.' She looked into a drawn, sad face. 'She asked specially for you, you know. Said she'd only show it to you. Said she thought you'd understand. Quite a feather in your cap, I suppose.' She turned to walk away, embarrassed. 'See you. Take care.'

14

Vicki and Gran Kincaid met head on in a doorway. Mouth downturned, Gran strode on, forcing Vicki to backtrack. Neither spoke.

Her end of the table laid, Vicki tilted her head to one side, cocking one ear at the bedroom above. She heard nothing. With a cluck of annoyance, she passed through into the middle room and the foot of the stairs beyond.

'Reggie, are you up?'

Her only answer was a creak of a bed and her first step on the stairs was accompanied by a snort of frustration. At the top of the stairs, she kept straight on into the back bedroom. As she entered, Reggie turned his back on her, pulling the bedclothes up over his shoulder, burying his head deeper into the pillow. The black stained floorboards groaned as she crossed to the window to open the curtains.

'What do you want to do that for?' were the first words of the day from her husband. The old iron bedframe rattled as he turned his back on the light.

'Are you coming?' Vicki demanded. She screwed her eyes tight and clenched her fists as she was ignored. 'Reggie, I asked you, are you coming?'

'What's the point?' Reggie didn't bother to open his eyes as he answered.

'Because I think you ought to.'

'Oh, bugger off.'

Vicki looked silently over the foot of the bed at her husband. His hair needed a wash, his beard was unkempt. It suddenly occurred to her that she was glad he had given up trying to make love to her any more. She didn't think she'd miss it. An over-rated pastime if Reggie's monotonously regular self-gratification was anything to go by. There were other things in life.

'If you are coming, you'd better get up now. I'm leaving in less than an hour.' She looked at her watch. 'They reckon on moving off at eleven sharp. And a right lousy day they've chosen for it.' She nodded towards the window. 'More like January than March is that outside.'

'I'm not coming.'

'Why not, Reggie? I don't know what's the matter with you these days, I really don't.'

'You don't?' Reggie roused himself sufficiently to raise himself on one elbow, lifting the blankets to send a waft of stale air through the room.

Vicki quickened at the first sign of fight her husband had shown in months. 'No, I don't, Reggie. You're not half the man you were. What's happened to you?'

'I'll tell you what's bloody happened to me. I was a hard working miner and now I'm an out of work criminal, that's what's happened to me.'

Reggie's spark of defiance soon burned itself out and he fell back into the bedclothes. Vicki tried to rekindle it.

'But that doesn't mean you have to give in to it the way you have. Others haven't.'

A surly defiance glowed for a moment more. 'But they probably haven't got wives off working all day, have they, instead of being at home, giving their husband a bit of support? What's that you call youselves? Women's

Support Group? And that's just about bloody right, women supporting each other. If you want to support a miner, why not start at home with me? What's that they say about charity starting at home?'

Vicki bit her lip. She had known it was going to be a difficult day, one way or another – she had been awake most of the night, her racing thoughts pursued doggedly by Reggie's snores – but she had not realised just how difficult. Reggie misconstrued her silence as being some degree of guilty submission.

'Didn't stop you taking on that job full-time when it was offered, did it?'

'Doesn't stop you eating the beef it buys on Sundays either.'

Reggie turned on his back to give his wife the full benefit of his scowl. He swung his head from side to side as if looking for somewhere to spit.

'Thought you'd throw that in my face sooner or later, you bitch; can't imagine what's taken you so long. Great like, wasn't it, spending my money in Majorca? Don't remember you complaining much then, by heck I don't. Nor driving round in a new car, neither.'

His wife's face softened. 'Fair comment, Reggie, love. I'm sorry. I shouldn't have said that.' She hurried on, seeing him turn as if deciding to quit while he was ahead. 'But I still think you ought to come this morning. There's still time if you hurry.'

'No.'

'Reggie . . .'

He sat half upright, as if anxious to settle the matter once and for all. 'I'll go on one condition, right?'

'What's that, Reggie?'

'That, if I'm nicked, you go to jail for me.'

'That's not going to happen. Several of the lads in your position are going; Bob Bullivant, Sam Vickers. The coppers are not going to do anything about it now. It's over, Reggie. Only the local police are going to be there, that's all; Badger told me so. They're not going to cause any trouble. If they had wanted to, they could have pulled you in a dozen times over already. I'm damn sure Badger's not the only one who's known about you lads and your trips down the Welfare. They know they've got to live with us again when all this has settled. They're not going to pick you up.'

'It's not only that neither, Vicki.'

'What's that then?' She looked more closely at Reggie's face, seeing his lower lip tremble, trying not to believe what she saw.

'I'm finished, Vicki. I'll not work again.'

'Don't be ridiculous. When this court case is over – and they'll never make that stick, they haven't a hope – you'll soon be back at work again; you wait and see.'

Reggie shook his head. 'They'll not have me back; even if there's still a pit to go to. They won't take me on again. Scargill's right; we're on a hit list and d'you really think they're going to take me on just to give me a nice fat redundancy payment a few months later? No way. I can see it now; no job, no pension, no lump sum. The only thing I'll bring home after a lifetime down a pit is a reputation as a trouble maker. No,' he sunk his chin on his chest as he kicked feebly against the heavy blankets. 'I'll never work again.'

'You're no trouble maker, Reggie,' Vicki said, softly.

'I know that, you know that, but try telling them that down the Job Centre. And anyway, what else can you do with those?' He held up callous palms for Vicki to see, as if there was no need of any other answer. Satisfied he had made his point, Reggie sank back into defeat and, sadly, Vicki watched him close his eyes.

Broadoak was going to return to work with pride, pride in the way they had fought a lost cause. There had been some who had not agreed with the strike, would have voted against it, but the Broadoak scabs could have driven to work in one car with room to spare. There had been countless casualties but only three deserters in what had been a rearguard action from day one. And now, if they could not have a victory parade, then their march would be the next best thing, a demonstration of the triumphant solidarity that had stubbornly refused to crack despite the hammer blows dealt to it by the combination of an effete leadership, resurrected from the 1920s, and a country turned in on itself. It was to be an occasion worthy of men who considered themselves the elite of the labour force, the Paras of the working class, proud men watched by their fellow countrymen as they had been brought to their knees by a pitiless government and one-eyed reporters. They intended to march with their heads held high, happy at least in the knowledge that, if there was anyone left sensitive enough to feel any shame at the whole sordidly unnecessary affair, it need not be a Broadoak miner or his wife or his child. The Union banner would be held high, the band would play and the drums would tell the world that the heart of a mining town still beat – at least for a while longer.

They only had two problems, where and when to march. Scarsby had grown around Broadoak. Dust from the mine lay thick on the pavements of the town square, the winding gear as much a part of the town centre's architecture as church tower or Town Hall. By the time the head of a marching column had reached Broadoak, its tail would still be outside Tesco. They had decided to start off in the opposite direction and circle around the football ground. A proposal to hold a rally in the football ground had been rejected; there would be no speeches, no epitaphs. The local MP had indicated his intention to be with them; the marchers had indicated their intention that he would not. The march was to be for miners, led by miners, not by some up-for-the-day Polytech lecturer. The Mayor could come and bring his chain – he'd been a collier for twenty years – and a year's heartbreak had earned the vicar his place.

As to when they should march, it had been planned that the men would return at their own convenience, a token few at the head of the column presenting themselves at a time not recognised as one when shifts usually reported for work. A few quiet words with a sympathetic pit manager had ensured there would be no difficulty over such a small final flourish of independence.

It was time to go, time to keep their heads held high under glowering clouds so low as to depress the cheeriest of spirits. But not before attention to one final detail. Jack Formby approached the Police Inspector.

'Morning, Inspector.'

'Morning, Jack.' The Christian name was spoken without a smile. Cautious, professional friendliness that could be cut off instantly at the first sign of trouble.

'You can call your lads off, Inspector. We're miners going back to work, not a flock of sheep being led to the slaughter. We don't need your sheepdogs. We know the way.'

The Inspector looked at Jack Formby long and hard and saw nothing more than pride. 'Fair enough, Jack. I'll see they don't bother you. We'll divert the traffic for you, see you don't get held up.'

Vicki Kincaid was still two streets away when she heard the first irreverent bars of 'Colonel Bogey' trumpet the miner's defiance. She began to run and was out of breath as she infiltrated her way into the side of the column. She was not the only latecomer but there was some subtle difference in her manner, her speech, her dress, that made her assimilation into the marchers less complete than the others. She was a miner's wife and proud of it but her reputation in the Support Group now set her apart in the eyes of the other wives who saw her with a mixture of respect, envy and dislike born of jealousy. There were no cheers or shouts as the marchers threaded their way between the terraced houses, just the sounds of murmured conversation and shuffling feet as the column gradually broke up into irregular groups. No one spoke to Vicki until she felt a tap on her shoulder.

'Where's Reggie then?'

She turned to see Sam Vickers's cheery grin. She smiled. 'Hullo, Sam. Nice to see a friendly face. I was beginning to think I had something your best friend doesn't tell you about.'

He fell into step alongside her, looking around him. 'Isn't Reggie here?'

'No, Sam; I'm afraid he isn't.'

'Why's that then?'

She shrugged her shoulders. 'Just couldn't face it, Sam.'

'Know how he feels, love. Bit pointless, like, for us, i'n't it. We'll never go down a pit again, Reggie and me, but I thought I'd come and support the lads, you know.'

'Do you really mean that, Sam?'

'What?'

'About not working again.'

''Fraid so, lass. Problem is, what else can we do?' He looked warily over both shoulders, like a stand-up comic about to tell a risqué joke, before whispering in Vicki's ear. 'One of our lot's already broken bail and got himself a job as a bouncer someplace in Manchester.'

'You won't do anything as stupid as that now, Sam, will you?' Vicki broke off for a moment to wave to Badger where he stood, poker-faced, on a street corner. 'You're bound to get off in due course. It's daft, is that, to treat you all like criminals.'

'Well . . .' Sam looked doubtful.

'Well what? My Reggie didn't do anything wrong.'

'I know that, love. Just plain bad luck, that was. They were picking the lads up at random, as if they'd been given a quota to fill and to hell with whether the lads had done anything to deserve it. And we all know Reggie, great big, easygoing ox that he is. We all know . . .' he hesitated for a moment to take a quick look at Vicki, 'let's face it, love, dear old Reggie's not bright enough to get into trouble.' He grinned at her to take the sting out of his words. 'Somebody trapped under a roof fall, nobody better to have around then than Reggie, but you wouldn't ask him to plan a bank robbery, now would you? But me now, not quite so easy is that.'

'How d'you mean, Sam?'

'Well . . .' Sam opened and closed his fists at the memory. 'I have to admit I gave this copper a fair old belter.' He held his hands like a golfer studying his grip. 'I found this piece of wood in some railings. We'd been pushed and shoved around for hours and we hadn't eaten all day. Then one of them kicked me on the knee and that was it. I caught him just there.' He pointed just below his left ear. 'So, you see, the best I can hope for is to be passed through in a job lot with all the other Reggies they pulled in. Not that I don't feel I haven't paid my debt to society already,' he scratched the back of his head ruefully, 'the going over they gave me back in the cells. By heck. Not much sign of Amnesty International around there that night, I tell you.'

'Couldn't you have reported them, Sam?'

'No chance.' He laughed bitterly. 'All them buggers look the same to me and, anyway, they'd all taken their numbers off their shoulders, just in case like. Still, they were very kind afterwards, gave us a nice wash and brush up before we saw the magistrate.'

'Aren't you afraid of being picked up again?'

'Not really; not for this sort of thing. Bloody prisons are full already and there must be hundreds like us breaking bail every day. That's not why Reggie didn't come today, was it? I mean, I've seen him down at the Club and in the Welfare often enough.'

'Of course not, Sam. It's just that I can hardly get him out of the house at the moment. Really down in the dumps is our Reggie, I'm afraid. Do me a favour, Sam; call round and try and get him out of himself a bit, would you?'

'No sweat, Vicki. I'll call this evening. We'll go for a pint.'

'Well, perhaps not this evening, Sam.' She could not think of a good excuse. 'But any other time.'

They almost walked into the marchers in front as, with the band falling untidily silent, the column crushed together like a collapsing concertina as its leaders reached the pit gates. Vicki and Sam were too far back to witness the token shift pass through, filing past the pit manager, the son of a collier, who seemed to swallow hard with each hand he shook.

When Vicki returned from work to 48, Bradbury Street, she felt like an outsider. She almost knocked before going in. As she hung her coat on the hallstand, she took a deep breath. She took another one before opening the door into the living room. Gran looked at her. Reggie did not. Neither spoke.

'Right.' She rubbed her hands, her face bright and cheerful. 'What do you want for your tea, Reggie?'

'He's had his tea,' Gran Kincaid answered for him. 'We thought we'd better get on. Never quite know what time to expect you these days.'

Vicki struggled to prevent the smile draining from her face. 'You know exactly when I'll be home, Gran. Not fair is that.'

'Never quite sure when you've got one of those meetings you're always going to these days. How did the march go this morning?'

'Well enough. You'd have been proud of the lads . . .'

'Always proud of the lads.'

'. . . and the lasses. I saw Badger, gave him a wave like. What time are you expecting him?'

'I don't know.' Reggie seemed to have displaced even Badger from her favour. 'Said he was going over the General to see that girl of his.'

Halfway through preparing her meal, Vicki stuck her head through the door. 'Anyone want a cuppa?' She swore beneath her breath as there was no audible reply. She ate alone. The only sign of movement from Reggie was when his eyes followed the course of the snooker balls on the TV. Gran, ramrod straight, sat staring into the past. Vicki washed her dishes and sat back at the table. The moment called for yet another deep breath.

'Fancy a drink, Reggie? Feel like going down the Club?'

'No.'

'Most of the lads will be there, last night an' all. Most of them start back tomorrow.'

'Exactly.'

'But I need to talk to you, Reggie. I've got something we must discuss.'

'It'll keep.'

'That's just it, it won't. We've got to talk this over before tomorrow.' Studiously, she kept her head turned from Gran. 'We need to talk it over in private, like. And I'm not going up in that bedroom; it's too bloody cold.'

'And nobody's going to turf me out of my own kitchen.' Gran went back to folding and unfolding endlessly the silver paper from the toffee she chewed.

Ignoring the old woman, Vicki's voice hardened. 'Please, Reggie, will you come down the Club with me, just for an hour?'

'No.'

'All right then.' Vicki leaned forwards across the table to speak more clearly, directing her words at the back of her husband's head. 'I've got the chance of a new job and I've got to give Mr Franks, the store manager, my answer in the morning.'

'So, what's that got to do with me?' Reggie twisted his head momentarily. 'Didn't ask me when you got the job first, did you? Nor when you went full time, neither.'

'But this is different.'

It seemed her husband had no interest in whatever that difference might be as he turned his attention back to the snooker.

'We would have to move from here.'

Slowly, Reggie turned his bulk in the chair sufficiently to be able to look at his wife over one shoulder. 'What d'you mean?'

'Exactly what I said; we'd have to move from here, go to Liverpool – at least for a while.'

'Move to bloody Liverpool?' Gran Kincaid forsook her neat folding movements to screw the silver paper into a ball as Reggie showed a rare flash of emotion. 'What the hell for?'

'I've got this chance of a supervisor's job but it means going on a course and the store here in Scarsby is too small for that. I'd need to go to one of the bigger branches in Liverpool.'

'And how long's this course then?'

'I'm not sure – few weeks, couple of months maybe.'

'You could travel then.'

'Too expensive, Reggie. They won't give me those sort of travelling expenses. I couldn't afford to travel every day.'

'Go in digs then.'

Vicki winced at the cold brutality but found it helped. 'I want you to come with me. I've talked a lot about it with Mr Franks. Been very kind to me, Mr Franks has.'

'Has he now?'

'He reckons this could be just the start, that I should do everything I can to stay on in one of the big stores in Liverpool after, not bury myself back in Scarsby. Very complimentary, he's been; reckons I've got it in me to be manageress, even buyer, one day. And there was no need for him to say that; no skin off his nose.'

'Quite sure?' Reggie sneered and turned his back once more.

The silence that descended was broken only by the click of snooker balls and the funereal whispers of the commentator.

'I'm going, Reggie,' Vicki said, quietly. 'I'm going to take that job.'

The silence returned.

'Come with me, Reggie. Please. We'd have to find a couple of rooms to start with but, who knows, after a while . . .'

Reluctantly, Reggie turned for the last time. 'How can I, Vicki? There's my bail.'

'I'm sure that could be changed. We'd see a solicitor, see if he could have the address changed. After all, what if this house burned down?'

'And there I'd be, stuck on my own in two rooms in a strange place, away from the lads. You've got to be joking.'

'Once your case was over, you could look for a job. You said yourself, you're finished as a miner.'

'What me? Find a job in Liverpool of all places? You've got to be flamin' daft, Vicki.'

He turned his back and Vicki knew she had a decision to make. She tried to put it off as long as she could but the silence drove her on.

'I'm still going, Reggie.'

'Please yourself.'

'So that's settled, then?'

Reggie said nothing. Neither did Gran Kincaid, now taking her time as she smoothed out the crumpled paper to begin folding it once more.

15

A plain-clothes policeman and a policeman in plain clothes are two very different persons. The one dresses and behaves so as to blend with his background. The other sticks out like a sore thumb. To convert from one to the other must take a conscious effort of will. The uniformed copper, off duty, is, to anyone taking the trouble to look, as readily recognisable as the off-duty nurse, or teacher, or social worker, or retired regular army major. A bus full of them cannot possibly be mistaken for anything else.

The bus ground to a halt and an explosion of compressed air heralded a jactitation of the folding door that was as violent as it was impotent. Jonathan stood back until, as a result of cursing manpower from within, the doors were jerked open to reveal Badger's grinning face.

'Hi.'

Jonathan squeezed passed him and threaded his way down the narrow aisle made narrower by beefy shoulders. He took a seat alongside Taff Evans. Badger followed to sit behind them. The next few juddering, rattling miles were taken up with talk of scrum halves and number eights, backrow moves and second phase.

'If you're going to play number eight, I'd better introduce you to our scrum half,' Taff said. 'That's him over there.'

Jonathan looked where Taff Evans pointed and frowned. 'Are they always like this, Taff? They're very quiet.'

'Bit uptight, some of them, I imagine. And some have just come off a shift and must be pretty nackered. But most of the hard boys are here. They wouldn't want to miss this one.'

'Why not?'

'Didn't Badger tell you?' They both turned round to see Badger grinning broadly. 'It's the semi-final today.'

'Semi-final?' There was horror on Jonathan's face, most of it genuine. 'Semi-final of what?'

'The local Brewer's Cup.'

'Who are we playing then, for heaven's sake?'

'South Scarsby Institute. Students. Usually very fit and tend to run us around for the first half hour but we usually manage to grind them down. There's a mining engineering department with lots of miners' sons – so watch out for yourself behind the ref's back.'

Jonathan looked appalled at the prospect.

The Institute pitch was better than Jonathan had expected. Within view of the red-brick college buildings, it looked quite civilised. Flat and close-cropped, it even had a small stand, already part full. There was a thin but animated band of supporters around the touchline with a higher-than-usual proportion of women, their gaily coloured scarves to the fore. Floodlights around the ground bore witness to strenuous evening training sessions and Jonathan suddenly wished he was somewhere else, anywhere else.

The changing rooms, one end of a Nissen hut type clubhouse, were up to the standard of any second-class rugby club, clean but stark, the concrete floor never quite dry, the air never completely free from the conflict between the heaviness of body odour and the all-pervading pungency of Oil of Wintergreen. The policemen trooped in with all the wary silence of a visiting team, showing all the reluctance to start changing of a team on whom no love is lost. They knew that, apart from the miners' sons they would be playing against, many of the girls in their scarves would be gifted daughters of proud miners. No one would boast of being related to a copper.

Out on the field, Jonathan looked at the opposition. Students seemed to have become much bigger and stronger than he remembered. Perhaps it could be explained partly by the broad transverse stripes on their jerseys but there was no gainsaying the awesome bulk of their full back whose face lay buried beneath a heavy black beard.

'What they call a mature student, I believe,' Taff Evans muttered as they lined up for the kick off. 'I wonder where they found him.'

To Jonathan, the first ten minutes were pure gasping, chest constricting agony. It came home to him that he had been a fool to think he could play in that class of rugby without any serious training. He was an unfit 27-year-old and he was playing against very fit 20-year-olds – and it showed. He did not get within five yards of the ball before it was gone, whisked away from him, seemingly always back the way he had just come. He was not too bewildered however to realise that, in Taff Evans, he was playing with a man in a class of his own. Taff had already left his mark on the opposing outside half who now only had one eye for the ball, the other being permanently fixed on this darting shaft of steel that tormented him every stride he took. It was only Taff's brilliant disruptive play and their policy of taking no chances that had kept the police on level terms after the first quarter but, inevitably sooner or later, served quickly from second phase possession, the student outside half found himself, for the first time, with the ball in his hands and freed from Taff's attentions. He made ground before serving his backs who had accelerated into space. Waiting, his hands already outstretched, was their wing. As the wing put his head back, rounded his man and headed for the corner, Jonathan, his lungs bursting, made for the corner flag. Halfway there, he was overtaken by Evans whose despairing tackle failed to prevent the wing slide across the line on one shoulder.

'Bit quick, that one, isn't he?' Jonathan gasped as they bent, hands on knees, to watch the fullback convert from the touchline.

As they jogged back to the halfway line, Taff got among the forwards. 'That's all right, lads. That was bound to happen sooner or later. Just keep playing it close. Don't give them possession.'

The brief rest had revived Jonathan and he found he was enjoying himself. He must get back to playing more often, he thought. He began to win a few balls at ruck and maul and swelled with pride at words of encouragement from Taff. Then it happened again, the ball jetting its way along their opponent's threequarters to the wing. This time, his marker's outflung hand tapped his heel and he stumbled. He was struggling to regain his momentum when he was caught by Taff, followed closely by Jonathan. A maul formed, the ball went dead and the whistle blew. As Jonathan got up, he heard a short gasp from below him. The two packs of forwards diverged, binding in anticipation of a set scrum, but the form of the winger remained, writhing on the ground, his hands around his ankle. Moments later and their trainer stooped over him, going through the ritual laying on of hands. Taff Evans, like any well behaved captain, ran over to make sure the wing was not seriously hurt, tousling the young man's hair in comradely sympathy before running back to his own side.

'D'you think I should go and see how he is?' Jonathan asked.

Taff Evans looked aghast. 'Bloody hell, no. You might cure him.' He turned to join in the sporting applause as the man bravely hobbled back to his position. 'That should slow him down a bit.' He glanced at Jonathan and an eyelid twitched happily.

Just before half time, the students went ahead again with their fullback thumping over a booming penalty from near the halfway line. Nine points down, Jonathan expected an atmosphere of depression but Taff was quite optimistic. Treating the backs like lepers, he took his pack aside. 'Now then, lads. We can win this, no sweat, as long as we don't make the mistake of giving the damn ball to our backs. We're about a stone a man heavier and they're already beginning to fade. We can grind nine points and more out of them if we just keep the pressure on.' The whistle blew. 'So now, play it close, wear the bastards down and be patient. It'll come.'

Taff's prophesy began to come true. The youthful chanting from the touchline became desultory as the students saw less and less of the ball and the rugby became duller and duller. Their pack began to go backwards, the police taking almost every strike against the head. A five yard scrum became a pushover try under the posts for the police, Jonathan having to do no more than fall on the ball to score. The other flanker scored close to the scrum, a try that went unconverted, and the police were one point in the lead.

Both sides now leaden footed with fatigue, play became so scrappy and disorganised that Badger, who until then had played with all the obscurity of the true hard grafter, suddenly found himself with the ball in his hands, only the full back to beat and Taff outside him, screaming for the ball that would give them the try to clinch the match. As if mesmerised, Badger thundered into the waiting arms of the last defender between the police and the line, not even sinking one shoulder as they collided. The fullback took the full force of the impact but somehow managed to gain possession and sent the police back to their own twenty five with a long raking touch kick. As Evans and Badger trotted back side by side, Evans treated his friend to a stream of Welsh oaths, some of which he had found no cause to use for years. They flowed again as one of the police centres knocked on in front of his own posts from the ensuing lineout. With all the options open now to the students, Taff, as he packed down, could see the match slip from their grasp in the dying seconds.

Before getting down to what was almost certainly the last scrum of the match, Jonathan scanned the opposing backs. Their outside half stood directly behind the scrum, as if signalling an attempt at a drop goal, but Jonathan had not been impressed by his kicking and there was a tension about the fullback's stance that would not have been there if he knew his colleague was going to kick for goal. The students put the ball in and the scrum held rock solid – no chance of a pushover try against much older men. As the opposing number eight kept the ball at his feet, the outside half went to Taff's side, taking Taff with him, while the scrum half dummied away the other side. Jonathan stood up but let him go. Foreseeing as if in some slow motion dream what was about to happen, Jonathan watched their number eight stand with the ball and give a short pass to the fullback who thundered down close to the scrum like a runaway train through a narrow cutting. There was no hope of taking him from the side; even if there had been enough room, the fullback's momentum would have carried him over. The only alternative to making some token movement that, to his team mates, would mean no more than waving the man on his way, was a full-blooded, head on tackle. Even as he lowered his shoulder and bent his knees, a vision of harrowed parents tending a quadriplegic son flashed before his eyes. He must have got it just right as, feeling hardly any shock, his shoulder squeezed out a grunt from a surprisingly flabby paunch that impaled itself upon it. Straightening himself, Jonathan lifted the man off his feet before both crashed to the ground. From ten yards away, Taff Evans's voice came loud and clear.

'Nice one, doctor.'

For a millisecond, everyone stood enthralled before piling on top and the final whistle went almost unnoticed. As they disentangled themselves, the fullback, last up, turned angrily to Taff. 'Did you say "doctor"? Have you got a doctor playing for you?'

The speed of Evans's reply was matched only by the innocence of his smile. 'What's the matter? Never heard of a police surgeon?'

As they walked, happy and exhausted, back to the changing room, Jonathan was treated to all the tribal displays of acceptance, ranging from the old-fashioned pat on the shoulder to the modern-day pat on the buttock. Within minutes the shower room was full of steam, laughter, foul language and obscene jokes. Jonathan stripped off, enjoying the ache of tired muscles, beginning to feel a few bruises. At least there were showers, not the communal bath where fifteen men wallowed together in a warm, scum-topped culture of Dhobi's itch and athlete's foot. He took his place in the line of hairy nakedness. Through the steam, above the babble, he began to hear his name.

'The doctor played well today, Alf.'

'He did an' all.'

There were sniggers and faces turned Jonathan's way as he tried to look as modest as his pride would allow.

'Man of the match, wasn't he?'

'By heck he was,' Alf agreed.

Someone further down the line took it up and, for the first time, Jonathan began to feel uneasy.

'Scores one try and saves another certain one, not bad is that, for a doctor like.'

'And that tackle. Bloody hell, did you see that tackle?'

'I really don't think we should let the occasion pass, do you, lads?' Alf came back and there was a shout of assent. 'I really think he deserves his colours, does our doctor, what d'you say, Taff? You're the captain.'

From the burst of cheers that rang through the murk, most of Alf's colleagues were in agreement that Jonathan should be given his colours.

Taff Evans appeared at Jonathan's side from out of the steam. Although he grinned, he seemed to be the only one to disagree. 'No, I don't think so, lads. Chwarae teg now, boys. He only played today to help us out and it does mean we're in the final now. Let's just leave it there, shall we?'

'For goodness sake,' an embarrassed Jonathan smiled at Taff. 'I didn't do that much. I . . .'

'I don't think you quite understand, doctor. Getting your colours in this club is not quite the same as what you probably have in mind.' Evans backed away in face of the inevitable.

Jonathan turned, hearing the slapping of wet feet as dripping bodies drove in on him. In a soapy, slithery rush he found himself pinned to the floor, the rough concrete raking his shoulders and buttocks. He struggled with little hope of success against the mass of cheering, grinning young men, trained in the art of physical restraint, and was soon spreadeagled with pinioned arms and legs. To a triumphant shout, a bottle of Wintergreen was produced and half its contents poured into Jonathan's crutch. The massage that followed, as enthusiastic as it was unskilled, produced a burning that made Jonathan's writhings so desperate as to delight his tormentors. After a while, the burning was replaced by a numbness that was even more terrifying as all knowledge of what they were now doing to him was denied to his senses. He tried to lift his head and look but a hand held him by the hair. Satisfied, the onlookers began to drift back to their showers and Jonathan found his limbs freed one by one. Able at last to stand once more, he hastened to wash the target of the colour ceremony and was relieved to find the physical signs of damage did not match up with the symptoms he had suffered. Even so, he found washing a strange experience, his hands disorientated in a weightless void in an area normally so sensitive.

The students observed all the usual courtesies, providing the statutory pasty and chips and the pint of beer. The bar after the meal was crowded but subdued. One policeman, at large amongst the gossip, can ruin the most innocent of parties; a coachload in a mining community still smarting from defeat after a year-long strike, could expect no more than the basic tribal customs. The bus left early and three young men, fit and untidy, sober but high on physical excitement, found themselves adrift in Scarsby town centre. Taff looked at his watch. 'Too early for Chalky's stag party,' he muttered. 'Where shall we go?' Minutes later they were in the back bar of the 'Prince of Wales'. When Jonathan returned to the table, drinks in hand, he caught the last few words of an argument Taff Evans had already started.

'What's this about the Community Centre then?' Jonathan asked.

Evans did not give Badger time to answer. 'He's in there half the time he's off duty, Jonathan, the bloody fool. I've been telling him, if he wanted to be a social worker why didn't he go in for one like everyone else?'

'But I thought you were encouraged to mix with the community workers?' Jonathan put the question to both Taff and Badger but it was Badger who was quick to reply, the corners of his mouth dragged down cynically.

'And that's another load of rubbish. The truth is we're positively discouraged from mixing with them but just do enough to make it look as if we are.'

'You don't get too close to them.' Taff Evans's beer slopped as his glass banged on the table in time to the words. 'Once a copper, always a copper.

If you don't like it, you shouldn't have joined. There's no two ways about it, to do the job properly, you've got to be something of a bastard.'

Jonathan smiled to himself, a picture of Dai Jack flashing across his mind.

'If you can't help some frail old lady across the road in the rush hour and then turn a deaf ear to her crying when you nick her for shoplifting ten minutes later, you should get out. I've tried telling Badger here the facts of life but he just won't listen to reason, the stubborn git.'

Badger turned to Jonathan for support. 'I just think it's a waste of time trying to rehabilitate some hardened old lag. I'm not so naive as to think you can do that; there's only one way to treat them, hit them where it hurts. But the youngsters, no. Most of the kids in Northend have been brought up by villains, they don't know any better, never had anything to look up to. They're the only ones worth bothering with. You should see them – it breaks your heart the way they accept losing. They've got it down to a fine art. It's all they've known and it's strange – the more they lose the more they seem to laugh it off, almost take a pride in it. But if we can't succeed with them, we are not going to succeed at all.'

'Bit like disease,' Jonathan said. 'I must admit I've always thought the only really logical branch of my profession is preventive medicine. Much more sensible to prevent a disease than treat it.'

'Now, for God's sake, don't encourage him, doctor. I've got to listen to this for hours.' Evans shifted in his seat as if he would rather talk of something else. 'None of us has any real hope without a radical rethink of the whole problem.'

'And I suppose you've got the answer to the whole problem.' Jonathan stifled the laugh that was intended to go with the statement as he saw Evans's face unusually serious.

'Yes, I have.'

There was a snort from Badger as if he knew what was coming.

'You can't expect to hit a picket over the head with a truncheon one day and buy him a drink in here the next,' Taff argued. 'You can't give a man the steel to shoot a terrorist one day and then turn on the compassion to handle a rape victim the next. You can't blame people for associating the "police" painted on the community panda with the "police" plastered all over riot gear.'

'So what d'you reckon's the answer?' There was nothing facetious about Jonathan's tone now.

'Two forces.' The words were spoken as if blindingly obvious. 'Two forces, quite distinct from each other, so distinct that one is not associated with the other. Keep the police as they have always traditionally been thought of, keeping law and order locally in their own community. Don't expect them to be a bunch of Jekylls and Hydes. Then have another force and call them anything you like, anything but "police". Give them a new name, give them a new uniform, anything but blue, and put them under a completely separate command with separate training. Call them paramilitary if you like, a sort of civilian SAS. Let's face it, the SPG and Instant Response Units only play with it.' Evans paused for breath. 'Arthur Scargill called Orgreaves a paramilitary operation and, of course, he was right. They reckoned there was upwards of ten thousand miners at Orgreave one day last June. Ten thousand. If that's not a military operation, getting ten thousand people from all over the country in one place at the same time, what is? And, if that was military style, I don't see that he can complain if ours was paramilitary. One thing's for sure, it certainly wasn't police work as young Badger here would like it to be. So, why not do it properly? Have regional squads around the country, ready to move to other areas if the local squad is not big enough to cope with the numbers.'

He stopped to laugh, his face flushed. 'Sorry, 'mechgyn i. Put it down to my passionate Celtic nature but, believe it or not, crouching behind a riot shield in some filthy old steelworks in the Black Country, being taught how to deal with petrol bombs, was not my idea of being a copper when I joined the force either. Village bobby would have done me fine.' He rattled his glass. 'Who's ready for another?'

'But what are they going to do all day long? There's not a riot every day.'

'There's not a Falklands war every day either. So do we do away with the Army and Navy? When your aeroplane crash-lands on the runway, you expect the firemen to be there within minutes, don't you? And how many aeroplanes go up in flames every year? There are a hell of a lot of people who earn their money sitting on their arses all day, waiting for things to happen, polishing their brasswork, doing the odd dummy exercise.' He rattled his glass again. 'Come on. We're too bloody serious. It's my round.'

They watched him elbow his way to the bar and the crush closed around him. They looked up, surprised, as he reappeared, empty handed.

'Let's get out of here. I've just seen Moggie Townsend, through in the other bar, drunk and with a crowd of his cronies. And he saw me.'

'Who's he, Taff?' Jonathan asked, already on his feet.

'Villain I helped put away about two years ago. I didn't think he was out yet.'

'So what. I fancy another beer.' Badger stared ahead, his thick lips pouting.

'You damn well do as I say. Pick your stuff up and let's get the hell out of here.'

Reluctantly, Badger did as he was told and Jonathan began to walk out.

'Not that way, doctor. Let's see if we can get out this way.' Taff Evans opened the door marked 'Toilets' and Jonathan felt a knot of fear tighten in his belly as they stood, eyes straining in the gloom of a rough, foul smelling courtyard.

'There are barrels in here,' Evans whispered. 'There's got to be a door.'

As their eyes adapted and as they felt their way along a narrow passage way, they found the door, locked.

'So much for fire exits,' Taff growled. 'Put your shoulder into it.'

But neither shoulders nor feet had appreciable effect. Jonathan jumped, startled, as the door into the bar slammed once more and a figure peered at them through the darkness until the urgency of his bladder overcame his curiosity.

'All right, lift me up.' Badger, his back to the dank, filthy stones, made a stirrup out of his hands and hoisted Evans to the top of the wall where, sitting astride it, he caught their holdalls and threw them down the other side. Repeating the procedure, with Evans hauling from above, Jonathan took his place opposite Evans. Between them they heaved Badger up and over the wall. It was as Taff jumped that Jonathan heard the rush of feet, the slamming of the door, the foul cursing. He saw the spite in dim faces beyond outstretched arms and, for the first time in a sheltered life, was exposed to a merciless hatred.

Propelled by fear, he fell to the ground awkwardly, feeling a sickening wrench in his ankle. Seeing him hobble, his companions took his bag from him and helped him make the safety of a wide, brilliantly lit street.

'You all right, doctor?' Evans asked.

Jonathan nodded, now near enough to being sick to be looking around, picking his spot. 'Just twisted my ankle. I'll be all right in a minute.' Deciding perhaps he was not going to be sick after all, he looked up to see the two policemen facing each other angrily. Badger was shaking his finger in his fury.

'Don't ever ask me to do that again, d'you hear? I don't run from anyone.'

'Then more fool you, that's all I can say.' Taff Evans was equally angry. 'Moggie and his friends will still be there tomorrow. It's only a question of time before we nail them again, but on our terms, not theirs. I've no intention of ending up in hospital just because of your stupid pride. He who fights and . . .'

'Bullshit.'

The two flushed young men, oblivious of Jonathan's pallor, stared furiously at each other.

'Let's skip it,' Taff Evans snapped. 'Let's go and have a last drink with Chalky.'

It was only when they began to walk away that they remembered Jonathan and his limp. The opportunity to break away and head for his bed was swept away as Taff hailed a passing taxi. He had no idea where in Scarsby they were, what sort of pub they were entering, such was the sickening pain in his ankle as he got out of the taxi. He settled gratefully on a bench in the corner but began to enjoy the beer that Badger brought him as he became involved in conversation with a pleasant middle-aged policeman alongside him. It seemed Chalky White was the oldest unmarried Sergeant in Scarsby and the lads intended giving him a send off he would never forget. Jonathan found, to his surprise, that he still had to pay for his beer when he hobbled to the bar in spite of being relieved earlier of a £5 note by a grinning, winking Taff Evans. He was introduced briefly to the impending bridegroom who already looked as if he was unlikely to remember a moment of what was going on.

An hour later, the room resounding to male voices, Jonathan found himself being propelled upstairs by the mass of bodies. On a dusty landing, he was surprised to see the heads of two women, one a mass of jet black curls, the other's hair dyed yellow – by no stretch of the imagination could it have been described as blonde. Jonathan could not be sure but he thought he could see the pink of bare flesh through the shoulders of their transparent plastic raincoats. Their voices were thin and pinched as they pleaded with Taff for just another gin.

Jonathan was beyond the point of no return when it began to dawn on him what he had contributed £5 towards. The room they entered was large and rectangular, a line of chairs along three walls, two chairs back to back at its centre. He had hardly found a seat when Taff Evans, their master of ceremonies, announced that, at enormous expense, they had obtained the services, all the way from Lesbos, of those international artistes, Starsky and Hutch. As Jonathan watched with a kind of awful fascination the grotesque writhings and judderings of sagging bodies that were urged on to greater and greater exertions, he hoped that the grin he felt fixed on his face like a death mask would not single him out as the women began to pick out their victims for individual attention from amongst their audience. He was one of the first to head for the door when Taff announced a short interval. He found Badger alongside him as he descended the stairs.

'What did you think of that?' Jonathan asked, his only reply being a look of disgust on Badger's face.

'I thought I'd make a run for it,' Jonathan admitted.

'I'll come with you.'

As they walked along the dark street, Badger slowed his stride to allow for Jonathan's limp.

'I don't think I'll get married,' Jonathan said, laughing. 'That sort of thing can put you off sex for life.'

16

There is no such thing as the British Standard Casualty Department; no two departments are the same. They vary in size from the big specialised centres like the Birmingham Accident Hospital to the one-man, part-time, seasonal facilities so handy for cut feet at some small seaside resort and so fiercely protected by the local residents. At the upper end of the scale are the large teaching hospitals in the highly populated areas, run by teams each with their consultant and thrusting, ambitious youngsters; at the lower end, the one room run by the on-call GP in a mining valley's crumbling geriatric unit, the vestigial remains of the once-proud Miner's Hospital that had looked after its own in the days of carbolic and GP surgeons operating in their pin-stripe trousers. Scarsby General came somewhere above the middle of the scale. Hospitals smaller than Scarsby have no casualty consultant, the casualty officers who run the departments being responsible to the consultant orthopaedic surgeons who visit the department only on request. Such had been the arrangement when Bob Bannerman had taken over Scarsby General's department, reluctantly sliding sideways off the promotional ladder towards orthopaedic consultancy. The orthopaedic surgeons, previously responsible, had handed over gladly to Bannerman, giving him a free hand to reorganise at his pleasure. For a while, the enjoyment of laying down the rules of procedure in his new little empire had dulled the pain of disappointment but it had not been long before he could think of no more innovations to introduce, no more clinics to set up in his efforts to give some variety to what he knew must become a nerve-stripping conveyor belt. As measured by all the possible combinations and permutations of their injuries, the variety of cases that came through the Casualty entrance was infinite but they came through the door with a grinding regularity that soon eroded the early enthusiasm, thinning it down to a self-protective crust that, to the ignorant, appeared to be, at best, hard cynicism, at worst, insensitive black humour. Once one has seen one battered wife, one has seen them all; once one has seen a child with 80 per cent scalds, one has seen them all. Mere variations on a theme.

There was no good reason why Jonathan should be any exception – and he was not. He had been working in Scarsby long enough now to look forward to his own personal follow-up clinic as a break from the seemingly endless queue of new patients. He considered it one of Bannerman's better ideas, to give the casualty officers the chance to see the end results of their own handiwork, take pride in their successes, learn from their mistakes. It was minor but gratifying surgery. It was encouraging to a young surgeon to see cut tendons move again, the small skin graft pink and healthy, the septic finger healed and mobile. It was a clinic of good results and high morale in patients frequently young and otherwise fit. For the first time, Jonathan was being totally responsible for a patient's treatment from first to last and, with the respect it brought him, he was also experiencing what went with it, the inevitable awe-inspired distance between himself and another human being. Jonathan never failed to be amused as the box of chocolates was always given to the pretty nurse on the way out from the final consultation.

He was gently laying down the law to a timid man whose septic finger he had incised some days before.

'Now move it, Mr Whittle, d'you hear? Move it. It's not going to come to any harm now; it's going to heal whatever you do to it. The only danger now is that you end up with a finger that is healed but useless because it's stiff. Do you understand now, Mr Whittle?'

He looked up and over his shoulder to see Sister Gaunt hovering like some dark predatory angel.

'Come and see me again next week, Mr Whittle, but remember now, move it!'

As the patient got up and left, Jonathan looked up to see Sister Gaunt raise her hand to prevent the nurse bringing in the next patient. He swivelled in his chair, surprise on his face.

'I'm sorry, Dr Brookes. I know you're busy but I need your help. Would you have a look at Mr Bannerman for me? I think he's . . .' she hesitated, 'I think he's ill. Would you come, please?'

He followed the flat feet and drooping shoulders along the corridor, guided by the sound of Bannerman's voice thundering above the screams of a child. They turned into the small operating theatre. A young woman, her face tear stained, sat on a stool near the head of the table, holding the hand of a squirming, bellowing, terrified youngster of about 10. She looked appealingly at Jonathan. Bannerman looked back over his shoulder as he heard them come in. His tone was booming, his mannerisms expansive.

'What's this, young Brookes? Finished your clinic already?' He looked at his wrist. 'S'not half-past two yet. Cured them all already?'

'You know me, Mr Bannerman.' It was not as important to scrub as thoroughly for a laceration as for a craniotomy but Jonathan glanced at Bannerman's watch, tight in the hairy groove between wrist and hand, before smiling reassuringly at the woman. 'I don't hang around. I just wondered, as I'd finished so early, whether you would like me to take over?'

'Why?' As he swung round in exaggerated surprise, Bannerman had to take a short step backwards as he swayed off balance. He steadied himself on a 10-year-old's shoulder.

Jonathan came alongside his chief and saw the laceration, a jagged cut running from the temple alongside the corner of the eye to the cheek. A piece of gravel, grey against the living colours, protruded from under one skin flap. Two clumsy looking sutures had already been inserted, the skin around showing the small pock marks of inaccurate previous attempts.

'That'll teach the young varmint to go falling off swings, won't it, mother?' It took a second or so for Bannerman's eyes to focus in an attempt to control a shaking hand.

'Fact is, Mr Bannerman, . . .'

'Why don't you call me Bob like everyone else, you prissy bastard.'

'All right, Bob then. But the fact still remains, we've got a problem we'd like you to sort out for us. It's Janet actually.' Jonathan extemporised. 'She's got in a bit of a panic and asked me to call you. I'll finish this off for you.' Jonathan began to take off his white coat.

'Our fair Janet in a panic? I just don't believe it. That cold fish? That'll be the day when anyone gets some emotion out of that girl.' Without a word of explanation to the child's mother, he put his instruments down and began searching in his pockets, muttering to himself. His face suddenly darkened with mock anger. 'What have you done with my cigars, Maisie? Maisie, where have you hidden them?' His voice rose theatrically. 'Shall there be no more cakes and ale because thou art a puritan?'

Seeing her chance, Sister Gaunt said, 'They're in your office, Mr Bannerman. I'll come and help you find them.'

As Bannerman left, a jerk of Jonathan's head brought Sister Gaunt to his side as he scrubbed. 'Well done, Sister,' he whispered. 'Just keep him there until I've finished and then I'll take him home.'

'And how do I do that, Dr Brookes? You know what he's like.'

'Give him another drink; probably the best way.'

'Where can I get one?'

'He didn't go out lunchtime.' He turned his head for a moment to give an anxious mother a topping up dose of reassuring smile. 'He must have been drinking in his room. That means there must be a bottle there. Filing cabinet is the classical place, I believe; usually a square or triangular bottle, one that doesn't roll around as the cabinet is opened and shut.'

Maisie raised one eyebrow as if wondering where a young man got such knowledge but she said nothing, turning to follow Bannerman. She had only taken one stride before Jonathan called her back.

'And get his car keys,' he whispered urgently.

'And how do I do that?'

'I don't know; just get them.'

Back at the operating table, Jonathan began winning back two people's confidence, explaining he was going to clean the whole thing up again and put some anaesthetic in this time to take the pain away. It might still hurt a little now and again but he looked a brave lad and footballers like Ian Rush had stitches all the time and who were his favourite team?

Quivering lips finally managed 'Everton.'

'Everton? That bunch of crocks? They couldn't . . .'

Jonathan smiled his farewell to mother and son at the theatre door, the mother too meek and too grateful to Jonathan to make any fuss. Hurriedly, he pulled his white coat back on and made for the follow-up clinic. He walked in just in time to see Bannerman, in his shirt sleeves, his head lowered to desk-top level, blow some ash that had fallen from his cigar, an 80-year-old lady looking enquiringly at a despairing Maisie as the fall out gently dusted the unhealed scald on her forearm. His voice and face hardening in youthful disgust, Jonathan strode to the desk and took Bannerman by the arm, trying to lift him out of his chair. Bannerman looked up at him, his eyes shuttering against the rising cigar smoke. 'Dear boy. Finished that case already?'

'You are wanted out in intensive care, Mr Bannerman.' He pulled at the back of Bannerman's chair. 'Please, Mr Bannerman, you're needed outside.'

Expecting an embarrassing struggle, Jonathan was surprised by a sudden smiling compliance, Bannerman allowing himself to be guided by the arm like a blind man. As they passed Sister Gaunt, Jonathan held out his hand 'I believe you've got some keys for me, Sister?'

Without a word, Maisie lifted her apron, thrust one hand in her pocket and came out with Bannerman's car keys.

'Will you carry on here, Sister?' Sister Gaunt nodded. 'And tell Dr James I won't be available for an hour or so.' Thoughts of how Janet was going to cope were of secondary importance to Jonathan, his mind preoccupied with how to keep a drunk colleague away from his patients. His only immediate idea was to get him in his own office and behind closed doors. As the door closed behind them, he stood, nonplussed, as Bannerman poured himself another drink and swallowed it with neither pleasure nor distaste. Bannerman sat at his desk to gaze up at Jonathan with a flat, meaningless smile.

'You are a prissy bastard, you know, Brookes.'

'So I believe, Mr Bannerman.'

'So I believe, Mr Bannerman,' Bannerman mimed. 'Still can't call me "Bob", can you? Nor "sir" either.' His face hardened. 'Never call me "sir", do you?'

'That's a term I reserve for a few very special people, Mr Bannerman. There has been no disrespect intended.'

'Not until now, eh?' Bannerman slowly, sadly, stubbed out his cigar.

'I think you ought to go home, Mr Bannerman. I'll drive you. Perhaps Mrs Bannerman will come back with me and pick your car up.'

'You're a hard bastard too, Dr Jonathan Brookes, Ph.D.'

'Not everyone would agree with you there, I'm afraid.' A mental picture of brown eyes and early morning mist was wiped clean as too precious to play a part in such a scenario.

'Then they'd be wrong. I've seen it before. All the boys who make it to the top have got it; and you're going to make it to the top, you take it from me. I've seen it all.' He looked longingly at the filing cabinet and Jonathan walked around the cramped room to close it and lean against it. Bannerman sniggered. 'This beer drinking, rugby playing, rich, handsome young bachelor stuff – bullshit, that's what it is. Just part of the charade. The establishment like it; fits in with the mental picture they like to have of themselves at that age. "Hell of a boy when he was on the house", that's how the most senior in the land like to think they were. And were they? Not on your precious life. All as careful as hell; never put a foot wrong. Never got tight one night, put someone up the spout, someone who refused to go off nice and quietly and have an abortion. Nothing like that ever happened to them. Oh, no. Much too careful.' He paused, his face twisting as if finding some reminiscence bitter in his mind, before looking accusingly at Jonathan. 'Did you ever get to find out the truth about our Gorgeous Gussie's knickers afterwards?'

'Come on, Mr Bannerman; let me take you home now.'

'Thought not,' Bannerman said with scorn, spitting a fragment of cigar leaf on to the desk. For what seemed to Jonathan an age, he glowered at the desk top, abstractedly cleaning his finger nails as he ground his way yet again through his unfair share of life's injustice. Looking up suddenly, he saw Jonathan between himself and the filing cabinet. He stood, took a moment to steady himself and was out through the door before Jonathan could gather his thoughts. By the time he had caught up with Bannerman, they were the centre of a busy department's attention as Bannerman took his generous farewells. In the casualty yard, Bannerman walked to Jonathan's car without a glance at his own, staggering, to the obvious amusement of a group of ambulance drivers, as he opened the door. While Bannerman sat, sphinx-like throughout, Jonathan was obliged to stretch across and close the passenger door, braving the smell of stale booze and cigars to fasten his chief's safety belt. He started the engine.

'I'm afraid I don't know where you live, Mr Bannerman. You'll have to direct me.'

The only response was an extravagant flourish through the windscreen at Scarsby General's stone wall. Out into the street and Bannerman waved right and left, the only sound he made being grunted heavy breathing as if in pain. Half a dozen turns and Jonathan felt he had driven that way before. Another right hander and the squash club came into view.

'Oh, no!' He accelerated sharply but his passenger, using his considerable strength against the car's momentum, opened his door and would have fallen out but for his harness. Jonathan braked and there followed a struggle for command of the door as the car swerved violently. He brought the car to an untidy halt and moments later was watching powerful, hunched shoulders recede along the pavement. Passenger door open, engine running, he pondered what to do. He felt he owed the man nothing. He had already done more than might be expected of him. Bannerman would find his own way home. He'd probably done that more than once. It was not as if Bannerman was going to be influential in some future appointment. If it had been one of the Liverpool consultants now, well . . .

'Oh, shit!' He pulled at the door viciously and drove into the squash club car park.

For more than an hour he was obliged to humour a bitter, disappointed man, murmuring inanely in accompaniment to wearying self-pity, longing desperately for Bannerman to show some sign of flagging. It was almost six o'clock by the time a front door was opened for Jonathan to present Bannerman's wife with a leering, wobbling husband. It had been his firm intention to cut and run at that stage but events overtook him once more. Bannerman's wife stepped silently aside as he tottered into the hall. She showed not the slightest surprise as he tripped to hurtle headlong across the hall and crack his head against the bottom banister. He lay on the floor, rubbing his scalp vigorously, his fingers coming away blood-stained. His wife stood, a disinterested spectator, as Jonathan heaved and hauled Bannerman to his feet. Without a word of thanks or a backward glance,

Scarsby's casualty consultant laboriously climbed the stairs and disappeared.

Jonathan turned to leave only to find his retreat cut off as Mrs Bannerman closed the door in his face. She walked passed him without looking at him and into a small lounge. Jonathan followed. He could do little else.

'Where did you find him?'

Jonathan thought quickly; there seemed little point in worrying her unduly.

'In the squash club.'

'Oh, there.' She pointed to a chair. 'Sit down.' With an economy of movement that would have warmed the heart of any time and motion expert, she lit a cigarette, inhaled and held her breath so long that very little smoke emerged as she sighed. 'That bloody place. Would you like a drink?'

Holding up his hand, Jonathan declined her offer politely. 'No, thank you, Mrs Bannerman. I have to drive back.'

'Dawn.'

'I beg your pardon?' Jonathan looked puzzled.

'The name's Dawn.'

Not knowing what to say, he fished in his pocket, withdrew Bannerman's car keys and held them towards her. 'Perhaps you would like me to drive you back to hospital to pick your car up?'

It was as if he had not spoken. 'You don't mind if I have one, do you? Are you sure you won't join me?' She left him, arm outstretched, keys dangling, as she turned to an assortment of bottles on a table beside the fire.

The Bannerman ménage had not been quite what he had expected, not what he had become accustomed to in the Liverpool consultants' Christmas parties. The crescent of semis had been built about the same time as the Northend estate, but for Scarsby's better-off tradespeople and bank clerks. As Jonathan had leaned down to help Bannerman where he had fallen in the hall, he had noticed the paintwork, fifty years of home decorating, layer on chipped layer. Through the window, there was still enough light for him to see a small unloved lawn and neglected flower beds.

'Well, and how's dear old Scarsby General then?' She sank languidly into her chair as if she intended staying there some time, thrusting out her legs, her jeans tight stretched across her thighs. She shook a soft white moccasin off one foot and wriggled her toes. With her free hand, glass and cigarette held expertly in the other, she pulled her jumper taut.

Jonathan decided she must have been very attractive once. He had second thoughts. She still was, peel away a layer of sloppy indifference, apply a little loving care. She was tall and slow-moving with straight auburn hair that would never look anything but tidy.

'The General? I can't say I see much of the hospital outside Cas but I don't imagine it has changed much since your day.'

She gave a short laugh. 'So you know all about that, do you? The old grapevine hasn't changed much obviously.'

Jonathan flushed. 'Well, you know how these places are.'

'I do,' she said. 'I certainly do.'

'Do you go back very often?'

'What, go back to the General? The girls would think I was slumming and the consultants would have nothing to do with someone who broke up a colleague's marriage. It doesn't take long to find out,' unhurriedly, she filled her mouth with smoke, removed the cigarette and sucked in air noisily through tight lips, 'that marrying a consultant isn't always a one-way ticket into high society.'

'Why don't you go back to work?'

Jonathan's question caught her as she stretched to stub out her cigarette. She paused to squint at him through eyes half-closed against the acrid smoke rising from the ashtray. 'You're sweet,' was her only comment. She stood and crossed to pick up the sherry bottle once more, passing close enough to make him tuck his feet under him. She raised it and one eyebrow, smiling encouragingly at Jonathan, but again he shook his head. She sat once more to gaze at him coolly. 'Are you really as sexy as they all say you are? Bob brings me all the news,' she explained.

Jonathan began to enjoy the novel thrill of being seduced. It was a change not to be the initiator – perhaps this was always the way with a married woman. She couldn't be more than a year or so older than he was.

'I'm sure I wouldn't know about that, Mrs Bannerman.'

'Would you consider going to bed with me?'

'I . . . I . . .'

Jonathan stammered, lost for something to say, as Bannerman's car keys fell from his hand to the floor. He heard her low throaty laugh as he stooped to retrieve them before getting to his feet. 'I must go,' he said, trying to overcome the tremor in his voice sufficiently to sound determined. 'If there is any difficulty about fetching the car, perhaps you would give me a ring?'

He had to wait as she took her time over getting up and leading him to the front door. For a moment, she stood with her back to it, barring his way.

'You're nice. You must come again. I'd ask you to come and have dinner with us one night except we don't have people to dinner. We ought to, shouldn't we? Isn't that what a proper consultant's wife is supposed to do, entertain all the little surgeons? Never mind' – the tip of her tongue appeared fleetingly between her lips – 'I'm sure we'll think of something.'

As Jonathan drove away, he found his palms cold with sweat.

Jonathan paced irregularly between kitchen and living room, trying simultaneously to cook himself an evening meal and watch the *Six O'Clock News*. He was passing the phone in the hallway as it rang. He picked it up to stand, phone in one hand, saucepan in the other. He had no time to speak before he recognised Janet James's voice, hurried and urgent.

'Is your TV on?'

'Yes.'

'What are you watching?'

'BBC News.'

'Turn to the local ITV. Quickly.'

The phone in his hand fell silent and he hurriedly dropped it back in place, strode into his living room to stab his finger into the remote control on the arm of his chair. A man's head and shoulders appeared and Jonathan, assuming that what the man was saying must be the reason for Janet's frantic call, listened intently.

'... were naturally very concerned about what they saw as a threat to their livelihood in the form of privatisation of the support services, in keeping with the heartless attitude of Thatcherism when it came to jobs. While the laundry workers fully realised their inability to influence central policy making in such a rigid, unfeeling bureaucracy, they had felt it necessary to make their point. That had been the sole purpose of the picket which would now be withdrawn at midday.'

Slowly, Jonathan closed a gaping mouth and swallowed hard as his astonishment grew. The man was black, his voice instantly recognisable and yet it had taken several seconds for Jonathan to accept what he saw. The screen might have been flat but it had given Gavin Prescott a new dimension, standing out as he so arrogantly did from the row of mutely self-conscious strikers who stood in a banner-wielding arc before the closed gates to some crumbling Victorian building. His astonishment waning, Jonathan went back to listening to what Gavin was saying, marvelling at the unhurried certainty of his speech, admitting to himself that he had heard leaders of national unions interviewed on the steps of TUC Headquarters who had sounded far less fluent.

'His members could always depend on the Union's support in their struggle against the run down of the Health Service. In the face of the Government circulars on competitive tendering, issued to the Health Authorities, the Union had co-operated with management in bringing about internal savings in the support services of between half and one million pounds. If, in spite of this, those services were to be put out to tender, then the Union would feel free to take whatever action was considered appropriate at the time. There would be no compromise, no picking off isolated services like the laundry just to placate their political masters. As he had made quite plain at the last meeting of the Joint Consultative Committee, if they wanted confrontation, they could have it.'

As Gavin's image faded, Jonathan switched the TV off, wanting nothing to dilute or trivialise what he had just seen and heard. As he ate a lonely meal, a new respect for Gavin Prescott made him wonder just how patronising his relationship with Gavin had been. For all his expensive education, for all the privilege and culture of his upbringing, Jonathan knew in his heart that he could never stand up in front of a camera and talk like that.

17

It was only Sandy. He was not all that well known at the General but at the Mental Hospital he was something of an institution. Sandy Ollerinshaw had been unfortunate enough to be born into a generation when the village idiot had gone out of fashion, had become socially undesirable, had been locked away with the insane where he belonged. When fashion changed and families were bullied and bribed into taking the harmless souls back into the fold, Sandy's family had moved on and he had nowhere to go. But Sandy had had one thing going for him — happiness to him was a sharp garden shears in his hand and a mile of privet hedge disappearing into the distance, or a spade and an acre of kitchen garden to dig. Another of Sandy's endearing characteristics had been his indifference as to whether the garden had belonged to the hospital or to the Medical Superintendent. A decree had been issued from the Superintendent's office that Sandy's services should not be lost to the hospital – something had to be done for him. So, while Sandy had continued to eat with the patients, a room had been found for him over the old, stone-built porter's lodge. For the first time, Sandy had found himself with a few pounds in his pocket and he had made one corner of the local pub his own.

The Mental Hospital's Records Officer had nearly fainted when Sandy had walked into her room and dripped blood all over her desk. His smile had still been warm and friendly as he had held out his hand with the gashed little finger. The morning ambulance to the General had already gone and the Sandy Ollerinshaws of this world do not warrant ambulances on their own merely for a split finger. Some bandage had been found, they had made sure he had enough money, and they had explained to him in detail how to catch the bus. He had waited placidly in the queue before being seen by Janet James. She had passed him on to Jonathan who was happy enough to work in theatre all day with such a cracking-looking nurse to help him. She looked not unlike Dawn Bannerman and was doing nothing to damp down a tense excitement that growled away deep in his gut, making it difficult to keep his mind on his job. All he could see was an attractive woman with her back to a door, smiling, saying, 'Time enough'. All was well with his world.

'This is Sandy,' the nurse said. 'Cut your finger, haven't you, Sandy?'

Sandy smiled the genuine, generous smile of the simple-minded when treated with kindness. Intelligent people don't look like that when they walk into a Casualty theatre with a bad laceration and Jonathan summed the situation up instantly. He pointed to the operating table.

'Jump up on there, Sandy, and let's have a look at it, shall we?'

Jonathan watched as the nurse removed the bandage. He took Sandy's right hand in his, turning it palm up. The pulps of the two distal segments of his little finger were split down to bone, the skin edges dirty and bruised. There was another small bruise in the palm of his hand. 'Can you move it?' he asked.

Sandy's response was a vigorous gripping movement that splayed widely the wound edges to reveal a flexor tendon glistening and gliding in its depth. The wound began to bleed quite vigorously.

'Woah. Hang on. Gently does it,' Jonathan laughed, and Sandy laughed with him.

'How did you do it?'

The smile only deepened.

'Can you feel that?' Jonathan asked, scratching the thick-skinned tip of a gardener's finger, but got no reply. 'All right then, Sandy. Just lie back and we'll look after you.'

It was the fifth laceration Jonathan had sewn up that morning. Surgery had suddenly got easy. He nodded as the nurse waved the bottle of local anaesthetic in front of his face. Sandy lay so still that, apart from the occasional smile of encouragement, Jonathan was able to resume his discussion of the merits of favourite pop groups which brought him to ask the nurse's opinion as to the best club in Scarsby on a Saturday night. Ten minutes later, his suture line looked so neat he was reluctant to cover it with a dressing, taking a moment to admire his handiwork as he rubbed the pallid base of the finger where he had injected the local anaesthetic.

'There you go, Sandy. Good as new.' He helped his patient off the table even though Sandy hardly looked the sort to faint on standing up. 'I'm afraid you'll need your jabs, especially as you're a gardener. Nurse will look after that for you.'

'Come on, Sandy. I'll show you where the canteen is, get you a cup of tea. Would you like that? How did you come in? On the bus? You wait in the canteen; I'll see if I can find an ambulance going your way. Going to have to stick a needle in your backside first though, I'm afraid.'

Jonathan whistled quietly to himself as he washed his hands.

Jonathan Brookes was no mean cook – living proof of the fact that it is possible to be good at something one does not enjoy doing. He had a healthy young man's appetite and he was hungry. It had been a hard day. Bannerman had been away at a meeting and Jonathan had had to do his clinics as well as the routine stuff. There had been no question of lunch. And the wok his step-mother Alison had given him for Christmas was proving a great success. He was also excited without daring to analyse the reason for being so. He jumped at the doorbell's discord even though he had been half-expecting it. Though not totally surprised when he saw who it was who stood in the doorway, he managed to appear so.

'Can I smell cooking?' Dawn Bannerman asked.

Jonathan was about to ask her in when she walked past him. A glance around her and she headed for the sound of cooking.

'Want any help?' she called back over her shoulder.

'No. I can cope,' Jonathan smiled.

'In that case, get a girl a drink and I'll have a look around. And don't take too long; I'm famished. You have got enough for two? You were expecting me?'

As she laughed at his confusion, Jonathan asked her what she wanted to drink. 'I don't keep sherry,' he apologised. 'Would a gin and tonic do?'

'Not that much of a specialist,' she murmured over her shoulder and when Jonathan found her to give her the drink, she was thumbing through a pile of his magazines. 'The *Autocar* and *The British Journal of Surgery*. That figures,' she said as she took her drink.

Back at his cooking, Jonathan heard her moving from room to room. He heard a cupboard door squeak; even the downstairs loo door opened and shut. She appeared at the kitchen door to lean against the doorpost.

'Nice,' she said. 'Much as I would have expected. Male without being too macho; plenty of books, not too tidy. And you're no poofter, though I did wonder.'

'How on earth can you tell that?' Jonathan laughed.

'No flowers and the curtains. Always look at the curtains. No woman would have chosen those.'

'Thanks; I'll remember that. You never know; that scrap of information might save me a lot of bother one day. Not that you're altogether correct as it was my step-mother who chose those when I moved in. I wouldn't know one curtain from another.'

'Then she must be very fond of you, your step-mother, because she was obviously thinking of you and not of herself when she did so.'

'That's very profound, Mrs Bannerman. Here; your supper's ready. D'you mind eating it out here in the kitchen?'

They both ate heartily with no thought of a world outside, their conversation becoming easier as their stomachs filled. There was no question of washing dirty dishes as Jonathan gave her the two coffee cups and told her to go through to the lounge.

'Remy Martin?' he asked.

'Beats hell out of the cooking brandy we have to settle for.'

By the time Jonathan handed her the brandy goblet, she had settled into his most comfortable chair. He raised his drink. 'Cheers.' His glass halfway to his lips, he hesitated. He saw her staring into the clear brown fluid she swirled silently with one hand while tracing with one finger of the other the pattern cut into the glass. 'Something wrong?' he asked.

She raised her eyes slowly.

'Are you coming to bed with me?'

She got no reply but one look at his face told her that, this time, there was to be no escape for him.

'Because, if you are not, and you are going to throw me out to drive home, then I cannot drink this – and I do so want to.' She drew the words out seductively. 'You've known as well as I have that my lord and master has this two day symposium in Oxford – I do hope the poor dear is not making a complete bloody fool of himself in the dinner tonight – so you are quite safe. No one is going to find out. And I am not in love with you so you need have no fear on that score. So; what d'you say?'

Jonathan tried not to make it obvious he had to moisten his lips but found he had to clear his throat before replying.

'Drink up, Mrs Bannerman. I would hate to be thought inhospitable.'

'Good. In that case, cheers.' She took a minute sip from her brandy. 'There's no hurry then, is there?'

A week had been long enough for a troubled conscience to have given way slowly to a recurrent, restless urge. For a few days, Jonathan had avoided Bannerman at all costs, unable to face him without a feeling of shame. As the days had gone by, he had begun to wonder how often his chief went to meetings. Now he was getting to the stage of not caring, subconsciously contriving all manner of clandestine assignations as he did his job with an air of abstraction that had not gone unnoticed.

'Peggy reckons you're in love. Is that true?' Badger had asked one night, grinning at the guilty confusion it had aroused. 'Good for you. Do we know her?'

He felt ten feet tall. He felt a man. He stood full square, confident in his own ability to tackle anything thrown at him. A man on top of his job. Someone who was going to be a consultant general surgeon – no sweat. And not just any old consultant surgeon but a top one. In his mind's eye he could see the jobs he would need to get, the qualifications he would need at each individual stage to make it impossible for any selection committee to refuse him. All he had to do then was to keep his nose clean.

In the meanwhile, there was the small matter of his follow-up clinic.

The first sign of trouble was the expression on the nurse's face as she led Sandy Ollerinshaw in. The second was the expression on Sandy's. The friendly smile was still there but it struggled gamely against the muddy pallor of severe toxaemia. His eyes, sunken and dull, looked anxiously at Jonathan. Sandy didn't enjoy feeling like this. Who was going to dig over the flower beds? No one did them the way he did. He felt ill. Was the doctor going to make it better for him? Jonathan's heart had turned over at the sight of Sandy's face. Now he struggled not to close his eyes, anything to shut out that look of implicit faith.

Sandy sat in the chair alongside Jonathan's desk, his shirt removed, the Medical Superintendent's old, discarded, pin-striped jacket draped over his shoulders. Outside, they had removed his dressing, replacing it with a temporary one. As Sandy lifted his arm on to the desk, his jacket slipped back to reveal the tell-tale angry red lines streaming up the inside of his arm. Momentarily losing control of his feelings, Jonathan closed his eyes. When he reopened them, the lines had not gone away. He slid a hand into Sandy's armpit to feel the swollen glands. He looked up at the nurse.

'Temperature?'

'Thirty-eight point five.'

Jonathan smiled encouragingly at Sandy as he steeled himself to remove the dressing, holding his head still against the instinctive reaction of pulling away from the stench that resulted from doing so. All his worst fears were confirmed. The little finger was black, the sutures, so neat and tidy one week before, now almost invisible where they cut into livid, swollen skin edges. Thin, bloodstained fluid leaked between the stitches and a brawny swelling extended back into the palm. Gingerly, Jonathan prodded the back of Sandy's hand with his finger, giving silent thanks when he failed to feel the crepitus that would herald gas gangrene.

'How long has it been like this?' Jonathan asked but only had a worried frown in reply.

'Why didn't you come . . .?' Jonathan's words tailed away as he realised he was just trying to shift the blame for his handiwork on to the patient. That hand was the result of his treatment, no one else's, and the sooner he accepted that, the better. The nausea he felt had nothing to do with the sight or the smell; he had seen and smelt wounds like that before but then they had been someone else's troubles, this one was down to him and no one else. He pulled the gauze back over the finger like drawing a veil over a disfigurement.

'That's going to need a bit more treatment, isn't it, Sandy?' The hypocrisy of each smiling word cut like a knife. 'Probably need another small operation but then you'll feel well again. You don't want to go round feeling the way you do at the moment, do you?'

The smile struggled back as Sandy shook his head. Jonathan turned to the nurse. 'Take those sutures out, soon as you can, please, nurse. Just let the wound gape. Don't pack it. I'll be along in a minute to give him some antibiotics but I'd like Mr Bannerman to see this.'

Bannerman took one look at the finger and handled the situation like the expert he was. 'You look a bit rough, old chap. Feeling lousy?'

Sandy warmed to this man who smelt of cigars.

'That finger – not much good to you any more, I'm afraid, old chap. I'm afraid you're going to lose it. Must have been some infection you got in it when you did it. Gardener, aren't you?'

Sandy nodded proudly.

'Yes; that would be it then. Don't worry. Dr Brookes here will look after it for you.'

Behind Sandy's back, Bannerman jerked his head at Jonathan and Jonathan followed him out and into his office. He closed the door behind him and Bannerman waved him to the chair. Jonathan sat, expecting the bollocking that he hoped would come to help purge him of an overwhelming feeling of guilt. All he got was a sympathetic smile.

'Drink?' The smile broadened into a grin as Bannerman pointed towards the filing cabinet.

'Oh, God, no, thank you.'

'I suppose it is a bit early, even for me.' He sat opposite Jonathan, stretched for an old cigar stub and relit it. 'Hurts, doesn't it?'

'What d'you mean?'

'Your pride.'

Jonathan tried to look as if he didn't know what Bannerman meant. 'The poor old devil looks so awful.'

'He'll be all right. And not so much of the old. He's not much older than I am. Is he on antibiotics?'

'Yes, I've started him intravenously and taken a swab.'

'Amazing to think, isn't it, that – what, fifty years ago? – he would be dead in another forty eight hours, with that lymphangitis. They'd have been debating whether to amputate his arm or not. Haemolytic strep would be my guess.'

'As it is, he's still going to lose his finger, isn't he?'

'Sure. But he'll be all right.' Bannerman looked closely at Jonathan, a kindly note in his voice. 'Do you want me to do it?'

'No.' Jonathan answered hurriedly. 'No, I'll do it.'

'He'll need a GA and he'll need to be admitted for a day or so. Find him a bed but arrange to do it down here; I don't imagine either the general surgeons or the orthopods will be too keen to dirty their hands with that one, so you won't have much problem. If you do, give me a shout and I'll sort the bastards out.'

'I suppose I'd better not excise the head of the metacarpal?'

'No. No point in risking spreading the infection by cutting through bone. Take it through the joint. I'd be inclined to leave the wound open, maybe do a secondary suture later.'

Jonathan hung his head. 'God, it's going to look awful.'

'Won't be too bad, once it's healed. Don't look so glum. After all, it's a daft-as-a-brush gardener you're dealing with, not some concert pianist.'

'Not the point.'

Bannerman laughed with something close to affection. 'Don't punish yourself. There's a good surgical reason for leaving the metacarpal; he'll be able to grip his spade much better with it than without it.' He took a last deep inhalation from a stub so small he could hardly hold it. He wheezed words of comfort as he ground it into the ash tray.

'It happens, Jonathan. It happens.'

'But, what did I do wrong?'

Bannerman stood suddenly. He held up his hand. 'Oh, no. None of that. I hold young surgeons' hands; I have always reckoned that went with the job. But I don't take confessionals. You saw the finger as it was, you know what you did to it, you've seen the result. You've got a far better brain than I have. You work it out.'

Jonathan picked up the phone and dialled a Liverpool number. There was no reply. He dialled another Liverpool number. This time there was.

'Royal Liverpool.'

'Dr Susannah Ridgeway, please.'

'Just a moment, sir.' A pause. 'Sorry, sir; Dr Ridgeway's away on leave.'

He went out, got in his car and drove. He pulled in to the curb, looked up at the light in Janet James's bed-sit, changed his mind and drove on. He thought of the Kincaids – an hour or so with Vicki would cheer him up – but then he remembered – Badger had told him she had moved to Liverpool. He only had one thought about the Bannermans. He had been a bastard to do it in the first place but never again could he make a cuckold of a man who had been so kind to him.

He parked in the centre of Scarsby and walked the streets, looking in coldly lit shop windows, hands in pockets, head down. A young policeman said 'Good evening,' suspiciously. He saw the pub he had run away from after the rugby match and went in. Badger and Taff's company had blinded him to just how seedy the place was. He drank a lonely pint of flat, bitter beer which did nothing to wash away the smell of necrotic tissue that would linger for days. He drove home, undressed, climbed into bed and prayed for sleep.

18

It was a still, clear Saturday morning in early May, breathless with the hope of summer to come. In Surrey, a boy woke to the dormitory's chill austerity, the youngest to be selected for the first eleven in living memory. In Hampshire, a boy woke to the thought of the new dinghy and the first club race of the season. In Gwynedd, a boy woke in the Spartan healthiness of an Outward Bound camp, his hands already itching for the feel of rope and canoe paddle. In Northumberland, a boy woke, hours away from his first outdoor athletics meeting.

Danny Shufflebottom just woke.

He wished he hadn't. His thigh hurt. He turned over, dragged the sheet over his head to keep out the sunlight and tried to pass some time in sleep. It was too hot under the sheet and it smelled. He thrust his head out again with a sigh of disgust and stared at the ceiling. There was one particularly big crack that started at one edge of the ceiling to branch again and again amongst the verdant damp patches, rather like the rivers he had seen in one of the maps in school. For a while, he shot rapids in a dug-out canoe, fighting off cannibals and pygmies, shooting crocodiles that were just about to eat his most faithful native bearer. As a vivid imagination stamped on a deadly snake that had struck from the jungle undergrowth, his real-life leg twitched in sympathy and he gave a yelp as real-life pain dispelled all thoughts of Central Africa.

A hell of a lot of use, those karate lessons, if he couldn't get out of the way of a drunken boot up the arse. He felt beneath his T-shirt, all he wore, pressed the spot and winced.

He looked at the sunshine outside, the blue sky smudged and smeared by the dirty window. He had tried going for a run like Gavin had told him, had felt quite proud of himself in the old tracksuit Gavin had lent him. He was never going to do that again. He remembered coming round the corner by the new snooker hall and running into the arms of that mean lot of bastards from Grimsdyke Square. Bugger that for a lark.

At such times there are no signs of Gavin Prescotts or Youth Organisers, no friendly village Bobby or urban Seventh Cavalry to appear and protect the individual's right to an independent existence outside the tribal street warfare that, for the majority of Northend's youngsters, was a pastime in which there was no close season.

Danny was hungry but knew that the moment he gave in to his hunger and went downstairs he was committed to the day, another bloody day. He closed his eyes, his hands caressing, fantasising that the love they brought was not his own. Gasping and empty, he cried, tearlessly, into the pillow and, the sun now strong through the window, fell asleep.

The noise from the next bedroom woke him the second time. He put his head under the pillow but still heard it, the rhythmic, wordless humping creak he hated. Within minutes, he had pulled on grey, stained underpants and jeans, ragged jumper and trainers, and was in the kitchen. He found the cornflake packet and opened the fridge door, closing it again with a sigh. He boiled the kettle, made a pot of tea and waited patiently for it to cool. He was pouring it on his cornflakes when his mother appeared. It was warm enough for her not to have bothered with her dressing gown.

'Any sugar, Ma?'

'Should be, Danny. Try on the shelf.' She sat, poured herself a cup of tepid tea and drank, her elbows on the table, staring vacantly, showing little evidence of post-coital bliss. 'What you doing today, then?'

'I'm going out.'

'Where are you going?'

'Got things to do, haven't I?'

'Now, I don't want you hanging round that bus station, d'you hear? I know that's where you go. I've seen you there. They're a bad lot, them; d'you hear me?'

'Yes, Ma.'

'That boy of Dolly Budge's. He was one of them lot. And you know what became of him. He was into drugs and that. Now you keep away from there, d'you hear?'

She shouted the last few words, trying to make them carry above the slam of the door.

The same sun that shone down on Epsom downs and the Hamble, on Snowdonia and Geordieland, warmed the back of a sensitive, gifted youngster who stood on a street, trying to decide whether to turn right or left, unwashed, with nothing in his pockets but his hands, devoid of anyone's concern where or when he ate next. The problem of the next ten minutes was solved by a mongrel, mostly whippet, which proved friendly, darting and running and teasing until it got bored, cocking its leg against a car wheel before trotting off, its tail erect as if showing what he thought of someone with so little to offer. The young lad from the house on the corner, the one that had won the Council prize for the best garden last year, was prepared to be friendly too, but a few words to him from Danny and a mother appeared at the door – he must come in and get ready if they were to go in to town, shopping. Danny watched the door close. He was dying for a drag.

'What you limping for then, Danny?'

'Fell over the cat, didn't I?'

Chico Morelli, from where he sat on the low wall surrounding the Catholic Church Hall, grinned his approval of such a clever answer.

'Bit clumsy, was that, wan't it, you karatein' an' all?'

'Yeah. Must have been the same cat you fell over when you broke that arm.'

Morelli's smile stayed unchanged; just his eyes hardened. 'Where were you off to? What you up to then?'

'Not a lot. You don't look too busy, neither.'

'My quiet time of the day, like, i'n't it. Things might look up later; you never know your luck.' Chico Morelli groomed the tassles that hung from his sleeve. 'How is the karate going then?'

'Brill.'

'Fancy trying some of it out on me, then?'

'Do me a favour, Chico. What d'you think I am, tired of life?' To the Danny Shufflebottoms of this world, as class conscious as any, the Wayne Morellis are in a different league but Danny felt sufficiently encouraged by Morelli's chatter to sit alongside the nearest to a friend he was likely to find that day. Physically, they were seven years apart; mentally, the gap was consideredly less. 'Got a smoke on you, Chico? I'm skint.'

'You smoke? At your age? Does my bastard brother know?'

'Is he really a bastard then, Chico?'

Wayne Morelli laughed, pausing to throw a stone at the Church Hall cat. 'Reckon his father was so small and so black me Mam never saw him in the dark. Anyway, he did the midnight flit, like, didn't he. What d'you smoke then?'

'Got some grass? I'll pay you. I know Budgie used to get his stuff from you.'

Wayne did not answer for a moment as a germ of an idea struggled to implant itself in very barren soil. 'How d'you manage then, living at home, I mean?'

'Got this place of my own, haven't I?'

'Oh, yes. Got ourselves a penthouse flat, have we?'

'Dead cosy, it is, honest. I only went home because – ' he eased a stiff leg as he chose his words ' – the filth got a bit too nosey.'

'Yeah. What's this with you and that big blonde copper then? Bit rum is that, i'n't it? What's going on between you and him? Fancy young boys, does he? Bent as a butcher's hook is he? It was him what fixed your karate up with my brother, wan't it?'

'They're not all bad, Chico. He's quite a nice guy, really.' A spark of loyalty survived. 'Him and Micky, they got me to go back to school, take these special spelling lessons.' He laughed bitterly. 'Fat lot of use they were, an' all; about as much use as the karate. I still can't bloody read.'

Morelli laughed as if he understood the problem. 'Where's this place of yours, then?'

'Got some grass?' Danny's face took on the sharp look of the street survivor.

'Have to go home, pick up some stuff, like. Where shall I see you?'

'You know the quarry behind the Centre?'

Morelli nodded.

'The sheds. The one they used to use as an office. When?'

'Four o'clock.' He saw Danny's face fall. 'Got things to do, some people to talk to. Any tinnies?'

Danny shook his head.

'Anything to eat?'

Wayne stood up as Danny shook his head again. 'Don't work for no charity, you know. You'll owe me,' he said, all vestige of a smile now drained away.

'Sure, Chico, I know that. You'll get paid.'

'With what?'

'Same way I always have. I don't owe nobody.'

The scramble bikes were, like everything of the least commercial value at the Centre, locked up securely. At first they had been brought out and used at weekends only and under the strictest supervision but, as the evenings grew lighter and the demand increased, so the supervision inevitably became somewhat more relaxed, while the track, worn into the rubble and the refuse, became irresistible to any Northend youngster fortunate enough to own a Susuki or a Yamaha. As a result the gap in the quarry fencing, which Council workers had struggled so manfully to repair, now gaped permanently, just wide enough for man and bike.

Danny, watching from the hut, hungry and desperate, saw Wayne walk through the gap in the mesh, a plastic bag in his hand. He moved the sheet of corrugated iron to let Morelli in, standing back not without pride.

His guest screwed up his face. 'Smells like somebody's crapped in here.'

'Somebody has. One of the stinkin' winos. You don't notice it after a while. Got some stuff?'

They sat against adjacent walls. Without a word, Wayne threw Danny a paper package. The pasty and the chips were almost cold and the first bolted mouthful stuck, giving Danny a dragging pain beneath his breast bone. Seeing him claw at his chest, Chico laughed, throwing him a can of lager. It took two such cans to sluice down the stodge and Danny had been outside to pass his urine noisily against the side of the shed before he settled again against the wall, the look on his face that of a guest at dinner who knows his host keeps good cigars.

Morelli sat, smiling.

'Come on then, Chico.'

'Come on what?' he teased, enjoying a rare moment of power.

'Chico. For Chrissake.'

Morelli sniggered as he threw Danny another, smaller package he dug out of his pocket. He watched, appreciating the expertise as Danny rolled himself the reefer. Danny hesitated as if enjoying to the full the last seconds of his craving, lit it and inhaled, his eyes closed, shutting out the drab filth around him. Morelli waited, anxious to be sure Danny was firmly on the hook, before indulging himself. It was Danny's turn to watch, benign curiosity on his face, as Morelli took from a pocket inside the leather jacket a small, shallow tin box. With a sort of reverence, he held the tin in front of him, removing the lid with care and respect. As if bound by the conventions of some strict religious ceremony, he laid out a small hand mirror and razor blade, both of surgical cleanliness in comparison with the surrounding squalor. The tin next divulged a rectangular plastic cachet, as neat and professional as a tea bag, the contents of which soon lay in a mound on the mirror. Using the razor blade with loving delicacy, Morelli divided the mound into lines and, through a pencil thin roll of paper, snorted his cocaine with an efficiency and economy undreamed of by any Regency buck and his anatomical snuffbox.

They sat for a while, seemingly oblivious to the racket of the scramble bikes outside, as they pursued their divergent emotional paths. Cannabis is a 'dirty' drug, a mixture of substances, all with varying effects, but Danny seemed to find the hedonic fraction he wanted, sitting, benign and at peace, seeking his own ill-defined Elysium. He did not get as far as to finish his joint, offering the soggy remnant silently to Morelli who waved it away as if he never touched the stuff. For his part, Morelli, his eyes bright and glistening, with no need of an artist's romantic notion of self-destruction to spur him on, seemed to be having difficulty controlling his limbs, his restlessness contrasting with the immobile, tiger like menace of his slack lipped smile.

'Let's go and show them how it's done, shall we?'

'Who? Show them what, Chico?'

'Can you ride?'

''Course I can ride.'

'Show me, then.' Morelli put the mirror and blade back in the tin, the tin in his inside pocket.

'Do we have to, Chico?'

'Bloody chicken, aren't you?'

'No, I'm not, Chico. It's just . . .'

'Come on then.'

The two riders, brought to a halt by Morelli standing astride the track where it passed closest to the sheds, took one look at his face and made no objection as they handed over the bikes. Morelli roared away to leave Danny trailing and it was not long before he had lapped the young lad. Quick-witted and coordinated, Danny felt the exhilaration sweep the fumes of cannabis from his brain as he got the hang of sliding the back wheel on the corners. Soon they were leaping over small jumps, raising two fingers to the knot of youngsters who had gathered at the back of the Centre to watch. Inevitably they tired of the same circuit and looked for fresh adventure. With a wild cry of delight, Danny saw Chico cut away from the well-worn path and duck beneath the gap in the fence. He followed, standing on the rests as he clattered across the pavement and on to the road.

There followed a wild chase between parked cars, along footpaths, through the sagging wire fencing of abandoned allotments, as they hurled profanity at raised fists and hooting car horns. They turned and headed back and Danny, well versed in every nook and cranny of the area, found himself ahead as they bored in on the gap in the fence once more. Braking and steadying himself, he lifted his front wheel over the gutter and ducked his head. He twisted his wrist, thrusting out his elbow as he gave a burst of throttle to take him through the gap, only to catch the sleeve of his jumper in a hook of cut wire. The bike crackled on from under him as he was dumped on his back just the other side of the gap. Morelli saw him fall, braked hard and was already sliding broadside as he hit the gutter. He curled into a ball as he was pitched across the pavement and into the lax fencing. Laughing, cursing, yelping with pain, they got up and half-ran, half-hobbled to be swallowed up in the maze of Northend's back lanes.

Badger had shifted the corrugated iron sheet and had smelled the smell, not only that from the wino's parting gift, but that sweeter, more clinging aroma from Danny's joint. He had pushed at the grease-stained chip paper with his foot and had not been surprised to see the unsmoked, flattened stub. What had surprised him somewhat was the small plastic envelope. They were usually more careful than that. He had picked it up, squeezed it open in his left hand and had tasted gingerly what had come out on the tip of his right index finger. Thoughtfully, he had put both articles carefully in his pocket.

Badger was in uniform. Micky Dunn saw him come through the door and nodded towards his office. He had more or less been expecting him. They stood facing each other.

'I expect you know why I'm here, Micky.'

'Frankly, Badger, I can think of at least half a dozen possible reasons. Which one would you like?'

'There have been complaints, Micky, from the residents around here.'

'Tell me something new,' Micky Dunn growled.

'We've had complaints about the noise ever since you got those bikes but, so far, we've been able to turn a deaf ear – and that was not meant to be funny. But this time it's different, Micky; we just couldn't ignore it any more. We've had complaints that those bikes have been ridden on the public highway and I know for a fact they are not licenced or insured. Not only that but it seems they made themselves a damn nuisance when they were doing it. And we've got descriptions, Micky; both of them seem pretty well known round here.'

'I heard about that, naturally. But I wasn't in the Centre myself at the time.' Dunn saw the look on Badger's face and added, 'Straight up, Badger. I wasn't here. Otherwise the two young bastards would not have got away with it.'

'So you know who they were?'

'The two bikes were found, damaged, near the gap in the fence, that's all I know for certain.'

'One was described as a slim youngster with black, curly hair. The other one had a very distinctive black leather jacket. Mean anything to you, Micky?'

'Look, Badger. Is this on or off the record?'

'Everything said here goes into a written report back at the nick. This was an official complaint and this is an official inquiry.'

'In that case, I've told you. If anyone breaks the law here in the Centre, I treat him or her like anyone else and I call you in. Anything that goes on outside the Centre – and I get to hear of things all the time – that is none of my business. If I were to tell you of everything I know that goes on in Northend, this place would be empty overnight. As far as I was concerned, there was damage done to the two bikes which has now been repaired. No one has owned up to the damage, no one will, and you know as well as I do that it is useless asking around; none of them will grass. So I'm sorry, Badger, I just can't help you.'

'You draw a pretty fine line of distinction, Micky.'

Dunn's instinctive reply of 'Don't we both?' was suppressed out of respect for a young copper trying to do his job. He simply shrugged his shoulders.

'And that's it?'

'That, Badger, is as far as I can go, yes.'

'Fair enough, Micky, so that's what goes in the report and, if it satisfies the Inspector, it's all right by me. If it doesn't, I'll be back.' Badger relaxed visibly. 'I intended coming to see you anyway.'

'Coffee?' Dunn invited.

'Just so long as you can promise me it's not being offered as an inducement to subvert the course of justice,' Badger smiled.

'You haven't tasted my coffee yet,' Dunn grinned back.

'As I said, I intended to call in. I wanted a word with you about Danny.'

'Is that so?' Dunn, his back to Badger, seemed to be concentrating on the kettle.

'He hasn't been turning up for his karate lessons.'

'That doesn't surprise me.'

'Oh?'

'He hasn't been turning up for rehearsals either. And he's not been back to his old haunt over in the sheds either, in case you were wondering.'

'I know that. I've already looked for him there.'

'Angela reckons she will have to call the play off, which is a pity.' He kept his back to Badger though the kettle had boiled long since. 'I rather think our Danny may have taken up with bad company.'

'The thought had crossed my mind, Micky.'

Micky Dunn poured two-day-old milk from the bottle. As he turned,

175

the tone in his voice was as if he was broaching a completely new subject.

'It's not often I admit defeat, Badger, – and I certainly wouldn't want to do that just yet with Danny – but there is another bright young spark where I really feel the time has come to throw the towel in.'

'Oh? Who would that be then?' asked Badger, his blonde eyelashes fluttering innocently.

'Young chap called Morelli, Wayne Morelli.'

'Ah, yes. I know him – or perhaps I should say he is known to us. The one they call Chico?'

'That's him. He's a downright bad lot, that one.' Micky's voice took on a philosophical tone. 'Isn't it the Catholics who say "give me a child until he's 7"? Well I reckon Satan had this one until he was 7. He's nothing but trouble whenever he calls in here. I can't ever remember trying to stop anyone coming to the Centre before but I wouldn't lose any sleep if I never saw him again.'

'Thanks for the coffee.' Badger stood up, placing his mug carefully on the desk, the undrinkable undrunk. 'Must get back. I loathe writing reports. I think I'll make a couple of calls on the way back, behave like the caring community copper they're all on about, show the uniform a bit, as you might say, like showing the flag in the old days. See you as usual next Thursday, Micky? Perhaps Danny will be here by then too.'

Micky Dunn held out his hand. 'Thanks, Badger. Somehow I thought you'd understand.'

Perhaps it is possible for someone to be too kindly to be a policeman. If that were so, then Inspector George Hardcastle would certainly qualify. It had occurred to him many times in a blameless career that he might be in the wrong job but now, within two years of placing the engraved clock on the mantlepiece, he was quite sure. He had joined the force to be a village Bobby, cuffing kids' ears for snitching apples, strolling around a cattle market in big boots and helmet, not to end up in charge of a nick in a down-at-heel council estate in a northern industrial town. But he had survived, his conscience intact, despite years of disenchantment that constant contact with the rougher elements on both sides of the law had induced. If one is to identify a bent copper, there have to be the George Hardcastles against whom to measure the degree of curvature. He was therefore in a better position than most to recognise that Police Constable Kincaid was as straight as a die. Young, idealistic, inexperienced and trusting, maybe, but bent? No.

All he could do was make the reprimand as unofficial as he could but he was not looking forward to it. Had it been one of the other young rookies, it would mean little to him. He would use language they understood and he would leave no scars. But an official reprimand just before going to the Staff College at Bramsill would go hard with Kincaid and what irked Hardcastle most was that it would all be based on information given by a greasy haired little copper's nark with form as long as your arm.

'Sit down, Kincaid.'

'Thank you, sir; I'd rather stand.' He did just that, staring unfocussed at the wall above his Inspector's head like someone who has just refused a blindfold at his execution. 'I don't imagine I'm here for a cup of tea.'

'You've been a bloody fool, haven't you, Kincaid?'

'I have, sir?'

'Concealing evidence; that's serious enough for anyone. When a copper goes and does it, it's ten times worse.'

'And what evidence would that have been, then, sir?'

Hardcastle sighed. When he spoke again it was in his most avuncular manner though it did not take long for suppressed irritation to show through.

'Kincaid, do yourself a favour. Grow up. You can do better than that. You're an intelligent man, not just another woodentop. So why not behave like one and then perhaps I'll treat you like one. But if you keep up that stupid attitude, then I'll go by the book and you can kiss Bramshill goodbye together with your dreams of becoming Chief Constable. Understood?'

'Yes, sir. Thank you.' Badger's rigid back and neck relaxed a little, allowing him to lower his eyes and look down defiantly at Hardcastle.

'Now, lad; what exactly is going on up at the Community Centre?'

The Inspector sat back as Kincaid explained his attempts to become involved in the Centre in his time off. He watched a young man's anger slowly rise at what he saw as the official reaction to his efforts.

'All very commendable, Kincaid, depending on just how far you have gone.'

'Sir?'

'Just how far have you been prepared to cover up for these young villains, that's what I mean, Kincaid? What happened about that complaint about them using those scrambling bikes on the road that I sent you up to look into? What happened there, for instance?'

'You had my report on that, sir.'

'And beautifully vague reading it made too. When you get yourself sacked, Kincaid – which is the most likely future I see for you at the moment – you could always turn to writing fiction. I know a good story when I see one. Do you know who was riding those bikes?'

'There was no positive identification, sir.'

'That's not what I asked, Kincaid. Do you know who they were?'

'No, sir.'

'From the descriptions I've seen, everybody in Northend would tell you who one of them was. I could tell you. Now, who was the other one? You must have questioned someone?'

'I interviewed the Youth Organiser, sir; thought he might know who it was.'

'Knowing damn well that Micky Dunn would never let on about what his lads might get up to outside the Centre, not that sort of thing anyway.'

Hardcastle paused and Badger gave a silent sigh of relief, feeling he had weathered that storm reasonably well.

'I'm not against you turning the odd blind eye if, in return, you get these youngsters' confidence, Kincaid. It's the way I saw myself at your age. But you've got to learn where to draw the line. Now what's this about drugs at the Centre?'

'Don't quite know what you mean, Inspector.'

'Now careful, Kincaid. Don't start getting smart again. Have you any evidence of drugs there?'

'I shouldn't think there's one boy or girl going there who hasn't smoked a joint in their time, sir.'

'Not what I mean, Kincaid.' There was in Hardcastle's voice a note of warning that he was running out of patience. He picked up his chrome paper knife, shaped in the form of a small sabre, and began prodding at a new, thin file as if he hated the sight of it.

'Look, sir. You know as well as I do the results of that university survey. Based on that, probably as many as two out of ten of those going to the centre are habitual users, let alone taking the occasional drag, but that doesn't mean Micky is running an opium den. What d'you want me to do, go on a witch hunt there that will empty the place for him?'

'But choosing not to investigate and concealing evidence once found; two different matters altogether, wouldn't you agree, Kincaid?'

'Of course, sir.'

'And what would you say if I were to tell you I have information that leads me to believe you have concealed evidence of drug taking?'

'May I ask the source of your information, sir?'

'You may not.'

Inspector George Hardcastle had reached the watershed. A few more questions and he would be committing himself to ruining a promising career. And for what? To satisfy the evil need of a hardened young criminal, intent on dragging a fine young man down with him. In disgust, he threw the paper knife on to his desk, smiling inwardly in relief as he saw it come to rest pointing away from Badger.

'Why, lad?' he asked, quietly.

Badger thought for a moment before answering. 'Is this off the record now, sir?'

Hardcastle nodded.

'Because I cannot stand the double standards we apply.'

'Such as?' Hardcastle asked, knowing exactly what Kincaid was going to say and trying not to show he was warming to such youthful honest intensity.

'Say, just for argument, we find some young kid smoking pot. What do we do? We nick him – no bother. His parents probably wouldn't miss him for a week and then wouldn't bother to come to court with him. Next day we walk past a café full of blacks where the smell of pot coming through the doors nearly makes you puke. And what do we do? Suddenly find something more interesting on the other side of the street because to walk into that café would cause too much aggro, maybe start another riot. If we have to turn a blind eye to the one, then we ought to choose to do so to the other. Either that or we walk into that café and take whatever comes.'

'You've got a lot to learn, lad.'

'And is this what I'm going to be taught at Bramshill, sir?'

Hardcastle didn't answer.

'If the Chief Constable', Kincaid's jaw jutted as if he had just burst through that café door, 'can do something about a golfing chum's ticket for speeding, why can't I do some young kid a favour?' He thought for a moment. 'I would get more satisfaction from keeping an underprivileged youngster away from a three-month custodial sentence than sending a hardened villain down for twenty years.'

Badger Kincaid had been fortunate indeed in his choice of Inspectors. 'God knows what made you join the police force, Kincaid.' It was obvious from his voice that the official business was over.

'Fancied the uniform, sir. Thought it would pull the birds.' Badger wondered whether he might venture a grin.

'I'm serious, lad. If you had to join, as a thinking man, why not go for the CID? What do you want to stick to the uniformed branch for? You'll find the ability to think a positive handicap at times in this job, take my word for it.'

Badger shook his head doggedly. 'No. I don't want to take anything away from the lads in CID but I want to be in the community, be part of the healthy side of it, not ferreting about in its filth. We've lost our way, sir. We need to get back to the days when the man on the street saw us as a guardian, not someone you can't trust as far as you can throw him.'

'See yourself jumping into freezing canals saving old ladies' lives do you?' And Hardcastle, a sensitive man, knew, from the look on Badger's face, just how much he had hurt an equally sensitive young man. He tried to make amends. 'Don't take it amiss, lad, but what would you say if I told you you'd made a mistake, that you're in the wrong job? You're not cut out for this job.'

'There's only one thing to do then, isn't there, sir?' His eyes were back, staring defiantly at the wall above Hardcastle's head. 'It's up to our generation to put that right, make the job cut out for us.'

SOUTH LANCASHIRE POST
Saturday May 4 1985

Health chiefs in South Lancashire could be facing a novel form of sanction, beginning next Monday, if plans drawn up by the National Union of Public Employees go ahead.

The dispute arises over the vexed question of competitive tendering for hospital services, such as laundry and office cleaning, in keeping with Government policy of privatisation of some parts of the Health Service. The industrial action against this policy is to take the form of selective sanctions against any members of the Health Authority who are known to have voted in favour of competitive tendering. Any such member who provides some form of service to the local community has been warned by the Union that its members are being encouraged to boycott all such services wherever alternative arrangements can be made. It is known that the Health Authority has at least one doctor, a milkman and a local baker amongst its members.

When interviewed yesterday, Mr Gavin Prescott, local Branch Secretary of NUPE, confirmed that the sanctions would be imposed unless the Authority changed its policy on competitive tendering. Mr Prescott maintained that, following talks with the Authority two years ago, his Union had cooperated fully in a process of internal savings which had already resulted in savings in excess of five hundred thousand pounds in the first year and was on target for savings of one million pounds in the current year. His members, Mr Prescott said, were dismayed by their jobs now being put at risk after cooperating in making such considerable savings and now fully intended doing a bit of competitive tendering of their own.

A spokesman for the Health Authority said the Chairman and members regretted that there was obvious misunderstanding by the National Union of Public Employees of the Authority's motives in investigating the cost effectiveness of certain of the support services. Nothing had been decided without the fullest consultation with the Union, but, as a result of the Authority's investigations, most members felt that they would not be carrying out their duties responsibly if they did not recommend limited competitive tendering for some of the services.

19

All young men – the ones that care – like to draw the bottom line. The equation must work out to a neat, definable result, written in black and white, or they must know the reason why. Like novice swimmers, they like to feel occasionally the reassuring sensation of solid ground beneath their feet.

Jonathan's car wheels crunched familiarly on the courtyard gravel. Inside the door, he was embraced like an only son by Alison, who then held him at arm's length.

'You've lost weight. You look tired. You're not eating properly.'

'Of course I am. Don't fuss.'

Alison stood back, her heart aching as Jonathan and his father radiated affection from where they stood, feet apart. No hug, no handshake, no touching.

'Hi, Dad. How are you?'

'I'm fine. How are you?'

'Great.'

Alison felt the urge to take one infuriating male in each hand and crash them together like cymbals. She sighed, shaking her head. 'Well, at least give your long-lost son a drink. I'm going to make the gravy.'

She left them to their awkwardness.

'Beer?'

Jonathan laughed to himself, wondering just how old he would have to be before he was offered spirits by his father.

'No thanks, Dad. If there's any wine with lunch . . .?'

'I've got rather a nice Mouton Cadet.'

'Sounds great, Dad. I'll have a glass of that. That will be enough to drive back on.'

'You could always stay tonight; get up a bit earlier in the morning. It's not that far on the motorway.' And it would be wonderful to hear once more noises from the bedroom next to theirs, the bed creaking in the small hours, the muttered word in a young man's sleep.

'I have to be back tonight, Dad.'

'You won't mind if I have another sherry, then?' Michael Brookes grinned at his son. 'Lissa tells me I'm drinking too much.'

'Wouldn't have thought there was much danger of that, Dad.'

'You wouldn't care to tell her that, would you?'

It was as if they had been manoeuvring for a reason to move into the kitchen, looking for Alison's catalystic chatter. Within minutes, they were in the steamy warmth, beginning to laugh as Jonathan described a rugby match he had played with the police and his fears for his boss's life on a squash court. An embellished account of his tackle on the fullback brought a frown to Alison's face as she told him to give up that rough old game and stick to squash. Soon it was a Sunday lunch of yore, with Michael carving the beef and Jonathan giving his considered opinion on tasting the gravy. The beef was cooked to perfection, the Mouton Cadet everything Michael had promised and the soufflé was a masterpiece. Jonathan pushed his plate away with a sigh.

'Lissa, that was superb.'

'A glass of port to round it off?' It was not so much an invitation as a plea; another moment to be shared. 'It's vintage, decanted with my own fair hand this morning. It's not often I have a patient who gives me a case and there aren't many bottles left.'

'Michael, he's driving.'

'Just one won't hurt, will it?'

Jonathan smiled. 'Not really. I needn't start back until quite late.' He watched his father pour with loving care, took the glass and sipped. 'Gorgeous. Like silk.'

It was as if the first sip had signalled the end of the meal and Alison leaned forward, her elbows on the table, her chin in her hands. 'Now then, tell me everything that's happened; not just that old rugby. I want to know everybody you've met; what you've been doing.'

'What she means is, how's your love life, have you got a girlfriend down there?' Michael laughed.

Alison glowered at her husband in mock fury. 'No, I don't.' She turned her attention back to Jonathan and, in a trice, changed her features to a mischievous smile. 'Have you?' she asked.

Jonathan found he could not look Alison in the eye and played with his glass. 'No, not really.'

'No, not really? What sort of an answer is that? I don't believe you.'

'I've only got one,' Jonathan laughed, trying to keep a guilty flush at bay. 'And she's in Liverpool.'

'Are you going to marry her?'

'That's the trouble, Lissa; she won't have me.'

'More fool her then. Have you asked her?'

'Hasn't really come to that.'

'Have you told her you love her then?'

Why was it so easy when someone like Alison said it and so painfully difficult for someone like himself to grind it out, Jonathan thought as he hung his head in silence.

182

Generous lips set in sudden anger, Alison looked across at the two men. She lifted her head, letting it fall back into her cupped hands with a slapping sound. 'You and your father. There's no way anyone could accuse poor Rosemary of having had an affair with the milkman. You both make me so angry at times.'

Father and son grinned at each other. 'How's the job going? Enjoying it?' the father asked.

'Very much, Dad, yes.'

'Learning a lot?'

'Yes; up to a point. It's getting a bit repetitive now.'

'You wouldn't like to do it for the next thirty years?'

'No, Dad, I wouldn't.'

'All jobs get to be a bit like that, you know, Jonathan. How does Bannerman feel about it?'

There was a pause before Jonathan answered, long enough to be significant to two intelligent people who, in their different fields, worked, day in, day out, on an endless conveyor belt of human emotions and reactions. Both recognised someone prearranging his thoughts, feeling the need to take care over his answers. An enquiring glance flashed between Alison and Michael. Were they about to hear the true reason for Jonathan's visit?

'I'm pretty sure it gets to him at times, Dad.'

Over the years, Michael Brookes had learned when to stay silent.

'It's partly due, I think, to the fact that it was not his idea to end up as a casualty consultant. I imagine it's different if that's what you want to do right from the start. But I get the impression he was very ambitious at one time, had high hopes of an orthopaedic consultancy in Manchester. I certainly don't think it was part of his plan to end up in Casualty in Scarsby.'

'So. Which was it? Booze or women?'

Astonished at the pin-point accuracy from someone who, in a young man's mind, lived in cloistered remoteness from the real world, Jonathan looked at his father's expressionless face, then across at Alison to see essentially the same reaction.

'Both, I suppose. He's divorced and married again but that only happened after he went to Scarsby. But he certainly has a drink problem.'

'Oh,' Michael said. 'One of those, is he? Is it interfering with his work?' He looked searchingly at his son.

Jonathan hesitated before answering. He was clear in his mind that Bannerman and his drinking was one of the reasons why he had travelled home, to use his father as a talking block on which to hammer out his own attitudes, to try to straighten out confused thinking by putting the thoughts into words. Michael Brookes might be his father, with attitudes, interests and emotions so similar to his own as to make them like two peas in a pod, but he was also a pillar of the surgical establishment, the senior surgeon of a District General Hospital with contemporaries amongst the north-west's medical hierarchy.

'Difficult to talk about it, really, Dad. Don't know just how much I can or should mention.'

Michael Brookes's face softened as Alison chipped in. 'Jonathan, darling; you don't imagine your father's going to betray your confidence. Nothing will go beyond these four walls.'

The story of Bannerman's drunkenness came out, his clumsy surgery in the theatre in front of a frightened mother, his totally unprofessional attitude as he dropped cigar ash over a patient in his clinic, his drinking at lunchtime and the bottle in the filing cabinet, the days off 'sick' which seemed to be getting more frequent. The facts were given accurately if disjointedly, rather as if he was emptying his head of the jumbled thoughts for his father to rearrange and put back in nice, neat compartments for him. He was to be disappointed.

'So. Nothing serious as yet.'

'Maybe not, Dad, but . . . I mean to say . . .'

'There's a lot of it about, Jonathan.'

'Is that all you can say about it?' The disappointment, bordering on disillusion, was clearly apparent.

'What d'you want me to say about it?'

'At least, that you disapprove.'

'I do. I most certainly do.'

'Well?'

'Well?'

Jonathan, fuming in youthful intensity of feeling, hardly noticed his father quietly refill his glass as if offering a peace token. 'But what does one do? Have you ever had to deal with it?'

'Yes.' Michael Brookes answered quietly and slowly and saw that his son was not going to be satisfied with that answer. 'Had a registrar once. Began to get hints from the nursing staff that he was acting a bit strange operating on emergencies at night. Then he was brought in one night to Casualty on a stretcher. He'd been found lying in a ditch, roaring drunk, with a Pott's fracture.'

'And then?'

'Then? A few quiet words with the Health Authority, given the sack and arrangements made for his admission to a drying out centre in Liverpool. God knows where the poor lad is now.'

'But what about when it's a consultant?'

'Ah, then,' Michael suddenly found something of intense interest in the centre of the table, 'it becomes very difficult.'

'That's no answer, Dad, and you know it. What does happen when it's a consultant?'

Jonathan had never known his father so evasive and his frown showed it. Michael felt the shadow over a relationship he cherished and did his best to disperse it.

'We had a consultant in Dunbridge some years ago – never mind who it was – and we had to suspend him on full pay for eighteen months while he got himself sorted out. He's back working full time again now; seems to be all right.'

'And you were involved in that yourself?'

'I was one of the so-called "three wise men"; not a very pleasant job, I assure you.' He glanced across at Alison and got the smile of encouragement he had been looking for. 'Everybody closes ranks around a drinker, Jonathan. I'm told it's the same with drug users, though I have no personal experience of that yet, thank God. But it's true. I've no idea why – something to do with the herd instinct perhaps – but everyone looks after their own. Perhaps we think, "there, but for the grace of God ..."; I don't know. What I do know is that we are not unique in medicine, though people who put their lives in our hands like to think we are; a purely selfish sentiment, I might add. But we're no different from, say, industry which harbours drunks and drug users from managing directors down to the shop floor. The legal profession here,' he grinned as he jerked a thumb in Alison's direction, 'was never noted for swelling the ranks of the Band of Hope and the clergy would be decimated if they had to swear an oath of abstinence.' His face took on an amused, contemplative look. 'I wonder, on one of these skiing holidays of yours, whether you've ever been flown by an alcoholic pilot.'

He had done nothing to dispel the seriousness on his son's face. Jonathan had seen nothing amusing in his father's attempt to keep the discussion as light as he could but he was taken totally unawares by his father's sudden change of mood.

'Do you want me to do anything about it?'

The directness of the question turned the tables, the son taking on the evasive air at the father's offer of immediate action.

'No. That's all right, Dad. I've less than three months to go and I expect I can manage till then.'

'When, of course, it will become someone else's responsibility.' The fact that he loved his son dearly did not mean he need not teach him the difference between idealism and realism. 'All I need to do is ring the senior surgeon in Scarsby; I've never met him but that would be no problem. Or, perhaps, the Prof. in Liverpool?'

'No, thanks, Dad. But it is a problem, isn't it?'

'It's not your worry, darling,' Alison murmured softly. 'It's up to the other consultants there to do something about it if it gets too bad. They're bound to know about his drinking.'

'Alison's right, Jonathan. You keep out of it. You stick to the clinical stuff and leave them to sort themselves out. As you say, you won't be there much longer.'

They looked for signs that their encouragement had succeeded but found Jonathan's face longer than before.

'Don't talk about the clinical stuff, Dad. I've just made the most awful mess of someone's hand.'

Michael Brookes was now certain of the reason for the trip north. He only had to wait and it would all come out. Alison reached across the table. 'If you two are going to talk shop,' she said, her voice full of quiet understanding, 'then I'd better get some more coffee.'

'What happened?'

'I stitched an old boy's little finger up and it went gangrenous. It was the most terrible mess you've ever seen and I ended up having to amputate it.' Jonathan paused. 'And I feel very bad about it.'

'I can see that.' Michael was having difficulty concealing his relief that it was nothing more dramatic. From the look on Jonathan's face, he had not known what to expect. 'But it could be worse. It happens. Why do you blame yourself?'

They both smiled their thanks as Lissa put fresh coffee in front of them. She sat once more, her face, intent and loving, sweeping from one to the other as they joined words again.

'I'd got too bloody cocky by far, Dad.' Jonathan relaxed visibly, as if he had longed to make such a confession to someone he knew would understand. His voice became less taut, the words coming more strongly, powered by his self-recrimination. 'The job had become too easy for such a bloody genius as me; that was the problem. I was doing it with my spinal cord. My mind was on other things.'

'That won't be the last time that will happen to you, Jonathan. What do you think went wrong?'

'Everything. He was a simple-minded old boy who didn't talk very much. He just smiled; he was so grateful for everything we did for him. That smile goes through me now, every time I think of it. But I was too cocky, too busy with my own thoughts to waste time with an old idiot who couldn't give a decent history. If only I had found time to struggle with him a bit, I might have found out it was a dog bite. It's bitten a couple more since then and been destroyed but I should have known without him telling me; all the signs were there, you know, those round, patchy bruises you always see around a dog bite? He had them in his palm and on the back of his hand.'

Michael Brookes nodded.

'If I'd only known that much, at least I would have put him on antibiotics.'

'But you don't put every laceration on antibiotics as a routine, do you?'

'No, but a filthy dog bite I would have.' Jonathan stared at his coffee getting cold in front of him. 'And I was so proud of the suture line; I can see it now, so neat and tidy. When you think of all those filthy bugs I buried in that wound.'

'Did he have his tetanus jabs?'

'Oh, yes.' Jonathan's tone was dismissive, as if anxious not to dwell on anything he might have done right. 'But, more than anything, there was the local anaesthetic. I should have had my wits about me there too.'

'Oh?' Michael's head came up sharply, as if they might be coming to the crux of the matter. 'What about the local?'

'There I was, complimenting myself on the best digital block I'd ever done,' Jonathan smiled ruefully. 'He didn't feel a thing. But it was no thanks to me; I put the injection too far up the finger.'

'Rather than on the safe side of the web where it can spread into the palm if under too much tension, you mean?'

Jonathan nodded. 'But that's not all. The base of the finger went dead white and I took no notice. I'm sure now the finger was as numb from ischaemia as it was from the anaesthetic. If I'd been on the ball, I'd have known then; I remember rubbing the damn thing, trying to get the circulation back.'

'You didn't use . . .?' Michael struggled with a question he was reluctant to ask.

'Adrenalin?' Jonathan finished the question for him. 'That's just it,' he said, bitterly. 'I don't know for certain.'

'Oh.' It was impossible now to hide an overtone of censure. 'How was that?'

'I remember the nurse showing me the bottle; I remember looking at it; I don't remember reading the label. What I do remember is laughing and pulling her leg about something at the time.'

'It might not have been adrenalin. It might have looked like that simply because you put just a drop too much local in.' Michael struggled to find loopholes through which his son could escape his self-chastisement. 'You don't use adrenalin routinely, do you?'

'No. They usually give us plain unless we specifically ask for adrenalin.'

'Well then,' his father argued but Jonathan was not to be comforted.

'No. I've walked the streets of Scarsby trying to convince myself that it wasn't adrenalin but it must have been. It was so dead white and I must have put too much in too high up the finger in a filthy dog bite I didn't recognise and then sewed it up too tight. And then sent the poor old sod off for a week without another thought. If it had been somebody important, I would have seen him the next day, made sure everything was all right.'

'Nothing you could have done about it by then. The damage would have been done.'

'I know, Dad, but the fact is, I didn't care. I could have tried, applied ice bags to reduce the metabolism, taken some of the sutures out, started antibiotics earlier – anything. And I think it's that lack of care that I feel guilty about as much as negligence.'

'Who said you were negligent?' Michael sprang immediately to his son's defence. 'Misguided in your management, maybe, but there's no proof that there was any adrenalin in that injection. That could have been explained easily by the finger swelling rapidly with the injection fluid in place.'

Jonathan looked affectionately at his father. 'Thanks, Dad. Nice try, but, let's face it, you and I, we both know I was negligent.'

His father did not reply for a moment and when he did, it was in measured, kindly tones. 'I think, after my little peccadillo a few years ago, I can claim to know just how you're feeling. There are two kinds of negligence, aren't there? There's the one everyone reckons they understand though they have enough trouble, God knows, putting it into words; that's the one that is measured against the law of the land. Then there's the other one, when inwardly you know you could have done better, should have done better, and some poor bastard of a patient has had to suffer for it. In all honesty, Jonathan, I think you might have been guilty this time on both counts – you might have had a bit of difficulty in a witness box on a couple of points there.'

Michael turned for a moment to smile at his wife. 'I think I have convinced at least one lawyer of the two kinds of negligence. Perhaps all doctors should marry lawyers and all lawyers marry doctors.'

'But you are going to have to learn to ride the bumps, Jonathan. You won't get far in surgery if you are going to get so upset every time something like this happens to you. Surgery's a tough racket. And there's no doubt it is going to happen to you again to some degree, in some form, however much you swear now it never will. You're not God. You've got to learn to put that gangrenous finger out of your mind as if it never happened, and that takes a certain hardness of heart that you will have to develop. At the moment, my son, you're looking into the patient's eyes too much. Try to spend more time looking at their disease and less at their faces. Don't let them take so much out of you, otherwise you won't stay the course.' He smiled, trying to be less serious. 'Here endeth the lesson. It's one of the problems with working under local anaesthetic, isn't it? You can't turn round and blame the anaesthetist.'

'Thanks, Dad. I needed that.' Something close to a grin spread back over his face. 'You have no idea how many times I have given up surgery in the last week or so and gone back to anatomy.'

There was a tiny sound in Alison's throat as she stretched a hand across the table towards Jonathan. 'Don't do that, Jonathan. Don't do anything hasty. I think it would be an awful waste. You were never cut out to be a dried-up academic. You wouldn't be happy.'

'Nothing could have been much worse than the way I've felt the last week, Lissa.'

'I know, Jonathan, but that will pass.'

'Does Bannerman know about this?' Michael asked.

'Yes, of course. I showed it to him immediately.'

'What did he have to say about it?'

'He was marvellous; handled the whole thing beautifully. Took me aside afterwards and told me not to worry about it. Made me feel even worse after the things I had been thinking about him. I think I would have felt better if he'd given me a right bollocking. Sorry, Lissa.'

'Never mind, Jonathan, it's all over now.' Alison stood up. 'Come and sit down and tell me what you're up to when you're not working. Your father can do the dishes after you've gone.' She drew Jonathan down beside her on the chesterfield, turning to look at him. 'Were you serious when you said you had no girlfriend down there in Scarsby?'

'Absolutely serious,' Jonathan laughed, a statement he felt he could claim now to be true.

'You mean you've met no one down there?' There was genuine disbelief in Alison's voice and Jonathan strove somehow to reassure her.

'Oh, yes. I've met quite a few very interesting people, my boss, the Casualty sister – a very sad woman I'll tell you about again – a fascinating little black hospital porter, self-educated, as ambitious as hell. But the chap I really get on well with is the policeman, Badger; the one I told you about playing rugby. I suppose it's because we are very alike in many ways. He tried the academic life too and didn't really like it; he was a teacher before he joined the force as a graduate. He's been selected to go on some special course soon and should make Inspector quite young. His mate, Taff Evans, reckons he's destined for great things.'

'Just like you.' Alison squeezed his arm.

'Interesting family altogether, ruled with a rod of iron by an aged grandmother, all five foot nothing of her. Then there's Badger's brother, Reggie, who's a miner.'

'That can't be easy, policeman and miner, brothers living under the same roof,' his father broke in.

'There's worse to come. Reggie couldn't go back to work as he is on bail awaiting trial after being arrested at Orgreave, and Vicki, that's his wife, has left him and got a job in Liverpool. And you can imagine what Grandma thinks of that though it's not strictly true to say she left him. Apparently she wanted Reggie to go with her but he wouldn't.'

'He'd rather stay at home with his Gran, you mean?'

'That's a bit hard, Lissa. He must be hoping to go back to the pit after his case is heard.'

'He won't work again. Not as a miner anyway.'

'Why do you say that?' Jonathan asked, raising his eyebrows in surprise only to see Alison just shake her head. 'But you can't help feeling sorry for him, Lissa. The life he has always known has come to an end as far as he sees it. The strike had meant nothing but ruin for poor old Reggie while I think you could say it has set Vicki free.'

Jonathan paused for a moment as he heard Alison mutter, 'Good for her.'

'A great girl, Vicki, mind you. A tremendous character. I suppose, in a way, it takes a certain courage to walk out on your husband like that; go it alone in a strange city. I'd like you to meet her. I think you two would get on.'

'I rather think we would,' Alison smiled, 'having once done much the same thing myself. Do you see a lot of your friend, Badger, then? What a strange name.'

'Not as much as I would like. We have a few beers together now and again but he has other interests; his girlfriend is one of our night Staff Nurses. But he's coming sailing with us.' Jonathan sat more upright, looked more alert at the thought. 'And that casualty porter, Gavin, I told you about. They're both coming on the race down to New Quay at the end of the month. I can't wait to sail *Gelert* again.'

'*Gelert?*'

'That's the name of the boat. I must admit, I'm dying to get away for a few days.'

'And that's with your girlfriend from Liverpool again?'

'Yes. Except she's not my girlfriend. I've told you, Lissa, she won't have me.'

'Bring her home here; let me have a word with her. What's her name? Susannah, is it?'

'Yes; Susannah Ridgeway. She's an anaesthetic registrar in the Royal Liverpool.'

'And it's her boat?'

'Well, her father's or, to put it more accurately, one of his boats.'

'Not anything to do with Sir Warwick Ridgeway, Chairman of your Health Authority, is she?' The question came dreamily from the depths of an armchair where Michael Brookes fought off port-induced sleep. These were rare moments. Time enough for sleep when his son had driven away once more.

'She's his daughter, Dad.'

'Good God. You should get stuck in there, my boy. The bits of Lancashire that chap doesn't own are not worth having.'

'Don't take any notice of your father, the mercenary old beggar.' Alison snuggled closer to Jonathan. 'Tell me about your Susannah. What does she look like?'

The shutter that fell as Jonathan almost curtly changed the subject told Alison all she wanted to know. She had met the reaction before, years before, when his father had turned aside all her probings as she had tried to coax her way into the lives of two people deeply devoted to each other. She was generous enough to take it not as a rebuff, but as a measure of Jonathan's feeling for the girl. Like father, like son; there would be no trivialising anything they held dear. If Alison ever hoped to be made privy to Jonathan's feelings about this Susannah, she would have to be patient. Any other girl and he would string along, laugh and joke about the affair. But this one, no. The signs were out; hands off.

20

The old-style matriarch in a mining community, tempered and shaped on the anvil of this century's early decades, was a formidable being. Typically, she left school at 14 with only a one in a hundred chance of living to draw her old age pension, going out to work in a community where nearly half the population were under 20 years of age. If she was lucky, she went into service at the house of the local doctor or solicitor or was taken on at the local milliner or shoe shop where, at first, she worked for nothing in the hope of better things to come. Some tradesmen even charged a few shillings a week for their 'training'. In the South Lancashire coalfield, if she was less fortunate, she probably ended up a 'pit brow lass', cleaning the coal as it came off the endless belt, picking off the mud with her bare hands under leaking roofs, with no heating in winter and no first aid for the remorseless trickle of injuries. It was little wonder they married young only to find they had exchanged one kind of drudgery for another. The man worked long and hard under dreadful and dangerous conditions and he expected his comforts when he came home. If they were so unfortunate as to be sufficiently fertile, the women found themselves pregnant almost continuously for the first ten years and more, some of them dying from malnutrition in the process. Spartan conditions engendered Spartan values and the wealth of a family was measured in the number and the strength of its sons. The family with but one man lived on a knife edge, its whole fragile economy liable to be crushed beneath a roof fall. The whip-round, offered so apologetically by four of his mates, was the last money the man brought his wife as his unwashed, mutilated body, covered with a blanket, was laid at her front door. As far as the mine owner was concerned, it could have been worse – it might have been a pit pony that had been killed. There were plenty of men only too happy to fill the vacancy, a good pit pony cost money.

Gran Kincaid was one of the few to survive it all.

But now her mind, still needle sharp and capable of the clear, dispassionate thought instilled by her upbringing, was confused, torn as she was between pride and doubt and anxiety. She stood on the pavement outside 48, Bradbury Street, enjoying the grinning attention of the two beefy young men who towered over her, one dark, the other so fair, a matching pair in their jeans, open necked shirts and lightweight anoraks.

'You take care now, d'you hear me?'

'Yes, Gran.'

'Don't go doing anything stupid now.'

'No, Gran.'

Jonathan lifted the hatchback as Badger heaved his bag, engrained with the mud of countless rugby matches, on top of Jonathan's. Badger saw the heaped packs of beer cans.

'Hell. I didn't think of getting any beer,' he apologised.

'No need,' Jonathan laughed. 'More than enough there.' He looked down at Badger's leather slip-on shoes. 'You will need some soft shoes though.'

'Got some trainers in my bag. Will they do?'

'They'll do. Couple of extra jumpers too?'

Badger nodded.

'Where's your car?' Jonathan asked, looking around him.

'In the lane. Thought it would be easier to pinch there,' Badger grinned. 'I could do with the insurance money.'

The hatch slammed down and they stood side by side on the pavement once more as if waiting for the order to dismiss from a parade. For all the pride the matriarch would have in a miner son or grandson, it was nothing as compared with the adoration she would bestow on one who had been clever enough to break the family mould. Anyone could go down the pit. In a street where no coming or going went unnoticed, not everyone had a son or grandson who could get his degree and become a teacher or be a graduate policeman going to Staff College with a glittering future ahead of him. In the past, Gran Kincaid would have seen to it that money earned at the coal face by one brother had been used to educate the other and set him free. But she knew that to set him free was synonymous with letting him go. By giving him the means to cut the umbilical cord, she would not know where her boy was, every minute, day and night. As she would sit, hour after hour, staring into the fire, she would not have the mental data necessary to imagine what he would be doing at any given time this coming weekend. Would he come back, still talk her language, after mixing with these rich strangers? It was no more than she had hoped and dreamed of, made sacrifices for, but it still unsettled her, seeing the posh new car parked just where they had put that bloodstained stretcher down so many years before.

'This boat of yours, doctor; quite safe, is it?' She couldn't bring herself to call it a yacht. To Gran Kincaid, yachts meant no less than Cannes, the Duke of Windsor and 'that woman'. She had visions of blazers and Oxford bags. She turned to her grandson. 'Those shirts; were they aired properly?'

By way of reply, Badger bent down and kissed a dry, wrinkled cheek. 'See you in a few days, Gran. Say goodbye to Reggie for me, would you? I looked into his room but he seemed to be still asleep.'

On impulse, Jonathan bent and kissed her too. 'Don't worry, Mrs Kincaid. We'll look after him. And thank you again for my lunch; I won't need to eat for another week.'

With hands clutching a shawl around her shoulders, the hem of her black skirt inches off the paving stones, the tiny figure stood and watched the car drive away down the long street, absorbing every last millisecond of visual contact. Knowing that a dozen pairs of eyes would have been watching their every move, she straightened her shoulders proudly before going into the house, closing the door and calling up the stairs to enquire if the only one of her household remaining was going to get up for his dinner.

'Bloody marvellous.' Badger stretched out his arms, rubbing his palms together enthusiastically before beating a joyful tattoo on the dashboard.

'What is?' Jonathan laughed.

'Just getting away for a few days. Couldn't have come at a better time.'

'What did Peggy think about it?'

'Said I could go on the strict understanding I didn't enjoy myself. What happens about grub?'

'All provided.'

'And you do this fairly regularly?'

'In the summer, yes.'

'Lucky swine.' A trace of an anxious frown remained on honest features as if there was still one small matter to be resolved. 'How many of you sail in this boat usually?'

'Just the two of us.'

'This girl, Susannah, and yourself?'

'Yes.'

'So how does she feel about having the two of us gatecrashing the party? I take it she knows about us?' There was a sudden panic in his voice.

'She's delighted. She said she was looking forward to having a bit of intelligent conversation for a change.'

'But you do fancy this girl?'

'I think you can safely say that, yes,' Jonathan smiled, but only just.

Gavin Prescott was standing on the kerb, ready and waiting, a small, battered, plastic suitcase in one hand, when Jonathan drove up. There was no argument over seating arrangements as Badger got out and tipped his seat forwards for Gavin to clamber into the back. As Jonathan accelerated away, Badger turned in his seat.

'Ever been to Wales before, Gavin?'

'Never.'

'Brought your passport, have you? We might get stopped at the border.'

Jonathan laughed with them but added a word of warning. 'No cracks about the Welsh this weekend. Susannah's mother was Welsh and she's very proud of it.'

'Was Welsh?'

'She's dead.'

'Right. We'll just have to stick to Irish jokes then.'

Jonathan had chosen to drive along what he called the Riviera route that followed the North Wales coastline. He drove fast enough for young men not to get bored, not so fast they could not relax. Bright chatter sped the miles and Badger was the first to glimpse the sea.

'I still can't believe I'm going to be out there tomorrow.'

Taking his eyes from the road for a moment to glance to his right, Jonathan grinned. 'Well, you're not, you blockhead copper you. That's Liverpool Bay. It's Cardigan Bay we'll be sailing in.'

'I know that. You know what I mean.' His voice hushed a little. 'It looks so lonely out there. I trust there will be some other boats going with us?'

'On the way down, yes. Coming back we'll be on our own.'

That seemed to give both his passengers food for thought and Jonathan laughed. 'Don't worry; the forecast is pretty good. There's a front out in the Atlantic but apparently it's very slow moving and they're not expecting it to go through for a few days yet.'

Conversation waxed and waned as the hours passed. It died altogether as finally Jonathan threaded his way through the narrow streets of Abersoch.

It would have been difficult to imagine either Gavin's or Badger's mental picture of a holiday cottage by the sea, but it was impossible to mistake their disbelief at their first sight of the actual thing. To Jonathan's obvious delight, two mouths gaped as he pulled into a gravel drive that swept in an arc to the portico of a large white, Italian-style house. He drew to a halt behind the pale blue BMW 323i. Parked in front of the garage was a steel grey Bentley Mulsanne. Jonathan nodded at the Bentley. 'Looks as if we've got company. That's Susannah's old man's car.'

'Would that be Sir Warwick Ridgeway?' a quiet voice asked from the back seat.

'As ever was,' Jonathan laughed.

'Oh, my Gawd.' Badger pretended to shrink down in his seat. He pointed to the BMW. 'And whose is that?'

'Susannah's. She calls it her Fallot.'

'Fallot? What's a Fallot?'

'A blue baby.'

They were hauling their luggage out of the hatch when Susannah, elegant in a plain red cashmere jumper and pleated tartan skirt, came out to greet them. The kiss she gave Jonathan was the affectionate welcome for a favourite brother she had not seen for some time. As she was introduced to Gavin and Badger, her handshake was friendly and firm. She led them into the house and turned to Jonathan. 'Gavin and Badger are in the bedroom next to yours. You're too late for tea but Mrs Rowlands has made a cold buffet sort of thing for later. Don't take too long. Come down and have a drink.'

As they climbed the stairs, Jonathan felt like a prefect detailed by Matron to show two new boys their dormitory. He smiled to himself as he wondered what they would make of the Headmaster. As he showed them their room, Badger's face already proclaimed to all his immediate devotion to Matron, while Gavin's had the wary look of someone expecting to be bullied. After a wash, they regrouped upstairs before making a united descent.

In one corner of the sitting room stood a sideboard crammed with food, in another, Susannah stood smiling in front of a polished oak table, laden with bottles.

'Beer, Jonathan?'

'Please.'

'What about you, Badger?'

'Same, please.'

'Gavin?'

'Would you have an orange juice by any chance?'

'I think we can probably manage one of those, yes, Gavin,' she smiled. Jonathan had told her all about their guests over the phone. Badger was just as she had imagined him to be, totally predictable. The one so dark, the other so fair, Jonathan and Badger could be the positive and the negative of the same photograph. But Gavin; that was a strange one. She wondered how that friendship had come about. Badger would fit in anywhere, his open face his passport to prince's palace or widow's bedsit. But Gavin had the look of someone anxious to learn how to behave, someone who would not be offended if she taught him to ask boldly for an orange juice and who would then look forgiving if there was none. 'Go on out on the terrace, the lot of you. I'll bring your drinks out.'

They passed out on to a terrace where a stone-topped balustrade was the only barrier to a sheer drop to the water below. Badger and Gavin had time only for a quick gasp at the view before two men rose from where they had been sitting, their drinks on a white-painted iron table, their faces turned eastwards over the bay towards the pink haze lovingly laid like a blanket on Snowdonia's mountain range by a setting sun. If the three young men's arrival was an unwelcome intrusion, they were too well mannered to show it. Jonathan introduced his two friends to Sir Warwick Ridgeway, a big man whose well-cut board room pinstripe made no concession to a weekend beside the sea. There was a welcoming smile on his face as he nodded, silently shaking their hands. In turn, Ridgeway introduced them to the other man, shorter than he, brisker, quicker in eye and hand.

'And this is Casper, a business friend of mine; Casper Schumacher.'

'Jonathan. Badger. Gavin.' Even without the name and the accent, the sheer professionalism of the handshake would have been enough. There was scant need of Ridgeway's explanation.

'Casper's over from the States.'

'Business or pleasure, Mr Schumacher?' Jonathan asked politely, taking a frothing silver tankard from Susannah.

'Please.' Schumacher looked pained. 'The name's Casper. Combining business with pleasure, you might say, Jonathan. Warwick here has been kind enough to help me trace my roots. My mother's side of the family, they came from Wales, back in the bad old days. Her maiden name was Llewellyn and she wasn't very keen to change it to Schumacher, I can tell you. Had to work real hard on that little lady.'

In some ways, Schumacher was a disappointment to Jonathan. Though his accent was unmistakably American and his voice ground out, Kissinger-like, from the back of his throat, scarcely modulated by his lips, his tone was moderate and cultured, nothing like the archetype Jonathan might have expected. Jonathan would have considered hard-nosed ruthlessness as *sine qua non* in someone Sir Warwick Ridgeway honoured with the title of 'business friend'. Somehow, Casper Schumacher didn't look the part.

'And what d'you think of Wales?' Jonathan asked.

They all turned towards the sea and the mountains and Schumacher, in measured tones that sounded a little too much like the considered opinion of a company's balance sheet, compared favourably what he saw to the Bay of Naples. When he felt he had given sufficiently generous praise to conform with good manners, he turned to what really interested him – people.

'You three young fellas; are you all doctors?'

He did not look put out by the laughs.

'Badger here,' Jonathan said, 'is a policeman and Gavin, he works with me in the Casualty Department.'

'I'm a porter,' Gavin stated simply.

'Not to mention a thorn in my side.' There was a deceptive softness in the voice of someone who was the head of a vast business empire but the quiet smile on Sir Warwick Ridgeway's face looked genuine enough. 'I've been wanting to meet this young man face to face for some time now.'

'Badger.' Susannah's voice came from behind them. 'I sense an eyeball-to-eyeball confrontation. Let's leave them to it. Come and help me get some stuff from my car.'

Left alone, Gavin and Jonathan took the two seats facing the older men, Jonathan seemingly relaxed, Gavin upright and watchful, placing his glass on the table as if anxious to have both hands free.

'Now; what's this about this young man being a thorn in your flesh then, Warwick? He doesn't look like trouble to me.'

Sir Warwick's description of the sanctions that Gavin had devised against members of the Health Authority was given with the evenhandedness that showed that it was possible to be ruthlessly efficient while still able to see two sides of an argument. Jonathan listened intently, ready to leap to Gavin's defence but found it was not necessary. Sir Warwick had been generous in his words and Gavin calmly nodded his approval. A discussion flowed of funding and cutbacks, privatisation and competitive tendering, socialist dogma and insensitive management. No finger was wagged, no table thumped, no voice raised. The argument was fuelled by growled, perceptive questions from Schumacher, the thrust and riposte directed without anger between Ridgeway and Gavin. The only one not to take part was Jonathan, who felt more and more isolated. As he sat back and listened, it came home to him how, yet again, he had patronised Gavin. His instinctive reaction had been to go with Badger and Susannah but he had stayed out of a conscious feeling of loyalty to Gavin. He could hardly leave this black hospital porter, penniless and uneducated, to face two such powerful men alone. He must stay and protect him.

But there had been no need. It was not only physically that Gavin Prescott could take care of himself. Silently, in his mind, in his imagination, he had lain awake many an hour training himself equally as hard for just such a confrontation as for any physical assault. Without malice, the honours shared, the argument subsided.

Ridgeway turned to Schumacher. 'So you can see, Casper, we're not dealing with the usual kind of hospital porter. That was quite obvious to me the first time I heard him speak on TV.' His head swung back towards Gavin. 'Where did you learn to speak like that?'

The earliest days of the Ridgeway business empire were now part of South Lancashire's folklore; the picture of the young boy with no schooling, pushing his barrow round the back streets of Liverpool, collecting rags and scrap metal, was an example thrust before the eyes of many an indolent Lancastrian teenager. Gavin's reply had a solid basis in fact.

'Where did you, Sir Warwick?'

The laughter that followed the moment of stunned silence began as short grunting sounds deep in Schumacher's chest. He suppressed them long enough to glance sideways at his host as if seeking permission for a guest to laugh at his expense. He need not have worried and both older men put their heads back and roared.

'And these sanctions this young fella's imposed,' Schumacher asked, breathlessly, 'have they been effective at all? Have they hit anyone where it hurts, in the wallet? What about the Chairman, for instance, Warwick?' He looked delighted as he saw Ridgeway grin guiltily.

'Only indirectly. The milkman on the Authority. He likes to make out it's his own business but, in fact, I own it.'

As if signalling he had heard enough jokes at his own expense, Ridgeway turned to Gavin.

'And what are your plans? I don't see you as a hospital porter for the rest of your days.'

'I have no intention of being a hospital porter all my life, Sir Warwick, but, for the next year or so, I have a family commitment which makes it impossible to do anything about it. After that, I intend taking up full-time trade union work.'

'Ever thought of coming down on the other side of the fence? Would a job in management hold any attraction for you?'

'And who'd give me a job in management with my background, my education and the colour of my skin?'

'I might. Sounds as if the colour of your skin bothers you more than it bothers me.'

'And get rid of a trouble-maker in the process, bring him into the fold where you could keep an eye on him? Find myself redundant at forty, too old to do anything else?' Gavin heard Schumacher chuckle. 'No, thank you, Sir Warwick. There's more future for me amongst my own lot, making it as hot as I can for you.'

'Good for you,' Schumacher muttered.

'I admire your loyalty, Gavin' – Ridgeway sounded as if he meant what he said – 'but you won't find fame and fortune amongst the working class, you know.'

'Sod the working class.'

The little gasp of astonishment, given by both men, caught Ridgeway as he was swallowing almost neat whisky. The fumes, aspirated into his larynx, sent him into an acute fit of coughing, forcing him to break wind noisily, leaving him with eyes streaming as he tried to speak. As he put his glass down, spilling some of its contents as he did so, there was no doubt who was in command of the moment.

'What has the working class ever done for me?'

With Ridgeway still wheezing, Schumacher took up the conversation. 'Am I correct in thinking then, Gavin, that you do not see the union movement as some sort of a crusade?'

'Personal crusade, yes; political, no. I think politics has become the curse of the modern working class, a cross it has had to bear too long, dragging it down with such bloody stupid concepts as equality and fraternity. I don't want to consider myself equal to some lazy bum who has no intention of doing an honest day's work in his life. And I've had experience of brothers. Give me a good honest enemy any day.'

Gavin paused but only for a moment before his ideas poured out, a handful of powerful unions charging realistic dues and cut free from political dogma to pursue profit for its members by forcing highly trained accountants of their own on to Boards of Directors. No cap-in-hand beggars threatening nothing but disruption but highly paid financial brains expert in every board-room dirty trick, as keen on a share of the profits for their members as the dividends for the shareholders.

It sounded naive even to Jonathan, who, taking scant interest in the investment of his own money, had little expertise with which to judge. If either of the older men thought the same, they were polite enough not to show it, both obviously affected by the young man's passion. Ridgeway looked sideways, smiling gently at Schumacher.

'Wouldn't you like to be young again, Casper; feel as strongly as that again?'

Schumacher thought for a moment, gazing into a glass of old Scotch as if the ability to afford such luxuries needed to be weighed in the balance. 'Not really,' he growled. 'It's much too painful a stage in life to go through twice, don't you think? Once was enough.'

Badger and Jonathan, flushed and sweaty in the close, muggy atmosphere common to all yacht-club bars on a Saturday night, sat in the wide bay window, inky darkness at their backs, crowded in on both sides by the crews from the New Quay boats. Most of the group had pint glasses in their hands, unable to put them down for the empties that crowded the table top. They stopped singing for a moment to shout their invitation to join them as Susannah and Gavin appeared. Smiling, Susannah shook her head, raising her voice to make herself heard.

'Jonathan, we're going, You've had nothing to eat. Are you coming?'

Jonathan's reply was drowned in the shouts of protest as restraining arms were laid across both his and Badger's chests. There was another burst of laughter as a drunken voice proclaimed his readiness to go with her. Laughing herself, Susannah gave up the unequal fight.

'God help you in the morning, that's all I say. First launch is at seven. The start is at nine. You make sure you're on board by eight, d'you hear?'

There was laughing chaos as several unsteady bodies tried to stand to attention and salute but, long before Susannah had reached the door, the empty glasses began to reverberate once more to the sound of 'Cwm Rhondda'.

Chico Morelli had begun to feel his new responsibility. Slowly, he had come to accept that his father would never be the same again, that he would never spend much time out of his wheelchair. Now he, Chico, would have to step out of his father's shadow and become the man of the house, the provider. He felt the same uncertainty of any young man on the threshold of his chosen career. His curriculum vitae was reasonable; not brilliant by many standards but sufficiently sound, he felt, to ensure a reasonable degree of future success. His first qualification, a conditional discharge for taking a conveyance without permission was modest enough, but Chico could take pride in the fact that he had been only 12 years old at the time. But things had improved. Although his passion for other people's motor cars had accounted for the bulk of his court appearances, there had developed a wholesome leavening of attempted burglary, theft and criminal damage to grace his form sheet. The charges of possessing cannabis had proved that he was not overspecialised in his interests but

Chico felt that it was most probably his latest sentence of six months prison, suspended for two years, for assaulting the police during the course of burglary and theft while carrying an offensive weapon that had finally confirmed his promise of greater things to come.

But he needed to recruit an accomplice, somebody quick, alert and hungry.

'You sure about this?' Danny asked.

'No prob. Two minutes' work. I've been sussing it out for weeks.'

'I don't know,' Danny said, looking doubtfully at the Balaclava helmet and pickaxe handle he had just been given. 'Never done nothing like this before.' He shook the wooden club tentatively. 'That could hurt somebody.'

'That's only to frighten them. No way you're going to have to use it. And there's got to be fifty, hundred quid in it for you, easy. For two minutes' work. Think how much grass that can buy. And don't forget how much you owe me,' he added menacingly.

'Dunno,' Danny muttered.

For all the violent element in Northend's community, Father Mulcahy had seen it simply as further evidence of His wondrous works that there had always been religious harmony in the vast sprawling estate. There were Catholic and Protestant churches, doctors, schools and football teams – but no ghettos – and it was to him a particular source of pride that the pensioners' Saturday night Bingo session in the Catholic Church Hall attracted as many Protestants as those from amongst his own flock. It was also a great relief to have at least one church function that ran itself. All he was required to do was to provide the cash float of about £100, all in coin, which was returned at Sunday Matins by the two retired bank managers who supervised the affair. He could never be sure whether the night would show a profit or loss – only that every penny would be accounted for – but the amount in the old canvas bag had never been more than £120 when the doors were locked at eleven o'clock exactly.

It was ironic that two men who had spent the last few years of their working lives presiding over hundreds of thousands of pounds and surrounded by security screens and burglar alarms, should suddenly find themselves confronted by Balaclava helmets and pick handles when responsible for £82.50. No one would have quibbled if they had decided the amount involved too trivial to defend, but they were made of sterner stuff. Without hesitation, shoulder to shoulder, they came forwards, inside the arc of the descending clubs.

'Sod this.'

From the corner of his eye, Morelli saw Danny drop his pick handle and run. Anxious to stand back so that he could swing his club, he tried to disentangle himself from an old man's instinctive fury. He had just bent his knee to bring it up in a defenceless crutch when the second man, freed of Danny's attentions, took up the attack. An arm that had held a rifle as a lean young man in baggy khaki shorts had picked his way through Rommel's desert minefields, swung a bag full of coin to bring it crashing on a black, evil eyed helmet. As the aged bag split, sending coins cascading into the gutter, a dazed Morelli grabbed it to wrench it from the old man's hand and run after Danny and into the darkness.

Danny laid no claim to the pitiful reward for the night's work that remained in the torn canvas bag. His face showed disgust and remorse as he stripped off the sweaty hood.

'You can count me out, Chico. I'm not cut out for this bloody game.'

'That was bloody obvious, wo'n't it? Great start to a partnership that, you sodding off even before it had started.'

'Stuff the partnership. There's got to be easier ways of making a living.' Danny looked with sudden loathing at what he held in his hands. 'First thing we'd better do is burn these things.'

'No, don't do that.' Chico sounded as if he had already forgiven Danny. He took the Balaclava gently from him. 'You never know when that might come in useful.'

21

Jonathan and Badger had overslept. With Gavin standing at her shoulder, Susannah, furious at their hangovers, gave them no chance to eat Mrs Rowlands's breakfast. By the time the launch hammered noisily away from the slipway, the anchorage was empty. The New Quay boats, their crews' enthusiasm for late-night carousal matched only by their passion for competitive sailing, were already weaving their way between the permanent moorings as they waited for the ten-minute gun. A bunch of businessmen, retired master mariners, pathologists, surgeons, pharmacists and dentists, they spent their summer weekends chasing each other around a part of the

Irish Sea that could be a mill pond one moment, a screaming fury the next. Faces plastered with sun cream often peered out of dripping hoods. The club's rules were as unpredictable as the weather, often seeming to change in the middle of a race, but one law remained immutable – anyone could join in; anyone, that is, prepared to pit his sailing wits against a wealth of canny racing experience.

Susannah was still tacking back to the start line against a keen easterly when the starting gun fired and the ribald remarks that came at them across the water as the New Quay boats surged past in the opposite direction made little concession to the fact that it was a woman at the helm. Over the start line and Susannah headed after the other boats, their spinnakers already set, as they made for St Tudwal's Sound, the gap between mainland and island that would set them free into Cardigan Bay.

'We've got a new reaching spinnaker,' Susannah shouted. 'Thought we'd try that today.'

Jonathan nodded and, a few minutes later, hauled hand over hand on the spinnaker halyard to draw out a vast expanse of bright red sail from its bag, like a conjuror producing an endless stream of silk. The sail filled with a smack like a flat, broad whiplash, making the boat lurch and sending Gavin and Badger grabbing for support. Jonathan looked at Susannah, trying to ignore the ache the sight of her always gave him. He grinned and got his first, slow, forgiving smile.

'Coffee?' was another way of saying he was sorry.

The wind freshened and the boat heeled as it set off in pursuit. Slowly, they began to carve their way through the haze that filled the gap between themselves and the back markers. As the haze thickened to swallow up all but one or two of the boats ahead, Jonathan turned to Susannah, frowning.

'Henry's very quiet. Haven't heard a thing from him. Unusual for him.' Henry Armitage, New Quay's cruiser captain, enjoyed a friendly chat with his fleet, especially if the visibility was poor, invariably if he looked like winning.

'VHF's not working; can't send or receive,' Susannah said. 'Rowlands only spotted it yesterday. Hasn't had time to get it fixed.' She smiled. 'Nice to have a peaceful trip for once.'

Another three hours and they were up amongst the tailenders, but it was Gavin, tense, silent and watchful, who first noticed the other boats turn suddenly to port towards the invisible coastline. It was he also who first heard the deep throb of the naval frigate that loomed out of the mist, seemingly suspended in mid-air in the horizonless haze. It passed across their bows twice, the second time close enough for its wake to slam into *Gelert*'s bows.

Jonathan raised his eyebrows. 'Do you think they're trying to tell us something?' he asked.

'I rather think we've wandered across the Aberporth missile range on a day they're firing,' Susannah replied.

'Seems to have lost interest.' Badger shielded his eyes as if to see further through the mist. 'He's off. What do we do now?'

'Press on. He's done us no harm. Look over there.' Susannah nodded to her left, grinning. 'It's given us half a mile on those boats. It only leaves those three up ahead to catch. See if you can get another half a knot out of that spinnaker. We might still just have a race on our hands.'

With the wind sluicing back off the bright red sail and with every inch of rigging taut and quivering, the boat heeled and raced through the water.

'Out of there, Gavin, and up on the side with you. And you Badger.'

Within ten miles of the finish, the mist lifted and they recognised New Quay head bathed in the evening sunshine. They knew they could not catch the leading boat, a big Sadler, but they were rapidly overhauling the other two who were now converging on the finish on their landward side. The last hour, as all four sat jammed side by side, was a breathless, rushing, hissing charge on the back of a thoroughbred. The thrill might not have the sudden exquisite intensity of the rider leaping at Becher's Brook or the ski jumper launching himself into space but it was a sensation stretched out far, far longer. Susannah, eyes shining, lips open, had ducked under the top guardrail, bracing herself over the top of it at each gust as she concentrated on keeping them in a straight line. At the first sign that she was being overpowered, Jonathan played the mainsail track with a coordination only possible between two people who had sailed a great deal together. The nearer they got to the finish, the louder Badger roared them on, giving them a running commentary as he snatched glances at the opposition over his shoulder. By the time they could distinguish the colours of the houses, looking down on the bay, tier on tier, like boxes at the opera, they were level and the last few minutes were a blur of pier and waving arms, moored boats and bright coloured dinghies as, after 45 miles of hard sailing, they squeezed home ahead of the other two boats by no more than a few yards.

As Susannah turned into the wind, Jonathan doused the spinnaker, reducing the vibrant driving force into an inert, unmanageable heap. He yelled at Badger to help him stow it through the narrow companionway but got no response as Badger stood, staring bemusedly back out to sea in the direction from which they had come. 'That,' he said, to no one in particular unless possibly to himself, 'was, without doubt, the most fantastic bloody sensation I have ever known. Is it always like that?'

'Unfortunately, no,' Susannah laughed. 'That was one of the better ones.

If only you two drunken slobs hadn't made us late for the start, we might have won that.'

'What happens next?' Badger asked, as if prepared to do it all over again.

A curry and rice, cooked by Gavin, and they made their way ashore. The yacht club bar heaved with warm humanity, friendly Welsh voices giving the humid atmosphere its own unique timbre. The day had been hot, more like July than May, and a small cheer went up as they pushed open the door. Chairs scuffed the floor as room was made for them midst the crews who had raced them down. Empty glasses appeared like a sudden rash as Jonathan offered to buy them a drink.

'Good thing you didn't win today,' said one face, red with sun and beer. 'I'd have protested.'

'Why's that?' Susannah had already guessed the reason but tried to look genuinely innocent.

'Not changing course when you were told you were crossing their firing range. Gave you quite an advantage. It would have served you right if you'd had an Exocet up your transom.'

'Is that what happened? We did wonder but our VHF is on the blink.' Her explanation was greeted with howls of disbelief.

'Yes, yes, we believe you.'

'The old Nelson touch, eh?'

After a day's hard sail, an hour of noise and beery warmth had their effect. When the singing began, Susannah decided she had had enough. She leaned over to Jonathan. 'I'm just going to have a word with my favourite harbourmaster and then I'm going aboard. I'll cadge a cast out. Don't be too late. Let's try and get an early start in the morning.'

Jonathan nodded happily, now accepting without question that Gavin would go with her.

It is equally possible to be woken from sleep when a noise stops as when it starts. Susannah looked at her watch to find it was well past midnight when the sound of singing no longer carried across the bay. It was another half-hour before she heard the giggling whispers. The boat rocked a little and there was a loud splash followed by gasping curses from one and suppressed laughter from another. Minutes later there was no mistaking the sound of wet clothes slopping on the deck above her. She smiled for the first time as she heard Gavin's welcoming comments as two equally drunk young men half-climbed, half-fell into the cabin, one naked, hairy torso dripping all over him as someone searched for a towel.

Susannah and Gavin were sitting in the cockpit, enjoying their breakfast in the blissful stillness of a late May morning. Gavin was as anxious as Susannah to be off and the appearance of two bleary faces in the companionway evoked neither sympathy nor offers to cook their breakfast. It became obvious who had fallen overboard the night before as Badger emerged in a strange mixture of Jonathan's and his own clothes. They both had obvious difficulty in swallowing the rough bacon sandwich they managed to make for themselves and gulped gratefully at the coffee Gavin forgivingly brewed for them. Thumping headaches made them close their eyes as they bent to stow the inflatable. It was obvious Jonathan did not enjoy the experience of weighing the anchor and took less than his usual care in stowing it and its chain in the anchor well on the foredeck. Susannah started the diesel and Jonathan stayed up at the bows, anywhere away from the thud and throb of the engine.

Onlookers on piers and jetties watch boats arrive with interest but find it an irresistible urge to wave as boats leave, especially if they are heading bravely out to sea alone. Three or four early risers, self-righteously sucking in chestfuls of fresh, salty air, were no exceptions. Gavin and Susannah waved back, Susannah smiling, the arc drawn by her arm becoming more purposeful, more personal, as she saw the unmistakable figure of the harbourmaster hurrying along the pier. His wave, both arms extended, crossing and uncrossing above his head, seemed a little excessive even for such a whole-hearted man but they were too far away to make any sense out of his valedictory shout.

'Made a bit of a conquest there, I think,' Jonathan shouted from the bows, feeling an ache in his chest that had nothing to do with his second hangover on successive days.

To Gavin the coastline passed by agonisingly slowly as, for the first two hours, the diesel drove the boat northwards over a glassy sea. Where exhilaration had carried them southwards the day before, silent boredom set in, Gavin with the tiller in his hand, his eyes riveted to the compass, Jonathan asleep below. Another two hours and Badger was dozing also when Susannah leaned across his legs to call into the cabin.

'Jonathan.' She waited for him to rub his eyes and stick his tongue out a couple of times as if he didn't relish the taste in his mouth. 'Come and have a look at this.'

Climbing stiffly out into the cockpit, he looked where she pointed, away to the north-west. Whatever word came immediately to mind, he suppressed it, tucking his shirt in his trousers, suddenly becoming alert, all vestige of hangover driven from his mind by what he saw.

'I've been watching it for the last half an hour,' Susannah said. 'It's coming at us like a train.'

'What is, Susannah?' Already there was anxiety in Gavin's voice.

'Something I suspect the harbourmaster was trying to warn us about. I think we'd better get ready.'

The watery pale blue sky immediately above them shaded away to the north-west, gradually darkening until it was almost black where it met a leaden sea. There was no honest line of benign white cloud, heralding the usual cold front, just dirty grey smudges like chalk on a poorly cleaned blackboard. From where they stood, the horizon already looked angry and serrated, the prodromal ripples beginning to whisper menacingly under their hull.

'What d'you think?' Jonathan asked.

'Two reefs in the main and a reefed number three – soon as you like – while I get dressed. Better too little sail than too much. Might be a bit hairy up on deck later though I suppose we had better have the storm jib handy too; we could easily need it if that weather is as bad as it looks. I'll take over from Gavin while you get those two dressed up.'

'What d'you think we'd better do?' Jonathan tried to conceal the unique combination of fear and excitement. 'Shall we run back to New Quay?'

'Back to New Quay?' Gavin showed unashamed alarm.

'It's going to get pretty tough if we go on.'

'No worse than my Inspector if I don't turn up for my shift tomorrow.' There was a genuine smile on Badger's face as if there was nothing Cardigan Bay could produce to match his Inspector's wrath.

'We must be somewhere just over halfway there.' Susannah looked at the three men. 'Do we press on?'

Two heads nodded.

'All right then. I'll mark our position on the chart so at least we'll know where we were when it started.'

The sight of Susannah clad from head to toe in foul weather clothing did little to reassure Gavin. With a grateful sigh, he handed her the tiller. The boat was already beginning to heel.

'When you've got your gear on, Gavin, d'you think you could boil up a few cans of soup and fill those two big thermos flasks?'

The boat began to butt its way into short steep seas, shuddering as it crashed into the occasional bigger one. Gavin, when he reappeared, looked like a black monk, his face shrunken and withdrawn within the hood of his oversized jacket. Jonathan, the webbing of his safety harness looped around his collar, winked at Susannah from the galley as he boiled the soup. A few minutes later, they sat, side by side, the coachroof closed, half the companionway sealed off. No word was spoken in the strange hush that followed the engine being switched off. For the best part of an hour, the boat sped through the water at much the same angle and speed at which it had speared in at the finishing line the day before but now there was a subtle difference. The wind in the rigging now moaned where it had sung. For an hour Badger, nearest the bows, took the brunt of the solid water that began to break over the bows, grinning as it slashed against his back. Next to him sat Jonathan, mainsheet in his hand. Gavin, his eyes staring with the fixity of imminent sickness, sat between Jonathan and Susannah, the latter wearing that look unique to someone who feels ultimately responsible for a boat and its crew. Time became meaningless, something not to be thought about; it was now no more than a question of enduring for just that length of misery it took to reach safety. It crossed their minds whether it still might not be wiser to turn and run back but they decided they were already beyond the point of no return. The wind now howled, whipping the tops of the waves into spume, ruffling the smooth backs of a long swell down which the boat careered. Gavin and Badger saw the other two taking increasingly frequent glances at the Decca Navigator repeater below one of the compasses on the bulkhead. Though the everchanging figures, bright in the grey gloom, meant nothing to them, it was obvious they were becoming vitally important long before Jonathan leaned in front of Gavin to shout at Susannah.

'Not going to make it, are we?'

'No. We're east of it already and the wind is veering north all the time.'

The words were whipped away from Badger and he heard nothing. Gavin looked for a moment as if he was going to ask what that meant but seemed to change his mind.

Anyone who sails regularly in the northern half of Cardigan Bay has engraved on his heart the latitude and longitude of the Causeway Buoy, that doleful sentinel, endlessly bobbing and swaying, which marks the outer extremity of Sarn Badrig, St Patrick's Causeway, ten miles of hungry reef that bares its fangs at low spring tides.

'The sooner we tack out the happier I'll be.' Susannah ducked as green water came over the side to sluice away beneath their feet. 'It's blowing harder than ever.'

'I'll go along with that,' Jonathan muttered.

'Does that mean going back out to sea?' A voice, controlled if faint, came from beneath Gavin's hood.

'Not for long.' Jonathan rubbed Gavin's back and shoulders as he stood up. 'Once we're round the buoy we can head back inshore and, with the way the wind is shifting, we'll start to get the shelter of the peninsula. Down hill all the way then.'

'Thank God for that.' Gavin had just found out how quickly and deeply one can become religious in a small boat.

All four had crossed over beneath the flapping, rattling bedlam of the tack when they all heard the sudden slithering crash.

For a second they stared at each other, anywhere but in the direction of the crash. Reluctantly, Jonathan looked up at the bows. He turned back to Susannah.

'Anchor's broken loose.' He unwound the harness from round his neck. 'I'll have to go and stow it properly. We'll be in a hell of a mess if that goes over the side.'

'Shall I go about?' Susannah shouted. 'Perhaps it might slide back in place.'

Jonathan shook his head. 'It seems to be jammed against the pulpit at the moment. If you go about, it might go straight over the other side.'

The sound of more and more chain escaping from the well cut short any further discussion. Sliding the clip of his harness along the guardrail, Jonathan grabbed at any hand hold he could find as he crouched and slithered along the deck. He had reached the bows and was moving his safety harness from the wire guardrail to the rigid toerail when a wave broke over the bows.

'Shit.'

The curse seemed to have been shouted from close behind him but he had to wait a second before the salt water drained away sufficiently to allow him to open his eyes. Badger's face, inches away from his own, also streaming water, grinned at him. Badger had to put his mouth almost inside Jonathan's hood to make himself heard. 'Thought you might need some help.'

'You bloody fool. Get back. You've got no harness on.'

Trying to reduce the angle at which they were heeled, Susannah had brought the boat's head up slightly into the wind but, if anything, it had made things worse as the boat lost its stabilising momentum and began to be thrown about at random, the foresail flapping and adding to the confusion. More chain emerged from the well and began to cascade over the side. Jonathan knew that to let much more go over the side was certain to drag the anchor after it from where it had wedged itself precariously against the pulpit. Stretching his leg across the deck, he tried to gain purchase against the opposite toerail only for a loop of chain to slide under his foot at the crucial moment. The boat lurched and he found himself falling, slithering feet first beneath the opposite guardrail and over the side. With the boat now steeply heeled, he was chest deep in the water by the time his harness arrested him and one instinctive haul on the toerail told him he had no chance of getting back on board on his own. With nightmarish slow motion, he saw Badger's one hand grasp the webbing, the other take hold of a stanchion alongside him. He lip-read rather than heard Badger roar, 'Now pull, you bastard,' before Badger threw his head back, his eyes closed, his thick lips spluttering with the effort of heaving Jonathan on board. The stanchion bent but did not break and soon they lay, two exhausted, dripping heaps of arms and legs entwined on the foredeck. Agonisingly slowly, they managed between them to recover the chain, stow the anchor securely and crawl back to the relative safety of the cockpit. Her face saying it all, Susannah stretched out a hand to hold Jonathan's for a moment. Gavin might have been carved in stone.

The sea had got under Jonathan's waterproof trousers and he felt every cold squelch as they battled out to sea once more. He felt better as he took his turn at the tiller and spirits began to rise as they decided they could safely go about once more. Though the wind still howled, the seas gradually moderated and three of them mustered the occasional few words and a smile. The Decca winked its encouragement from the bulkhead, measuring steadily decreasing distances to safety.

It took a little time to convince all three of them that it really was the St Tudwal's light that came and went like a will-o-the-wisp amongst the troughs and crests that heaved, mile on mile, over their port bow. Another half an hour and they were sure and did their best to involve Gavin in their soaring morale. Susannah lifted the corner of his hood to display a picture of abject misery.

'Nearly there, Gavin.'

The statement from deep inside the hood that never again would he step foot in a boat under ten thousand tons, followed by a long-drawn-out theatrical groan, was made not so much in the voice of fear as of true conviction born of hour after hour of unmitigated misery.

Susannah felt the peaceful exhaustion she had craved in the wasted years and wondered how long it would last before she had to come back for more.

Badger wondered what were his chances of being asked back again. He had seen danger tackled in the only way he knew how – head on. They had not turned and run away. He had thrilled to every crash and shudder as the little boat had refused to be denied the course it had taken. But he knew that had only been possible by dint of Susannah's and Jonathan's knowledge and experience. Now he wanted to learn too. Would they teach him or would they resent his intrusion into their strange relationship? Of even greater importance, what would Peggy say about it? Peggy and Susannah? He just didn't see it. Hell, he'd worry about that tomorrow. Badger began to finger his bruises, prodding enthusiastically through the thick layers of clothing. Already he could feel the hot soapy water, the first draught of beer in the back of his throat.

And Jonathan, feeling Badger's honest warmth and strength alongside him, decided he had never known such happiness.

22

Badger had welcomed Micky Dunn's cryptic phone call as an excuse to get out of the house. Danny wanted to see him, not at the Centre; did Badger know that lane that ran behind the snooker hall?

As Badger's old car crawled groaning along the lane, Danny appeared from the vandalised ruins of a row of lock-up garages, useful now only for glue-sniffing sessions and teenage sex self-education. He jumped in the car, slammed the door and crouched like a hunted animal.

'What's all this, then?' Badger asked as he switched the engine off.

'Want some help, don't I?'

'What sort of help, Danny?'

'You said you would.' Danny turned his face accusingly. 'Or was that all bullshit like everyone else?'

'Bullshit yourself. What happens if anyone does help you? You stick it for a couple of weeks and then chicken out. Gavin tells me he can't be bothered with you any more, that you hardly ever turned up for his lessons, and Micky tells me you're living rough again. Why should I bother with you any more?'

'One more chance, please, Badger.'

'Why? What's happened?'

'Nothing. Oh, shit!' Danny crouched lower as a group of youths, jostling and slouching their way from a day of penniless boredom to a night of mischief, turned the corner into the lane. A strange car parked in a back lane, the faces of two conspirators pale through the windscreen, was an unexpected bonus, a gift sent from heaven to help fill a few moments of vacant existence. Even better, as they came closer, the big blonde bugger in the driving seat was an off-duty copper, and wasn't the other that round-arsed fairy that was one of Chico Morelli's lot? The car rocked as underemployed muscles were exercised. The occupants' ears sang as the roof reverberated to the blows of open palms. As serious doubts were joyously raised as to Danny's gender and grim fears expressed as to Chico's reaction when he heard of Danny's affair with another man, a slobbering wet kiss was implanted against the driver's window. By the time Badger had opened his door, they were in full flight, turning, twisting, taunting as they went.

Danny waited until Badger closed the door once more. 'That's bloody torn it.'

'That lot friends of yours?'

211

'Do me a favour.'

'Why so upset then?'

'Because Chico's going to know about us meeting like this before tonight's out.'

'And that bothers you?'

'You've got to be joking. Of course it bothers me.'

'Why?' Badger persisted doggedly.

'Because he's likely to beat the shit out of me, that's why. It's all right for you; you don't live in this hell-hole. It's just a game to you. You come and go and get paid for it. I live here twenty-four hours a day and don't get paid for it.'

'There is a solution, Danny,' Badger said quietly.

'What's that then?'

'He's on a suspended sentence. A bit of help from you and we could get him off your back for a nice tidy stretch, long enough to get you organised, probably away from here.'

'Nothing doing, Mr Kincaid. I may have realised I'm not cut out for a life of crime – that's why I'm here – but that doesn't mean I'm a grass either. It's still a case of us and them and, whether I like it or not, at the moment I'm still one of us. But I want out, Badger. I'm desperate. I'll do anything to get out.'

'Including going back to school?'

'Yes.'

'And karate lessons again if Gavin will have you back?'

Tight black curls shook as a head was nodded.

'And go into care?'

That took longer to answer. 'If I have to.'

There was no doubt in Badger's mind as to what he should be doing, what any right-minded copper would do. There had to be some good reason for Danny's sudden change of heart. It didn't take any great intelligence to guess it probably had something to do with Morelli – Danny would be unlikely to be the prime mover in anything very adventurous. He should take him in. Who could tell what Danny might not come up with after half an hour on his own in the interrogation room with a couple of the hard boys putting the frighteners on him? It could mean the absence of Morelli from Northend for some considerable time and a feather in PC Kincaid's cap as he left for the Staff College. But what would it mean for Danny? Wrung out of all useful information by methods that would alienate him for ever more to all forms of authority, forced to give evidence in court that would alienate him equally from his peers, he would be thrown back on the streets like an undersized fish to develop until he was big enough to worth netting once more. And what were those high-sounding words Badger had said to his Inspector? He would get more satisfaction from keeping an underprivileged youngster away from a three-month custodial sentence than sending a hardened villain down for twenty years? Is that what they had been, just high-sounding words?

He leaned forwards and started the engine.

'Where are we going then?' Danny demanded.

'To see Micky; tell him you're agreeable to going into care, find out exactly what we can do about this dyslexia of yours. After that, to see Gavin; ask him if he'll take you on again. We'll try the General first and, if he's not there, his home.'

'But Chico'll be there.' Danny's voice screeched in alarm.

'You're going to have to learn to stand up to the Chico Morellis of this world, Danny.'

'That's all right if you're built like a brick shithouse like you. But what about poor little sods like me?'

Badger laughed as he let in the slipping clutch.

Anger and concern fought for control of Taff Evans's face as he sought to look anywhere but at Badger. 'Hardcastle wants you. You great brainless idiot.'

'What for?'

'On the double. He's in no mood to be kept hanging around.'

The Inspector was uttering monosyllables solemnly into his phone as Badger knocked and entered his room. At a wave of Hardcastle's hand, he went out again to stand waiting the other side of the closed door. A barked command from Hardcastle and Badger stood before his desk once more.

'You'll never learn, will you, Kincaid?'

Abruptly, Hardcastle stood to face Kincaid across the desk. 'Did you come in by car this morning?' he asked.

Surprised, Badger raised bushy, blonde eyebrows. 'Yes, I always do.'

'Where is it? In the yard?'

Badger nodded.

'Right then. Let's get it over.'

'Get what over?'

Without answering, Hardcastle strode out of the room. As they traversed corridors and stairs, heads swung their way and conversations dipped as if in sympathy. Along one side of the yard, Panda cars were parked in a row, neat, business like and spotlessly clean. Opposite them stood a motley collection of private cars. Badger's would have stood out amongst them even if Taff Evans had not been standing alongside it, hands in pockets, moodily kicking at its tyres. Hardcastle turned to Badger and held out his hand.

'Keys?'

'It's open.'

With a cluck of despair, Hardcastle nodded to Evans.

Taff started by raising the boot of his friend's car, throwing on to the ground an assortment of dirty rugby socks and a damp towel. A muddy Jock strap and battered gum shield Evans picked out between finger and thumb. By the time spare wheel, jack and foot pump had been removed, his hands were smeared with oil and dirt. He looked at Hardcastle and shook his head.

Inside the car, Taff began on the back seat but found nothing. With one hand under the front passenger seat, his expression froze. Reluctantly, he withdrew his hand, refusing to look at what it held as if the very touch of it had been enough.

'All right, Evans. Let me have that.'

Sliding one hand inside as if pulling on an oversized black woollen mitten, Hardcastle spread his fingers. Pink flesh gleamed through three large holes. 'This yours?' he asked quietly.

'Of course not. Never seen it before.' Badger looked at the balaclava with stunned fascination.

'Can you give any good reason why it should be there?'

'None.'

'Short while ago, two young thugs wearing these things mugged a couple of old dodgers coming out of a Bingo hall. But one of them lost his bottle and legged it and he was seen to have some sort of yellow stain on the back of his mask.' Slowly, Hardcastle turned his hand over, using the other to stretch the stitching to the full, the loose knitting giving way except for where it was matted beneath the smear of caked and cracking yellow paint.

'As from now, Kincaid' – no judge passing the death sentence could have been more solemn – 'you are suspended from duty pending further inquiry. You will report to me daily but you are relieved from all duties indefinitely. An investigating officer will be appointed from outside this Division and you will not communicate with any possible witnesses in the meanwhile.' For a moment, the real Hardcastle broke through. 'I suggest the sooner you get in touch with the Federation, the better.'

'Bloody nonsense.'

Hardcastle turned on an irate Welshman. 'You keep out of this, Evans. He's been warned before. More bloody fool he if he didn't take any heed.'

'But, for God's sake.' Taff was not his usual articulate self, his words struggling against his fury. 'You'd have to be deaf, dumb and blind not to tell that that thing was planted there. He's been fitted up and you knew all about it.'

'Evans, I said watch it.'

'You even knew what we were looking for.'

'If it's that obvious to you, then it will be just as obvious to the investigating officer, won't it? And Kincaid will have nothing to worry about, will he?'

'And how long is that going to take? What are his chances of going to Bramshill now?'

'I warned him, Evans. Now leave it at that. He's suspended and that's the end to that.'

'Do you have the power to do that?' Badger's stubborn defiance was overcoming his disbelief at what was happening.

'You can do better than that, Kincaid. I've already had verbal authority from the DAC. We'll have it in black and white for you by tomorrow.'

'On what grounds?'

'Discreditable conduct, bringing the force into disrepute, concealing evidence. I don't know,' Hardcastle sounded weary, 'but I'm sure they'll come up with something.'

'Sheer bloody madness.'

Inspector George Hardcastle would dearly have liked to agree but he let Taff Evans have the last word.

Jonathan had done his best. He had played squash with Badger once or twice, allowing him to wreak vengeance on a small black ball that could never be hit too hard. They had gone out one night with the sole expressed purpose of getting mindlessly drunk and had failed, however hard they had tried. But Jonathan had been a busy man with limited time off-duty. It had been the same with Peggy. She had taken the brunt of his misery until she had barked at him, told him to grow up, and seen him turn and walk away without a word. Peggy had cried but had not been too worried; the great soft idiot would be back. Micky Dunn had found him an embarrassment, a reminder that, if he had not got him interested in the Centre in the first place, Badger would not have been in the trouble he was. He had put it to Badger, would it not be wiser to keep away from the Centre, and especially from Danny, while the investigation was taking place? Badger had taken the hint. There was only one place he now fitted, sitting between his brother and grandmother, staring into the fire that glowed in shadows that still defied the sun of early June.

His regular report to the station was the highlight of his day, the only purposeful activity left to him. He always delayed it until the afternoon, trying to draw it out as long as he could by chatting up his old mates. But he was beginning to sense them turning away, busying themselves suddenly, as soon as he appeared round a door. To see fresh faces was the chance of human contact and Badger's spirits rose as the patrol car swept into the station yard, its tyres squealing as the driver parked the powerful vehicle amongst the tiny Pandas. The navigator played scrum-half and there was affection and respect in the grin as he opened his door and clambered out. He leaned his elbow on the car roof, tipped his hat on the back of his head, a woman's voice intoning monotonously from the radio behind him.

'Hullo, Badger. How's it going? Sorry to hear of your troubles. I know lock forwards are not supposed to both push and think but you've taken it a bit far, haven't you? What have you been up to then?'

A young face, already hardened by service in the cutting edge of any police force, grew angry as he listened sympathetically to Badger's story.

'But that's got to be crazy, Badger. What the hell does Hardcastle think he's doing?'

'To be fair, he couldn't do anything else really.'

'But he must have known as well as anyone that was all set up. Who d'you reckon did it? Who the hell would have that sort of grudge against you, of all people?'

'I've got a pretty good idea.'

'And you've had a word with him?'

'Dare not; not yet. Later perhaps.'

'Anything we can do? Just say . . .'

He stopped and three heads jerked forwards, inching instinctively nearer the car's radio receiver. It is not often emotion creeps into the disembodied voice of a radio operator in a police communication centre but evil that threatens one policeman threatens them all, even a young woman secure in the heart of police headquarters. It was the semitone rise that drew their attention even before they registered what she was saying, that a police vehicle had been involved in a road traffic accident at the junction of Theobald's Way and Gordon Road, a witness had reported the driver seriously injured. All available units to proceed. Ambulance already requested. Message timed 14.05.

The car door slammed and Badger had to leap back from the bonnet that swung at him as the driver reversed out. Its siren wailed before it reached the road outside. Gordon Road was no more than a quarter of a mile from the station and, as Badger thrashed through the gears in game pursuit of the patrol car, a sickening premonition filled his belly.

Taff Evans loathed solitude almost as much as silence. He was happiest when in company, prodding, goading, provoking people into passionate but good natured disagreement. That was why he missed Badger so much, the great easygoing bloody fool that he was. Badger had been the only really intelligent close friend he had ever had. It was rare, the combination of brains and good nature. The brighter they were, the less time they seemed to have for the company of such a run-of-the-mill copper like himself. That's why the last few months had gone so quickly – he had dreaded the time when Badger would leave for Staff College to be replaced by some bonehead like himself. But to lose his company due to suspension on evidence that everyone in Northend's nick would tell you was planted, was more than he could bear. He had thumped the steering wheel as he had kept to the speed limit in Theobald's Way's outside lane, snarling in his mirror at the queue of cars building up impatiently behind him. He had concentrated his ill humour on the red Audi Coupe that suddenly had overtaken him on the inside. In an angry, reflex motion, he had switched on the flashing roof light and given a short burst on the siren. For a moment it seemed to have had the desired effect, the other car slowing down for Taff to come abreast of it. As he had leaned across to wave the driver in to the side, he had found himself staring at the arrogant grin he had seen in his mind's eye all day. There had been no mistaking the slicked back hair, the black leather shoulders. There had been no doubt either about the message as two fingers had been raised and the car had sped away once more.

Thanks to Evans's restraining influence, the road ahead had been empty and the two cars had roared forward. As the more powerful Audi had pulled away from the Panda, Evans had bared his teeth as he had urged a screaming engine to greater effort. In his adrenalin-boosted hatred of the man he had been chasing, determined to nail the bastard even if he had to ram him to do so, it had not occurred to him to call for assistance. It had only added to Evans's fury to see Morelli slow down and allow him to catch up before raising his fingers and accelerating away once more. There was little doubt that, whatever his failings, Chico Morelli, as a driver, was in a class of his own. Another time, another place, and he could have been a world-class rally driver. Where Evans had sat, tense, half blind with anger, Morelli had stroked his car in and out of the traffic, the God-given coordination of hand and eye augmented by the transient clarity of cocaine. The chase had become more and more desperate as both men had taken greater and greater risks. Morelli had seen more sport in the lanes and squares and avenues of the estate and had sniggered as he had dropped a gear before hurling his car at the turning into Gordon Road. He had applied opposite lock as the back end had broken away and had bellowed his own twisted victory cry as he had thrust at the accelerator to pull himself straight. Evans's turn had been sudden, jerky with anger, and his belly had tightened as the car had begun to slide. The fleeting sight of a terrified old lady on the street corner and his hands had twitched again. He had felt the car begin to roll but had not seen the street lamp it hit. His next sensation had been of a strange peace and the distant smell of blood and dust in his nostrils.

When Badger reached the scene, Taff Evans was being lifted on to a stretcher. The ambulance men were having difficulty with his right foot which dangled from his leg like a package on a string. At the other end, a young local doctor had a mask over Evans's nose and mouth. As Badger leaned over, Evans became agitated, struggling and waving his arms. The more he struggled, the tighter the mask was pressed to his face. It became obvious to Badger that Evans wanted the mask removed and Badger took the doctor firmly by the wrist and pulled it away. Evans said one word.

'Morelli.'

There was a fatalistic calm about the way Badger Kincaid walked away from his friend. There was no sign of haste or anger as he picked his way between wreckage, police cars and ambulances and out through the ring of voyeurs to where he had abandoned his car. There was no fumbling as he strapped himself in, simply a sudden resolute jab as he closed the clasp. There was a ponderous certainty in his movements as he drove off, like someone who knows he is in plenty of time for an appointment. Tucked away in a lane where he could see the gap in the fencing, he stopped, turned off his engine and waited.

Eyes that had stared through a windscreen for ten minutes did not flicker as they watched Morelli duck through the gap. Badger did not move for a couple of minutes more as if allowing Morelli to herd himself into a corner. Unhurriedly, he got out, slammed the door behind him and walked tall towards the fence.

A few yards from the shed, the sound of the corrugated iron sheet being dragged aside brought him to a halt. In the doorway stood Morelli, legs astride, hands thrust deep into leather pockets. A fixed grin gave way to a sneering laugh.

'Rather hoped it would be you.' His eyes changed their focus to somewhere over Badger's shoulders. 'Where are your friends? Sorry; I forgot. They're not talking to you any more, are they? Been a naughty boy, haven't we?' He suddenly stopped his taunting as he saw Badger slowly move forwards towards him. 'What's this; fancy yourself do you? Come on then. Come to Chico.'

Withdrawing his left hand, he extended it towards Badger, palm up, flexing and extending the fingers as he drew Badger towards him. His eyes darted once more as the sudden wail of sirens and skidding tyres was followed by distant shouting. The sounds drove the smile from his face and he retreated into the gloom, his back against the far wall.

A small frown of disbelief creased his forehead as Badger followed, stepping remorselessly towards him. Morelli drew his knife to hold it stiff armed in front of him as much to keep Badger at bay as with any intention of using it but, as he saw nothing more than a tightening of Badger's lips, he began to draw small circles in the air with the knife's tip, taunting him, begging him to keep coming. The knife's movement stopped as if Morelli had made a decision and his taunting ceased as he bared his teeth. Neither heard Hardcastle's 'leave it, Kincaid' from the doorway as drug-driven lunge and blind courage met. Badger looked with innocent surprise at the blood from the wound in his neck, his eyebrows bunching as if showing puzzled interest in the whirring sound as crimson jets spattered a black leather jacket in front of him. As his knees buckled he grabbed Morelli for support, to feel the knife grate on a rib as Morelli pushed him away. The sight of Badger on his knees before him drove Morelli into a frenzied shout as, his back arched, the knife held in both hands high above his head, he gathered his strength for the final plunge into Badger's back. He would not have heeded the shouted warnings if he had heard them and he died with a look of hate on his face as the police marksmen found their target.

Jonathan Brookes had never thought of Taff Evans as having relations let alone next of kin. It had not even crossed his mind to question how he had come to join a police force so far from home. It seemed there was only an aunt in some unpronounceable village in a Swansea valley but, for all Jonathan's compassionate explanation of the orthopaedic surgeon's instant verdict – one glance had been enough – Taff Evans was not going to agree to the amputation of his foot until he had heard that soothing lilt, if only over the telephone.

'Brought me up, my Auntie Blod,' Taff explained, his face sharp and wild in spite of the morphia. 'My father shoved off and Mam died.'

'I'm sorry, Taff, I had no idea.'

'Weren't to know, were you?'

'Anyway; nice cushy desk job for you from now on.'

Taff Evans jerked his head and gave a short laugh with the black humour with which his countrymen have faced disaster for generations. 'Not so worried about that but where am I going to find a team so bad they'll pick a one-legged flanker?' He tried to smile but morphia does not touch the sort of pain that crossed his face.

Jonathan stayed with him. Casualty had been quiet and Janet would cope. He left the bedside for a time, conscious of eavesdropping on a telephone conversation even when spoken in a foreign language. When he came back, Evans seemed more at peace and was dozing.

'Casualty on the phone for you, Dr Brookes. In Sister's office.'

He hadn't heard the nurse come up behind him.

'Will you come down straight away, please, Dr Brookes?' Maisie had been persuaded to call it a day. Her replacement was young, of another generation. To Susan Drake, doctors were not subjects for idolatry.

'Yes, of course, Sister. What's the problem?'

'Now, please, Dr Brookes.'

The phone went dead but not before Jonathan had heard the background sounds of confusion. He heard the raised voices, the scurrying feet again as he neared the department. He was surprised by the number of police in the corridor, raised his eyebrows at the bloodstained uniforms. He headed for the centre of activity, the intensive care unit.

He had seen it often enough, the patient with torn, bloodstained clothing, both arms out on boards like a crucifix, restless enough to require restraint, reassuring voices slowly rising to a point somewhere short of impatience. Someone sat at the head of the couch, someone Jonathan did not recognise, but the back of the doctor leaning over the patient's right side was familiar enough – Bannerman's shape was unmistakable. From somewhere, hidden behind Bannerman's bulk, came a sucking, bubbling sound and there was rather more blood around than usual. Janet was working on the outstretched left arm. The Sister and two nurses bustled around. Nothing that Jonathan might not have expected in a place accustomed to the unexpected.

But the same could not be said for the atmosphere. High tension is the normal background to such a scene, the medium in which maximum efficiency develops and decisions, right or wrong, are made swiftly and executed dexterously, the sort of stress that brings out the best in one. But there is a subtle difference between stress and strain. There might not be overt panic but there was no doubting the strained, anxious silence that Jonathan sensed as he walked through the door. Eyes that glanced his way pleaded for help.

As Jonathan walked to the patient's side, it was doubtful which struck him first, the smell on Bannerman's gasping breath or the patient's blonde hair and bushy eyebrows. Blood caked on fair eyelashes shook as recognition and hope increased Badger's restlessness. The bubbling beneath Bannerman's hands intensified as Badger tried to speak. As Jonathan stood, numb with sorrow and disbelief, his mind cleared and, slowly, he began to assess what was doing on. He turned to Bannerman.

'What's the problem?'

It was only when Bannerman looked up from the wound in Badger's neck that Jonathan grasped the reason behind the ambient tension. Bannerman was drunk. The sluggish unfocused eyes were not those of a man with excited, exaggerated movements that might result in some positive, active mishap, rather those of a man drugged into impotence. With both hands pressing swabs into the wound, Bannerman was slouched over his patient, his breathing deep and noisy, the attitude of someone who had ground to a halt. As he took his right hand from the wound, blood, bright jets amongst the dark, welled to overflow on to the couch. From beneath his left hand, came a blowing sound interspersed alternately with that of sucking and bubbling. When Bannerman removed this hand also, Badger heaved in a spasm of coughing that filled his neck veins and turned the flow into a torrent. With ponderous movement, Bannerman took a large swab and temporarily stemmed the bleeding once more.

Jonathan saw the thick, blue lips, usually so red, and frowned at the young man at the head of the couch whom he now took to be an anaesthetic registrar.

'He's cyanosed,' he snapped. 'Give him some oxygen.' He got no more than a shrug of the shoulders in reply. As if in mute explanation, the registrar took the mask he had been holding and placed it over Badger's face with no improvement in the colour of the lips.

'Why's that?' Jonathan asked.

'Because he's hardly breathing up here at all. His trachea's open, maybe his larynx. Nine-tenths of his respiration is coming through there. Add to that his pneumothorax and you can understand why he's cyanosed. I can't do anything about it.'

'What pneumothorax?' As he asked the question Jonathan saw the pad on the left side of Badger's chest wall amongst the leads to the cardiac monitor and cursed himself for a blind idiot. He tore at his white coat and rolled up his sleeves. 'For God's sake, give me a catheter and introducer, Sister.' He turned his wrath back on his young colleague. 'Why in hell haven't you done anything about it before?'

'Because he won't let me. Says it can wait; let him stop the bleeding first.'

'But why the hell didn't you get on and do it anyway?' A perfunctory wash of his hands and Jonathan was already choosing his spot where to plunge the catheter.

'Because he's a consultant and I'm only a poor bloody registrar, that's why. He's supposed to know.' Bannerman appeared totally oblivious to his two juniors discussing him. 'Frankly, I think the whole bloody thing is a shambles. The coppers that brought him in did a better job than he's doing. This patient was under control when he came in and should have been taken to main theatre, his pneumothorax treated and the neck explored under GA.'

'Then why don't you get on and give him a general now?' Jonathan roared, knowing the absurdity of the question, feeling the inertia of suddenly working in an emergency with someone he had never met before.

'Oh, sure. Have him asleep without a tube down and then he aspirates half a pint of blood and that's it. I'm not taking the responsibility for that.'

'Where's your consultant?'

'On the way down, I hope.'

They noticed Badger had become less restless. He was holding his head still but was following the dialogue with his eyes. Ashamed of their outburst, their voices felt to a murmur.

'Wait until I finish this and I'll get a tube in his trachea for you.' Jonathan bent down to connect his catheter to a bottle containing water that would act as a one-day valve for the air in Badger's chest. He grunted his satisfaction as a stream of bubbles rose noisily to the top. The re-expansion of the underlying lung drew a larger volume of air in through the wound and another fit of coughing coincided with Bannerman removing both hands to stare with vacuous calm. As blood was sucked into the open windpipe, the coughing become uncontrollable and Jonathan found himself shouting at his chief to staunch the flow yet again. As if determined to show his authority, Bannerman delayed reapplying pressure and turned towards Jonathan, his face, for the first time, showing emotion – hatred.

For a few moments there was a lull as everyone stood, waiting for a lead. Janet James stooped, still manipulating the drip in the left arm. Sister Drake and the nurses looked from one doctor to another, anxious to help. As they did so, the door was flung back and into the silence strode a tall, angular man in a well-cut, plain grey suit. Without looking to right or left, he walked to look over the anaesthetic registrar's shoulder. Sharp eyes above a fiercely hooked nose took in the scene.

'What the hell's going on here?'

'Stab wound of neck, sir.' The registrar stood up, still carrying the mask, as if only too glad to hand it to anyone. 'He's lost a fair amount of blood but it's reasonably well controlled by pressure. I've had no chance of getting a tube down as he has an open trachea or larynx.'

'Why the hell wasn't he admitted then?'

The question was directed at his junior but the consultant anaesthetist turned his head to look at Bannerman as he spoke. As Bannerman raised his head and his consultant colleague saw his face for the first time, the anaesthetist swore, the instinct to protect a colleague suppressing the words into a tight-lipped hiss.

'Oh, bloody hell.' He leaned forward as if to make sure Bannerman could hear him clearly. 'You can't cope with that without a GA, Bob. We can't put a tube down from up here. If you put a tube in his trachea for us, we'll put him to sleep and connect up to your tube.'

There was no sound from Bannerman, simply his noisy breathing coming from a face set in mulish obstinacy.

'I did ask him to do that, sir.' The registrar's tone was pained, as if anxious to rid himself of all responsibility.

'Bob.' A note of despair was creeping into the anaesthetist's voice. 'Put a tube in that trachea. Soon as you can.'

'Got to stop the bleeding.' Bannerman's first words were growled, deep in his throat. 'Sister, give me some sort of retractor. What about a bit of service round here. Where the hell's Maisie?'

'Bob.'

'Bugger off, Dick. Who the hell's th'surgeon? Don't tell you how to do your job.'

Richard Monks, vastly experienced senior anaesthetic consultant, Chairman of Medical Staff Committee, looked for help to Jonathan Brookes, junior Casualty Officer, only there to satisfy the Fellowship regulations. The look in his eyes was half-appeal, half-order. Jonathan walked round Badger's feet to come up behind Bannerman.

'Can I help, Mr Bannerman?'

'Bugger off, I tell you.' The words came back over his shoulder but an angry twitch of his hands resulted in another splash of blood and Badger groaned. There was urgent fear now in Monks's face.

Jonathan went and scrubbed rapidly once more. He turned and walked purposefully back to stand behind Bannerman.

'I think you'd better let me put a tube in, Mr Bannerman. If we can get an airway established, then Dr Monks can put him asleep and we can perhaps wheel him up to Main Theatre where they'll be in a better position to explore the neck.'

'Hand him over to the experts, you mean.' Bannerman looked away from where he was trying to insert a retractor, sobering up enough to turn from wooden inactivity to angry paranoia. 'Someone like you, you mean. You bastards think . . .'

'Bob.' Monks's hand went instinctively towards the wound as there was fresh bleeding. Dumbly, he appealed to Jonathan once more as it became obvious that Bannerman was losing control.

Jonathan moved alongside Bannerman, spreading his feet as he forced himself shoulder to shoulder. 'Let me put a tube in. You're sick, Bannerman. Leave him to me.'

'Get away from here, you bastard.' Jonathan felt the saliva on his face as Bannerman spat the words, his breath stale with whisky. 'I don't need your help.'

A sudden surge of bleeding made up Jonathan's mind for him and he gave a shove that would have sent a smaller man reeling. But Bannerman was a big man, jammed in the angle between Badger's outstretched right arm and his chest wall, and he hardly moved. As Jonathan stretched round him, trying to reach his wrists, Bannerman lifted both hands from the wound to take Jonathan by both shoulders and hurl him backwards across the room. A crack on the head as he stumbled backwards and fell, left Jonathan dazed. It took some time for him to hear and see the panic.

As Bannerman had swung towards Jonathan, a finger, caught in a ring of the retractor, had dragged it with him. Its curved points had clawed at the trachea, pulling it open just as the release of pressure had released the flow of venous blood. In seconds, Badger had been drowning in his own blood, his face grey, his pupils already beginning to dilate.

This time, Bannerman put up no resistance as Jonathan pulled him away, standing back as if suddenly awakening to find he had been sleep walking. Jonathan reapplied the pack as Badger jerked and shook in his asphyxia. Looking round for help, Jonathan stared into a face that stared abstractedly back – Janet James seemed unable to move. Monks's unwashed hand came over Badger's head to take over the pressure – sepsis was of secondary importance now. Sister Drake pushed the tracheostomy tray within easy reach.

As Jonathan was pitched into a procedure he had never even seen done before, a high-pitched voice screamed in his head, the words slow and distinct. 'Please God, no. Please God. No, no. Please, get me out of this – please.' Not that there was any great technical difficulty – there was a wide hole in a big man's windpipe, easy enough to intubate – but it was an operation always associated in a surgeon's mind with the razor's edge of life and death.

The thrust of the tube down the windpipe brought a 'Well done, lad,' from Monks. 'Now get some suction down there, quick.'

But putting the tube in place had been the easy part. Trying to suck out the blood from the lungs would be much more difficult, the suction via the catheter Jonathan now inserted being far less efficient than one or two good belly coughs from Badger himself. He could only hope that the tickling the catheter produced would result in Badger giving just such violent coughs – and that would depend on whether his cerebral anoxia had already knocked out his reflex centres.

The sharp, jabbing jerks that Jonathan gave the catheter became more and more desperate as they produced no response from Badger, inert and flaccid beneath their hands.

'Oh, God.' Monks already sounded defeated. 'Keep trying, lad.'

'Cardiac arrest.' The registrar behind Monks's back made it sound like a logical statement of fact.

The voice still screamed in Jonathan's head as he went through the ritual movements of cardiac massage, knowing them to be of no possible consequence in someone who could not be aerated. It was obvious that the anaesthetic registrar thought he had given up too soon as he took over the massage as Jonathan walked away from the couch to stand back and survey the scene. As Jonathan put his head back, the shout of agony he gave was as much to drown the shriek in his head as to call off the registrar.

'Leave him. He's dead. Leave him alone, I tell you. Badger's dead.'

23

The summer weekend invasion over the border into North Wales was in full swing. Jonathan drove with a care and concern for others that he did not feel for himself. Watching a post-mortem carried out on one's closest friend is an event likely to affect the most insensitive of men and the self-imposed deadening of emotion that had been required to bear the sight of Badger's body being ripped apart could not be switched off like a light.

He drove like a robot, the car following a route as if it had been programmed long before Jonathan had put a foot inside it. The North Wales coastline was as beautiful as ever but he never gave it a glance, feeling the rub of broad shoulders alongside him, hearing a laughing voice. He drove into the public car park, high on the cliff, locking the car and walking away as if he always did that when he went to Abersoch. He climbed down through the Yacht Club and on to the slipway. The young lad in the launch raised an eyebrow at Jonathan's grey suit and leather shoes, took one look at Jonathan's face and decided it was none of his business. Once aboard, Jonathan found the key in the usual, obvious place – tucked in the corner of the gas bottle compartment – opened the cabin and went below.

An hour later, anyone watching from the shore might have admired the expertise as a single-handed yachtsman, scorning the use of an engine, slipped his moorings to glide out of sight between the islands.

A gentle, fitful easterly teased the sails, making the boat's speed through the water vary between slow ahead and slow sideways as the motionless craft was swept down by the tide, conditions guaranteed under normal circumstances to drive any active, impatient young man wild. Jonathan seemed content so long as what wind there was was on his back and the last, precious warmth of the sun on his face. The sun's sudden plunge brought a drop in the temperature and a constancy to the breeze, making the flat water under the hull zip like a slender bough swept through a pond. He shivered. By the time he had attached the automatic steering and settled on a westerly course, he shook with the cold. In the cabin's hollow confines, as he searched amongst the lockers and pulled on some foul weather trousers, boots and an Arran jumper, he had to endure the echoing laughter and the wisecracks, the good natured pushing and the shoving. As he heated up his tins of stew and baked beans, he smiled affectionately at the comments about his cooking. He even gave a little laugh, short, sad and reflective, when someone said 'cheers' when he opened a can of beer. He climbed out into the cockpit, coffee in hand.

He had slept on board over night often enough, but always at anchor. He threw the dregs of his coffee away and looked up at the sails. A decision made, he dropped the mainsail and secured it around the boom. He waited to be sure the boat still made steady headway under the bellying genoa before fishing out his sleeping bag, still dank and musty from the New Quay race. With a sail bag under his head, he settled on the cold, hard comfort of a cockpit locker, above him a cloudless night sky. He felt as if he would never sleep again and made no effort to overcome the feeling. He tried to think, to marshall his thoughts, to speak to himself out loud if necessary, and failed. Each time, pain brought him to a grinding halt. He tried to cry and couldn't, grinning instead as Badger hauled himself out of the cabin, shaking his head as if his hangover was bursting his skull. Jonathan laughingly offered him a can of beer only for Badger to put his tongue out and pretend to vomit. The next moment they were brawling on the cockpit floor, Susannah, from where he stood at the tiller, frowning her disapproval at such childish behaviour. As the boat heeled sharply, Badger began to slide, clutching for guardrails that melted away under his hands, but, even as the water swirled round his shoulders, there was an unconquerable strength in his grip on Jonathan's wrist. The vice like clamp around his wrist remained as Jonathan watched Badger's face, disembodied, flat on the water's surface, drift away, questioning, perplexed, as if demanding an explanation of why Jonathan could allow this to happen. Jonathan sobbed bitterly as he hauled desperately on the hand that held his wrist so tightly, hearing above the sound of the water cascading from the body he pulled safely aboard, the wheezing, coughing gasps he knew so well. He pushed Bannerman aside, recoiling from his gratitude, to rush to the stern and shriek his friend's name. The second shout woke him with a start and, with his tears, he poured out grief and guilt and shame and self-recrimination.

Alison and Michael Brookes sat eating a leisurely Saturday breakfast, wondering what to do with their weekend when the phone rang.
'Shepworth 720743.'
'May I speak to Mr Brookes, please?'
'Speaking.'
'Good morning, Mr Brookes. My name's Susannah Ridgeway. I'm a friend of Jonathan's.'
'Oh, yes. Good morning, Miss Ridgeway.' Michael Brookes made faces at Alison who had put her newspaper down, sat up straight and looked interested.
Susannah heard the confusion in Brookes's voice and he almost felt her forgiving smile over the phone. 'I'm the one he goes sailing with.'
'Ah. Of course. Forgive me for being so slow. Jonathan has spoken of you many times.'
'You're very kind, Mr Brookes, but I'm sure he hasn't, not if I know my Jonathan. Has he rung you in the last day or so?'
Alison now stood besides Michael, trying to piece together what was being said the other end of the phone. 'No. He rang just after the Bank Holiday weekend, couldn't stop talking about the sailing, seemed full of the joys of spring. It all sounded very exciting.'
'He hasn't rung you about his friend, Badger, then?'
'Was that the policeman who was killed?'
'Yes, it was.'
'Susannah, I am sorry. We did wonder when we heard it on the local news. Then we saw in the paper he had been taken into Scarsby General so we thought Jonathan might have been involved. We tried to have a word with him but he gets very cross if we ring him at work and we got no reply from the house. I imagine he's very upset.'
'That's really why I've rung.' The hesitation that followed brought a look to Brookes's face that had Alison reaching for his hand. '*Gelert* has gone.'
'*Gelert?*' Perplexity joined anxiety in Michael's voice.
'I'm sorry. *Gelert* is our boat. It's gone from Abersoch. The man who looks after it for us rang last night to say it had disappeared from its mooring. We left it until this morning to see if it was back but there's no sign of it as yet.'
'And you think Jonathan has taken it? Is that what you mean?'
'The lad running the launch that took the man out to the boat last night did not know Jonathan – he's new, someone earning a few bob during the holiday – but his description would do very well for Jonathan.'

'And does that mean that he's been out at sea all night?'

'Don't worry. He can't possibly have come to any harm. We always keep some food and drink on board in case of emergency – what we call our "iron rations" – and it was a lovely night. I only wish I could have been there with him.'

'You don't think . . .?'

'He's going to do anything stupid? No, not for a moment. Not Jonathan.'

Mixed with the fear engendered by a mental picture of a beloved son alone at sea in a small boat at night, was a tinge of jealousy at someone who presumed to know his son better than he.

'Where are you speaking from?' Brookes asked.

'From Abersoch. I came down last night.' She tried to make it sound as if she would have done that anyway. There was a moment's hesitation before she spoke again.

'Look; why don't you come down for the weekend, wait for our errant boy here. There's no one else here and the weather's perfect. You can give him a piece of your mind over a beer when he finally decides to come home. Please come. In the meanwhile, I'll ring round and make a few enquiries.'

The traffic was nose to tail most of the way, unnervingly fast on the motorways, plodding behind the slowest caravan off them. Alison sat quietly, conscious that any threat to Jonathan was still the only thing her husband would not share with her. It was early evening before they reached Abersoch and if they had not been so road-weary, hungry and scratchy, they also would have been impressed as they finally found the house and turned into the drive. The pleasant looking woman who answered the door, ushered them in.

'Mr and Mrs Brookes.'

'Thank you, Mrs Rowlands.'

As Susannah came in from the terrace, she had the light behind her and Michael Brookes wondered whether that had been contrived. First impressions would be formed with her guests under the microscope while she still preserved a degree of mystery. Even so, he could see she was tall and proud of it, elegant and self-assured as she walked towards him, her hand outstretched.

The kiss that Susannah stretched to give was as natural as a daughter's. 'Don't worry,' she smiled. 'That precious son of yours is perfectly all right. We're just making a great big fuss over nothing.' She turned towards Alison. 'And you must be Lissa. I've been terrified of meeting you.'

'For heaven's sake, why?' Alison laughed as they too shook hands.

'Judging by Jonathan's descriptions, I've got an awful lot to compete with and – if I might say so – I can see what he meant.'

Alison saw an open, frank smile and felt shame at her moment's instinctive distrust in one woman's compliment to another.

'Is he back?' she asked.

'No.'

'Have you any news of him?' Michael Brookes cut in.

'Yes.' She teased him gently with silence but quickly relented. 'He's in Barmouth.'

'Barmouth?' His father made it sound like the end of the world. 'How d'you know he's in Barmouth?'

'I rang New Quay, spoke to the harbourmaster there.' She stopped and laughed.

'And he told you? How would he know?'

'All I got from him to start with was a right telling off – left me in no doubt what he thought of sailors without VHF going off without checking the weather forecast with him first. That's going to cost me a couple of glasses of Guinness the next time we meet. But he was a Coastguard himself once and said he'd ring around quietly, try to find out without creating too much of a fuss. He rang back about an hour ago to say *Gelert* had just anchored in Barmouth.' Her voice softened as if she were talking to herself. 'It is very strange; I was convinced in my own mind that he was heading back to New Quay.'

'And do you have any theories why he should have chosen Barmouth?' Alison asked, studying Susannah's face intently.

'No.' The lie came promptly, a little too promptly to convince Alison. Trying to avoid Alison's gaze, Susannah saw suddenly how tired Michael Brookes looked. 'Forgive me,' she said. 'You've driven a long way. Which would you prefer, a wash or a drink? We've got something cold for later.'

'I would like a very large gin, please, Susannah. I'm not too fussed about what you put in it. It's been a very long twenty-four hours.' Alison's relaxed honesty set the seal on friendship.

Susannah looked at Michael Brookes and raised her eyebrows.

'Bit early for me. Is it too late for a cup of tea?'

Shaking her head, Susannah pointed to the terrace. 'Go and make the most of the sun.'

The conversation murmured on as between old friends, stopping only from time to time as Snowdon's range of mountains demanded their attention, excelling itself in its subtle combinations of a spectrum refracted from a setting sun. Later, indoors, refreshed and fed, Susannah and Alison sipped their coffee. Michael showed his approval of Sir Warwick's choice of Scotch.

'So you reckon something must have happened in that ICU?' Michael sank drowsily into his chair.

229

'Yes.'

'Why do you say that?'

'I've had a word with Gavin and . . .'

'He's the black casualty porter Jonathan's spoken about?'

'That's right . . . and he's saying nothing and that, in itself, is significant; normally he's never short of a word. I'm sure you know better than I do the atmosphere when everyone is shutting up like clams.'

'I most certainly do. But you've no idea what it was?'

'None.'

'Well,' Michael sighed as if it were of lesser importance, 'the main thing is we know Jonathan's safe, at least for the moment. How can we get in touch with him? Can we call him on the radio?'

'No.' The sharpness of Susannah's reaction brought more of a surprised look from Michael than from Alison. 'No,' she repeated, more softly. 'I think we should leave him alone.'

She saw the disappointment on his face and her face softened. 'I intend ringing the Barmouth harbourmaster first thing tomorrow morning and, if the boat is still there, I thought I might drive down to Barmouth for the day.' Her face flushed. 'Just to make sure he looks all right. I have no intention of letting him know I'm there.' There was no doubt she was looking directly at Michael as she added, 'Would you like to come with me?'

Brookes looked pleadingly at his wife.

'Don't look at me, darling. I've got to be back at work, nine o'clock Monday morning – I must go home tomorrow – but I haven't met a consultant yet who couldn't fiddle a day or two off just by picking up the phone. No doubt, when that wandering son of yours finally decides to make his way back,' – a feeling of exclusion brought an edge to the voice of the most generous of souls – 'he can give you a lift back to Liverpool. You can catch a train from there.'

The Barmouth harbourmaster said he'd looked fine. Had been ashore and payed his harbour dues like a good boy. A bit quiet. Didn't seem to want to talk much. Had gone off and done some shopping but had stayed aboard ever since. Was there a problem? Did they want him to give him a call? Said he thought he'd be leaving on the early morning tide. Yes, the forecast was still good for the next few days. It was his pleasure, he assured Miss Ridgeway.

The boat looked trim, the sail cover neatly in place, the rigging taut. They both snatched for the binoculars as a figure emerged into the cockpit. Susannah smiled. 'Go on. After you.'

Michael Brookes put the glasses down like a thirsty man drawing breath after his first few gulps of water. 'Seems to be all right,' was all he could say after so many hours of anxiety.

Susannah took a long hard look, speaking while still holding the binoculars to her eyes. 'I wonder what the hell's going through his mind, sitting like that out there. Mean devil, going off on his own like that. Why are men so selfish? Why do they always want to keep some little part back?'

She lowered the binoculars and turned, expecting no more than the usual male shrug of the shoulders, to find gentle firmness.

'And you have no secrets?'

'No. Not from him, at least. Not now.'

The questions that followed logically in Brookes's mind he was too sensitive to ask. He simply grunted.

'What was that for?' Susannah laughed.

'I was wondering just how stupid my son could get. If I were his age again . . .'

As she leaned to kiss his cheek, he realised it had never occurred to him how nice it would have been to have had a daughter too. 'Come on,' she said. 'I'm hungry. Let's find somewhere to eat.'

As they threaded their way through the crowds and picked over an indifferent meal, their conversation was trivial but never strained. Back on the quay, they saw Jonathan exactly as they had left him, his feet up on the cockpit locker, his back against the bulkhead. Susannah took hold of Michael's elbow and turned him round. 'Come on. We're not doing any good here. Let's go home.'

Barmouth's harbourmaster's forecast had been quite correct; it was another beautiful day. Sun poured in as Susannah pulled back the curtains. As she put a cup of tea on the bedside table, she smiled at a sleepy, unshaven face that was trying to make the polite noises appropriate to being woken by a beautiful woman, already vitally alert.

'Good morning. Did you sleep well?' she asked.

'Yes, I'm afraid I did,' Michael confessed.

'No need to feel guilty about it. No need to keep awake in case the baby cries any more, you know.'

Stubbly jowls creased in a grin. 'I rather think I owe your father a bottle of whisky.'

'He can stand it. Come on; it's a lovely morning. Breakfast in half an hour. We're going for a walk along the beach while the tide's out. He'll be coming up on the tide – that's why it's so nice to have a lifting keel around here to get out over the bar – even so he won't be in for several hours yet.'

'Something tells me I will have to learn something about boats just to stay in the conversation in this place.'

'Give you your first tutorial this morning, if you like.'

Michael Brookes remembered another walk along another beach – at Westmere. When had that been? 1974? How long ago was that? Eleven years? As long as that? He had the same feeling now as then, strengthening with each slow stride along the hard, wet sand. But the love he felt was not the covetous force he had stretched out towards Alison. This time he was extending the love he felt for his son to enfold someone he sensed loved Jonathan too. He was surprised how readily he was prepared to do so, squirming with a touch of conscience – he had not been so generous with Lissa. The gap between them closed as slowly, words coming hesitantly at first in ragged, uncompleted sentences, Susannah was drawn into sharing confidences with a born listener. The nightmare of her Oxford days was relived, her constant fear of falling prey to her addiction once more laid bare, the mystery of the scar made plain. By the time they had turned back, the protective arm around Susannah's shoulders, something never contemplated with his son, said it all.

Michael Brookes saw to it they were hours early for their vigil from the terrace. He sat with the binoculars almost permanently to his eyes, watching everything that moved. Susannah had no need of the glasses as the tiny shape emerged from St Tudwal's Sound.

'That's him.'

As Brookes stood, agitated, Susannah put a hand on his shoulder, pushing him back into his chair.

'You stay there. I'll go down to the slipway, make sure he doesn't sneak off.'

When Jonathan stepped off the launch, he looked more like a rep who had had a rough weekend in London at the firm's annual convention, than a sailor. He held his grey jacket over one arm, his shirt limp, creased and grubby. His shoes were slippery and he was glad of the hand Susannah offered as he stepped on to the wet concrete. They looked at each other long and hard. Neither gave an inch.

'Had a good trip?' Susannah felt she had to say something.

'Not bad. Not much wind coming back. Had to motor most of the way. I owe you a couple of gallons of diesel.'

'Where have you been?'

'Barmouth.'

'Oh? There's someone up at the house who wants to see you.'

'Who's that? Dad?'

'It is.'

'Hm. Something told me he wouldn't be far away. Better get it over with then, hadn't I?'

Michael Brookes had his back to an empty fireplace when his son walked in. The smile Jonathan gave him was as loving as ever but shorter, more compact. Susannah, hovering behind Jonathan, watched them as they stood and marvelled at the bridge of deep affection that bound them but which neither seemed able to cross.

'Hi, Dad. You all right?'

'Yes, of course I am. Much more to the point, how are you?'

'I'm great. Why shouldn't I be?'

'What d'you mean, going off like that, without telling anybody where you were going? Making everyone worry about you.'

'Why?'

'What d'you mean, why?'

'Why should you worry about me?'

'Because . . ., because . . .'

Tears welled in Susannah's eyes as she saw Michael struggle to say it and fail.

'I'm a big boy now, Dad,' Jonathan said, quietly. 'Let me go. I'm not a child any more.'

'Can I see you a moment? I've been looking for you for the last two days.'

Gavin discounted the milling mid-morning crowd. If Jonathan could disappear for days and expect others to cover for him, he could spare him a few minutes.

Jonathan looked around him and then at Gavin's face. 'All right – let's go in Bannerman's room.'

With the door closed behind them they stood facing each other, watchful, uncertain how to react.

'I'm sorry about Badger. I don't know any other way to put it.' There was no doubt Gavin meant what he said but he conveyed in his tone that the admission was of sorrow alone. Jonathan was not to misinterpret one word as implying a feeling of responsibility or blame.

'Yes. It was very sad.' There was steel in Jonathan's voice also, as if making a legal statement without prejudice to whatever position he might have to take later.

What had already become obvious was just how powerful a catalytic force Badger's good nature had been.

'You had a rough time by all accounts. Sounded a complete bloody shambles.'

'It wasn't very pleasant.'

'Was Bannerman as drunk as they say he was?'

'And how drunk do they say he was?' Jonathan asked, his face expressionless.

They had said little but it had been enough to redraw the boundaries between rising star and lowly hospital porter.

233

'How's the family taking it?' Jonathan's enquiry had the politeness of the junior officer taking a dutiful interest in a squaddy just returned from compassionate leave. 'Can't be very pleasant for them.' He raised an eyebrow at Gavin's laugh.

'My mother still hasn't quite made up her mind whether to be proud of Chico or not, but there's no such doubt in my beloved step-father's mind. You should see his face when my mother pushes him up to the cemetery every Sunday afternoon after the pubs shut. It's as if he's visiting a shrine, a war memorial. I'm sure that's how he sees it, how he'd describe it if he was articulate enough to put it into words. As far as he's concerned, Chico is just another casualty in their war against an oppressive police force that protects wealth and privilege.'

He looked across at Jonathan and saw the scepticism in the downward curve of his mouth.

'You don't believe me, do you; think I'm making all that up. But then, how could you? How could you possibly understand their attitude of mind?'

'And Linda?'

'Having a rough time in school as you can imagine. Thank God it didn't happen this time next year.'

'So.' Jonathan fell silent as if there was nothing more to be said but Gavin made no move to leave.

'You can't blame me for Badger's death, you know.' The face suffused beneath the black skin. 'It had nothing to do with us being friendly. That wasn't why Chico had it in for him. That was just coincidence.'

'Now who on earth would think that? It has never crossed my mind for a moment.'

'Badger was a bloody fool.' Gavin paused for a moment, watching Jonathan struggling to control his anger. 'He should have grown up. I don't understand it; it wasn't as if he had all that cushy a childhood – couldn't have been all that easy for him. Not like someone like you. He should have learned when to come in out of the rain.'

'Perhaps you don't recognise an honest man when you see one,' Jonathan snapped.

'Coming from my background, d'you mean?' Gavin laughed bitterly. 'You people don't realise, honesty is a luxury not everyone can afford. No' – he relaxed as if suddenly regretting the path the conversation had taken – 'I just didn't understand Badger. I liked him, I really did. The only copper I've ever respected. But I couldn't make him out. How someone could be bright enough to get a degree, be a teacher and be accepted for that Staff College place and then behave out on the street as if he was as thick as a plank, totally defeated me. I couldn't help but compare him with youngsters from my part of the world who really are as thick as a plank but are so quick, so sharp, because they know that's the only way they are going to survive.'

'He just saw everything in black and white – no crime in that, is there?'

24

Her Majesty's Coroners go back a long way, tracing their origins to the twelfth century when the duties of the *custos placitorum* were to safeguard the King's property. Over the centuries their function has become more and more limited, their task now being essentially to hold inquests into violent and unnatural deaths, deaths of unknown cause and deaths in prison. Broadly speaking, coroners come in two forms, medical or legal, depending on whether they have obtained their basic training in medicine or the law, though a few have a foot in both camps. It is unusual for a lawyer to study medicine; many doctors enjoy the law.

For the perfect example, one need look no further than Colonel Noel Fergus Burkinshaw, OBE, TD, MRCP, Barrister at Law.

Born on Christmas Day in 1920, the eldest son of a local Honorary Physician, he had been brought up in a household where the ethics of medicine were as important as its practice, the reputation and integrity of the profession were principles to fight and die for, at a time when doctors could do no wrong. He had taken pride in carrying on the tradition of his father and grandfather at Cambridge and Guy's, warming himself in the adulation that a fistful of prizes had brought him when he qualified in 1943. The young man had a fine mind. A glittering future must lie ahead.

A strong sense of duty had made him join the army without waiting for any house appointments. He had enjoyed the last two years of the war, a smart young officer in his service dress and Sam Browne as he had walked down the aisle with the daughter of his father's closest friend, the doyen of the local general practitioners. The first niggle of doubt in his father's mind had made itself felt when Noel, a serious-minded young man who obviously enjoyed discipline and respect, had not taken his discharge but signed on with a short service commission. With the passage of time, however, the acquisition of a higher degree and rapid promotion had allayed the older man's fears – it would be nice to have the Director General of Army Medical Services in the family.

But the Army and Major Noel Burkinshaw had parted company. amicably and with much regret on the part of both. Only Noel and his wife, Mary, knew the true reason. The serious, almost staid, young officer had an Achilles heel and the endless round of parties on foreign postings with gin at throw-away prices had found it. He had got out while he could. From the day he had walked away from the RAMC Depot, he had not touched alcohol in spite of rising to command the local Territorial Field Ambulance.

Too late to join the hospital rat race, Burkinshaw had accepted gratefully his father-in-law's offer of a partnership in his practice. A kindly man, considered a bit old fashioned when it came to the dignity of the profession, always immaculately turned out, he had settled into a sort of childless contentment. After a while he became restless. Someone had suggested he should read law and he had laughed. And then he had thought again and had found another world of order, discipline and respect open to him. He had sought the position of police surgeon and had got it. The chance to become one of Her Majesty's Coroners had come his way and he had leapt at it.

Colonel Noel Burkinshaw might be a bit of a stickler for behaviour but he had been spared the priggishness of the converted. The fact that he was a drinker who did not drink did not preclude him from feeling compassion for those who found themselves unable to overcome the problem. Though the amount of time he now spent practising medicine was getting less and less, he was still very much in the mainstream of the local profession and therefore privy to all the local medical gossip. Like everyone else, he heard about this doctor and that, who the womanisers were, who gambled more than they should, who the drinkers were. An honest, upright man himself, he still felt no censure for such colleagues – he just wondered how they managed to cope.

He had often wondered about Robert Bannerman.

'Please rise for Her Majesty's Coroner.' The Coroner's Officer, stocky with a neat beard, small mouth and thin lips, enjoyed the moment as a row of senior police officers were amongst those in the crowded courtroom who stood at his request. Colonel Burkinshaw entered, climbed the dais and stood for a moment as if assuming command. His Officer waited until the Coroner had settled in his chair before deriving deep satisfaction by ordering his Deputy Chief Constable, amongst others, to 'be seated'.

'This inquest today ...' Burkinshaw cleared his throat and started again, staring at a reporter, one of a dozen packed into the jury benches, who had just dropped his notebook. 'This inquest today continues from that adjourned from June 10th of this year, when formal identification was obtained, and is into the death of Police Constable Cecil Kincaid which occurred at Scarsby General Hospital on Thursday 6th June of this year. Before this court proceeds any further, I would point out that our duty today, in accordance with the Coroner's Rules, is to establish the time and place of the incident, the nature of the injuries sustained and the place and the manner of his death. I would stress again that it is not the function of this court to apportion blame, simply to establish the facts.' He shuffled some papers as if to emphasise he did not expect to have to refer to that again. He looked over his glasses at the front of the court. 'If any legal representatives be present, would they stand and be recognised?'

A young man stood. 'Andrew Jamieson, sir. I represent the Police Federation.' He looked well turned out, stood up straight, short hair, no beard. Burkinshaw nodded his approval.

Except for the Federation's solicitor, Michael and Alison Brookes had been the first to arrive, tucking themselves into the far corner, Alison trying to make conversation, Michael wishing she would not, both sitting tense and upright, memories of another courtroom flooding back. Reporters had straggled in and spread themselves around only to be herded into the jury benches by the Officer as a phalanx of policemen, silver braid much in evidence, had taken over the body of the court. Jonathan Brookes had seen his father as he came through the door, nodded – and found a seat as far away as possible. Richard Monks had come and sat beside him. The last to arrive, the Home Office pathologist, Allan Kelsey, was the first to give evidence after Burkinshaw had outlined the events and summarised the evidence he intended to call.

Kelsey took the oath, stated his name and sat down, fishing in the inside pocket of a crumpled sports coat for an equally crumpled sheaf of notes as he identified himself.

There was nothing crumpled about Allan Kelsey's evidence. Within that shaggy exterior lay a keen and analytical mind. He began with a systematic account of a post mortem carried out with the infinite care brought to any case where future litigation was inevitable. Reciting all his normal findings first, he summarised by saying that, at the time Kincaid had met his death, he had been a healthy young man, free from any form of disease.

'I now come to the details of his injuries. The bruising in and around the heart was that only to be expected after cardiac massage. I found a stab wound in his left fifth intercostal space, a small laceration in the left lung and blood in the pleura, all consistent with being caused by a long-bladed knife. An intercostal catheter was in place and the lung fully expanded.'

'For the benefit of the court, Dr Kelsey, could you put that in lay terms?'

'Police Constable Kincaid had been stabbed in the chest and his lung punctured. This had collapsed but had been re-expanded again by the tube inserted by the surgeons.'

'Thank you.'

'His major injury was a stab wound situated just above the inner end of his left clavicle. The wound was an incised one, five centimetres long, though the ends were more ragged, consistent with attempts at surgical enlargement.'

'Attempts, Dr Kelsey?'

'Consistent with surgical enlargement, sir.'

'Very well.'

'The sternal muscles on the left side had been almost entirely divided and there was a large wound in the trachea involving to some degree the left lobe of the thyroid. Behind this and in line with it, there was a small wound in the oesophagus involving all layers. The point of the weapon had come to rest against the anterior surface of the vertebral column. To the lateral side of the wound, there was considerable laceration to the major veins in the region of the junction of the internal jugular and subclavian but, surprisingly, the major arteries, the carotid and subclavian, had been pushed aside and escaped damage. Thick chyle, consistent with a recent meal, had been seen in the wound and could be expressed from damage to the thoracic duct.'

'And the cause of death, Dr Kelsey?'

'I'm coming to that, sir.'

Colonel Burkinshaw accepted the answer as no more than one would expect from a doctor who dressed like that, but he had to be careful. A copy of the post mortem findings had been in his possession for some time, long enough to brush up on relevant facts, but he had no intention of being drawn into a discussion of the anatomy of the root of the neck. He said nothing.

'The lungs were congested and oedematous with evidence of basal consolidation and collapse. In the trachea and major bronchi I found a quantity of blood. In my opinion, Police Constable Kincaid died as a result of respiratory obstruction secondary to the wound in his neck.'

'In other words, he died from drowning in his own blood arising from the wound in his neck.' Proud of having reduced a lot of technical mumbo-jumbo into words anyone could understand, Burkinshaw made it a statement, not a question, and looked pained when Kelsey disagreed.

'No, sir.'

The Coroner waited for an explanation but did not get one until he asked for one, the tone of his voice that of a commanding officer addressing a junior officer late on parade.

'Well?'

'It is not uncommon for death by drowning to occur with the victim's airways to be perfectly patent at the time of death. If the victim is recovered from the water, his airways cleared and normal respiration restored, he can still die hours later from the metabolic disorders that absorption of large quantities of water from the lungs produces. That was not the case with PC Kincaid. He died, as I said, from respiratory obstruction due to blood in the trachea and bronchi. The deceased did not drown, sir, he choked.'

The Coroner would have liked to have taken the sloppy devil down a peg by telling him he was splitting hairs but he had sufficient wisdom to realise Kelsey was not nit-picking. The distinction was an important one. He turned to the Federation's solicitor. 'Any questions for Dr Kelsey. Mr Jamieson?'

'No, thank you, sir.'

The smile Burkinshaw had given the young man who had stood to attention when he replied was wiped away before he turned back to Kelsey.

'You are released, Dr Kelsey. I now call Inspector George Hardcastle.'

From the way Hardcastle went through the preliminaries, it was obvious he was no stranger to the witness box either. Indeed, it was less than a week since he had stood there before, giving evidence in the inquest on the villain, Morelli. Burkinshaw remembered the clear, concise manner in which the Inspector had justified the carrying of firearms by his men, the fact that Morelli's father had been known at one time to possess a gun which had never been found. The Coroner felt an immediate rapport with the distinguished-looking man in uniform. As might have been expected, his account of events commencing with Police Constable Evans's accident and ending with Morelli's death was given in terse, disciplined jargon. Turning to the tragic death of Police Constable Kincaid, he stated that the Force could ill afford to lose such an able, dedicated and universally popular officer. Burkinshaw thanked him, turned and smiled at the Federation's solicitor.

'Mr Jamieson?'

'One or two questions, if I may, sir.' Andrew Jamieson turned to face Inspector Hardcastle. 'It is true, is it not, Inspector, that Police Constable Kincard was suspended from duties at the time of his death?'

'That is correct.'

'On what charges, Inspector?'

'He had not been charged.'

'So, can we be quite clear on this point, Inspector? At the time of the constable's death, although he was suspended from duty, he was still employed as a policeman against whom no charges had been brought, let alone substantiated, and therefore, having not been found guilty, must be presumed to have been innocent.'

'At no time was I ever in doubt of his innocence. Badger Kincaid was a very fine officer.'

'Thank you, sir.' Satisfied his part in the proceedings had gone well, Jamieson sat down.

That left two witnesses for Burkinshaw to call, the young Casualty Officer and the Consultant Anaesthetist. Logically, if one followed Kincaid's fatal progress, he should call the casualty officer first, but Monks was a senior colleague, chairman of several local committees – they had served together on various charities.

'I now call Dr Monks.'

As Richard Monks took the oath, Burkinshaw wondered why Monks had bothered to come himself. As a rule, consultants fell over backwards to avoid having to give evidence – he had never seen Monks in the witness box before. It was usually the registrar who was detailed off to attend. He presumed it must be the seriousness of the case. He wouldn't want to risk a registrar making a fool of himself in front of the Press.

'You are Senior Consultant Anaesthetist at Scarsby General Hospital, Dr Monks?'

'I am.'

'And you were present at the unfortunate death of this young officer?'

'I was. May I, in my own words, give you an account of what happened?'

'Please do, Dr Monks.'

'At the time the patient was admitted to the casualty department, I was engaged in another case in the main theatre. One of my registrars was in attendance, however, and called me immediately he saw the seriousness of the injury. When I got there, Mr Bannerman was dealing with the wound in the neck and a casualty officer had just successfully drained the pneumothorax.'

'By that, you mean the re-expansion of the lung?'

'Quite so.'

There was nothing hurried about the way Monks stopped to take breath, going on as if reciting a well-rehearsed statement.

'While my registrar was putting me in the picture, explaining the obvious difficulty of intubation and, therefore, the impossibility of general anaesthesia, it was becoming apparent to Mr Bannerman that the nature of the injuries were much more serious than he had anticipated. It was while we were discussing the best course to take towards inducing general anaesthesia – we had just decided that establishing a tracheotomy . . .'

'A direct opening into the windpipe?'

'Exactly. Establishing a tracheotomy and transferral to the main theatre was probably the best option – that the patient developed his acute respiratory obstruction from which he died despite every effort on our part and on the part of the casualty officers.'

Monks let his voice fall away as if that was the end of the matter. He had no real hope that the Coroner would leave it at that but he thought it worth a try.

'You have heard the pathologist say, Dr Monks, that the cause of death was respiratory obstruction due to blood entering the trachea. Do you have any comment to make on that? Would you agree with Dr Kelsey as to the cause of death?'

If Monks took a deep breath before answering, he managed to hide it skilfully.

'There is no doubt, sir, that some blood entered the trachea. It would have been inconceivable that some should not. From the police testimony – they mentioned the coughing and going blue – there must have been a considerable amount of blood aspirated before he arrived in hospital. But I have an alternative theory.'

'Yes, Dr Monks?' Burkinshaw kept it short, anxious to conceal the fact that he too would be glad when this point had been disposed of.

'There is an unusual condition which may cause death, sometimes quite sudden death, arising out of material being aspirated into the lungs. It is usually, but not invariably, associated with pregnancy where childbirth under anaesthesia takes place soon after a meal. It is called Mendelson's syndrome. Aspiration of gastric content, quite small quantities if the acidity is high, can cause a reaction in the lung tissue which can produce a kind of respiratory obstruction that can be easily overlooked at post mortem if not specifically suspected. Dr Kelsey mentioned the thick chyle coming from the damaged thoracic duct which would suggest a recent meal; one could understand an increased acidity that excitement and fear might produce, and there were wounds in both windpipe and gullet in close juxtaposition.'

Drawing himself up to his full height, looking over glasses balanced on an impressively hooked nose, he summed up with the solemnity of a reasonable man.

'I do not deny for a moment the importance of the blood in the trachea but I suggest that other important factors, not now verifiable, could well have come into play in this man's death.'

The Coroner had a problem, a decision to make and make rapidly. The

Home Office pathologist might look scruffy but he was a first-class brain. Would he have looked specifically for this syndrome? How obvious was it at post mortem? He would certainly have mentioned it in his report if he had seen evidence of it. But he had released Kelsey. To bring him back might result in no more than an unseemly argument between two eminent doctors with no real impact on his final findings. After all, Burkinshaw had already decided what his finding was going to be – he had very little option really. It was going to be 'unlawful killing' at the end of the day whatever had been in the young policeman's lungs. He looked at Monks, erect, well dressed, widely respected – and smiled.

'Thank you, Dr Monks.' He turned to the court once more. 'Mr Jamieson?'

'No questions, thank you, sir.'

There was a relaxation in the court as the young Casualty Officer took the stand. One or two people left the court room, the swing doors thudding behind them. Jonathan Brookes took the oath to a background of low, murmured conversation. With the exception of a man and a woman in the far corner of the room, few looked at him. The Coroner did. An astute, sensitive man, the experience of countless general practice surgeries behind him, his eyebrows furrowed in interest. As he studied the young man's face, there returned that niggling anxiety he had suppressed towards the end of Monks's testimony only to have it reinforced when he had seen Monks go back to his seat even though released from the court. He was used to the trembling hesitancy of some young houseman finding himself in a witness box for the first time. But this was different. The Casualty Officer was not all that young, the look on his face not that of fear. He was tense, certainly, but if Burkinshaw had to describe his attitude, he would have called it resolute determination. His name, as he gave it – Jonathan Brookes – for some reason sounded familiar.

'And what is your position at Scarsby General Hospital, doctor?'

'I am one of the Casualty Senior House Officers, sir.'

'And you were in attendance at the time of PC Kincaid's death?'

'I was.'

'And were you in charge of his management, Dr Brookes?'

'No, sir. Not at first, that is.'

Burkinshaw's next question came quickly as if anxious not to hear Jonathan's last five words, as if they did not fit in, as if they suggested mud at the bottom of a tranquil pool, best left undisturbed. 'Who was present altogether?'

'Apart from the nursing staff, there was Dr Monks and his registrar, Mr Bannerman, the Casualty Consultant, and Dr James, another Senior House Officer.'

'And what injuries did you find in the deceased when he was admitted?' With Kelsey's minute description on record, Burkinshaw would have been happy to accept, in fact hoped for, a generalisation from Brookes that would help wind up a case about which he was suddenly becoming apprehensive. 'Do you have any reason to disagree with the account you have heard given by the Home Office Pathologist?'

'No, sir. But then I was not present myself at the exact time Police Constable Kincaid was admitted.'

'You were not?' Burkinshaw sensed that the court had gone much quieter, some of the reporters reopening closed notebooks. Now he was not the only one to suspect that, not so much by what Brookes had said so far as by his manner, his tone of voice, that this young Casualty Officer had a tale to tell. The coroner shifted in his seat as conflict grew in his mind between an inborn desire to protect the good name of a profession he loved and his duty as a coroner to get at the truth of how Kincaid died. 'Perhaps you would explain.'

'I was seeing a patient on one of the wards when they rang to say I was wanted urgently in Casualty.'

'D'you mean there was no one on duty in the department at the time the constable was admitted?'

'No, sir, of course not. I knew Dr James was there. When I left, things were very quiet and I made sure they knew where I was going.'

'And Mr Bannerman, of course; he was there?'

'I imagine he must have been but I have no way of being sure.'

Burkinshaw had a growing fear he was handling things badly, that he would never have got himself involved in the present line of questioning if he had the chance to start again, but one glance at the intense interest on the faces looking up at him told him that he could do nothing now other than go on.

'But Mr Bannerman was in charge of the theatre when you arrived?'

'The Intensive Care Unit, sir,' Brookes corrected his senior. 'Kincaid was never transferred to a theatre. Yes, it is true to say that Mr Bannerman was present when I got there.'

The coroner was not the only one to hear the qualified answer, the implication in the tone.

'So, when you got there, there were already two doctors present. Why then did Mr Bannerman send for you so urgently?'

'He didn't.'

'Who did?'

'Sister Drake, one of the Casualty Sisters.'

'And why would the sister send for you?' There was a slow, solid authority to Burkinshaw's voice now, signalling his decision that his sense of duty as a coroner was now paramount. If the questioning of a colleague was going to prove distasteful, so be it. 'Are you sure Mr Bannerman did not instruct her to do so?'

'Quite sure, sir.'

'Why, then, should she do that on her own initiative?'

'Because she was unhappy at the way Mr Bannerman was conducting the operation.'

In the silence, Burkinshaw leaned over his desk, the pencil in his hand turning over and over as he drove the ends alternately into his pad. He searched Jonathan Brookes's face for malice or hatred but saw nothing but honest, stolid determination.

'I feel I should warn you at this stage, Dr Brookes, about the dangers of giving evidence in a Coroner's Court when, in doing so, you impugn a colleague's ability or integrity. Though the proceedings in this court are privileged absolutely against defamation, it is not the purpose of this court to hear evidence that might be considered actionable. This court is interested in the manner of Kincaid's death, no more. Do you understand?'

'Perfectly sir. I am giving evidence on oath. The evidence I will give will be restricted to fact as I saw it but I too feel it my duty to Ba..., to Police Constable Kincaid that the true facts of his death should be known.'

'Very well, but Mr Bannerman is neither here himself to speak for his actions nor is he represented. I am given to believe he is unwell and not able to attend.'

'He has not worked since the day in question, sir. A matter of recurrent attacks of viral pneumonia, I believe.'

'Yes.' The coroner's remark was languid, as if he shared Jonathan's ideas about such a diagnosis. 'What, then, did you find when you reached the Intensive Care Unit? Careful now, Dr Brookes; just the facts.'

'Mr Bannerman appeared to be dealing with the wound in the neck, Dr James was putting up intravenous lines and the anaesthetic registrar was attempting to give some oxygen.'

'Not Dr Monks?'

'Dr Monks had not arrived at that time.'

'You said attempting.'

'The patient was very blue but the registrar was unable to give much oxygen as most of the patient's respiration was through the wound in his neck.'

'And there was no tracheotomy at that time?'

'There had been no tracheotomy at any time. The registrar had requested one but had been over-ruled by Mr Bannerman who apparently could not be convinced that the bleeding was not the immediate problem. It was only then that the patient's pneumothorax was pointed out to me and, with the patient so cyanosed, I thought I could help most at that stage by putting a chest drain in – which I did.'

'And then?'

'And then Dr Monks arrived. When he saw the situation, he advised Mr Bannerman to put a tracheotomy tube in, transfer the patient to the theatre and explore the neck under more favourable conditions.'

'And Mr Bannerman's reaction?'

'He didn't seem to hear, sir.'

'What did you do then?'

'I scrubbed up and went to the couch to see if I could help Mr Bannerman in any way.'

'And were you able to?'

'That was the problem, sir. He refused any assistance even though he was making no progress. In fact, except for small enlargements to the wound, he had done nothing at all. He had frozen and could not be reasoned with. The patient's condition was deteriorating with constant significant blood loss and was obviously in urgent need of something being done to secure an airway that could be made watertight. I came to the conclusion that Mr Bannerman must be ill, time was running out and it was up to me to do something. I tried to get my arms around in front of him at the same time as trying to elbow him out of the way.'

'And did you succeed?' Seeing the strain that was tearing at the young man, Burkinshaw's voice was gentle and considerate but audible to the farthest corner of his court.

'No, sir. It has been on my conscience ever since that my action may have brought about Kincaid's death as Mr Bannerman, in resisting my attempts to take over the operation, turned and threw me to the ground where I lay stunned for a while. It was during this time that Kincaid died. I do not know exactly what happened. What I do know is that he died as a result of his own blood flooding into his trachea and whether you call that drowning or choking would seem to me to be a bit academic. We tried all the usual measures but there's precious little you can do if the airway is completely blocked.'

'So there's nothing in Dr Kelsey's findings with which you would fundamentally disagree?'

'No, sir.'

'And were you present at the post mortem?'

'I was.'

'So you must have seen the extent of the wound in detail. In your opinion, Dr Brookes, with regard to the injuries to the blood vessels in the neck, were they compatible with survival if a safe airway had been established early on?'

245

'In all honesty, sir, I do not know. I have wondered many times since what I would have done if I had found myself alone in those conditions. Would I have coped? The wounds in the veins looked much smaller than I expected but then I imagine they always do when the veins are collapsed and empty. It's a very different matter when the patient is coughing and straining and the veins are full and distended. I think I would have been in the most awful difficulty as I have no experience in such major vascular surgery, but if an experienced surgeon had been operating under general anaesthesia, I rather think . . .'

In the utter silence that followed, Burkinshaw, oblivious to the rest of the court, peering compassionately at the pale, drawn face, wondered at a young man who, on the threshold of his career, had been so imprudent as to speak out as he had when he could so easily have simply followed the party line. Why? Even as he asked the question, he did not realise he had got it right.

'Dr Brookes, did you know the deceased?'

'He was one of my closest friends.'

Burkinshaw turned away as if he could not stand the look of pain any more. 'Mr Jamieson?' he asked.

The solicitor stood, shook his head but said nothing.

The crowded court room watched the coroner push and prod with his finger tips, fidgeting until the pile of notes in front of him formed the perfect rectangle. He raised his head, having decided what he should say, only to find Jonathan Brookes still in the witness box. He smiled his apology. 'You're released, Dr Brookes. Thank you.' He watched as Jonathan took his seat once more beside a stoney-faced Consultant Anaesthetist.

'This court will be adjourned until some time to be decided in the future. I think there is little difficulty in piecing together the manner of this young man's unfortunate death but it may be that there are others who would wish to give evidence on their own behalf and it would be wrong for me not to give them the opportunity to do so. Should this not be the case, however, this will be the last public hearing. I think it only right therefore that I should take this opportunity to commend publicly the actions of the local police force. Such cases as these only bring into focus the dangers that face the ordinary man on the beat these days and it was only in the best traditions of the force that Police Constable Kincaid, even though not on duty at the time, carried out what he saw as his duty with the utmost disregard for his own safety. I would also include in my commendation the officers and ambulance men who dealt so skilfully with such terrible injuries. This inquest is adjourned.'

By the time Michael and Alison Brookes had fought their way through the mass of burly policemen, Jonathan had gone.

25

'For God's sake, sit down. You're like some caged animal. If you don't sit down and relax, I'll go crazy.'

Michael Brookes took scant notice of his wife's pleading. He stopped his restless pacing only to look out of the window. 'He could at least ring. That's not too much to ask, is it? Why won't you let me ring him?'

'Because, if he had wanted a shoulder to cry on he would have stayed to talk to us after the inquest yesterday.'

'Perhaps he didn't see us.'

'Don't be ridiculous. Of course he saw us. Don't crowd him. He'll come when the time's right. I've told you, unless he's on duty this weekend, my guess is he'll be here about teatime today or tomorrow. Now go and cut the lawn; go and do something useful.'

'I cut it only two days ago.'

'Well, cut it again. What about all those hedges? There are plenty of those out there that need trimming.'

'Bloody tyrant,' Michael Brookes muttered as he kissed his wife.

The physical effort under a summer sun together with the monotonous rhythm of the shears helped Michael Brookes through the afternoon. The clipping stopped the moment he heard a car turn into the Close. He was already walking up the garden towards the courtyard when tyres made the familiar sound of crunching through gravel. He saw his son heave himself out and, without hesitation, walk towards him. The feel of the arm across his back, the power of the hug, overwhelmed him and, as his own arms closed round his son, he struggled for words.

'You're half an hour early.'

Surprised, Jonathan stood back but without relinquishing his hold across his father's shoulders. 'What d'you mean?' he grinned.

'Lissa – she said you'd be here teatime.'

'Just shows what a clever, perceptive woman you married then, doesn't it, Dad? It's nice to know you can still get the odd thing right now and again.'

'Cheeky young beggar – you always were. How are . . .?'

He stopped as, over his son's shoulder, he saw Susannah standing beside the car, smiling hesitantly as if not sure of her welcome, her eyes darting uncertainly between Michael Brookes and Alison who had come out to join them. Jonathan stood aside, delighting in the welcome Susannah was given. Inside the house, Alison looked them up and down before they settled in their chairs.

'When did you eat last?'

Jonathan laughed. 'We've just driven up from Scarsby, Lissa, not from somewhere in the Third World. What is there about me that always makes you want to feed me?'

'You've lost weight again.'

'I have not.'

'Are you staying the night?'

'No, Lissa.'

'But you'll stay for supper?'

'No, thank you, Lissa.'

'You're on call tonight?' Michael Brookes sounded as if he longed for that to be the reason.

'No, Dad.' No explanation. Just a look at his father to say that he loved him but that his home was in Lymm now, that he was just visiting. 'But we've got to get back.'

While his father struggled to stop his face from sulking, Alison smiled as she sat beside Jonathan on the chesterfield, slipping her arm under his.

'We were very proud of you yesterday, darling. You haven't a hope in hell of that stupid great father of yours up there ever telling you that, but you can take it from me, we were.'

'Thanks, Lissa.'

'What d'you think, Susannah?'

'I'm not sure he's told me everything that went on but, reading between the lines, it sounds as if he did very well.'

As if anxious to be true to form, Michael Brookes glowered at his son. 'Can't have done you much good, you realise that, don't you? Must put a cloud over your future,' he growled.

'At least I've got a future, Dad. More than can be said for Badger.' He felt Alison squeeze his hand and there was no immediate response from his father. 'Dad, Badger Kincaid was one of the most honest, upright men I have ever met, probably ever will meet. I couldn't let him die with a lie hanging over his grave.'

'No one lied at that inquest, Jonathan.'

'And nobody told the truth either, not the whole truth anyway. Well, maybe the pathologist. His evidence was pretty straightforward. But the way the Establishment closed ranks – Monks and his Mendelson's syndrome – really. When did you last hear of a case of that?'

'I know,' his father smiled. 'Real rocking horse manure stuff that, isn't it. But you realise Monks is Chairman of the local Medical Staff Committee, don't you?'

'So what?'

It was Michael who broke the silence that followed. 'I take it this man Bannerman was drunk?'

'Absolutely stoned, Dad. He could hardly see. And, once again, the dreaded word was never mentioned. Everyone, including myself, managed to get right through that inquest without saying the truth, that the surgeon was drunk. It's quite incredible.'

'I don't think there was much doubt in anyone's mind in court what was wrong with Bannerman. I shouldn't think there was anyone who didn't get the message.'

'But it was never admitted, Dad.'

'It couldn't be, Jonathan.'

'I would have said it if asked.'

'And then you would have been really in trouble. That would have called for an opinion from you and the coroner was quite right to make sure you stuck to fact. There was no way you could have produced proof that Bannerman was drunk – he could have been ill.'

'Do me a favour, Dad.'

'No, Jonathan. There, in some ways, I think you're wrong. You were in an inquest yesterday, not a court of law. I was impressed by the coroner – he was as anxious to protect a young doctor as he was to determine the truth. There may come a time when you will look back and feel grateful to him.'

'Rubbish.'

'If anyone is guilty, I am,' Michael said, slowly.

All three looked at him, surprised.

'If I had done something about it when you told me about Bannerman's drinking problem some time ago, perhaps your friend might still be alive.'

'What could you have done?' It was the first time Susannah had intruded into the conversation.

'Had the courage to get up and tell the truth, get him suspended, maybe find some desk job for him. I should have said something.'

'Does that mean you are going to be careful not to make the same mistake again and tell them about me?'

There was neither the snide satisfaction in Susannah's voice of someone making an unanswerable point, nor a heart-rending plea for clemency, simply the weariness that she should cast a shadow over the loving atmosphere of the old house. Jonathan, realising for the first time that he was not the only one to know of Susannah's troubles, looked from Susannah to his father who sat, stuttering wordlessly. Slowly, Michael found his way out.

'But that's different. What I mean is, you've got things under control; Bannerman hadn't. Quite different problem.'

249

'Is it? What I didn't tell you was that it's not so long since I nearly fell from grace again – it was only Sir Jonathan in shining armour who rode up and saved me. What if I go and do it again when he's not around? What if he finally gets fed up with the way I treat him and tells me to get lost? What happens then? Do you turn me in? Or perhaps Jonathan?'

'Don't talk rubbish,' Jonathan snapped.

'Will someone kindly tell me what's going on?' There was the hurt look of the excluded as Alison looked at a husband who could keep secrets from her. 'What are you all talking about?'

Her pained expression only deepened as the other three appeared to ignore her.

'Is it rubbish? What if I went off the rails again and did something dreadful – killed a child maybe – and then it all came out that you both knew about me all the time and let me go on working in an anaesthetic department of all places?'

'But you're all right now. You're over-reacting,' Jonathan said, angrily.

'But am I? You weren't so sure that night, were you? You had a good look round that night, didn't you? I could tell the next morning. And don't imagine I put it down to telepathy that my father appeared on my doorstep at 9 a.m. the next morning. Does that sound as if you had total confidence in me? Would you ever be sure of me?'

'Will someone please tell me what is going on?' Alison repeated, speaking slowly and distinctly.

'I too have a problem,' Susannah explained, quietly. 'Correction – I have a drug problem. I must remember to keep saying it. Booze I can handle. My difficulty is that I can't just leave it there. I find getting drunk a bore; it's not enough; I want to fly.'

'But that's all over,' Michael insisted. 'As I said, the problem with Bannerman was that he was hopelessly out of control. You are not. If and when Bannerman can show he's dried out, then I'm sure he will be reinstated and back at his old job – there are plenty of precedents.'

'Quite.' With a deprecating look, Alison waved her hand as if wanting to minimise what Susannah was saying to proportions that could be swept out of mind. 'The odd bit of pot smoking; most young people experiment these days; it's not . . .'

As she saw Susannah slowly shake her head, a weary smile on her face, Alison stopped, her mouth hardening slightly as she receded from the conversation to become more watchful. She stared stonily as Susannah gave her a brief account of her troubles. As Michael made soothing noises, Jonathan noticed how his stepmother said nothing as she rose, simply making the excuse of getting tea as Jonathan tried to change the subject. When she returned, shaking her head at Susannah's offer of help, the tea cups brought with them a half hour of stilted, tautly polite conversation before the subject inevitably reverted.

'D'you really think that will happen to Bannerman, Dad? He's a hell of a nice chap in many ways and a good surgeon beneath it all. It was very difficult not to like him.'

'Well, I know he was dealt with locally immediately after your friend's death. There's no doubt several members of staff will have known of his drinking for some time and this event would only have brought things to a head. He would have been interviewed by "the three wise men", one of whom would have been Dr Monks, and sent off on indefinite sick leave and his case reviewed in a few months time. Now, after a certain young man's evidence yesterday, he'll almost certainly be suspended indefinitely on full pay. No further action provided he goes and gets dried out. Could well be back at work in a year.'

'But what about the law, Dad? Where does he stand legally?'

'That would depend on whether there is anyone to make a complaint. Even if they did, it would be very difficult to prove. Even your evidence would be a matter of opinion. Did Badger have any dependants?'

Jonathan shook his head. 'An aged grandmother whom I haven't yet plucked up the courage to go and see. A rather ineffectual brother. I don't see them doing anything about it.'

'What about the Police Federation? I wonder whether they would take it up on their behalf? Their solicitor was in court.'

As if unable to face the thought of being dragged through the affair again, Jonathan suddenly stood, looking down on his father. 'We must go, Dad. Before we do, are you favourably disposed towards me at the moment? Can I ask you a favour?'

'What's that?'

'It's something I know you hate doing.'

'Try me.'

'Do you remember me telling you about the black porter in Casualty I got very friendly with – Gavin Prescott?'

Michael Brookes nodded.

'Well, he's going to Liverpool and taking his sister, Linda – Linda Morelli is her full name – taking her with him. It was Gavin's half-brother who killed Badger and I can well imagine his reasons for wanting to get out.'

'So what's this got to do with me?'

'I'm coming to that, Dad. Linda's got her name down for Med School in Liverpool. She should be coming up for interviews shortly. D'you think you could put a word in for her?'

His father's reaction was predictable as he stood to face his son.

'You know how I hate that sort of thing. I wouldn't do that even for you.'

'You didn't need to do it for me, Dad,' Jonathan grinned. He turned his head. 'I seem to remember – just the two of us in this room – I told you I was going to make them an offer they couldn't refuse.'

'But those days of nepotism and patronage are gone, Jonathan, and a good thing too. It could even go against her. I'm told there are Deans who have refused to consider someone just because they have heard the name mentioned in conversation. Anyway, I don't know anyone in the Medical School now.'

'Come on, Dad. Don't tell me it doesn't go on, even now. You must have one or two old cronies you could ring. What about my old chief, Alex Tibbs?'

Michael Brookes showed signs of weakening. 'She'd have to get the grades they ask for. There's nothing anyone can do if she hasn't got those.'

'Thanks, Dad. Now, we must go.'

The bear hug he gave his father confirmed that the one on arrival was not to be considered an isolated event. He kissed his stepmother. There was no doubting the sincerity of Michael's invitation to Susannah to come and see them again soon, nor the affection in the hand laid gently on her shoulder as she walked towards the car. Susannah's and Alison's unsmiling farewells were exchanged without physical contact of any kind.

Michael Brookes sat in bed, his hands folded in front of him, staring at Alison's back as she brushed her hair at the dressing table. She had hardly spoken a word all evening. Between strokes, she sneaked glances at his reflection in the mirror. In the previous four years, she had learned a thing or two about this complex man she had married, one being that it was impossible to make him discuss anything he did not want to discuss. To try to force him to talk on any subject was only to invite stubborn, grunted monosyllables.

She wriggled down beside him but had to wait awhile until he too slid down and turned off the light. They stared up into the darkness.

'Want to talk about it?' Alison asked.

'About what?'

'Don't be stupid, Michael; Jonathan and that girl.'

'That girl is it now? Bit different from the way you talked about her after Abersoch.'

'That was before I knew about this drugs business. Surely you can't be too happy about it yourself – you wouldn't want Jonathan to go marrying a drug addict, now would you?'

'She's not a drug addict. And who said they're going to get married?'

'She is – she admitted it. I suppose one's got to give her credit for that. But, take it from me, Jonathan is very much in love with her.'

'But she's all right now. I think she's a tremendous girl.'

'Men,' Alison snorted. 'Would you think the same if she wasn't so beautiful?'

'I'm sure we can leave it to Jonathan's good sense. He's grown up all of a sudden. I was quite worried about him a couple of months ago – that day he came home to lunch. I felt then that if he went on like that, feeling every knock the way he was, that he'd have to give it all up. General surgery would have killed him. If he was going to get so upset when somebody lost a finger, just imagine what he'd be like if someone lost his life.' Michael paused for a moment. 'If someone dies after an operation you've done, an operation for something a bit troublesome but certainly not life threatening – say a young breadwinner drops dead from a pulmonary embolus ten days after you've done his varicose veins – then you've got to be able to advise that same operation to an identical patient who walks into your clinic two days later and look him straight in the eye when you're doing it. And I'm not talking about courage – it has got nothing to do with guts and certainly nothing to do with technical ability which is what most people think surgery is all about. It's to do with the ability to harden your heart and not sit around thinking of the widow and orphans of the man who would have been still alive except for your advice. It's the sort of attitude of mind that makes you stick to your guns when you think you're right and everyone else thinks you're wrong.'

'Bigotry, you mean.'

'No.' Michael reacted sharply. 'I don't mean bigotry. That's hanging on to an opinion without listening to reason. What I think it takes is the ability to listen honestly to what everyone says then make up your own mind and to hell with them if they don't agree.'

'And what on earth has all that got to do with Susannah and her drugs?'

'Nothing directly. It's just that he's changed and for the better. In many ways I feel I'm only just getting to know him. I get the feeling that, given the circumstances, he'd turn round and tell me to go to hell – and I'd love it. It's going to be a relief not having to be so eternally protective. And, with that sort of change of character, if he says Susannah is all right, then that's all right with me too. I'll back his judgment.'

Though Alison kissed Michael first, she turned away without reply.

26

It was late evening when Jonathan answered the phone. The voice on the other end was not that of someone used to making social calls.

'Is that Jonathan?'

'Yes.'

'Warwick Ridgeway here. How are you?'

'Hullo. Good evening.' He still did not know what to call him.

'Sorry to hear about that young friend of yours. You mustn't let it upset you too much. I regret I didn't have the chance to talk to him more that weekend – he looked a fine young man.'

'He was.' There did not seem anything else to say.

'It's the other one I'm ringing about; your black friend. What's his name, Prescott? What d'you make of him?'

Suddenly asked to put into a few words something he could not decide himself, Jonathan played for time. 'In what way?'

'He's rung me; asked me if I can get him some sort of job in Liverpool. Tell me; what's his background? What sort of a chap is he really?'

Jonathan hesitated for a moment then listed facts as if summarising a clinical history.

'Desperately deprived childhood – made him a ruthless survivor – highly intelligent – self educated – burning ambition.'

'Reliable?'

'Utterly – so long as it is in his own interest or, possibly, his sister's. If he ever finds himself in a position to wield any form of power, I would hate to stand in his way.'

'But deserves a bit of help?'

'I think all he needs is a toe in some door. He deserves that much.'

'Hmph.' The length of time the line went dead became embarrassing. When Sir Warwick Ridgeway spoke again, it was hardly in the clipped, decisive tones of a successful industrialist. 'Wish it was you I was going to do something to help. Not the type to ask though, are you? But I owe you. Like sometime to be able to . . . Wouldn't want you to think I don't appreciate what you're doing for Susannah . . . If ever there's anything . . . She's all I've got, Jonathan.'

If it had not been spoken with such real emotion, Jonathan would have laughed at such a statement coming from one of the richest men in Lancashire. But Sir Warwick had not had his last stuttering word.

'Damned if I know why you two can't get your act together. If you don't buck up I'll be too old to enjoy my grandchildren.'

'I'll say "goodbye" then.' Gavin Prescott walked into the room and thrust out his hand.

Jonathan, taken aback by the suddenness of the gesture, did not take the hand in his. 'But I've still a couple of weeks to go,' he smiled. 'I'm not going yet.'

'But I am.'

The slender, black-skinned hand was still extended and Jonathan shook it formally, too surprised to be enthusiastic.

'Where are you going? Liverpool?'

'Yes. And I've got myself a job. I start on Monday.'

'In a hospital?'

'No; in a sports centre. Part-time karate instructor, part-time on the administrative side. I'm taking Linda with me. I'm over the moon.'

'That's great.' Just in time, Jonathan remembered to look suitably surprised and delighted and to ask how he'd managed it.

'Influence in high places, how else?' Gavin grinned. 'That and the sheer power of my personality.'

'I'll give you a ring as soon as I'm settled. I'll show you round. Will you come?'

'Of course.'

'Promise?'

'Promise.'

'You must be looking forward to going back to Liverpool.'

They sat, Janet James and he, side by side on one of the couches, swinging their legs idly on one of those rare occasions in a casualty department, a few minutes of total peace and quiet.

'Yes,' Jonathan admitted. 'I suppose, if I'm honest about it, I am glad to be going back.'

'Of course you are. You've never really fitted in here.'

Too surprised to be angry, Jonathan turned sideways, his mouth agape, to see the same friendly, cherubic smile, without a trace of malice. 'That's a bit hard, isn't it?'

'I don't think so. You've never been anything more than a bird of passage. It would have been different if all you had ever wanted was to be Casualty Consultant but you're ambitious – a permanent appointment here and you'd almost certainly end up like poor Bob. Poor Bob,' she repeated, her voice low and full of true sympathy. 'I wonder how his wife is coping with him at home all day?'

If Janet thought Jonathan's silence covered vague mental pictures of marital stress, she was quite mistaken. He saw it all in crisp detail. The face at his front door, the snarling, naked hatred as Dawn Bannerman had hurled herself at him, scratching and punching. The way she had broken free when he had finally caught her wrists. He heard again, word for word, the obscenities she had spat at him as she had backed away to her car, becoming more and more unintelligible, merging as they did into howling grief as she drove away.

'And what about you?' he asked Janet. 'What are you going to do next?'

The same, fixed smile belied the sadness in the way she shrugged her shoulders. 'I can always stay on here, I suppose. They've offered me the job of locum consultant while Bob is away.'

'That's great' – Jonathan looked and sounded genuinely pleased – 'as long as that is what you want. I don't want to hear that you've started drinking,' he grinned.

'No chance of that, I'm afraid. I just haven't got the passion and it's the passionate ones who become the drinkers. I know they say it can happen to anyone, but you don't often see it in cold, hard-headed skinflints, do you? It's as if alcoholism only thrives in the warmth. The pity is that, by the time they have become recognised drinkers, they have made such awful nuisances of themselves that people forget what they used to be like.' She paused for a moment, her face unusually earnest. 'Bob must have been very much like you in many ways when he was young. You both feel very deeply, you are both very likeable people. You made more friends here in a week than I have in a year. I won't be the only one sorry to see you go.'

She slid slowly to her feet to stand, buttoning up her white coat. 'Come on, Dr Kildare. Sounds as if they've found some more customers for us.'

A lacerated milkman, his red spotted trail easy to follow from the delivery van parked in the yard to the theatre – the factory girl's avulsed finger nail – the screaming young lad who had torn his scrotum climbing over a spiked fence – the city fat cat in his Saville Row suit, travelling north on business, feeling trapped in an NHS hospital by the pain in his chest – the fat, kindly housewife wondering how she would cope with Grandma now she had put her back out, lifting the old lady out of bed – the old man with the gashed forehead, living rough, being slipped a coin by the junior nurse. Any casualty department mid morning.

'Attempted suicide on the way in, Dr Brookes.' Sister Drake did not seem too put out at the prospect.

'Hell. That's just what we need. What sort, d'you know?'

'Cut throat.'

Jonathan heard the trolley go past in the corridor outside and hurried after it, not knowing what to expect. He was immediately encouraged by the degree of 'flap' ahead of him. There wasn't the extreme urgency about the movements that always attend a life in imminent danger. The patient was not fighting to get off the trolley. The voices were soothing and encouraging rather than clipped and decisive.

There was a fair amount of blood around – a nurse, pressing a sodden pad to the left side of the neck, seemed to be hindered by a man's thick red beard. Another pad and bandage surrounding the left wrist seemed to be doing the job by itself. When Jonathan leaned over to speak to the patient, there was no sudden backward start of recognition, no sudden indrawing of breath, not even the raising of an eyebrow. It was almost as if he was meeting Reggie Kincaid by appointment.

Reggie's face was equally impassive as Jonathan gingerly lifted the pad on his neck. The wound was about the same size as his brother's but a little further out. It was little more than skin deep, all the blood coming from a small nick in the external jugular vein. Nodding his relief, Jonathan handed the pad back for the nurse to press on once more while he undid the bandage at the wrist. Again, only skin deep, it would need no more than a couple of stitches. He smiled at an immobile face.

'No sweat, Reggie. You'll live. I'm afraid we're going to have to shave a bit of that beard of yours. Give you a short back and sides the same time if you like. No extra charge.'

He might as well have saved his breath. A few more attempts at getting through and Jonathan gave up, tidying up the sticky, hairy gash in silence while Janet came in to suture the wrist.

Vicki was waiting for him, sitting patiently on a bench, still managing to look subtly different from those around her. She was one of those people who could never be one of a crowd. There was space each side of her in the surrounding bustle and it would have been difficult to decide whether she had spoken to no one or no one had spoken to her. She stood up as Jonathan approached, holding out her hand, composed, self-assured.

'Good morning, Jonathan. How is he?'

'He's fine. No great damage done.' He smiled admiringly. Her clothes were still distinctive but more subdued, her makeup more subtle. She was learning fast. He looked round. 'Let's go somewhere a bit more private, shall we?'

The best they could find was an empty cubicle. Jonathan leaned against the couch as Vicki sat in the chair alongside. Beyond the curtain a grown man yelped and hissed as he had his stitches removed.

'Well, Jonathan, what's that husband of mine done to himself?'

'Nothing too terrible. Cut through the skin on the left side of his neck. Nicked a vein but no real damage done. Small cut across his left wrist – again just skin. Hasn't cut anything of importance, thank heavens.'

'Much as I expected. I couldn't really see our Reggie making a good job of anything. Typical is that.' She laughed at Jonathan's disapproving frown. 'Poor Jonathan. You must have had a bellyful of the Kincaid family since you came here. When does this job of yours finish?'

'Next week.'

'And you'll be glad to get away, I'm sure.'

And Jonathan suddenly found that, in all honesty, he could not deny it.

'Yes, I'm sure you will be. Get a breath of fresh air. I haven't regretted moving away, not for a moment.'

'How on earth did you manage to get here so promptly? He couldn't have done it more than an hour ago?'

'I came in the ambulance with him.'

Jonathan raised one eyebrow.

'I got a phone call a few days ago from one of Reggie's old mates, one of the bunch that got arrested with Reggie, chap called Sam Vickers. Seems our Reggie got up one day last week, put on his working clothes and managed to get through the pit gates unnoticed amongst the early shift. But he was soon picked up like, and taken to the manager's office. The manager, by all accounts, was very kind and understanding but poor Reggie soon found himself outside the gates again and then they saw him, on his hands and knees, blacking his face with coal dust and crying his eyes out. Seems they put him in a car and drove him home at that. Sam rang me, told me I'd better come home like, and I said I'd come over this morning. But I think he must have told Reggie because, as I was knocking on the door, Reggie was out in the bathroom, cutting his throat.'

'How awful for you.'

'Not really. He'd had the kindness to get into the bath first so there wasn't too much mess like. The ambulance was there very quickly and they coped beautifully.' She smiled once more at the look on Jonathan's face. 'I know. I'm a hard bitch, aren't I? I suppose my only saving grace is that I realise the fact. But be reasonable, doctor. You know as well as I do; he had no real intention of taking his own life. You know he was doing nothing more than looking for sympathy – as usual. But, even if he had found the guts to make a good job of it, I couldn't have been upset for long, not if I was honest. To me it would have been the ultimate selfish act, designed purely to punish me for the rest of my days. Well, he's bloody well not going to do that to me.'

'What about old Mrs Kincaid? How did she take it? The shock of something like that could kill an old lady that age.'

'Not that generation, Jonathan. They were made of sterner stuff, by heck they were. I've learned a lot from her over the years. She might hate my guts but, by God, I have nothing but respect for her.'

'Respect?'

Vicki nodded. 'She sat there, mouth shut like a vice, her chin stuck out, saying not a word. I watched her – she didn't bat an eyelid as they carried the stretcher past her through the kitchen. I bet, if you walked in now, you'd find her sitting there, in total silence, hour after hour, just like after Badger died.'

'I must call and see her. I've been trying to pluck up the courage ever since Badger died.'

'I wish you would, Jonathan. She'd be so glad to see you. It would keep her going for weeks, would that – just mulling over your visit, what you said, what you were wearing, like some old cow chewing the cud. But,' Vicki sat up abruptly, 'what happens now? What's the routine?'

'The routine is to get Reggie seen by a psychiatrist. If it had been a more serious attempt, I'd say we ought to admit him until he had been seen. But, even though we know he didn't try very hard, he's obviously very disturbed at the moment and we don't want him going away and doing a better job of it next time.' Jonathan hesitated as if unsure how his next remark would be received. 'I don't think he ought to go back to 48, Bradbury Street.'

'Don't worry, doctor. I'll take him off your hands.' Vicki Kincaid smiled ruefully. 'The silly bastard. One of the reasons for going to see him was to tell him I had a job for him. I've managed to fiddle him a place in the stock room. They've promised to find all the heaviest weights they can for him to shift, make him feel he's really working again. I came to beg him to take it. Now I'm going to tell him he's bloody well got to. I'll take him straight from here to my place in Liverpool. We'll get a taxi. We'll . . .'

'If you could wait until I'm off duty, . . .'

'Certainly not. You've done enough for the Kincaid family. If you're lucky, this will be the last you see of us. Knowing Reggie though, he'll probably rupture himself lifting some washing machine and . . .'

They both laughed and Vicki stood, offering her hand once more. 'Thanks, Jonathan; you've been a love.' Her parting was no embarrassed peck, no sisterly brush of the cheek, but a kiss full mouthed on his, lingering just long enough to leave Jonathan wondering.

There was ample parking space in front of 48, Bradbury Street. Jonathan wondered what they had done with Badger's old banger. As he got out of the car, he saw a curtain drawn back on the other side of the street. He stood to stare pointedly at the window until the drapes fell back in place again. He laughed quietly to himself – Badger would have enjoyed that. He knocked on the door and walked in, calling 'Hullo' every few steps through the shadows in his anxiety not to surprise the old lady. He need not have worried. She looked at him as if he came in at the same time every day.

'Good evening, doctor. It's good of you to call.' Her only movement was to point. 'Sit you down over there.'

The lifeless cushions, rigidly moulded into Reggie's shape, were uncomfortable and Jonathan found himself sitting bolt upright. He looked across at Gran Kincaid, motionless except for the heave of her breathing and the slow, rhythmic caress of one thumb on the other.

'I must apologise for not coming to see you sooner, Mrs Kincaid, after Badger died like that and now Reggie.'

'Yes, indeed.'

There was no note of censure, just the stoical acceptance of things that happen. Jonathan felt the blanketing silence of the house.

'But I'm going back to Liverpool in a couple of days and I felt I couldn't leave without coming to see you.'

'Thank you, doctor.'

'I was very sorry about Badger's death.' The statement sounded flat, trite, meaningless. But what else could he say? 'And now, with Reggie leaving you, you must be very lonely, Mrs Kincaid. This house must have been so full of life at one time.' He looked around him. 'It must be full of memories for you.'

At first there was no flicker of emotion in her face, the only sign of what was to come the change in the caressing thumb, its gentle, comforting stroke intensifying to a gouging thrust that furrowed the lax, wrinkled skin. She began to rock slowly back and fore and her first real words of communication, the first thoughts to seep through a crack in her defensive shield, took Jonathan by surprise.

'God could never have made coal any other colour than black, could he, doctor?'

'I'm sorry . . .?'

'You said this house must be full of memories for me. I'm sure you think of me sitting here with all those memories to help me through the lonely hours. Well there were some happy ones – the birth of my Edgar, the birth of my grandchildren, small, pink, fresh life amongst all this black and grey.'

Gran Kincaid put out her hands as if she were holding a newborn child again but the tenderness in her face disappeared as they dropped into her lap again to turn into white-knuckled fists.

'And then there are the other memories. I must have seen a thousand times my husband going through that door there –' she pointed '– with a shoebox under his arm, our first stillborn son inside it, going to the council incinerator because we couldn't afford to bury it. The woman next door, sitting there –' her finger swung towards the table 'gibbering with fear, her husband coming in and dragging her out by her hair. We heard him through these walls, beating her all the way upstairs. She used to lock herself in the coalhouse every time he went drinking after that. I was lucky there, that at least was something I didn't have to worry about. And then the knock on the front door and the stretcher outside – what every wife feared most. I still remember trying to wash my husband's corpse without feeling the grating of broken bones. And then the police, big in their uniforms, standing in this room, telling me my only son was killed, with Reggie and Badger in bed upstairs. And now they're gone too.'

There was silence while a young man struggled impotently for words. When she spoke again, it was with the expression of someone looking genuinely for an answer.

'Why me, d'you think, doctor? What has God got against me? Why am I being punished by living so long?'

'You never know, Gran. Vicki and Reggie might be back yet. I can't see them away for long. They were very much part of the community here, weren't they?'

'No. I pray to God they never do.'

Jonathan could accept without difficulty the sudden transformation back from black, introspective despair to the old fighting determination. He could not conceive of anything to which the redoubtable old lady would succumb for long. What he couldn't understand was the reasoning behind the surging fervour.

'But, surely, you'd like to have Reggie back, wouldn't you?'

'No. I hope she sticks it out.'

'Who, Vicki?'

'Yes.' Gran sat, as hard and straight backed as the chair she sat on. 'That girl's got guts. I just wish I'd had her guts when I was her age. If I'd ever had a daughter, I wouldn't have asked for anything better.'

'But,' Jonathan spluttered, pointing vaguely in the direction of the table, 'I mean – when I came to lunch that Sunday – I got the impression you didn't get on together very well.'

'We don't. We're too much alike. That's why she always needles me about the old days. What she's saying really is "If you're so strong, why didn't you do anything about it?" And the reason why I sound so proud of what we put up with is that I know I have no answer. And, of course, she's right, doctor, though I'd die before I'd admit it to her. We were fools. When I think of the way we were treated. The men stayed in one night a week to look after the kids so that we could go to the pictures. The other nights they were out drinking their wages away. If you weren't married you would be locked out if you weren't home by nine o'clock. One trip a year to Blackpool on the charabanc was all we got, where we still ended up looking after the children because the men were too drunk. That was our life then – where no wife, even the childless ones, dare suggest they go out and get a job of their own. That idea would soon be beaten out of you. It's the only thing the unions and the bosses have ever agreed on.' The rocking motion stopped as if its driving force had run down. She nodded her head knowingly. 'No. She won't come back. She knows she wouldn't dare face me. She won't let me down.'

Gran Kincaid sank back into a reverie that completely discounted Jonathan's presence. When she spoke again, it was more to herself than to her visitor.

'It is a shame though, after all the family's been through. All coming to nothing. I suppose if they were going to have a family they would have had one by now. Vicki's not likely to want children anyway now, they'd only slow her down. That girl's got things to do and I wouldn't blame her. But it is a pity, to think of the Kincaid family all gone – after so much suffering.'

'But who said the Kincaid family was going to disappear?'

The question was almost whispered in its gentleness and Jonathan smiled as an old lady's sharp wits brought sudden acute attention back to her face.

'You had another grandson, you know. Reggie wasn't the only one.'

'Yes, doctor, but . . .'

'And, in a few months' time, you are going to have your first great-grandchild. That was another reason for coming to see you. Peggy asked me to. She wasn't sure what sort of a reception she would get if she came herself. She was worried what you'd think of her. She thinks of you as being very strict. She thought you might not approve. And you needn't worry,' Jonathan added, smiling, 'She's a good, hard working girl and a miner's daughter. Her name is Peggy Wells.'

As the rocking motion began once more, Gran Kincaid's arms folded across her chest as if she could already feel the warmth of a child once more. Tears squeezed through tightly closed eyelids to run silently down her cheeks. It was some time before she could speak.

'Ask her to come, doctor, please. Soon. Tell her to make it soon.' She opened her eyes. 'To think of the number of times I have lain in my bed asking the Lord to take me in my sleep – and, now, I want to live more than ever. May He forgive me.'

Jonathan sat for a moment, staring through his windscreen, still moved at the memory of the old lady he had just left, rocking and crooning softly to herself. Jerking himself into life, he banged on the steering wheel, speaking aloud to himself before driving away.

'That leaves one more, Jonathan Brookes. Just make sure you don't make a mess of it.'

There was no handle to the door. He was just about to knock when a youngster came alongside him, put his shoulder to the door and barged it open. Jonathan followed him in.

There was no mistaking Micky Dunn from Badger's description. There was no doubt either that he considered the matter he was discussing with two teenagers more important than Dr Brookes's visit as, although acknowledging Jonathan's presence with a nod, he made no attempt to break off his conversation. Badger had said Micky Dunn was good at his job, trying to make youngsters feel important, building up their self-esteem. An important decision finally made, Micky came towards Jonathan, a friendly smile on his face.

'Dr Brookes. You wanted to see me?'

'If I may, Mr Dunn. I'd appreciate your help.' A couple of months before, there would have been a smile on Jonathan's face that would have signalled his anxiety to please.

'If I can. Come in.'

Facing each other in his office, Micky remembered another such interview with someone about the same size and build. 'What can I do for you?'

'I was a close friend of Badger Kincaid's.'

'I know. He told me about you. Very sad.' Micky Dunn existed in a world where life had to go on. 'So?'

'I want to trace a lad called Danny Shufflebottom. Can you help me?'

'No problem. He's next door playing pool. Why d'you want to see him?'

'I'd like to see him in private. I'd appreciate it if we could use your office. It shouldn't take long.'

They stared long and hard at each other. Slowly, Micky rose to his feet. 'I'll send him in,' he said, quietly.

While Micky Dunn was out of the room, Jonathan crossed and took his seat at the desk. He fixed his eyes on the open door. The youngster that came through it was small, with black, tightly curled hair. He stood in his worn T-shirt and jeans, his hands in his pockets, perky defiance on his face.

263

'Micky said you wanted to see me. And who the shit are you?'
'My name is Jonathan Brookes.'
'So what does that make you then?'
'I'm a doctor and I'm going to be a surgeon. And what are you, Danny?'

Jonathan could see what Badger had seen. The question had gone home. From nine out of ten Danny Shufflebottoms he would have had a quick foul-mouthed reply but not from this one. Beneath that paper thin layer of bravado, Danny cared about what he was.

'Sit down, Danny. And close that door behind you.'

Warily, Danny did as he was told, never taking his eyes off Jonathan. 'What you got to do with me, then?' he asked. 'What's in this for you, then? I don't know you from nobody. I've done nothing wrong.'

'I was a great friend of Badger Kincaid's.'

'Oh, sod it. Why does everyone have to keep talking about him? I didn't have nothing to do with that. I told them.'

'But he had a lot to do with you, isn't that true, Danny?'

'Don't get me wrong,' Danny wriggled in his seat. 'He was – well, he was great. But he didn't know his arse from his elbow really. All his fancy ideas. Special teachers. Thought he could put it all right with a few karate lessons. What a bloody hope he had in this place.'

'That's why I'm here. I'm going to see his hopes come true.'

'Do me a favour.' Danny put his head back and gave a short, hooting laugh. 'What you going to do, then, fix up a few more karate lessons for me? You're going to have a job because even the local instructor has had the sense to bugger off out of Northend.'

'Frankly, Danny, apart from cleaning up your language, I haven't the foggiest idea where to start. Are you in any kind of trouble at the moment?'

'Course not.'

'And you're not involved with the police in any way? After all you were a friend of this Chico Morelli, I'm told.'

'I'm clean. Like I said, I told them all I know. They don't want to see me no more.'

'Where are you living? You were living rough, weren't you?'

'I'm at home. I couldn't go back to that place no more. But what can you do to help? What can you do that Badger couldn't?'

'I don't know but I have got one advantage that Badger didn't have.'

'What's that, then?'

'Money. Not an infinite amount but far more than I need for myself. But, perhaps even more important than money, I have contacts, people with influence – one man in particular with fingers in all sorts of pies, someone who started off very much like you, someone who, I know, will help.'

'Bullshit. Who the hell would do all that for me?'

'Nobody will be doing it for you. We're both going to do it together for a man I loved very much. And, if I get any trouble from you, Danny Shufflebottom, I'm going to hammer you within an inch of your worthless bloody little life.' As he began to choke, Jonathan raised a clenched fist. 'You and I, Danny Shufflebottom, we're not going to let Badger down a second time.'

27

Whether one feared him, respected him, admired him or worshipped him, one did not ignore Sir Ralph Buchan. Liverpool's Senior General Surgeon looked the part. He was not a vain man, though there was no doubting his pride in his good looks, always immaculately dressed, his thick silvery hair carefully groomed, his neat moustache trimmed with military precision. His operating was in character. Those colleagues who laughed behind his back – no one laughed to Sir Ralph Buchan's face – sneered that he only knew three operations, that he referred everything else to others. Like all snide remarks, there was an element of truth in it. His repertoire was limited but what operations he performed he did with great skill and integrity, always in sepulchral silence, his deft, positive technique always leaving his registrar wondering how his chief always managed to get the easy operations to do.

Predictably, he was a punctual man.

Jonathan Brookes half-ran, half-walked along the corridor, his hand clutching at his white coat pockets as their contents threatened to spill on the floor. He breathed deeply, not from the exertion but from excitement. Blissfully happy, he was back in a job he adored, working under the same roof, sometimes in the same theatre, as someone the very sight of whom, walking towards him down a corridor, made him catch his breath. Now he met Susannah several times a day, their paths crossing by happy chance, not as a result of stilted telephone calls. It all seemed so easy now. Where, before, his thoughts of her had always been driven by a frenzied longing, he now felt a quiet assurance that, given time, she would come his way. Wary barriers were coming down. They touched.

There was also a competitive air to the whole place that he found stimulating. He was not yet halfway up a pyramid of keen, ambitious young doctors, a pyramid that had a very wide base and a fine point. If he didn't stay within its central core, he would soon find himself slipping down the outside. And there were those two cases he'd admitted during the night that he must examine again before showing them to Sir Ralph.

He got little or no sense out of Sister Vera. A ward sister for twenty years, she was known to flap only on Sir Ralph's ward round mornings. She still remembered with horror the morning she had given him his clean white coat with two buttons missing.

'Good morning, Tommy. Did you get to bed afterwards?'

But Tommy Hutchinson, house surgeon, with half a dozen lots of blood to take before the Chief arrived, had no time for Jonathan either.

At ten o'clock precisely the ward doors swung open.

'Good morning, Brookes.'

'Good morning, Sir Ralph.'

There were smiles and a few words for the Sister. The houseman got a nod. The students were ignored as became their status.

Wally Young was the fourth patient on the left. A hard man, he had smoked and drunk his way through most of the money he had earned as a Liverpool docker and it was not in his nature to complain at the consequences. In fact he was quite pleased with himself in having lived so long.

'Good morning, Mr Young.'

''Morning, Sir Ralph.' The words bubbled to the surface from deep inside a barrel chest, ending in a bout of coughing that had the patient reaching apologetically for the sputum mug. He had only been in the hospital a matter of hours but Sister Vera had already instructed him in protocol.

'Yes, Hutchinson. Tell me about Mr Young.'

Prop forwards are not renowned for their rhetoric, at least not when sober. Tommy Hutchinson kept it short. 'Mr Young is a 72-year-old ex-docker, Sir Ralph, admitted during the night with abdominal pain and vomiting. No real bowel symptoms. There is a past history of two severe coronary thromboses, treated in hospital, and another suspected one for which he refused admission. He smokes and drinks. He is a chronic bronchitic with creps at both bases and some oedema of his ankles. He has a pyrexia and a mass in the right iliac fossa. He was seen by Dr Brookes at three o'clock this morning, put on antibiotics and a decision made to treat him conservatively until you saw him today.'

Sir Ralph waited until Sister Vera had folded back the bedclothes for him. That was part of her job. Gently, combining his examination with a few quiet, pertinent questions of his own, Buchan felt Young's abdomen. Satisfied, he looked up, his eyes sweeping the line of students who seemed to shrink, trying to merge with the background like hostages avoiding the eye of the hijacker making his selection for execution. He chose the prettiest girl.

'Now, my dear. Come around here and examine this abdomen for me.'

Sir Ralph was a teaching hospital Consultant who taught. Though he would have found difficulty in giving one the normal value for the serum level of creatinine, he had a love of and an aptitude for the demonstration of physical signs in the abdomen that had endeared him to generations of students. His love of teaching – he had described it once as his only hope of immortality – did not rest with his students. While his senior colleagues fought tooth and nail to secure for themselves the services of a senior registrar that would ensure they would not be called from their beds except for VIPs, he had got rid of his own, saying he was fed up with trying to teach somebody who knew more than he did, that he wanted a younger man he felt he could help mould.

He watched quietly as a flushed young girl tried in vain to control her tremor. Self-consciously she laid a pale, gentle hand on a thick-skinned, hairy belly under the critical gaze of nine pairs of eyes. As she stood, having ground shakily to a halt, Sir Ralph motioned to his Sister who pulled the bedclothes over the abdomen again as if her last chance had gone.

'Well? What did you find?'

'His tongue was coated, his breath fetid.' The girl glanced at the patient as if apologising that she had to say such things about him.

'Good.'

'In the abdomen, on inspection, I thought I could see a swelling in the right iliac fossa but no general distension and no definite peristalsis.'

'Excellent. Go on.'

Wondering about all the stories she had heard about Sir Ralph and his attitude to women students, the young girl blossomed and excelled herself in her description of the palpable mass – firm, slightly tender and fixed.

'And what d'you think it might be, Miss . . . Miss . . ?'

'Burton.'

'And what d'you think it might be, Miss Burton? Careful in your choice of words now, Miss Burton.'

'I think it is either an appendix abscess or a neoplasm of the caecum, sir – Sir Ralph.'

'And I would agree with you, Miss Burton. And if you were a betting girl, which I'm sure you are not, which of those would you put your money on?'

'Appendix abscess.'

'Why?'

'Because Dr Brookes has drawn a circle in Biro around it to see if it's getting bigger or smaller.'

Letting the laughter roll around the bedside, Sir Ralph contributed a small chuckle of his own. 'And you have implicit faith in Dr Brookes?'

The girl, losing her nervousness smiled back. 'Of course.'

Sir Ralph glanced briefly at Jonathan, standing at the foot of the bed. 'I'm sure Dr Brookes is a big enough man to stand a little public debate over his management of Mr Young so far. Do you agree with what he has done so far?'

'Yes.'

'You don't think he should have operated on Mr Young last night?'

'No. If this is an appendix mass, then there is every chance it will subside on its own and the patient is not an ideal candidate for operation with his bad chest and history of coronary thrombosis.'

'Very good, Miss Burton. Just one more thing. Try not to refer to the person in the bed as "the patient". Always remember, the patient has a name. Use it whenever you can. Mr Young is not here just for you to learn medicine on, you know.' As the student returned to the ranks, slightly crushed, Sir Ralph Buchan smiled at Wally Young. 'All's well, Mr Young. Dr Brookes was quite correct in not operating on this abscess of yours last night. I'll see you again the end of the week.'

As Sir Ralph walked round the foot of the bed to move towards the next patient, Jonathan stood back to let him pass. As he did so, one side of his chief's mouth moved.

'Leave him, Brookes. Don't touch him. If you do, you'll kill the old bugger.'

'Yes, Tommy. What's the problem?'

'It's Wally. He's a bit crook.' The house surgeon sounded as if he knew of better ways of spending Saturday afternoons.

'What's the matter with him?'

'The pain's back and he's moaning like hell. Been sick a couple of times.'

'How bad's the pain?'

'Pretty bad. Colicky, I reckon. He's a tough old sod – not the sort to moan. I think it's gen.'

'Right, Tommy; I'll come over. Could you organise a straight abdo erect in the meanwhile?'

'Done it. The films are on his bed.' The line went dead.

Wally Young was still cheerfully respectful but now there was about him the subtle anxiety of the patient who suspects he is very ill. Jonathan had already learned to recognise and respect that most important physical sign.

'Hullo, Wally. What's the matter, the pain back?'

' 'Fraid so, doctor.' He gasped and his face screwed up as another spasm twisted to a climax. 'Been sick a couple of times too.'

'What sort of stuff have you brought up?'

'The last time it was horrible brown stuff.'

'When did you pass wind last, Wally?'

'Can't remember. The young doctor asked me that. 'Bout this time yesterday, I think.' Hollow-eyed, Wally Young searched Jonathan's face for reassurance. He tried to summon a grin from a face distorted in pain. 'Hell of a thing, isn't it, doctor, when you can't enjoy a good fart?'

Jonathan laughed as he pulled back the bedclothes. Wally's abdomen was a little distended now and Jonathan squinted over it to see the rippling surface. The lump was not quite so easy to feel and Wally squirmed under Jonathan's hand. His stethoscope rasping in amongst the hair, Jonathan heard the tinkling sounds that rose to a crescendo in time with each spasm of pain. He covered Wally up once more.

He picked up the X-ray films from where Tommy Hutchinson had left them. Wally Young tried to look at them with Jonathan. There was no mistaking the central, small fluid levels, as straight as if drawn with a ruler, and the absence of gas in the large bowel.

'I'm afraid we're going to have to put a tube up your nose to stop the vomiting, Wally, and a drip in your arm so that we can give you some fluids that way.'

'Fair enough, doctor. And will that put it right?'

'It might, Wally.'

'And it might not?'

'Let's just hope it does. I'll come and see you again this evening.' Jonathan turned to walk away but Wally stopped him.

'And if it doesn't, that would mean an operation?'

'It might, Wally, yes. We would certainly have to consider it.'

'So be it, doctor.' You don't frighten easily someone who lived through Hitler's bombing of Liverpool's dockland. 'But what would Sir Ralph say? Don't forget what he said about killing the old bugger.'

Jonathan put his head back and laughed loudly enough to make Hutchinson look up from his notes in the Sister's office. 'You weren't meant to hear that, Wally.'

'Always had good hearing, doctor.'

Tommy Hutchinson didn't stop writing as he listened to Jonathan's instructions. Putting his pen away, he turned. 'What d'you think, boss?' Front row forwards tend to be irreverent people. 'I think he's obstructed.'

'I agree, Tommy.'

'So?'

'So?'

'So are you going to operate on him?'

'I think we might have to, yes.'

'But you heard what our glorious leader said?'

'I did. But I don't see the sense in leaving him if he's going to die anyway.'

Tommy shrugged his shoulders. 'If you're determined to get shot at dawn, it's no skin off my nose. An hourly check on what they get up his tube and on his pulse rate, you said?'

Jonathan nodded.

'But no enema?'

'No, just in case it is an appendix abscess.'

'But you don't think it is?'

'No.'

'Sir Ralph Buchan, K.B.E., thinks it is.'

Jonathan didn't answer.

'How's it going now, Wally? Any better?'

'Rough, doctor.'

'Has that tube made the pain any better?'

'No. Worse.'

'Passed any wind?'

Wally Young shook his head. No time for joking now.

Jonathan studied the charts at the foot of the bed. He lifted the sheets for a brief examination of an abdomen that Wally could have told him was getting worse by the hour.

'Just going to have a look at your X-rays once more, Wally.'

There was the trace of an understanding smile as Wally nodded. The young man had to have time to think. It was quite a decision he was having to make.

Back at a desk, Jonathan flicked through Wally's file without seeing a word, his mind full of the image of what he was sure was going on inside that abdomen. He was equally sure it was not the same image that existed in Sir Ralph's mind. Sir Ralph was a senior surgeon with power of life and death over a young man's career but Jonathan felt fortunate in one way. At least he was working for someone known to be as straight as a die. Sir Ralph might be an old-fashioned pedant but at least he left his juniors in no doubt where they stood with him – there was no question of all smiles and Christian names one day and stab in the back the next – Sir Ralph had treated Jonathan so far with the respect due to someone rather older than the usual registrar, someone with an excellent academic record and the ability to have a promising future. But Jonathan was still relatively inexperienced. He did not even have the final FRCS. Thin ice rather than solid foundation. The easy option was to let Wally Young die. It was, after all, no more than everyone was expecting, including Wally. He stretched for the phone and dialled a number.

'Hullo. Dr Ridgeway here.'

'Susannah, this is Jonathan. You are on duty, aren't you?'

'Yes.'

'Would you have a look at somebody for me?'

'Who's that?'

'Patient called Young, up here on the male ward.'

'I've seen him.'

'You've what?'

'I've seen him. Your house surgeon asked me to.'

Jonathan clucked down the phone. 'That guy always seems to do things just before I think of them. What did you think of him?'

'Not much. Surely you're not thinking of operating on him, are you?'

Et tu Brute? 'I might.'

The silence from the other end of the line said it all.

'How would you feel if I asked you to give him an anaesthetic?'

'I would do it but very, very reluctantly. I'd get him off the table for you – these bad chests are often better oxygenated under the anaesthetic than when they're awake – but I wouldn't answer for what might happen afterwards. It's when they refuse to cough afterwards because of the pain it gives – that's when they get into trouble. Are you going to do him?'

'Yes.' The simplicity of the final decision, when it came, took Jonathan by surprise.

'Does Sir Ralph know about it?'

'Not yet.'

'Jonathan put the phone back on its stand, stared at it for a moment, picked it up again and dialled the switchboard.

'Sir Ralph Buchan, please.' His mouth went dry as he heard the ringing stop. 'May I speak to Sir Ralph Buchan, please? It's Dr Brookes, his registrar.'

'Dr Brookes.' In two words, low, rough and languid, Lady Buchan conveyed gin and tonic and thick cigarette smoke. 'You're the poor new lamb who looks after this husband of mine. Do you want him? You must come to dinner sometime. And your wife. No, he told me – you're not married. Girlfriend then. Now don't you dare drag him away, d'you hear? Expecting guests any minute for dinner and bridge. Old friends. Here he is.'

'Yes, Brookes.'

'I'm sorry to bother you, Sir Ralph,' – Jonathan paused long enough for his chief to say it did not matter but there was no sound – 'but it's Mr Young, one of the patients you saw on your last ward round, the one with the mass in the RIF.'

'I remember. The appendix abscess.'

Jonathan searched for the courage for direct confrontation and failed to find it. 'I'm afraid he's obstructed. Faeculent stuff coming up his Ryles tube, visible peristalsis, no flatus.'

'Hm.'

'It was the only sound Sir Ralph made though, in the background, Jonathan could hear Lady Buchan's strident welcome to her guests. 'I know your feelings about him, Sir Ralph, – I wouldn't have bothered you otherwise – but I would like your permission to operate on him.'

Buchan was impressed. The young man had behaved properly – always of paramount importance to Sir Ralph – by ringing. He'd shown good manners while having had the guts to hold his own opinion. And he hadn't asked his chief if he thought he ought to operate, hadn't implied he wanted Sir Ralph to come in and do it. He'd made up his own mind, more or less telling his chief what he would do if left on his own. Sir Ralph had heard of that business in that inquest over in Scarsby and he didn't hold it against the boy. That had taken guts too. The boy shouldn't have been left in that position. But there was an air about him – he looked like being his own man. Just like his father, looking back. He remembered Michael Brookes, just two years ahead of him in the rat race. So long ago.

'Very well, Brookes. Go ahead. I'll be here if you want any help. The absolute minimum though, d'you hear? He's probably just got a loop of small bowel stuck to the abscess. A small incision over the abscess and just drain it. He'll have to take his luck with the obstruction.'

Sir Ralph did not wish his registrar good luck.

Back at Wally's bedside, Jonathan tried to look as old and as sage as he could.

'I've looked at your X-rays again, Wally. This trouble of yours is getting no better, is it? I think the time has come to do something about it.'

'Bad as that, is it, doctor?'

'Yes, Wally, it is. I just don't see you getting better if you don't have something done. I've rung Sir Ralph and he agrees with me now.'

'And will you be doing it?'

'Yes, I will, Wally.'

The two men stared at each other for a moment. 'But you don't altogether agree with Sir Ralph, do you?' He held up his free hand as Jonathan began to protest. 'Come on, doctor; you can't fool me. You don't think it is an abscess on my appendix, do you?'

'No, I don't.'

'You think it's something much worse, don't you?'

'Yes, Wally, I do.' The dreaded word was never mentioned – there was no need.

A slow smile spread across the older man's face. 'Seems to me,' he said, 'we're the only two in favour of this operation, doctor.' He held out his hand. 'I say we go for it, all the way. Good luck to us both.'

An hour later, Jonathan stood at the operating table, Tommy Hutchinson and the night theatre Staff Nurse opposite him, Susannah Ridgeway quietly watchful at Wally's head. 'Can I start?'

Susannah nodded, silent in her concentration.

The skin prepared, the house surgeon, skin forceps in hand, began to arrange the drapes to leave a small window on Wally's right side but found his hand being pushed aside.

'Hang on a minute.' Jonathan dug his hands into Wally's belly, now soft and unable to resist. He grunted as the mass beneath his fingers moved. He shifted the drapes, arranging them along the midline. 'I'm going to do a paramedian.'

Tommy Hutchinson shrugged his shoulders. 'If you say so, boss. But Sir Ralph . . .'

'Sod Sir Ralph.'

The sudden defiance took the housesurgeon by surprise and the abdomen was opened in total silence. It took a few minutes of delving, pulling and snipping before the cancer of Wally's caecum was displayed in Jonathan's hand.

'As you said, boss, sod Sir Ralph.' There was a new respect in every word.

'What are you going to do?' Susannah asked. 'Short circuit it?'

'No. I'm going to take it out.' Wally's words rang in his head – 'all the way' he had said. But he also had good surgical reasons for his decision. 'I can't really just bypass it and leave it. Look there.' He pointed with a forceps. 'It's leaking there already, that's why it behaved like an appendix abscess. If I drop that back and he survives, he'll almost certainly get a faecal fistula that won't close if he doesn't die of peritonitis first.'

'So it's shit or bust whichever way you look at it, as you might say.'

Hutchinson's earthy humour cut through the tension, helped Jonathan relax as he began an operation he had never done before. Under supervision, he had done the early stages once or twice. He had joined various parts of bowel together, again under the eagle eye of a consultant or senior registrar. Never before had he taken the total responsibility of both the decision and the execution. But his love of anatomy came to his aid in finding the correct planes of cleavage and in laying bare the bowel's blood supply as he removed the diseased segment of gut and rejoined the cut ends. All anxiety as to the consequences of his decision, either to Wally or to himself, was lost in his total absorption in the technique and it was with a sigh of regret rather than relief that he dropped the remaining healthy bowel back, leaned straight armed against Wally's chest and thigh to blow out a long, delicious sigh. He turned to Susannah. 'How is he?'

'He'll do.' She paused before adding quietly, 'So will you.'

'I'll second that, boss. Bloody great.'

'Thank you, Tommy.'

There is a feeling of deep content, unique to surgeons, one that does not dull with age, when an operation has gone well against all the odds. Others in stressful occupations may feel similar but never identical emotions. It is like the aftertaste of a fine wine that lingers and is extinguished only with reluctance. Surgeons sit in their theatre clothes, savouring the atmosphere for as long as they can. It makes up for the crushing despair felt after the routine operation that has gone tragically awry, a taste of defeat that nothing will expunge.

Susannah found Jonathan Brookes sprawled in a chair, sweat-stained and happy. She walked across to lean over him and kiss him. In the kiss was a tenderness he had not known. As he stood to face her, the restlessness had gone from brown eyes that held his in quiet appeal.

'Jonathan Brookes is dead,' she smiled. 'Long live Jonathan Brookes.'

'Just so long as Wally Young isn't dead along with him, that's all,' Jonathan laughed. 'Otherwise I'm out of a job.'

'I just won't allow him to die. We've got him as far as the ICU and I've got the duty physiotherapist crawling all over him already. Another couple of hours and I think our Wally will wish he was dead.' Susannah paused to give a little chuckle. 'I'd love to be on the next ward round, see Sir Ralph's face when he sees Wally sitting up in bed.'

'Let's not tempt providence, shall we? There's still a long way to go. And, who knows? Perhaps the old boy will take it the wrong way and give me the sack for proving him wrong.'

'I don't think so somehow. I get the impression Sir Ralph Buchan is a bigger man than that. No; I think you may have got a very powerful man on your side from now on.'

As Jonathan contemplated the prospect, Susannah took the step that separated them to do what she had always found impossible, to yield gently to physical attraction. There was no shrinking from bodies separated only by flimsy layers of cotton as she put her cheek to his shoulder.

'My poor, dear, gentle old Jonathan. I hope he isn't dead altogether. I was very fond of him, you know.'

Reluctantly, Jonathan pushed her away just far enough to raise his hand and draw one finger gently over the scarred eyelid. 'And what about you? Do you think perhaps the time has come for you to have something done about that?'

Susannah took hold of his hand and kissed it. 'I think so now. It's the least I can do, isn't it – prove I've grown up too? I don't think I need my prop any more.'

'And we can go back again, right to the beginning?'

'Oh, yes, please.'

'I love you, Susannah.'

'That,' she said, 'will do for a start.'